PRAISE FOR GENERATION MANIFESTATION

"Heartrending twists."
—*Foreword Clarion Reviews* (4/5 rating)

"A richly realized dystopian worl
The Hunger Games meets
—Ryan Porter, *The Toronto*

T0288800

"It's like the lovechild of *1984* and *The Chrysalids*."
—Joe Pedro, *Passport* magazine

"A fun, engaging read about a strong heroine fighting her way through a disturbing and unique future world."
—Todd van der Heyden, CTV News

"A refreshing and at times heartbreaking exploration for anyone who has wanted to be more than they are."
—Nicole Demerse, Award-winning screenwriter/producer (*Mohawk Girls, Degrassi: The Next Generation, 6Teen*)

"Bereznai's prose keeps the heart and mind racing. His superhuman characters are unabashedly flawed and perfectly relatable idols for the 22nd century."
—Elio Iannacci, *FASHION* magazine

GENERATION
MANIFESTATION

(Originally published as *I Want Superpowers*)

A **Gen M** Novel

Book 1

STEVEN BEREZNAI

First Printing I Want Superpowers: 2016

First Printing Generation Manifestation: 2021

Jambor Publishing

Cover by Demented Doctor Design

Copy editing by Andrea Németh

Author photo by Mitchel Raphael

ISBN 978-1-989055-04-5 (paperback)

ISBN 978-1-989055-05-2 (ebook)

Names: Bereznai, Steven, author.
Title: Generation manifestation / Steven Bereznai.
Description: Toronto : Jambor, [2021] | Series: Gen M. | "Originally published as 'I want
             superpowers'" (Toronto : Jambor Publishing, 2016).
Identifiers: ISBN: 978-1-989055-04-5 (print) | 978-1-989055-04-5 (ebook)
Subjects: LCSH: Teenage girls--Fiction. | Teenage boys--Fiction. | Genetic screening--Fiction. | Women
             superheroes--Fiction. | Superheroes--Fiction. | Supervillains--Fiction. | Good and evil--
             Fiction. | Genetics--Fiction. | Genetics--Moral and ethical aspects--Fiction. | Ability--Genetic
             aspects--Fiction. | Mutation (Biology)--Fiction. | Adaptation (Biology)--Fiction. | Biological
             fitness--Fiction. | Dystopias--Fiction. | Young adult fiction. | LCGFT: Bildungsromans. |
             Science fiction. | Dystopian fiction. | Apocalyptic fiction. | Action and adventure fiction. |
             Romance fiction. | Graphic novels.
Classification: LCC: PR9199.4.B4695 G46 2021 | PS8553.E6358 | DDC:
             813/6--dc23

For my mom and dad.
Thank you for all your support.
I could not have done this without you.

Special thanks to: Joey Wargachuk for his ongoing enthusiasm, advice, and graphic design/marketing skills—you keep me inspired; Jamie Sherman, for his font wizardry; Andrea Németh, for her insightful edits, and Demented Doctor Design for the awesome cover.

CHAPTER 1

"I look ridiculous," I say, holding up the edges of my flouncy dress in an attempt to keep the hem from catching on our apartment's rough wooden floorboards. My mom kneels beside me in the dimly lit, one-room flat.

"Yes," she agrees. "You do."

Other moms would coo or reassure. Mine's a sledgehammer with hearts etched into the handle.

Our drop-down bunks are latched against the wall to give us a bit of space. The chipped and faded countertops in the kitchenette are scrubbed, and our breakfast bowls dry in a small sink with a rust stain down its center. According to the label on our rations, we ate oats, though they were so pulverized, it's hard to say for sure. Rumor is, they mix in sawdust.

"There will always be rumors," my mom often says.

We're both clothed in head-to-toe red—me in the dress, she in her work coveralls. Above her left breast is a round patch with the image of a cog on it, marking her as a factory worker—not the best of positions but not the lowest either. Still, it's a far cry from when my father was alive.

She stands, turning me this way and that. At sixteen, I'm taller than she is, which is weird. I'm used to looking up to her, not down. I'm big boned and meaty where she's porridge thin. I take after my dad that way.

"Stop fidgeting," she says, sliding a pin into place.

Her tone puts me on amber alert. I try something new—I keep my mouth shut and wait to see if her impatience will balloon into something more.

Here it comes, part of me warns.

But today's a good day, and the tirade doesn't erupt. Sometimes it's like that. She's... unpredictable. My mother keeps working, and I let myself breathe. The only thing having a blow-up at the moment is the booming thunder outside. We barely notice. It emanates from the roiling black clouds that hover beside our borough, clouds that sit there, day after day. I see them through a small window, patched with duct tape and grimy from the billowing smokestacks of the factory where my mom works. The mass of condensed vapors never expands nor contracts, never intensifies nor dissipates. They've been floating there, stuck, since before I was born.

"They're left over from the war," my dad told me when I was little. "Boy, did they make you wail when you were a baby!"

Oh, Papa, I think.

Today, his absence is like a slowly leaking faucet—a bead of sadness gently gathers until it has enough mass to drip, and then *plop*. Other times, I'm flat out angry. But, it's been so long, the feelings are usually like the storm out there. Never gone, but after years and years of enduring it, mostly relegated to the background.

Look at me coming up with a metaphor—or is it an analogy? I wonder. The question is eclipsed by the storm itself.

Our borough was established precisely on the border where the clouds end. On that razor line rises an electrified chainlink fence, separating us not only from the billowing storm but also the remains of a broken and crumbling city, doomed long ago by the phenomenon above.

In our old neighborhood, local kids and I dared each other to step over the clouds' shadow when it crept onto our side of the fence; when one of us did, we'd all run away squealing.

"That should do it," my mom says. Her voice draws me back into the present as she steps arm's length to admire her handiwork.

"Give us a twirl!" my brother says enthusiastically. His name's Nate; Nathorniel Jarod Feral when he's in trouble.

He's 12, with big brown eyes that give him a spooked owl look; they make him appear younger (and more innocent) than he is. His frame is such a perfect combination of our parents, a mad scientist must've spliced Nate's DNA together in a test tube rather than, you know, that *other* way. He gets all the luck. Currently, he's showing off his walking handstand, feet in the air, wearing a pair of pink underwear and nothing else. They were white until they accidentally got washed with Mom's coveralls. They've been his favorite ever since.

He maneuvers around the small wooden kitchen table on his hands with the same dexterity as if he were on his feet, making good use of his ridiculously broad shoulders. Those he got from our dad. Combine that with our mom's narrow waist, and his set of etched abs (honestly, what 12-year-old needs that kind of muscle tone?), and the kid looks like he jumped off the cover of a comic book.

Some people were born with the proportions to be awesome, I sigh internally. Petty jealousy aside, I love the brat and give him what he wants, spinning until the hem of my dress flutters around my ankles. He lands nimbly on his feet and claps.

"Caitlin! Caitlin!" he chants.

"Please," I say, making shushing motions with one hand while the other eggs him on. He presses his cheek against the fabric covering my belly and wraps his stupidly muscled arms around my back.

"It's so soft!" he gasps with wonder, as he still does at so many things, practically a teen, but still a big kid. "And slippery!"

My mother grabs his wrist and yanks him away, making me trip into the side of the table.

"Ow!" I say.

The move is so sudden and harsh, it takes me a moment to switch gears. For the hour it took to help me prepare, she was a mom born of some dream. She fussed, but she didn't call me "chunky" as she struggled to zip up the back. When we found a rip in the side, she didn't break into hysterics, demanding to know, "How the eff am I supposed to raise two children alone?" Instead, she smiled and reassured me she'd get it fixed in plenty of time for Testing Day. She tricked me into lowering my guard.

"Are the headaches back?" I ask cautiously. Maybe it's a safe question; maybe it's not.

"I'm fine," she says, her jaw tense. She's trying to convince herself as much as us. Her brow creases in pain, and she forces herself to let Nate go. Her lips twitch. Invisible strings pull them into a marionette's smile.

"I'm fine," she repeats, patting his head with jerky, mechanical motions.

She's trying, I remind myself. *It's hard for her.*

"Okay," Nate says, testily brushing her arm away.

She eyes me, her internal pressure sensor veering from the far-right danger zone to the far-left safe zone—and back. Finally, it settles somewhere in between. Her face relaxes. Unlike the lightning cloud on the other side of the fence, this storm seems to have passed—for now.

"You need to finish getting ready for school," my mother tells Nate quietly. I can tell she feels bad for flipping out. She's low on meds, and she's been splitting the doses. End of the month is always the worst for rations.

"Yeah, yeah," he replies. It's his new favorite saying. I'm not sure where he picked it up, and, though it's a bit sassy for my mom's taste, it's hard to tell him to stop when both of us have taken to imitating him.

"Yeah, yeah," my mom echoes, and it's as if the air comes back into the room. Unlike me, Nate has a way of breaking the tension. Mom smirks and points to the wardrobe we all share. It's built-in next to the worn kitchen cabinetry. "Put some clothes on already."

He decides to be obedient, in his Nathorniel way. He performs a couple of dance steps, utterly unabashed. His feet are a blur as he twirls around me and does a majestic leap. He manages to be both a vision and a donk (what my mom calls a "dork") at the same time.

He moves aside his chess set and pulls clothes from his drawers, holding shirts against pants as he plans his outfit. Nate sings as he dresses, a tune our mom used to croon to us, but he's changed around the lyrics. It was a lullaby about jumping over the moon. He's transformed it into a love song. It's raw and childish, but his pitch is perfect. There are rare moments where his voice breaks on a note he can't quite hit; somehow, it makes the song more true. My mother's frown deepens. She's worried. The kid's got talent, but is it the regular kind, or the *special* kind?

I put a hand on hers, trying to be reassuring. The gesture feels borrowed from what I've seen other people do. We're not the touchy-feely type and, true to form, she takes her hand away, resting it above her heart.

"His first testing isn't for another year," I say.

"I know," she says, "I just wish he wouldn't—"

"I know," I reply. "But if you try to stop him—"

"That *would* go badly, wouldn't it?" She shakes as if the consequences were too horrible to contemplate. "At least I don't have to worry about you for much longer," she says, adjusting my dress around my shoulders. "Sweet sixteen. Get through today, one last time, and then you're safe. Right?"

Safe. The word hangs in the air like a set of manacles.

"Sure," I say, because I know that's what she wants to hear.

She nods in relief and gives me an awkward hug. It's so rare, I keep my arms at my side. The important thing is she believes me. If she knew what I was thinking, it would only make her worry. Saying the right thing is a skill I'm developing. Growing up, adults taught us to always tell the truth. I've come to realize *that* is a lie. People don't want the truth. They want to hear what they want to hear. And, the truth can be dangerous.

"I'm glad we're past last year's nonsense, and the year before that," Mom says.

"And the year before that," I add.

4

"We *are* past that nonsense, aren't we?" she presses. "You've come to your senses? No more funny business?"

"No more funny business," I agree.

"Good. That stunt you pulled last time nearly did me in," she says. "Caitlin, it's okay to fail their test, no matter what they say about what an honor it is to pass."

"Of course," I lie again. My rib cage twists because if I pass, they'll take me from her and Nate, forever.

Maybe she's right. Maybe I'm better off as I am.

"And, Caitlin," she says, "please come back in one piece."

On that point, she and I agree. The final testing is the most rigorous. Broken bones, scars, and head trauma are expected. Disfigurement is a possibility. Forcing a Manifestation is not a delicate process.

"Cross my heart," I say, tracing an X over my chest. I leave the rest of the expression unspoken.

Mom nods, but she's stopped paying attention to me. Now that one child is almost safe, her fretful nature is honing in on a new target. My dad used to say she wasn't happy unless she was worrying about something. I follow her gaze and watch my brother deciding between two equally garish tops. Is his thing for color and textures an indication that he's "special" or merely one of his quirks?

There are so many alerts about signs to watch for, it's impossible to know what's bunk and what's not. One year, it was, "Allergic reaction to shrimp causes girl to glow in the dark," followed by, "Boy projects own shadow after winning bicycle race." For a year after, anyone between 13 and 16 years old received packets of desiccated shrimp in their rations and biking was a required extracurricular.

"One more thing," Mom says. "This is for you."

She hands me a worn decorative box with a ratty pink bow.

"Presents!" Nate says, bustling over. He wears yellow pants and a green shirt—no socks or shoes as yet. "Open it! Open it!"

I lift the lid, and my eyes sparkle at what's inside.

"I know it's a little on the girly side for you," Mom says. Her jaw clenches; sometimes it's she who braces for *my* moods.

"I love it," I say, and that is the truth.

It's a simple plastic coronet, but it looks like gold if you ignore the peeling paint. I place it atop my blandly black hair, tied back with a strip of red ribbon.

"It was mine when I was a girl," Mom says.

"Did you wear it at your Testing Day?" Nate asks as he puts on mismatched socks.

My mom has a faraway look in her eyes. "There was no Testing Day when I was young. *You*'re Generation Manifestation. Pass or fail, you're defined by your results." She says this last with a defeated sigh.

"Gen M," I say. "Yay for us." My sarcastic tone hides the hope within— not that Mom's paying attention.

"I got this before the war ended," she says, touching the coronet with such gentleness, it's as if she were afraid of turning the most wonderful dream to dust. "I wore it to a costume holiday called Halloween. There weren't many celebrations in the refugee camps, but, sometimes, we found a way. I was younger than either of you are now. Of all the things for me to still have, I can't believe it's this. I dressed as a princess, if you can imagine."

I can't. My mom's hair is shaved short—saves her from wearing a hairnet at the factory—and her coveralls? Hardly royal material.

"Look at you," she says to me. "You're a princess too."

I gaze at my reflection in a cracked mirror between our bunks. I squint to create a filter that distorts reality so I no longer see me. I don't see a fairy princess either. I see *her*. The me I wish to be, a girl with a cape and a hero's circlet around her brow. A girl who can fly, or lift a bus, or teleport away. Maybe all three.

Today is my final Testing Day.

Today, I find out if that's the girl I get to be.

CHAPTER 2

At school, I pass a poster in the hallway with Supergenic hero Captain Light on it. He's dressed in form-fitting silver. A lightning bolt's emblazoned on his muscular chest. In big letters, the poster reads, BE STRONGER. BE FASTER. BE SMARTER. BE GEN M!

That's the plan.

Our teacher Mrs. Cranberry eyes us as we enter a classroom made of the same concrete slabs as the rest of the building.

Her arms and legs are broom-handle thin, reminding me of the stick people we draw on the chalkboard when playing hangperson. She sees me, and her bony fingers touch the emblem of a book and ruler on her suit jacket as if the symbol of her station can give her strength—even though *we're* the ones being tested for the final time.

She brushes back her grey curls and eyes my dress and coronet. Her thin lips purse; wrinkles gouge her face. I give her a twirl, mostly because I know it will annoy her.

"Acceptable," she snorts, waving for me to take my seat.

I reach my desk and pull out my stool, taking a moment to examine it to make sure it's safe. The girl one desk over notices and smirks. Her black hair is shiny and lustrous. Mine is a pit where light goes to curl up and die. My brown eyes bug out, like I'm constantly surprised; hers are delicately lidded at a demure angle. And her dress—it's a vibrant yellow that brings out the flecks of gold in her hazel irises. I bet her gown is brand new.

Her name's Lilianne. She's the worst.

In second grade, she gave me the nickname "Puddle Pants" after I sat in a pool of water she'd left on my seat. All the kids chanted along with her.

Puddle Pants, Puddle Pants!

Today, the seat is dry. I plonk myself onto it and focus on the pamphlet sitting on my desk. All of us have the same one. One classmate turns his into a paper airplane. I read mine.

TESTING DAY: What it means for you!

On the front flap is the image of a smiling boy with wings and a girl shooting lasers from her eyes.

Mrs. Cranberry does a headcount and releases a rare grunt of satisfaction. "Good. Everyone's here."

She sounds relieved. Incidents happen. Years ago, a classmate of mine spontaneously Manifested and jumped out a window in front of all of us. We're not supposed to talk about it.

I also remember a story that *everybody* talks about—of a pimply boy named Lore and his little sister. They were big news in our borough. They failed to show up for testing because their parents tried to run away with them after discovering Lore could communicate with butterflies. We never found out his sister's powers. Whatever the case, the family got past the security fence. All the stories—official and otherwise—agree on that.

According to the infocasts, protectors caught them in the Yellow Zone, executed the parents, and sent the kids across the river to be with their own kind. And then there are the rumors. One is the family got as far as the Red Zone only to be slaughtered by ravenous mutated animals. Others say they found land not irradiated in the Genetic Wars with potable water and soil to till, but nobody believes that. I choose to accept the siblings are safely in Jupitar City, happy with their own people—and Lore with his butterflies.

I smile as I picture it; as usual, Mrs. Cranberry ruins my reverie.

"Look at the lot of you all dressed up," she says.

I'm not surprised she's pleased. Ties leash the teens who identify as boys; frayed dresses turn the girl-identified into a kaleidoscope of "little ladies," and stiff hand-me-down jackets, cinched skirts, and unnecessarily tight suspenders force everyone else—no matter where they fall on the gender spectrum—to sit straight. Mrs. Cranberry kicks the foot of anyone who fails to keep their knees together. Leg spread? Not on her watch.

The students with parents who earn more credits wear the newer, fanciest clothes—like Lilianne.

I'm not jealous, I assure myself.

A moment later, my lie turns true. I forget all about Lilianne when a pair of testing officials arrive at the open door. Sleek helmets are strapped to their orange form-fitting hazmat suits, which bear the symbol of six lightning bolts in the shape of a star. Students shift on their stools. The guy who made the paper airplane freezes mid-launch; the craft falls from his numb fingers and nosedives into the floor. Lilianne's social station doesn't insulate her; she grips her faux-crystal purse and swallows heavily. My skin prickles excitedly.

8

The older of the two testers attended my previous testings. The hunching of his back, the paunch at his belly, and the thickness of his round spectacles give him a mole man quality. The second tester is new. He's young for the position—and handsome. His hair is like shiny gold spun from a fairy tale, matching his metallic skin. He looks so fresh out of a box, curly bits of foam should be sticking to him.

Anyone who's into boys sits up straighter in their chairs. I realize I'm one of them. So is Mrs. Cranberry. Golden Boy consults the electronic pad in his hand.

"Normand Bamford?" he calls.

We all look at Normand at the back of the class. He stands, scraping his stool on the floor. My body's dense, but he's heavy-set, which is unusual since everyone's on rations. His parents are bureaucrats, which means more credits, more food stamps, more everything. His suit's brand new and freshly pressed, but an awkward fit on his lumbering frame. His bowl cut almost looks like a wig. He squeezes antiseptic gel into his hands. That's one of his things. I can't imagine how much of the stuff he must go through in a year.

What a waste of credits.

His leg brace creaks with every limping step of his turned-out foot. He's been like that for all the years I've known him. I used to think his brace was so cool because it made him look part robot. He avoids looking at anybody as he plods to the door. He's the one student who's weirder and less popular than me.

We watch him go, each of us wondering, *Will he be back?*

The minutes tick by; the air grows heavy; the smell of teen sweat permeates. No one attempts to crack a window; the wooden frames are warped and sealed shut from years of paint.

I doodle in my notebook, drawing an image of myself in a superhero costume—a corset with a lightning bolt emblem on it, knee-high boots, a cape (obviously), and Mom's coronet about my brow. I exaggerate the length of my legs and inflate my breasts. I smile as I write underneath *NOT TO SCALE.*

I admire it, my daydreaming deepened by the hypnotic whir of the small fan on Mrs. Cranberry's desk, decidedly pointed at her. She's leaning back in her chair. I'm sure she's fallen asleep. Lilianne and her crew of girlfriends whisper and look at me.

Lilianne leans over.

"Nice tiara," she says. Her friends giggle. Why is she like this? She's beautiful. Shouldn't that make her too happy to be mean?

"It's a coronet," I correct.

"It's garbage," she replies.

"Just like me," I say.

"Just like you." She stops, eyes narrowing. I beat her to the punch line. She doesn't care for that.

The way she scans me for weaknesses, I swear she must be Supergenic. Not that she needs x-ray vision to find my flaws. There are plenty up front, from my potato face and creepy-crawly eyebrows to my big feet. But Lilianne's cruelty is growing more refined. She dismisses my obvious defects. They're too easy. She notices my sketch. I snap my workbook shut, but it's too late.

"Oh, Puddle Pants," she says. "You think *you're* going to Manifest?"

I blush. "I have as much chance as anyone." The retort is, as my brother would say, "weak."

"Is wetting yourself a superpower?" she quips, burrowing through my thick skin like an irradiated tick. She looks to her friends; they titter approvingly.

I stand and slam my palms on her desk.

"How about if I punch you in the face?" I ask. My mom's not the only one with a temper.

Lilianne's eyes widen. Her fleeting fear is satisfying for less than a second.

"Does your mom want to start treating raw sewage?" she asks. "My dad can make that happen, and my socialista mom can turn yours into a pariah."

"Caitlin!" Mrs. Cranberry shouts, very much awake now. "Sit down!"

She points her ruler at me. She wouldn't dare use it on me though, not on Testing Day. Would she?

"I will *not* have you making a fool of me again this year!"

I grudgingly take my seat.

"I own you," Lilianne says under her breath.

If I were a hero in a comic book, I'd turn the tables on her. I'd outsmart her, or win her over, or defeat her in a race at the end of the school year.

But this is real life.

I don't have to do any of those things, I reassure myself. *All I have to do to beat her is Manifest. The lowliest Supergenic is still higher than the most powerful of dregs.*

Everyone stares at me. I nervously finger the pamphlet on my desk. Beyond the dirt-caked windows that won't open, across the river, I spy the tall gleaming towers of Jupitar City. People fly amongst the buildings, mere specks in the distance.

I lose myself in their dizzying motion until the classroom door creaks open. Mole Man looks at his electronic pad. Golden Boy's arm is wrapped around Normand, holding him up. His nose is crusted with dried blood. Final Testing Day is especially rough.

"You okay to walk on your own?" Golden Boy asks.

"Stop fussing," Mole Man snorts. "The dreg's not our concern."

Golden Boy looks ready to argue.

"I shall be fine," Normand says in that formal way of his.

He takes a faltering step, wavers, and his knees buckle. He grasps at a nearby desk, but his fingers are devoid of strength.

"*Damnare!*" he says. Talking gibberish is another one of his quirks.

I join the collective gasp as he collapses to the floor.

"Normand?" Mrs. Cranberry stands, looking from the Supergenics to Normand, then back to the Supergenics, waiting for them to tell her what to do.

Golden Boy moves to help, but Mole Man yanks him back. Golden Boy jerks his elbow free, glaring and ready to argue. Mole Man holds up a silencing finger. "He is *not* our concern."

"Of course he is," Golden Boy insists.

"A word," Mole Man says. He closes the door, which barely muffles his shouts of "fall in line," "we have a quota," and "there will be consequences."

I risk Mrs. Cranberry's wrath and go to Normand's side. I tap him on the shoulder. "Normand?"

His eyes flutter open.

"I passed out, didn't I?" he asks, gazing at the ceiling.

"You did," I reply.

I offer Normand my hand; he squirts alcohol gel into my palm and gestures for me to rub it in. Even my mom isn't this much work.

"Caitlin!" Mrs. Cranberry snaps. "Help the boy up!"

I am *not* going to miss that woman.

I get my arm around Normand—and nearly crumple under his weight. After much grunting, I help him to his feet. He winces as he slides into his chair, but I convince myself he's all right, until his whole body shudders. Not once but twice, then a third time, followed by a fourth and fifth.

"Normand, are you okay?" I ask.

He may have a concussion or worse.

He shudders again, and again, and again. His eyes roll back in their sockets, showing their whites.

"Mrs. Cranberry," I say, "I think he needs—"

His body jerks once more before his eyes pop back to normal. He grabs my forearms and yanks me in close.

"Caitlin," he begs. "I can't go through that again; I *can't!*"

Our classmates stare. I ignore them.

"It's over. This is your final testing," I remind him. "You never have to do it again, not ever."

He pulls me closer, his mouth to my ear. This is the guy who wouldn't take my hand without disinfecting it. He's *really* terrified. "I barely got out of there. They're not afraid to kill us. They're not afraid to kill *you.*"

"Normand, that goes against the Treaty," I say.

I want to quote how the Supergenics can only test within reasonable parameters to find members of their kind, but he shakes his head. "They don't care. They're desperate."

He looks ready to say more, but the door opens. Golden Boy stands there, handsome even in his hazmat suit. He rubs his arm as if it's in pain. Mole Man is gone. Golden Boy looks at the e-pad in his free hand.

"Caitlin Feral?" he calls.

"Caitlin," Normand hisses. His grip on my forearms tightens. "Whatever it takes, live."

"Is Caitlin here?" Golden Boy asks. Confused by the lack of response, he says to our teacher, "I was assured you had full attendance today."

"Caitlin!" Mrs. Cranberry shouts.

I try pulling away from Normand; his grip is surprisingly firm.

"Promise me!" he hisses.

"Normand!" I snap.

"Now, Caitlin!" Mrs. Cranberry slams her ruler onto her desk. "Don't keep the young man waiting." She blushes apologetically and holds her hands up helplessly, giving Golden Boy a cracked laugh. "She's utterly

12

impossible!" To me, she levels a look I know all too well, promising me I'm going to pay for this latest embarrassment. Everyone sees it. Lilianne and her friends smirk. The tester's golden brow lifts. Normand is oblivious.

"Fine," I say to appease him. "I promise."

He lets me go, and I clumsily stagger back, jabbing my hip into a desk.

"Ow," I say.

Golden Boy winces. More giggles from Lilianne and her squad. I smooth my dress. Mrs. Cranberry stares like she's trying to shoot me with death rays. I tilt my head defiantly, the hero to her villain.

"Wish me luck," I say to her.

Her hand grips the ruler so hard it trembles.

"I'll see you soon, Caitlin."

CHAPTER 3

Outside the school, I do my best to forget about Mrs. Cranberry and Lilianne. Normand is tougher to put out of my mind. What did they do to him? What are they going to do to me?

It doesn't matter, I assure myself. Normand is weak. I am not. *So why is my heart beating so fast?*

I focus on Golden Boy as I follow him across the cracked asphalt of the recreational yard. It's a black sea surrounding the square, concrete school behind me. A rusty chainlink fence pens us in. A bus trundles by, and thunder booms. Golden Boy flips his fingers across the surface of his e-pad, not giving me a second glance.

The things Normand said rattle me more than I'd care to admit. What if he's right? What if the rules have changed? Am I willing to die on the off-chance of Manifesting? Is it worth my life? The answer isn't "no," but is it "yes?"

We approach a squat building set on the far end of the yard for safety. The last serious Testing Day incident was a decade ago, but we all know—and retell—the story. Officials used to take over a classroom and fill it with their gadgets and probes. One day, a kid turned feral. Wild with fangs, claws, and quills, he slaughtered three testing officials, two teachers, and half his class before protectors contained him in an electrified net. The Supergenics took him away, compensated the families of the victims, and, from then on, testing has taken place outside the school.

"There have been significant advances in testing protocols since then," Golden Boy says, sounding like a manual.

His words yank me from my thoughts. I look at him. He's still focused on his tablet.

"I didn't say anything," I yammer, which makes me realize—he's a telepath.

I remember the mind reader from the previous three years. He was older and smelled of alcohol. He didn't seem able to catch my thoughts unless he was touching me.

"Ah yes, Neville," Golden Boy says. "He's… retired."

Liar.

Golden Boy shrugs at my unspoken accusation. "It's not easy being a telepath. One's own thoughts can be too much, let alone someone else's. Neville became… overwhelmed. I'm Joshua, by the way."

He pulls off the glove of his hazmat suit and holds out his shiny hand, as golden as the rest of him, for me to shake. I hesitate.

"I'm more powerful than Neville," he explains. "I don't need physical contact to read minds, though it heightens the psychic connection."

I try to be comforted, but it's more than unsettling having someone creeping around my thoughts, even if they assure us Testing Day isn't a mind audit.

Joshua's hand hangs there. I force myself to take it. I'm surprised by the softness and warmth of his palm; not cold at all despite the metallic hue. Is he reading that reaction in my mind? Instinctively, I mentally sing a lullaby.

Two little puppies dancing in the rain—

"Please stop that," Joshua says. "It's irritating and hardly the way to fool a telepath."

It's possible to fool a telepath?

His cheeks blush rose gold as he lets go of my hand. "Best you forget I mentioned that, or you'll get us both in trouble."

We reach the squat testing building. I want to ask more.

"You always want to ask more, don't you?" he winks, pulling out a Supergenic i-dent card. It's shinier than ours.

"Mrs. Cranberry once said she wished that curiosity *would* kill the cat," I reply glumly. "I was the cat."

He laughs, and I can't help but smile.

"Well, I for one hope that the feline in question has many more lives," he replies. His words give me a warm glow inside.

He slides the i-dent card through an electronic lock and punches in a code. I hear half-a-dozen thick bolts pull back.

"Just in case," he winks.

He is ludicrously handsome.

"Thank you," he says.

I flush.

"That's not fair," I say.

"Life's not fair," he agrees amiably. "Take you, for example."

He gestures up and down at me.

"What?" I ask, looking to see if I've spilled something on my dress.

"Do you have any idea how predictable Testing Day is? I've been at this for months, school after school, and the closest I've come to getting anyone to Manifest is a 13-year-old with purplepox. You were supposed to liven things up for me."

"Me?" I demand.

"Yes, you. You're Caitlin Feral. Subject CF 1554 DASH 8. At least you're supposed to be. Where's the girl who showed up for her first Testing Day with blue skin after staining herself with wild berry juice? Or how about the following year when you plastered feathers all over your body with industrial glue?"

I remember both incidents all too well.

"My mom got the can of adhesive from the factory where she works. She brought it home to repair a mug," I reminisce. "It took two months to get all the feathers off, and another three for the skin to heal."

"Now *that's* what I'm talking about," he says. "*That's* the Caitlin Feral I was expecting. This is your last chance to Manifest. You know that, right? I figured you'd go all out. I've been looking forward to this for weeks, and all I get is this," he waves at me. "Another average girl in a hand-me-down dress. You're supposed to be a legend."

"A legend? What? No. Really?" I ask.

"Caitlin," he says as if he can't believe he has to tell me this. "You're *in* our training manual."

I can't help but be a little proud. *At least I'm good at something.*

"Exactly!" he says, his golden eyes shining. "So *be* good at this."

I consider his challenge.

"You've got a plan, don't you?" he asks with excitement. "Don't tell me. Don't *think* about it. I want to be surprised."

I want so badly to impress him. He's a handsome Supergenic who is not only paying attention to me, he thinks I'm a legend. It's a dream come true. I want to drag this moment out for as long as I can. Of course, I muck it up. *That* is my superpower.

"This year is different," I say.

He contemplates me. Who knows what his psychic powers are picking up. Nothing good as his golden brow furrows in disappointment.

"Yeah," he says. "I guess it is. Just my luck."

Joshua shrugs in acceptance. I'm no longer a legend. I'm a silly girl in a silly dress.

16

"Perhaps it's for the best. I doubt my colleague would have the patience for your special brand of creativity, this year in particular." Joshua rubs his arm as he says it—makes me curious about Mole Man's power. His ability is a matter of considerable debate in my class. In three years of testing, none of us has seen him use it. I'm thinking that's a good thing.

Joshua grips the door handle to the testing building and jerks his head toward it. "Your classmate Normand had reason to warn you about what to expect in there. We've had too few Manifestations. This year is worse than last. We need a win. Each classroom we've tested, my colleague has pushed the kids harder, made the tests more aggressive. We have the highest number of injuries on record. The dreg monitors are there to make sure we don't take it that far, but they're too terrified of him to say anything. And me, well, I'm the new guy."

"You're not supposed to be telling me this, are you?" I ask.

"No," he admits. "But what he did to that kid before you, it was nasty business. And my colleague was going easy. You won't be so lucky. He remembers you—not fondly. He's going to push you harder than anyone."

Hard enough to kill me? I wonder.

Yes, I hear Joshua in my mind.

My heart pounds wildly. No jokes, I could die in there.

"Listen, I was teasing you about putting on a show," Joshua says. "If you have to, you beg us to stop. Maybe that will get the monitors to intervene. And *don't* antagonize him."

"So, basically, don't be me."

"Yes!" Joshua agrees with relief as he yanks the door open. "Exactly."

Inside, there are Mole Man and three other officials in orange hazmat suits, all with the icon of the star made of lightning bolts. Their helmets hang from their belts. One tester's seated at a desk inputting information on a data terminal; another is setting up a drip bag; the third is waving for us to enter. We step through, and all the hairs on my body lift from the electrostatic decontamination sweeper.

The security door clangs shut, stealing any natural light, leaving us with a dozen cones of luminescence from the LEDs in the ceiling. Everything is shiny stainless steel—a contrast to my usual world of grit and concrete. A vibratory hum runs through me as someone activates a containment field strong enough to smother a D-bomb.

I recognize some of the testing devices—a treadmill, a lounge chair on a hydraulic lift, and a silver sarcophagus leaning against a wall. A metallic hula hoop sits on the floor.

That's new.

Joshua hands me a vacuum-sealed foil packet containing my testing suit. He turns to talk with his fellow testing officials. Two of them are dregs, here to monitor and supposedly look out for me. The third would have powers, in case I Manifest and have to be restrained. And, there's Mole Man.

The tester at the desk motions me toward a door. What's left of his grey hair is slicked back, and a thin beard covers his cheeks.

"You can change in there," he says. "And fill this half-way."

He hands me a plastic pee bottle with a cap. I go into a room eight measures by eight measures, what my mom refers to as feet, which is a weird unit because everybody's foot's a different size. It's all gleaming white tile, with a porcelain toilet and sink, steel shelf, and hooks in the wall. The smell of bleach burns my nose. I reach behind me, unzip my dress, and step out of it in relief.

I can breathe.

I hang the dress on a hook then rip open the foil packet to pull out a thin pair of track pants, disposable socks, a t-shirt, and collapsible rubber shoes. I dress quickly. Lastly, I take off the gold coronet and place it reverently on the shelf.

Soon, you won't need a crown to feel special, I assure myself, peeing into the bottle.

When I emerge, the testers wear their helmets. One of them takes the bottle from me; another attaches pads above my organs and an IV drip in my arm.

"We'll start you on the treadmill," the tester says, his voice coming through hidden speakers in his helmet. It's Joshua. His broad shoulders and lean waist are a dead give away. I wonder what it would be like to date a mind reader.

The question dissipates as I step onto the machine, and the track whirs. I jog lightly.

"Faster," Mole Man barks. Joshua turns a dial. The machine speeds up. I sprint, sweat dripping down my face while the heart rate monitor beeps at a satisfactory rate.

Satisfactory is for losers.

"Faster!" I order.

What did I tell you? I hear Joshua in my mind.

"You heard the subject," Mole Man says.

I'm a legend, remember? I think at Joshua.

He sighs and turns the dial.

The monitoring devices beep louder and quicker. A red light flashes.

I'm doing it! I think.

The pads all over my body heat up as a variety of energy waves bombard my muscular, endocrine, and central nervous systems, prodding them to do something out of the ordinary. Energy builds within me. I smile and grit my teeth against the burning in my legs, pushing harder.

It's happening! I think. *I'm Manifesting!*

I'm on the verge. I know it. I *feel* it. I give it everything I've got, wondering what sort of power is about to emerge—until my left leg cramps. I cry out in pain. My thigh's rigid as concrete.

Maybe it's turned to organic granite!

My foot hits the spinning rubber pad at a funny angle; my ankle gives under my weight, and alarm bells erupt in my mind. I'm going down.

"Abort!" Joshua orders. His palm slams a big red button, but it's too late. I fall chest first, ripping the IV from my arm as the spinning tread tosses me onto the floor. I land hard, knocking the breath from me.

I did it, is the only thought in my mind. *I Manifested.* I wait for the cheers and congratulations welcoming me into the Supergenic Family; cold silence greets me. This is not what the brochure promises. Circulation is coming back into my leg. I touch it through the track pants. It feels normal, but it can't be, can it? I whole-heartedly believed it had turned into living rock.

"Augmented acceleration, fail," Mole Man says, making a note on his electronic pad. I realize my stupidity. Of course, that's what they were testing for—super speed, not geomorphication—but other Manifestations were possible. Joshua helps me to my feet.

"Are you all right?" he asks.

"Let's move on," Mole Man interrupts, directing me to a hydraulic chair. I sit, and Mole Man fastens restraints about my ankles and wrists.

You've got this, I assure myself.

He clamps cold, metal pincers to my eyelids, forcing them to remain open as he squeezes a bottle, releasing acidic droplets onto my exposed eyeballs. It burns. I want to blink more than anything; trying makes the pincers bite more deeply. The pads on my temples grow hot as pokers. Pressure builds in my skull. I whimper. They're pushing me to exhibit ocular emissions such as lasers, x-rays, or hypnotic waves. My eyeballs bulge beyond their sockets, threatening to explode.

Is this what an optic blast feels like? I wonder—until my vision blurs. I pull involuntarily at the wrist straps. *Am I going blind?* It's happened to others.

"It's too much," Joshua says. The world goes darker and darker. "Nerve damage is imminent!"

"Fine," Mole Man concedes. "Ocular emission is a fail."

Joshua presses a button; the pressure decreases, and the room comes back into focus. Mole Man throws a pencil at one of the dreg monitors. The dreg cowers.

Joshua hands me a variety of gemstones. I clutch one after the other.

"Mineralization, fail," Mole Man grunts.

He puts a respiration mask over my mouth and nose, and I breathe in a chemical mist; it's a cheese grater against my throat and lungs.

"Sublimation, fail," Mole Man says.

Electrodes attached to my adrenals jolt me with electricity; I writhe and gasp.

"Shapeshifting, fail," Mole Man says. The pace of testing accelerates, as do the pronouncements.

"Telepathy, fail. Lycanthropy, fail. Weather control, elasticity, and flight… fail."

They bombard my brain with delta-waves in the hopes of triggering special cerebral abilities. I go into synaptic shock, convulsing as froth bubbles over my lips.

I hear Normand in my head. *They're desperate.* I taste iron as something warm drips from my nose into my mouth. *Blood*, I realize. The monitors remain silent. It's Joshua who yells, "Enough!"

Mole Man lifts a finger and sighs, "Agreed."

I have a sprained ankle, sunburnt skin (apparently, my epidermis does *not* absorb UV and convert it into other forms of energy), and a migraine. I'm not sure what's worse, the pain of the tests or being told how utterly ordinary I am. Not subjectively. *Clinically.*

When they inject me with amphetamines, I feel like they're going through the motions.

I'll show them.

The pads all over my body supercharge my endocrine and central nervous systems as I attempt to deadlift a metal bar with plates pulled downward by a magnet. *This* is my moment. I growl in defiance and yank the bar upward. My heart hammers, the room swims, and numbness spreads from my arm into my chest. I barely feel the weight slip from my fingers or hear it clang to the ground.

"She's going into cardio-pulmonary failure!" Joshua yells as everything goes black.

When I come to, Joshua's gesticulating at Mole Man. He has his helmet off. They all do.

"You're taking this too far!" Joshua yells.

"Need I remind you what's at stake?" Mole Man asks.

"You're not the one who feels their pain," Joshua replies. "And you!" he points at the monitors. "Why are you here?" They cringe, glancing from him to Mole Man uncertainly.

"You need to calm down," Mole Man says, reaching for Joshua. Joshua smacks his hand away and steps back. "Don't you *ever* touch me again."

"Or what?" Mole Man snorts. "Your powers don't work on me." He lunges toward Joshua. I intentionally knock over a stainless steel pan. It clatters on the ground.

Everyone stops and turns. Mole Man contemplates me, then angles his body back toward Joshua. "She's awake. Let's get back to work."

Joshua kneels beside me, a prince in bearing and looks.

"We restarted your heart," he says. "You can ask us to stop."

A lock of his hair is out of place, stuck to his sweaty forehead. I resist the urge to fix it.

"No," I say, standing up. "I can't."

I'm woozy, but I stay on my feet.

"Hold this around your body with your arms straight out to the sides," Mole Man says, handing me the glittering hula hoop I noticed earlier. I grasp it as instructed. He presses a button, and the hoop projects an energy sphere around me, gluing my hands and feet to the edges of the pulsating ball.

"I haven't done this test before," I say. "How does it work?"

"Hold on," Mole Man says—as if I had a choice. He turns a dial, and the sphere spins me every which way. He increases the intensity. I can't tell what's up, down, or sideways. I see the testing officials from every angle, then the floor, ceiling, and the walls. I'm going to throw up.

It gets worse. The gyroscopic device expands, pulling my arms and legs. At first, it's a light stretch, but the pressure builds in my joints. The pain is unlike anything I've known. *They're pulling me apart!*

"Stop!" I howl. "Please stop!"

They don't hear, or they don't care. The force grows. They're killing me.

"Please!" I beg louder.

Something pops. I'm about to be quartered when the pressure on my body eases, the sphere contracts, and the spinning slows. The hoop grows still; the energy globe sparks then winks out. I immediately drop the torture device and sway in place. My legs are jelly—not literally, unfortunately—and I fall to one knee. The hoop twirls on the floor around me.

Joshua steps forward with a stainless steel pan and holds my hair back as I barf into the receptacle. He and the other testers have removed their helmets. I glare at the hoop.

"What is that testing me for?" I ask. I've already done, and failed, the elasticity test.

"Nothing in particular," Joshua replies. "It's a last-ditch effort to rip the power out of you."

"Last-ditch? You mean—"

"You can go change," he says. If only that were true.

"Remove the dreg," Mole Man says. He holds a hand mirror, checking his teeth for food. "Prep the facility for the next subject."

"No!" I shout. "Put me back in the hoop. Give me one more chance. I know I can do it."

I expect Mole Man to order me out. He lowers the mirror and contemplates me. I see his truth. He *wants* to hook me up again. Joshua sees it too.

"Get this dreg out of here," Joshua barks, drawing himself to his full height. "We have much more promising subjects to focus on."

Please, Caitlin, I hear his voice in my head. *Go while you can.*

"Wait a moment," Mole Man says, gesturing for Joshua to settle down. "I've always believed if our subjects were to endure a little more discomfort, we'd have a higher success rate."

"The data speaks for itself," Joshua snorts. "She's a waste of our time."

I glare into his golden eyes. He glares back.

Mole Man drums his chin as if running an algorithm, calculating the cost-benefit ratio of time and energy spent on each subject versus Supergenic found. After all, every minute spent on a dreg who will never Manifest is time he could invest in someone who does have enhanced abilities. But how can he know for sure? If I push, I'm convinced he'll let me try again.

He'll kill you, I hear Joshua in my mind. *I won't be able to stop him.* It reminds me of what Normand said to me in class, begging me to live.

I'd rather die, I reply.

I'm about to say so when I get a vision of my little brother prancing around in his pink underwear. I step toward the hoop, but that's as far as I get. Invisible hands hold me back. Is Joshua using his telepathy to short circuit my motor functions and freeze me in place? No, this is me having second thoughts. I look at the hoop lying on the floor. I feel it ripping me apart. Blood and pain fill my world—then nothing.

It will *kill me*, I realize, *because I* don't *have superpowers.*

The epiphany does what all their invasive tests could not. It breaks the protective casing inside me that sheltered my beautiful lie, the one that gave me a hope I was willing to die for. Exposed, my delusion curdles in on itself, transforming into sour, stinking truth.

"There's no point," I say. The words come unbidden, as if I've been through this already, and I know this on some imprinted level. "There's nothing special about me. I'm a dreg." Mom will be so pleased.

There's a long pause. I'm more shocked than anyone. Mole Man snorts and turns his back on me. A wave of panic strikes.

What have I done?

I open my mouth to say I've changed my mind (again); Joshua cuts me off. "Go," he says. "You're finished." I deflate, and he adds, "For what it's worth, it was a pleasure meeting The Legend." He's trying to make me feel better. Like myself, it's a fail.

"Yeah, sure," I reply.

I keep my head up and shoulders straight as I walk to the washroom. My attempt at dignity is pointless with a telepath who knows that all I want to do is assume the fetal position. I don't bother singing about puppies in the rain. After the humiliation of the past hour, I've got nothing to hide.

The washroom door closes; my tear ducts open.

No, I say. Burns cover me, inside and out, broken blood vessels clot my eyes, and bruises ache, but I won't walk into that classroom a cry baby. I'm not giving Lilianne the satisfaction.

Fall apart later, I order myself.

I yank off the sweaty tracksuit, shove it into a mesh bag with a drawstring, and struggle into my stupid gown. *Why the eff do we have to dress up for this?* It's bull is what it is—all of it.

It takes a lot of pulling, but I get my dress over my hips and my arms through the sleeves. I twist and grasp the zipper, triumphant in this at least —until I yank and hear cloth ripping.

No!

In the mirror, I see the white of my underpants through a tear in the backside. Now the tears come. As I lack any other power, I'm devoid of the strength to hold them back.

It's not the dress that makes me crack. It's the black void inside me. Before, I could dream of a better tomorrow. Now, I know I'm stuck being me for the rest of my life.

My mother's plastic coronet sits on a shelf, a final remnant of her previous life, a time when she was allowed her fantasies, dressing up and pretending to be a fairy princess. I take the coronet in my hands. It's so light and insignificant, an illusion of something more. I contemplate it for a moment, squeeze my hands on either side and snap it in half.

I shove the broken pieces into the trash, and I don't look back.

CHAPTER 4

I emerge a mess from the washroom—eyes bloodshot and flushed cheeks stained by my tears. Mole Man ignores me now that he's confirmed I'm powerless.

I hand my bag of testing clothes to a dreg official. I consider asking if I can keep the track pants since I ripped the back of my dress, but I know the answer to anything that contravenes testing protocol. The female official shoves the bag into a chute connected to a bin in the back of the building.

Adding to my humiliation, Joshua walks with me back to the school. I would rather be alone, but part of his job is to make sure I return to class—and to fetch the next subject. At least Mole Man stayed behind.

Thunder booms above the crumbling buildings beyond the security fence. Attached to the chainlink, a battered mutant alert sign glares at me. The triangular warning bears the stylized black outline of a trio of growling animal heads—hound, lizard, and giant cat—budding like polyps within the triple crescents of a biohazard symbol.

"Do you ever get used to it?" Joshua asks, gazing at the storm. "The thunder, I mean."

I want to ignore him, but I might seem like I'm sulking.

"It doesn't wake me up anymore," I say. "So, I guess so."

"It's amazing," he says. "People can adapt to pretty much anything."

I suspect that's for my benefit. I wait for him to tell me it's all right to fail the test because my soon-to-come work detail will make me a valuable member of society. I prepare to bite my tongue to keep from yelling at him for such nonsense, but he says nothing of the sort.

He stares at the broken city behind the fence, beyond the signs warning of mutated animals, out at the dilapidated buildings where the lightning strikes.

"From Jupitar City, we see the storm in the distance. I always wanted to get up close. It's scary amazing."

Shadowrens wheel and dive amidst the lightning. The birds are so fast, their forked tails look like flying shadows—hence their name.

"I sometimes forget how powerful the storm is," I say. "Powerful enough to destroy a city."

He nods. "It wasn't dreg bombs alone that broke our planet."

I stop breathing. Nobody speaks like that, nor is that what I meant.

"The Supergenics were acting in self-defense," I say quickly.

He neither agrees nor disagrees.

"Do you ever wonder what it was like?" he asks. "Before the war, I mean. Back when that city was full of people going about their lives, off to work, buying groceries, planning birthday parties. And then something caused the first Manifestations, right in the middle of all that. There was no Supergenic state. We all lived together."

My reply is automated.

"When the first Supergenics Manifested, it should have been the dawn of a new golden age," I say, reciting the words all dregs knows by heart. "But instead of seeing potential and promise, the dregs looked at their superpowered children in fear. When given the chance to nurture, the dregs tortured. When given the chance to evolve, they sought to cure. When given the chance to understand, they imprisoned. They did so in the name of Science. In the name of God. In the name of Family, Tradition, and Society. In truth, they did so out of Ignorance and Fear."

"And how is that different from what the Supergenics are doing to the dregs now?" Joshua asks.

I step away from him and look about for black-clad agents to come swarming out with protectors at their sides to take me away. Joshua doesn't need to be a telepath to see my fear.

"I'm sorry," he apologizes. He sounds tired and sad. "It's not a test to gauge your loyalty. But it was unfair of me to ask because it *is* a question with consequences, for Supergenics and dregs alike."

He resumes walking toward the school. I want to ask more; for once, I keep my mouth shut. Silence is safety. Say nothing, and you can't say anything wrong.

We reach my classroom, and he pauses.

"I want you to know something, Caitlin Feral," he says. "I don't need any of those tests to see you're different. You *are* special, and we could use more people like you."

Before I can ask him what he means, he opens the door. My classmates stare at my bloodshot eyes, the suction marks all over my face, and my blistered skin. Even Mrs. Cranberry is shocked—as if in her tiresome career, she's never seen a testing go this far. Whatever pity she might feel, she shakes it off.

"Well, Caitlin," she says with satisfaction. "I guess you'll be with us for a while longer."

Her hand tightens on her ruler. I'd forgotten about the bottom beating saved for me. My testing is done—no need for her to hold back. No matter how rough I look, she's determined to get her licks in. The woman can hold a grudge. I expect her to make an example of me (again) here and now. To my surprise, Mrs. Cranberry points the ruler at my desk and says, "Take your seat."

Finally, a bit of luck. I scurry past, afraid she'll change her mind. Normand is staring through me, wide-eyed, his palms pressed to his cheeks.

"*Miraculum*," he murmurs in disbelief.

He's so weird! I expect Lilianne to eye me up and down with amusement and disgust; thankfully, she's distracted by something in her lap. Probably a nasty note about me. My dress flops around my ankles as I set my bottom down quick as I can in the hopes she won't see the rip in my backside. I realize my mistake immediately as cold wetness soaks through my underpants.

Lilianne strikes again. Now her blank gaze is fixed on me. She and her friends laugh. Mrs. Cranberry gazes at me with a cold smile; she was in on it. Joshua contemplates them with an unimpressed arch to his golden eyebrow.

"Ow!" Mrs. Cranberry says, putting her hand to her temple.

Joshua gives me a wink. Now it's my turn to smile. I wonder what he looks like stripped of his hazmat suit. Is he golden *everywhere*?

I heard that, he says in my mind.

I refuse to blush. *Good*, is my reply.

I like you, Legend, he tells me. *Let's have some fun at your classmate's expense.*

"Lilianne Whisper," he says.

Lilianne's head pops toward him in surprise.

"Yes, that's me," she says. Everyone else is confused too.

He gestures with one finger for her to join him. She gets up hesitantly. Usually, we go alphabetically, and she would be last. She eyes my blistered skin; it's no longer funny because she's next. She grips her purse, not leaving the side of her desk.

"Well, hurry up, Lilianne," Mrs. Cranberry says. "Don't keep the young man waiting."

Lilianne takes tiny steps to reach his side. As they leave, Joshua says to her, "I hope you've got a strong stomach." A better person than I wouldn't be gloating.

As the clock ticks, I wait gleefully for Lilianne to return. Testing time varies from teen to teen, but usually not by much. Normand's took half-an-hour. I was longer because of my stubbornness. Lilianne should be back by now. More than an hour later, Joshua opens the door. Mole Man's with him. They must've tortured her something special. I almost feel bad. Almost. I'm ready to "console" her when I realize Lilianne isn't with him. Joshua's face is ashen; his golden hair has lost a shade of luster. Mole Man's the opposite, smiling and rubbing his hands together excitedly.

I expect Joshua to say something in my mind; he's psychically silent.

"Eric Graymoor," he calls out.

A scrawny boy covered in freckles and wearing a pair of cracked glasses gets up. He walks forward, not taking his eyes off Lilianne's empty seat. I stare at it too. She's not coming back. I look at Mole Man's triumphant face.

But that means…

I choke the pamphlet on my desk. *It can't be!* Yet, it is.

Lilianne's Manifested.

CHAPTER 5

Walking home, I keep my eyes down, averting them from the order-enforcing protectors in their form-fitting copper uniforms. On their chests is the symbol of a fist clutching the all-seeing eye. More of them are out than usual, at most street corners and driving around in sleek patrol cars or skimming by on hover attack vehicles. A truck rumbles through the streets, pulling a twenty-measure long metal wagon. Strapped to it is the corpse of a gigantic lizard with three tails that end in rows of deadly spikes—a mutant killed out in the Red Zone. Cancerous nodules and ice burns cover its skin.

The protectors kept the beast in a cavernous freezer, ready to pull out on an occasion such as this. It reminds the population what's out there, why we need to follow the rules, what the protectors guard us against, and why our alliance with the Supergenics is so important.

I stop at a corner where people are gathered, looking up at a public info monitor on a lamp pole.

A video plays of Lilianne waving goodbye as she boards a hovercraft, her yellow dress fluttering around her as the vehicle powers up. This is cause for celebration. The Supergenics will send extra rations for the whole borough, including cake. I'd rather chew on rusty barbed wire than have a bite of Lilianne Whisper's Manifestation Day cake, even if it is chocolate, which it better be. What idiot serves vanilla? In a close-up, her eyes are clearly bloodshot. Joshua and Mole Man flank her in their orange hazmat suits. No word on what her power is.

That should be me, I think.

"What a happy day for the people of Borough 5," a stone-faced info clerk reports matter-of-factly on the screen. A touch of putty holds his short hair in place. His jacket bears the emblem of a video monitor. "Appearances would indicate that someone's been crying tears of joy. How lucky she must feel. We go now to the male citizen who contributed half of Lilianne's DNA to hear his thoughts on this wonderful occasion."

An image appears of a broad-shouldered man with thinning salt and pepper hair. He wears a bureaucrat's navy blue suit and tie. The emblem on his breast pocket is a pointing finger pressing a circle—a button that guides the rest of the labor force. I've seen him with Lilianne. She never tired of talking about how important her parents are. Of course, now that Lilianne's Supergenic, they're no longer legally her parents. He's a sperm donor. Her mom not only gifted the egg, she had the added honor of incubating one of the genetically superior. Ms. Whisper stands behind her husband. She's lean like her daughter, with the same delicate features. She wears a rose dress with a necklace of fake white pearls. A perma-smile is plastered to her face, and a drugged look glosses her eyes—not what I'd expect from a woman of her station. She nods continuously as her husband speaks.

"This is an exciting day for our daugh…" He catches himself and lowers his gaze, focusing on a his e-pad; from then on, he reads it verbatim, not daring to look up. "This is an exciting day for Lilianne. It has been an honor for my wife and me to be her caretakers for the past 16 years." He pauses, wiping at his eyes. If it were my mom up there, she'd be having a full-on meltdown.

But he's a bureaucrat, so he understands Lilianne's better off with her own kind. How could he hope to raise her now? What does he know about superpowers? It's a hard truth in a world of hard truths.

All the same, the transfer doesn't always go this smoothly. Not every parent is so willing to give up a child. There are the misguided runners who never make it past the Yellow Zone and are executed on the spot. There have been riots, the protectors coming out with their shields and electrified batons; hence tonight's preemptive increase in security. A short-range cargo transport lands on the roof of a ration center to stock it up.

On the screen above, Lilianne's waving goodbye. The people around me wave back. I do not.

I walk away, staring at the ground and picking at my peeling, burnt skin. I automatically step off the sidewalk to put some space between me and the protectors directly ahead.

To my right is the electrified security fence with guard towers every two-hundred measures. I barely notice the warning signs for radioactivity and mutant animals. Beyond the fence is the Yellow Zone, where a once-great city sits in ruin.

The ever-present storm clouds rumble with thunder. A network of energy siphons poke up amidst the rubble, sucking in the blasts of electricity from above. The Supergenic who created this phenomenon is long dead, but what the individual's power called forth remains. The lightning hits huge orbs of specially tempered glass set atop massive pylons, drawing the power into the electric grid that feeds the boroughs and Jupitar City.

I stare at the light show as I walk, wondering what it would be like to shoot lightning bolts from my hands or to summon a hurricane with a thought. I sigh. Today is the day I put such thoughts aside, like when I was 12, and I packed up my small box of toys to give to the little girl three doors down.

I'm so caught up in myself, I don't see the protector step in my way until his copper uniform fills my vision. The emblem of the fist holding the all-seeing eye glares at me.

"I-dent card," he says, his voice coming through the mic and speakers in his helmet.

My heart beats faster. I pull my plastic identification pass from my worn-out purse. He swipes it through a card reader attached to his on-the-go device. I've done nothing wrong, but I feel more guilty with every passing second. They have a way of doing that—making a person believe they've committed an infraction by merely pulling them aside.

He hands the card back and waves me along. I scurry away. He laughs at my ripped dress with the wet patch on my bottom. I pass two more groups of protectors on my way home, but none of them glance at me. I struggle not to think about what comes tomorrow.

Instead, I cling to the hope of a late Manifestation. I mean, it *could* happen, though the odds are against it. At my age, it's a million to one. With every passing day, month, and year, it gets exponentially less likely. Worse, if I were to Manifest after sixteen, the older I get, the higher the chance my power would be a pathetic nuisance, like incurable halitosis, or so powerful I'd die in the Manifestation—and take a chunk of my borough with me. A few years back, an explosion two buildings over blew up a housing unit. A man in his fifties stumbled out, belching fire. He died moments later from organ failure; his heart turned into coal.

It's one of the reasons for Testing Day, to force Manifestations before they burn too low or too hot.

I enter the concrete hallway of my tenement building and shove these thoughts aside.

Get me out of this dress.

The lift is broken. Again. We live ten stories up. My Testing Day legs are ready to dissolve by the time I reach our flat. I unlock and open the door, barely missing a rack of drying clothes. My mom stops kneading dough for dumplings and rushes to wrap me tight in her arms. That's two hugs in one day.

"I'm so relieved," she says, disengaging and handing me a dented can with a homemade ointment in it. "For your skin," she explains. "When I heard about your classmate, I thought for a second it was you."

"Lilianne," I say with distaste. She's all that anyone will talk about for the next month.

"That poor girl," my mother says, cutting chunks of dough and tossing them into a pot of boiling water.

I say nothing about my disappointment because I know it will upset her.

"Can you undo my zipper?" I ask. I'm afraid if I do it myself I'll rip the dress more.

"Of course, sweetheart."

It's a relief to feel my full breath as I hear the *zzz-vitt* sound of the metal prong drawing down interlacing teeth. I slide the sleeves off, careful to keep the fabric clear of my damaged skin. Mom doesn't ask about the wet spot on my butt, either because she doesn't see it or because she knows better. Either way, I'm relieved. I have my pride.

I hang the dress on a hook. She'll mend the garment then sell or trade it. I pull on a pair of worn jeans and a plain white shirt. I stare at my mom's red coveralls thrown over the back of a chair. She notices.

"Soon, you'll get a pair of your own," she winks.

I force a smile, fooling no one, but we pretend.

We don't wait for Nate to get home to eat. He's at that age where he's encouraged to pursue any hint of talent in the hopes it will lead to Manifestation. Tonight it's dance, followed by choir. Competitions are held throughout the year. He's won loads of awards, which is how he's managed to accumulate so many colorful clothes. He's a flower in a sea of grey, but that's encouraged—for now. Poor kid has no idea what's in store if he doesn't develop powers.

Effing Gen M, I think.

Mom examines the tear in the dress, planning her attack to repair it.

"Honey, where's the coronet I gave you?" she asks.

Crap. I'd forgotten about it. She steps back to stir the dumplings.

"It broke," I reply. It's not exactly a lie.

"Damn it, Caitlin!" she shouts, picking up the pot of boiling water and slamming it on the counter. Spray hits the window. She glares at me, hand on her hip.

"Well, let's see it," she snaps. "Maybe we can glue it back together."

"I... I threw it out," I say.

She shakes her head. "You did *what?* It *meant* something to me!"

"I... I'm sorry, Mom. I should've brought it home," I stammer.

"*This* is why you have no friends," she says.

The verbal slap catches me off guard. She's right, though. Breaking the coronet was childish. It's probably all she had left of that different time.

"Well, at least you still have me," I say, trying to lighten the mood, but it's hopeless. That's Nate's power. The anxiety Mom's been feeling all day drowns her relief that I failed their test. In an instant, whatever's been propping her up drops out from under her.

"Lucky me," she grumbles under her breath.

So begins the first day of the rest of my life.

CHAPTER 6

We eat in silence, and I think about my dad; things would be so much better if he were here. Maybe if he hadn't died, Mom never would've developed her mood swings. We definitely wouldn't be living in this dump. After dinner, I wash the dishes, and Mom starts mending the dress.

I put on my windbreaker jacket. My mom doesn't ask where I'm going, and I don't say goodbye.

Outside, I run through a series of back alleys, avoiding the protectors. I cut across a parkette with a towering stone statue of several legendary Supergenics. Their uniforms consist of tights and capes that accentuate their perfect bodies as they hold up the world, saving it from us.

Minutes later, I reach my destination—the library.

Most buildings in our borough are made of cinderblocks coated in spray-on insulation and grey stucco. Not so with this repository. The edifice is a marvel of architecture and craftsmanship. Seemingly carved from a single piece of luminescent marble, graceful columns grace the facade along with whimsical fairies, fiery demons, avenging angels, scaly dragons, and armies of elves, wizards, and dwarves.

"It's a pity project," Mom once said as we walked by, but I could tell, she was impressed.

A famous Supergenic author, Marigold Mapleton, led the campaign to have it built. She came for the ribbon-cutting, her purple hair sticking out like a pair of horns, praising the written word, and extolling the virtues of reading books in print instead of on a data screen.

"You simply *must* have that tactile experience!" she assured us.

I walk up the library's translucent steps. Everywhere my foot touches, the marble glows with circles of light that ripple outward. Sometimes, I prance up and down these stairs for fun until the librarian shoos me away. I reach the top, and a pair of stainless steel doors etched with pixies slides open without a touch. Inside, I inhale a slightly musty odor that swells my chest and widens my eyes. It's the smell of a building full of printed books.

The interior is as fanciful as the exterior, lit by floating glow globes. Marble columns crawl with stainless steel vines while copper bees and gemstone butterflies pollinate shimmering metallic flowers. I wander amidst the stacks of books on shelves of wood so black, I pretend they're ruptures in space.

I come to a data terminal atop a lectern, and I type my requests. A green checkmark appears alongside the instruction to "PLEASE PROCEED TO THE WITHDRAWAL DESK."

At the front counter is the librarian, Mrs. Sicklesop. She could pass for Mrs. Cranberry's crankier older sister. She takes my i-dent card and swipes it. An unusual BEEP makes her pause. She looks at the reserves I've placed, then at me.

"Aren't you a bit old for comic books, dear?"

"No," I reply.

"I'm terribly sorry." She's not. "But your access to comic books and other such literature has expired. That's what happens after you fail your final Testing Day." There's an "oh dear, what can I do about it?" hint to her tone. "Time to grow up. Those are the rules, and we mustn't break the rules. Would you like to enter another request?"

She slides her keyboard toward me like it's a chess piece closing in on my king.

I tilt my head, look at her primly, and tap her screen.

"My access doesn't expire until midnight," I reply. "It says so right here." I slide her keyboard back at her. Checkmate. Her eyes narrow; she looks like she wants to shake her fist at me, a clichéd villain bested by some clever brat whose spunk and big heart make up for her rough edges.

I smile. "Those are the rules, and we mustn't break the rules."

She grunts and disappears into the back stacks, returning an unreasonably long time later with five creased comic books. She takes her time scanning them. I keep looking at the clock. She notices and goes more slowly, fussing over one barcode that's crinkled, eventually entering it in manually. When she's finally done, I grab my reading material. She slams her palm on top of the pile, preventing me from taking them.

"We close in 35 minutes. Returns are over there," she points as if I didn't know.

"Thanks," I say with sarcastic cheer, yanking the comic books out from under her hand.

She scowls and pushes a cart of books into the back. I escape to my favorite reading place, a comfy blue seat that's practically a couch. I set my stash onto an end-table and reverently take the comic book on top. It has a muscular woman on the cover. She holds a glowing spear and wears battle armor reminiscent of a one-piece bathing suit that pushes her large breasts up and together. The outfit is stylized in yellow, black, and red; a dazzling crescent moon shines in the middle of her chest.

She stands beneath the bold title *Lady Strength*. I've read it dozens of times, yet my eyes linger, and I turn the pages with intentional slowness.

I'm at the best part, where Lady Strength's captured by the evil semi-sentient soldiers of the monstrously mutated Greyhounds. They tie her in chains and threaten a thermonuclear detonation in the boroughs.

Lost in the story, the ache in my battered body dims until a clomping tread echoes through the stacks, breaking the fantasy. I groan. It's my loser classmate, Normand Bamford. I can call him that because I'm a loser too.

I hear him before I see him, his bum leg slamming into the tile floor with every step. I roll my eyes. Yes, I jumped to help him when he fell this morning, and he did warn me about the new aggressive testing protocols, but we're not friends. To call him annoying is generous.

The creaking of his leg brace draws closer, and I instinctively curl into myself—as if that can protect me from the socially awkward scenario that's about to unfold.

"Greetings, Caitlin," he says in that nasal, overly formal way of his, pushing his oversized glasses up his upturned nose. As always, he doesn't look at me when he talks, but rather at some ghost over my right shoulder.

"Normand," I force myself to say.

He holds half-a-dozen comic books of his own, including one called *The Good Guy*. On the cover is a muscled man in a torn costume; he stands amidst a pile of monstrously deformed Greyhounds, dead at his feet. Normand sets down his stack of comics and picks up mine. I bristle as he flips through the titles.

Stop touching my stuff, I want to say—though my sense of ownership is laughable. Library comic books can't even be taken home.

"This one has merit," he says, pulling out an issue of *Polarmight*. On the front, the title character is shooting blasts of ice from her hands.

He's ready to settle into reading one of *my* comic books.

You've got your own! I want to shriek.

He hits nerves I didn't know I had. I grab the comic book back.

"I'm going to read that one next," I lie.

He blinks in surprise.

"Am I to surmise from your tone that you are expressing displeasure?" he asks.

He sounds like a computer program when he talks. I'm convinced he was dropped on his head as a kid. Only now do I notice how battered he is, with a black eye and swollen lip. Today was surely the toughest Testing Day in history, and let's face it, Normand's something of a wimp, so I can only imagine how much rougher this must've been on him.

"Sorry," I say, handing the comic book back. "It's been a bad day."

"Indeed," he agrees. "Testing Day is… stressful. And disappointing for most."

He's the first person to acknowledge to me that it sucks.

"Yeah," I agree. "And then Lilianne Manifests? How unfair is that?"

"Statistically, it is neither fair nor unfair," he replies. "It simply is. Someone must beat the odds. Why not Lilianne?"

Why not me? is my sullen, unspoken reply. Clearly, our brief bonding moment has passed.

"I wonder what kind of cake we'll get in our extra rations," he muses.

I refuse to admit I wondered the same thing. We *don't* have that much in common. Besides, I need to enjoy my comic book time. After tonight, I won't be allowed to sign them out anymore. I could get Nate to do it for me, but that's pathetic, like an eight-year-old who still sucks her thumb.

"Normand, it's almost closing time," I say. "I just want to read."

"*Tempus edax rerum,*" he says earnestly in his gibberish. "Time, devourer of all things."

He taps the gold watch on his wrist as if to give special emphasis. The timepiece has moving hands instead of digital. Word is it came from Jupitar City. He's constantly looking at it, and I want to shout at him, *Yes, we get it! You have a watch!* Even Lilianne doesn't have a watch.

"Time, devourer of all things," he says. "Tomorrow is a big day."

"Job assignments," I agree. "Goodie."

"Remember, when courage triumphs over fear, anyone can be anything. Even a hero," he says. "Someone told me that a short long-time ago."

I roll my eyes. *Whatever.*

He looks at his leg in its brace. It makes me wonder how much harder that's made life for him. For the first time today, I stop feeling sorry for myself.

"Normand, I…" Surprising myself, I reach to pat his arm. He shifts away.

"No need to spread germs." He stands, giving me an archaic bow. "Until the 'morrow."

He's so abrupt, I'm not sure if I'm relieved or insulted. He limps and disappears amidst the stacks. The creaking of his brace dissipates, and I turn back to my comic books.

Way too soon, the floating globes flash, indicating the library is closing. I flip shut a copy of *Amazingonians*. I check to make sure I have all the comics I checked out. I do *not* have the credits to pay for a replacement.

I finish counting. This is wrong. I have six issues, but I only signed out five. I guess Normand left one of his comic books behind, which is as likely as the sun forgetting to rise. Testing Day did a number on him. I will return it for him, but…

Get it together, Normand! You're going to be starting work detail soon!

I walk toward the front desk and slide free the comic book he forgot—curiosity and all that. The crone at the front counter sees me and dings the bell on her desk, waving for me to hurry up. I freeze on the spot.

"What the eff?" I whisper.

I hold a comic book unlike any I've seen, and I've seen them all—numerous times. We get so few issues, I even read the titles I don't like (including that annoying goody-goody RinRin and his cat Pokey). But *this*? What is this? The title of the comic book is *Tigara*, likely a play off the word tiger. Its principal character, as revealed on the cover, is a half-naked woman in a cone of light. She pulls on an orange, black-striped, elbow-length glove with claws at the end. The rest of her tigress inspired outfit lies on the floor.

I am instantly and utterly mesmerized.

I touch the cover with disbelief. It's almost too good to be true. There's barely a crease on it. This must be brand new! How could I not know about this? The red alert in my mind goes off. Something isn't right here. I spy the release date, and my heart pounds faster.

1993.

That can't be. That was *before* the Genetic Wars. Decades before. This must be a gag from the comic book publisher, involving a time-traveling Supergenic, though everyone knows time travel's impossible, even for them. The publisher has gone all out to achieve a historical feel. All sorts of things are off. The colors are less saturated, the style of art is gritty and harsh, an ode to a more primitive time perhaps, and the paper is different. Thinner. Frailer. These are the details I can explain. There is one I cannot. The sticker barcode—stuck on by Mrs. Sicklesop on every single comic book, no matter if it's covering up the villain's or hero's face in mid-battle (I swear she must do it on purpose)—it isn't there.

"Sweet Louise," I cuss under my breath.

This isn't part of the library's collection.

"The library is closed!" Mrs. Sicklesop shouts. I should hand the comic book over to her. I should report Normand (where did he get this? And why leave it for me? Brain damage or not, he's too much of a fusspot for this to be a mistake). I imagine giving the issue of *Tigara* to the librarian, and I know I can't. There's no telling what she'll do to it. Certainly, I'd never see it again. I turn my back on her, and I slip the mysterious comic book into my satchel.

Mrs. Sicklesop bangs harder on her bell. I wonder how much force it would take to shove it up her you-know-where. *Then* let her ding her bell.

Breathe, Caitlin, I tell myself. *It's just a comic book.*

It's a lie, and I know it's a lie. This is contraband.

Pony up, I tell myself, slowly releasing my breath.

I do a half-pirouette to face the librarian and walk to the counter as sweetly as I know how. I return the comic books I checked out. She yanks them from my hand.

"I have better things to do than wait around for you all night," she snaps.

"Do you?" I challenge.

Her jaw juts, and her eyes narrow. For a second, I think she's going to insist on searching my bag.

Crap, crap, crap!

"Get out of my library," she says, pointing at the door.

I don't argue. I want out of here as fast as I can. I back away and bow. That makes her glare. I get to the door. I'm almost safe.

"Caitlin Feral!" she shouts. I stop, heart pounding. I'm not a kid. Now that there's no hope of Manifesting, the protectors won't be lenient on me for breaking the rules. This comic book could land me into forced labor in an irradiated zone.

"I hope tomorrow you get assigned to garbage detail," she shouts.

"With my luck," I answer over my shoulder, "I will."

CHAPTER 7

The walk home is excruciating. I want to yank the impossible comic book from my bag and read it cover to cover. I pass protectors and pretend everything is normal. The symbol of the all-seeing eye held in a fist on their copper uniforms glares at me from every direction.

My eyes dart all over the place. *Are they staring at me?* My guilt feels like a flare. All viewing material goes through the Critic's Bureau, which oversees the dissemination of books, plays, and screenings. They boast, "We decide what you see so you don't have to."

It's one comic book, I assure myself. *What harm could it do?*

But as innocent as a comic book may seem, I'm sure it would be deemed against society's best interests. Almost anything from before the war is. A few cultural artifacts of "merit" are tagged and stored. The bureau destroys the rest "to prevent another gene war."

Normand would be in so much trouble if they found out I got this from him. *Where did he get it? Why would he give it to me?* And… *does he have more?*

The possibility is soda pop in my spine—bubbly, oh so sweet, and bad for me.

I pass a set of protectors a block from the library. They loom over me, their visors turning my reflection into a distorted mask. A few steps past, I'm ready to breathe easier.

"What's in the bag, girl?" one of them squawks. Her voice is inhuman through the speakers in her helmet.

I freeze. *Why would she ask me that?* Because I'm clutching the satchel as if it has the most precious cargo in all the world—which it does.

"I'm talking to you!" she repeats.

I can't move, yet I have to. I turn with the clunkiness of an overused windup toy. I slide the strap off my shoulder and hold the satchel toward the protector—best get this over with. It's an oddly perfect end for the worst day ever. Lilianne gets her powers and new life while I'll be cuffed and turned into an example.

Be stone, I tell my trembling hand.

It's a futile thought. Fear squeezes my bladder, making me worry I'll lose control of that too. I hear Lilianne in the back of my head.

Puddle Pants, Puddle Pants...

The protector jerks the bag out of my grasp, flips open the sash, and rummages through my belongings. There's not much—a half-eaten nutrition bar, my i-dent card (which she gives to her fellow to swipe through his on-the-go), an empty beverage bottle, and a bronze ribbon I won in a race. I like to keep it on me for good luck.

Clearly, it doesn't work. The protector yanks out the comic book and stares at it.

"Where did you get this?" she demands, flopping it in my face.

"The library," I say. It's sort of true, but she's not buying it.

"Since when can you check out comic books?"

She's right. That was a stupid cover story, one the librarian would happily deny.

The protector points her blaster at me. She's clearly noticed the real problem. The comic book lacks a seal of approval. "On your knees. Hands behind your head."

My lips tremble; I lower myself to the ground, one leg at a time. It's hard to keep my balance with my palms pressed into the back of my neck. Passers-by pick up the pace, heads lowered and shoulders hunched.

"No more lies," the protector says. "Where did you get it?"

She lifts my chin with the blaster, settling the blunt tip into the soft of my throat. I stare at my warped reflection in her visor. My cheeks are scraped and puffy from today's testing.

"We can do things to your mother," the protector says, looking at my i-dent file. "Make you and your brother watch. Like when we took your father away."

My cheeks burn from the memory.

"That won't be necessary," I say.

I'm sorry, Normand, I think.

"A classmate gave it to me."

"I need a name," she says, jamming the gun deeper against my throat.

"Normand," I yelp. "Normand Bamford."

Her partner types the name into his on-the-go and shows it to the protector who has me at gunpoint. She turns to the screen, then back at me. Thunder booms.

"On your feet," she says.

I get up and lose my balance; she grabs me and sets me right, shoving my bag and the *Tigara* comic book into my chest.

"If I find out you stole it from him…" she draws a finger across her throat. "Do you understand?"

I nod vigorously, struggling to believe that she's giving the comic book back to me. *Hasn't she noticed there's no seal of approval?* The rank of Normand's parents must make the protector too nervous to realize or care.

"Good," she grunts. "Now get out of my sight."

I hide around a corner and press my back against the wall. I pant, drenched in sweat. I stare at the cover of *Tigara*. I could blame Normand for all of this, but I'm the one who chose to keep it. I could've handed it over to the librarian, or left it in the library, or thrown it into a trash bin. But no. I could not have done any of those things. I take in Tigara's fierce countenance. Her athletic physique. Her ferocious costume.

You better be worth this.

I'm already convinced she is.

When I get home, Mom looks up from patching the dress.

"I was getting worried," she says. She's speaking to me again. She slides the dress onto a hanger. Nate's holding a wall handstand, counting under his breath and ignoring us both.

"That came for you," Mom says, nodding at a package wrapped in plain brown paper, sitting on the table.

Nate lands on his feet.

"Open it! Open it!" he says.

"Sure," I say, though I know he's going to be disappointed by what's inside.

I unwrap the parcel, and there it is—a plain charcoal jacket and grey skirt with a matching tie. My new school uniform. It's patched and worn in places, like everything I own. The Bureau of Education is passing it on from last year's graduating class.

"Put it on! Put it on!" Nate says. The kid loves clothes in a way I never have.

He sees my lack of enthusiasm. I knew this day was coming, but I convinced myself it would never come for me.

"Don't worry," he says, putting a hand on my arm. "We'll find a way to add some color."

The next day at school, Lilianne's desk is conspicuously empty. Oddly, so is Normand's. My eyes are heavy from not enough sleep. Last night, once Mom and Nate were breathing softly, I snuck behind the toilet screen and, using a flashlight Nate won at a ballet competition, I lost myself in Tigara's world. In the end, Tigara is broken and bloody after being betrayed by her evil twin sister. Goons surround the urban heroine, and it's a wonder I could sleep at all, wondering what happens to her next.

Now, I fidget at my desk and look over at Normand's empty seat. I'd been planning on grilling him about the comic book.

Is he okay? I wonder. *Did the protectors get him? Was that their plan all along? Let me go with the contraband comic book and follow me up the supply chain?*

I fidget and pull at my tie. We're all dressed in our uniforms. It's a first step away from the self-expression that might've helped us Manifest. Now, our diverse Gen M potential is being wedged into conformity. Those who identify as boys wear grey trousers held up by suspenders, white shirts with charcoal vests, and matching ties. Those who identify as girls are similarly attired, but in skirts. Those who are non-binary, well, they had to decide ahead of time how they were going to present for work studies—no one gets two looks, and everyone's uncomfortable. The bureau has access to our exact measurements from our Testing Day data, yet our uniforms are either too tight or awkwardly loose.

I play with a bright yellow bracelet of interlocking elastic bands around my left wrist. Nate gave it to me. He made it a few years ago during a "crafternoon." As promised, he found a way to sneak some color into my drab ensemble.

"All right, class," Mrs. Cranberry claps. "We have a lot to do this morning."

My hand is in the air before I realize it.

"Caitlin…" she sighs.

"It's about Normand," I say. Kids look to his empty desk. We all show the aftermath of testing—bruised and swollen faces, cut lips, stitches, bandaged heads, and broken limbs. My classmates might think Normand's recovering at home, but I know better. "Is he okay?"

"I would worry less about Normand and more about what I'll do to you if you keep interrupting," Mrs. Cranberry replies.

It would've taken less time for her to answer the question. She is so frustrating!

"Yes, Mrs. Cranberry," I force myself to say. I eye the door, wondering if I'll be the next to disappear.

She hands each of us a sheet of paper.

"These are your vocational proficiency scores based on your school results of the past several years," she says. "They will help determine which workstream we funnel you into. You will see five potential occupational outcomes listed. They are in order of demonstrated aptitude. One is most likely the best fit for you. Five, the least."

My hand shoots into the air. She towers over me as she places my aptitude results face down on my desk.

"You may *not* request a vocation that is not on your sheet."

I lower my hand and stare at the paper. My future is on the other side. Mrs. Cranberry pauses next to Normand's empty desk—and then keeps walking.

"You may turn your sheets over," Mrs. Cranberry barks.

I push Normand from my mind and flip the paper face up. I stare at my list, starting at number 5 and working my way to the top.

5. Laborer (aptitude for heavy lifting)
4. Clerical (proficiency in reading)
3. Janitorial (minimal sense of smell, strong stomach)
2. Assembly Line Worker (able to perform repetitive tasks)
1. Protector (above average dexterity and physical stamina)

This can't be right. I check the name in the upper right-hand corner. Caitlin Feral, followed by my birthdate and address. But this *can't* be the sum of my abilities. With each number, the list gets worse and worse. How can protector be my number one occupational aptitude? They're the ones who took my dad away. They're the ones making life miserable for us all.

"You will each have one night to think about it," Mrs. Cranberry says. "Tomorrow, you will choose three out of the five options listed. Keep in mind that while research demonstrates greater output when citizens have a level of choice in how they will contribute to our society, it is *strongly* recommended you include your top two proficiencies in your selection."

I roll my eyes. So typical.

Why pretend this is up to us? Tell us the top two are mandatory and be done with it.

I stare at the paper and think of what Mom said about Testing Day. I failed; now I'm defined by that result. Being Gen M sucks.

Mrs. Cranberry keeps yapping.

"You will receive preliminary practical training and evaluations in the three vocations of your choosing to determine your suitability for further development in *one* of those fields of work," she says.

I stare at my proficiencies. Janitor is one of the worst. Laborer could be fine while I'm young, but their bodies get so battered they wind up in too much pain to stay on the job and are left to survive on the most meager of pensions. Clerical would be fantastic if I could get a job at the library, but fat chance of that happening. There's only one in the whole borough and a lineup to take Mrs. Sicklesop's position when she dies, which at the rate she's going will be never. Assembly-line worker would mean I'd likely wind up working with my mom. I have a vision of her fussing over me amidst the conveyer belts, shouting, "No, not like that, like this. Oh, let me do it. Honestly, Caitlin! You're going to get us both reassigned."

Which leaves protector. Dark memories twist my stomach.

I can't be a protector, I think to myself. *I* can't. Not after what they did to my dad. And yet, I'm expected to try. As upsetting as that is, another thought takes precedence.

Mom is going to kill me.

CHAPTER 8

"Well," my mom says the moment she gets home. "Let's see it."

I stand by the hotplate, stirring a pot of stringy noodles. Nate hands me the foil flavor packet.

"It's on the table," I say.

Mom picks up my sheet of aptitude results and possible workstreams.

Here we go.

She gazes at the list.

Nate senses the obvious. Something's up, and it's not good. He slides his fingers into mine. We stare at our mom.

The word *protector* might as well be written in my father's dripping blood. Her grip tightens on the paper, and her lips purse. I brace for her to yell at me—and to shout back. I didn't create the list; *they* did. She'll sob, *Have you forgotten what they did to your father?* I'll comfort her when what I need is for her to comfort me.

She sets the paper down, takes a marker from her pocket (here it comes!), and calmly marks a black X next to Clerical, Assembly Line Worker, and, to my shock, Protector. She doesn't cry or rant. She hands me the paper.

"But—" I start.

"It's what they want," she interrupts. "You'll get basic training in all three disciplines. They'll score you, and then the Bureau of Contribution will assign you to a work detail based on your results and societal needs."

"So…" I begin, knowing there's a connecting thought she's leaving out, something she thinks is obvious, but which I'm not getting.

"So," she says with exasperation, "when you do your basic training to be a protector, you do the absolute worst job possible. You make sure you flunk. Do you understand, Caitlin?"

This is so contrary to the way I expected this conversation to go, I hesitate in my reply. She shoos Nate away. He retreats to his bunk and pretends to work on a sketch, but keeps looking at us, ready to intervene. Man, I love that kid. Mom grabs me by the shoulders and gives me a hard shake. Nate tenses, ready to spring into action. I hold my palm to him in the "let's see how this plays out" signal.

"I'm not fooling with you, Caitlin," my mother warns. "I *won't* have one of *them* in my home. I *will* disown you. Do you understand?"

"Yes, I understand," I say. She stares me in the eyes, gauging if I mean it, which is insulting. How could I want to be a protector? They say they protect us from what's beyond the fence, and from each other, but they're *always* watching, begging us to screw up. That's how they got my dad, and I never saw him again.

My mother lets me go, and I allow myself to breathe.

The next day at school, Normand still isn't there. My worry for him—and myself—grows. I watch the door, expecting protectors in their copper uniforms to come for me—all over that stupid (wonderful) comic book. Mrs. Cranberry briskly collects our vocational picks. When she yanks mine from my hand, her eyes fall on my selections. Her sour lips purse.

"Protector," she mutters. Her bony fingers tighten, and I brace for a smacking because I've once again done something wrong despite following her instructions to the decimal.

"Sit up straight," she says half-heartedly.

I note it. I *will* figure out the grown-up world.

"Today," she addresses the class, "you will begin with your lowest scoring vocational option."

For me, that means clerical, which is my preferred choice. The pay is decent and the work conditions better than most vocations. I have to ace that placement while sucking at the other two.

Mrs. Cranberry divides us into six groups. I stand with the stockier boys and girls from my class, which seems odd. Our scholastic scores are publicly posted. We all know how we rank in everything because it encourages competition, and so I can definitively say three of the students in my group are not clerical material.

"And this lot," she says to my cluster, "are headed to the Growing Lands."

I gape. "But, I didn't pick farmhand," I protest. "It's not even on my top five list!"

She raises a liver-spotted finger. "We have a deluge of *much* more qualified candidates for clerical positions, and a shortage of laborers. No, no, I think you'd do well getting your hands dirty."

"But you said we couldn't pick anything that wasn't on the list!" I argue.

47

"You can't. But, *I* can make recommendations. It's all arranged." Her face is triumphant. "Make me proud."

I rage inside as we walk in a clump to the train station. Streams of other teens merge with us. Groups of those who identify as boys push each other playfully as we walk, and groups of those who identify as girls whisper together in conspiratorial huddles. I'm conspicuously alone, and I'm surprised to be missing my classroom. There, I always had something to read, an assignment to work on, or daydreams of better days ahead. I could forget nobody liked me. Here, every laugh is a razor to my ears. My shoulders hunch, and if I could pick a power right now, it would be to pass through solid objects so I could sink into the ground.

Grey-clad overseers greet us at the grimy train station doors. The emblem on their chests is of three arrows, each pointing from the center in a different direction. They shout out the various occupational groups while standing under signs representing them—a pickaxe and light for the miners, a sheaf of wheat for farmhands, a set of cogs for the factory workers, a fist clasping the all-seeing eye for the protectors, and so on.

I hand an overseer my i-dent card. She swipes it through her card reader, nods, and hands me a beige armband with a sheaf of wheat on it.

"Track 8, car 52," she says, waving me toward the inside of the station.

I head in. The train station is one of the few grand buildings in our borough. It survived the war and is majestic with its sweeping staircases, antique giant clock, and steel girders that look more like works of art than structural support. Grime taints everything, and many of the window panes in the domed ceiling are broken, replaced with wood or rusting steel. Red-bellied shadowrens flutter in dizzying patterns overhead.

Their chirps echo all around. I imagine being part of their flock, a thing of speed and grace and precision, which is when I feel the wet and squishy plop of bird poop landing on my cheek. Several peers point and laugh.

I fish around in my pocket for something to wipe off the droppings. I've got nothing. I look at the armband. It'll have to do.

"You may want to reconsider that course of action, Caitlin Feral," a familiar voice says.

I turn and stare into a round face with doughy skin framed by a bowl haircut. I feel relief—and reflexive annoyance. It's Normand.

"Normand, where have you been?" I ask. "I was worried. Why weren't you in class?"

He gazes to my right, avoiding eye contact, and blinks like a cursor on a screen.

"No need for concern, Caitlin," he replies. "Because of my superior intellect, I'm exempt from the traditional selection process. My permanent workstream has been assigned." He indicates the armband around his charcoal jacket with a screwdriver and data monitor on it.

"Okay," I say, wanting to point out that in addition to his "superior intellect," he's got a crap leg. It's not like he's a great option for most manual labor positions, and he's got bureaucrat parents pulling strings beyond the reach of most dregs. It makes perfect sense he's assigned to a cushy tech position. He hasn't Manifested, but he's got it made.

Caitlin, I say to myself, *for once, keep your mouth shut and let him have this.*

"You still have bird feces on your face," he interjects, gazing at my cheek. "It would be advisable to remove it. Birds are known carriers for a host of diseases. For instance—"

I raise my hand.

"Normand, this is not the time."

"*Veritas*," he says in an agreeable tone, looking at his watch. "We are on a ticking clock. But it would be rather *fowl* to use your armband as a sanitary wipe."

His shoulders jerk up and down, and he releases a sound like he's having an asthma attack. This is him laughing. All around, teens with armbands hurry to their platforms. He stops wheezing as if someone had flicked an off switch.

"Here," he says, staring over my shoulder as he offers me a plastic container with a moist tissue poking out. My family rations gritty soap that practically dissolves our skin, and he's got wet wipes?

"Thanks," I say, pulling one free and using it to clean the bird poop off my face.

"Did you know birds defecate and urinate all in one?" he asks as if this should be the most fascinating thing in the world. The nerd in me is intrigued, but I refuse to let on.

"I should get to my train," I say.

The stream of teens around us lightens. The trains are all scheduled to leave soon. I'm screwed if I miss mine, yet there's something I have to ask.

"The last time I saw you at the library, did you... leave anything there?"

My eyes dart around, noting where the protectors are, faceless with their visors. Can they hear us? Probably, with their spying tech, but there's a lot of noise in here. We should be safe—I hope.

"What an unorthodox query," he replies, looking at his watch.

My heart hammers. A protector stares; he walks our way. Is this what they've been waiting for? To catch us to together? Are they recording what I'm saying? What exactly did I say? The protector closes in. Teens veer around him.

"Oh, well, never mind," I stammer. The protector is ten measures away. Sweat soaks my shirt. I step away from Normand. "I should go."

"I left you the *Tigara* comic book," he blurts. He doesn't see the protector. "I'd think that would be more than apparent. Did you find it to your liking?"

"Very much so," is what I want to say, but the protector is two measures away.

"Would reading issue two be of interest to you?" he asks.

He talks loudly to be heard over the din—or to sell me out. The protector doesn't need tech to hear us now. He's right next to me. Teens give us a wide berth.

I force myself to laugh. It's too shrill and hysterical to be real. My theater teacher would be disgusted.

"Oh, Normand," I snort. "You're so funny!"

He blinks rapidly, trying to process.

"What's happening now?" he asks.

"Vintage Normand," I say. "Such a clown."

I wipe imaginary tears from my eyes. My farce fails. The protector grabs my arm, ready to drag me away, like others of his kind did to my dad. Is that why they've set me up? Because of the crimes of the father? It's the kind of innately mean thing they would do.

"Why are you two loitering?" the protector demands.

I look to Normand, waiting for him to turn on me. He shudders twice like he sometimes does.

"What's wrong with him?" the protector asks.

My mind races. Can I use Normand's weird health issue to our advantage? Normand stares at the protector's visor.

"Why did the chicken cross the road?" Normand asks.

My eyes widen. The protector's grip on my arm tightens. Normand's telling a joke? We're as good as dead.

"Why?" the protector's voice crackles from the hidden speakers in his helmet.

"To get laid," Normand replies.

Silence drags. I close my eyes. I can't watch. The protector's helmet speakers emit a muffled chortle. My eyes pop open. Am I hearing this right? Is he *laughing*?

"That's terrible," the protector says. Playfulness tints his tone, and his hold on my arm weakens. "Did you kids hear that story on the info update about the guy who got hit in the head with a can of soda pop?"

Normand's eyes widen in alarm. "No, I am unaware of—"

"It's okay," the protector cuts him off. "It was a soft drink."

Normand gets it before I do. His shoulders rise up and down, and he wheezes out a laugh. The protector releases my arm, and it's my turn to wonder, *What's happening now?* I'm too surprised to play along. I look from Normand to the protector and back.

Hold up. Is Normand *saving the day?*

"All right," the protector says through his mic. "You two move along."

His tone is brusque, but his bark lacks bite. He waves us on with the indolence of an indulgent uncle. I wait for him to change his mind as we rejoin the thinning crowd, but when I glance over my shoulder, the protector's walking the other way.

"Did that happen?" I murmur.

"The evidence would indicate yes," Normand replies.

His leg brace creaks as we walk. I'm noticing it less and less. He stops at a set of stairs. "My track is in this direction."

Am I sad to see him go?

"Well, have a good day." It's such a banal farewell after our mini-adventure.

"A good day to you as well," he replies. "And before we were interrupted, I was asking if reading *Tigara* issue two would be of interest to you?"

My mouth is so dry I barely get the words out. "Yes, it would."

He gazes at his watch.

"Good. Then it's decided. Until then, fare you well."

He grabs the handrail and creaks his way up the steps.

"Wait. What?" I stare at his back. "What's been decided?"

He reaches the top of the stairs, and a grey-clad overseer asks for his i-dent card. Yellow lights flash around the station, and a voice crackles over the intercom.

"Five minutes 'til departure. Five minutes."

"Effing geez," I curse. *Why does Normand have to be so weird? And why am I diving in?*

CHAPTER 9

The hall is empty except for a few overseers and several protectors. I run, reach my track, and join the stragglers clambering on board.

The car's more dilapidated than my housing unit. Grime smears the train windows; bolts in the floor are more rust than iron; the lights flicker.

I slide onto a seat. A spring pokes into my bottom. Did someone go out of their way to make this ride as miserable as possible? The wiry fellow next to me seems oblivious. He presses his face to the window.

Like everyone else in our car, he wears the armband with a sheaf of wheat. I put mine on as he turns to me with wide eyes. The bridge of his nose is splattered with freckles; his black hair is a mess of beautiful curls.

"I've never been on a train before," he says with the chumminess of two people who've known each other for years. "I'm Bradie Lopez Nettle." He's cute in a boyish way, getting squinty-eyed when he smiles—which is often. It makes him look a touch simple.

He offers his hand. The gesture's unnecessarily formal, but unlike Normand's quirks, it's also strangely charming. I'm instantly suspicious— charming people get away with far more than they should.

"Caitlin," I say, making sure to keep my guard up.

"When I was little, my brother would take me to watch the trains," he continues in his familiar way. "We'd make up their destinations; the more impossible, the better—other planets, the center of the earth, cities beyond the Red Zone. Secret cargo would spark a series of brutal murders on board; turns out the ticket taker did it."

He momentarily wins me over with his enthusiasm, his talk of his brother, and the whimsical fantasies that remind me of the way I want to disappear into a world of cowls, capes, and masks. But the part of me that sabotages any attempt at getting close to anyone whispers in my ear, *He's an idiot. He's talking to you because you happen to be here. Don't think that he likes you.*

I shrink from him.

The other passengers chirp excitedly; the PA system squawks incomprehensibly, and a busybody type two seats behind primly tells everyone to take their seats because "the train's about to start moving." A mechanical grunt preludes a lurch, and we chug out of the station.

"Where are your friends?" Bradie asks.

I squirm.

"They were given different work assignments," I lie.

"Oh, that's too bad," he says.

"What about you?" I ask. "Where are *your* friends?"

If he's going to put me on the spot, I'm going to do the same to him.

"They're in Borough 10. I moved here two weeks ago. I'm living with my aunt. It sucked when my brother became a protector and moved away for his work placement. After our parents died, he pulled some strings so I could be closer to him."

His brother's a protector. I'm instantly horrified.

"We can trade seats if you want the window," Bradie offers.

"I'm good," I deflect.

He suctions his face to the window as we pull out of the station.

"Check that out!" he says loud enough for the whole car to hear. To my surprise, our fellows turn to see what's so exciting. He's barely arrived, and he already has more clout than me.

The ever-present storm clouds crackle on the other side of the security fence. The broken remains of a city decimated by the war with the Supergenics sit below the roiling black mass. We see that all the time. But today *is* different.

We head directly *toward* the storm and the forbidden city it destroyed.

The track leads to a mesh gate topped with barbed wire and flanked by massive guard towers. Signs warning of radiation, toxic waste, and mutated animals plaster the security fence winding left and right, separating the boroughs from the adjacent Yellow Zone.

The gate opens; Bradie grabs my shoulder as if he needs an anchor.

"We're going outside the fence!" he says.

Teens murmur "no way," "effing geez," and "badass." One boy shakes, eyes bubbling with tears. I'm keenly aware of Bradie's fingers holding me.

Should I touch him back?

I lift my hand, unsure where to put it. I hesitate and lose my chance. He lets go, pressing both hands to the window. I run my fingers through my hair as if that's what I meant to do all along—not that anyone's noticing. Like a bunch of cattle, they're mesmerized by the opening gate.

Why are they in such a tizzy? I wonder.

We're on farm duty, so obviously we have to pass through the Yellow Zone. This isn't a surprise. Despite my condescension, I grudgingly recognize this *is* momentous. None of us has been on the other side of the barrier. We speed through the opening, traveling under the black clouds that terrified us as children.

We're on an elevated track, which puts us above the streets of the decaying metropolis. I wish I'd accepted Bradie's offer to switch seats. I see the Yellow Zone in a way I never have before, gazing down at a pile-up of cars, toppled buildings, and the ever-present red-black wrens that have made the city their home. Lightning flares around us, but the many pulsating orbs dotting the city keep us safe. The concrete towers supporting the orbs put them almost level with the raised track. A burst of energy smashes into a globe ten measures away, making it crackle with electricity.

"Effing eff," Bradie curses.

I agree, especially as the journey turns from wow to weird. A residential area is flattened except for one roofless house. The yard is impossibly manicured with shrubs and flowers that almost look lacquered, and the rooms inside are perfectly preserved—a bed is made, a crib holds stuffed animals, toothbrush and paste sit on a washroom sink next to a clawfoot tub. The whole property pulsates with an ethereal light.

Further on, a bell tower has a giant lowercase "t" on it, which seems to be a symbol of some sort. Beyond a broken window, I'm sure I see a shadow cast by something with long limbs and goat horns dancing suggestively.

The creepiest is a public square filled with black statues of people trying to flee, eyes and mouths wide with terror; they're frozen in mid-run. My chest constricts. I don't think they're statues.

We leave them behind.

Our attention diverts to what's ahead. We approach a second security barrier, so formidable it makes the one around the boroughs look like a baby's playpen. That one is electrified chainlink. This is a wall of steel and concrete, rising 20 measures high, armed with sonic mutant repellants that make our ears vibrate with a rising hum the closer we get. It has huge mutant warning signs with the heads of a wolf, lizard, and lioness ensconced within the crescent moons of the biohazard symbol.

An imposing gate rumbles open, and we speed through—into the Red Zone.

I'm met by a landscape unlike anything I've seen. Beyond the concrete confines of our borough and the smashed remains of the Yellow Zone is a vista of golden wheat billowing in the breeze. We speed by apple orchards, rows of grapevines, and pasture land with cows and sheep, like in our farming books at school. It goes on and on.

"I don't understand," I say.

"What do you mean?" Bradie asks.

"There's so much of it."

"So?"

"So," I reply, "why do we end up with so little?"

For the first time, Bradie's smile withers.

Now what have I done? I wonder.

"Don't say that," he whispers. "Don't ever say that."

I'm about to ask why, but I don't. I know why. Dotting the farmlands are squat watchtowers, each bearing a flag with an emblem of a fist holding the all-seeing eye. The protectors inside ostensibly keep watch for prowling mutant animals. We all know they're watching the farmhands as much.

You're not a kid anymore, I hear my mother say. *You need to shut your mouth.*

"Our little secret," Bradie winks. He's back to his smiling self, but the smile doesn't reach his eyes; when he banters with the girls behind us, he's a bit too loud; a bit too gregarious; a bit too forced.

He's scared.

I have bigger chickens to poach. *How much of the food are the protectors taking?*

The train pulls to a stop, and a grey-clad overseer opens the door to our car. He barks at us, "Come on, farmhands. Let's go."

We leave in orderly rank and file, like at school. We crowd the open-air train platform, and the overseers direct us down a wide flight of stairs. When the farmhand trainees like Bradie and me have disembarked, the train whistles and chugs toward the mountains in the distance.

The baby-faced teens still on the train look at us enviously. A few wave. I wave back, sad for them. Those chosen to be miners will eventually die of black coughs, their lungs full of dust. For farmhands, it's the chemicals used to treat fruits and vegetables we need to worry about.

They get us from the inside or the outside, but in the end, they get us all.

CHAPTER 10

Overseers give us beige coveralls to wear over our uniforms, along with work boots, all of which fit poorly. We spend the morning standing in front of a rumbling conveyer belt, sorting apples into various categories.

I'm accustomed to the half-rotting fruit in our rations pack, so it's no surprise the most bumped and bruised specimens go in bins marked DREGS. If any look mutated, we set them in a biohazard bin to be sent to a lab. It's the other apples that amaze me with their glossy unmarked surfaces, firm bodies, and the promise of succulent interiors.

I stare at one in my hand. I've seen apples like this in pictures and assumed the images were digitally altered. I had no idea an apple could be like this in real life. The cartoon apples with smiling worms poking out seemed more realistic.

"Don't get any ideas," a woman with grey hair and a stained apron says next to me. "They'll be happy to beat you."

She jerks her head at the protector by the door. His visor glints at me, and he touches the baton at his hip. Of course. Produce like this is for people like him. I'm about to put the apple in a bin marked Protectorate when Apron Lady snorts.

"They wish," she says. "That one there, hon."

She points at a barrel labeled *Jupitar City*. It's brimming with hundreds of perfect specimens.

This can't be right, I think as I add it to the container.

"Okay, help me seal it up," Apron says to me.

I hold a circular lid above the canister while Apron applies a device that seals the top into place. Dozens of tubs are marked for Jupitar City.

Everyone knows the various boroughs and Jupitar City are trade partners. We ship some of the food and manufactured goods we produce across the river. In exchange, the Supergenics keep the boroughs and the surrounding land radiation-free and neutralize any mutated animals the protectors can't handle. Only now do I question how much the Supergenics are getting out of the deal. The answer, it seems, is a lot.

"You're catching on quick," Apron says to me.

"Yes," I agree. "I believe I am."

Later that day, pickers take us into the orchards, and we spend hours pulling apples from trees. I keep thinking about all the perfect fruit headed for Jupitar City instead of to the people who farm it. There must be some mistake. The Supergenics are heroes. Maybe they don't know how often we go hungry. A group of giggling girls pulls me from my thoughts, their high-pitched laughter grating my ears. Bradie is at the center of the fawning cluster, making an already irritating task worse. I try to refocus my attention. The trainee who picks the most apples gets a prize, and part of me thinks, *Maybe this time, it will be my turn to win.*

An overseer snaps her fingers at their group.

Good.

I should know better than to let my attention wander. I grope for an apple deep in the tree, the corner of my eye on Bradie. I overreach, my ladder teeters, and I know my efforts to right myself are doomed. The ladder falls from under me; I grab a branch in the nick of time, jarring my shoulder, and my feet flail in the air. Mrs. Cranberry is a train ride away, yet I hear her yelling at me to "Get down from there."

I dangle, hesitant to drop to the uneven ground below for fear of spraining my ankle. I'm about to call for help when a loud siren deafens and silences me. For a second, I think it's sounding because I've screwed up, and the protectors are coming for me. Deeper down, my pounding heart knows this is worse. We do drills several times a year. Whether it's here or in the boroughs, that siren means one thing—a perimeter breach.

I spin my head, searching for the safety shelter. All the other teens are doing the same. The overseers gave us cursory safety training when we arrived, but they've disappeared. Signage of stick figures fleeing a triple-headed beast point toward evac zones. The workers wave at us, shouting, "This way, this way."

I think of gymnastics class and let go, landing like a springy cat. *Nailed it.*

My heart pounds my ribcage as I run. I get less than five measures when my foot catches on a tree root, and down I go. I hit hard, knocking the breath from me. I struggle to inhale as someone helps me up. I look into Bradie's dark eyes.

"There," he says, pointing toward a set of stairs leading to the train platform.

58

People run up them, the experienced workers quickly but calmly, the trainees screaming and shoving their way in between.

"Ready?" Bradie asks.

I nod.

We sprint. I'm fast. Bradie's faster. I struggle to keep pace.

"Come on, Legs," he winks.

I push harder, wanting to show him what's what, weaving and jumping amongst thick roots. So does he. I dart around a tree and take the lead. I'm so exultant I block out the sirens and the panicked shouts of the other trainees. It's Bradie and me alone, racing for no other reason than to see who is the fastest, which is when I smash into a copper-uniformed protector. He's not much bigger than me, and I bowl him over.

"Effing geez!" he swears through the mic in his closed helmet.

He grabs my arm and yanks me to my feet. I think he's going to demand to see my i-dent card and formally charge me. He points to the crowd, "Go!" he shouts. "Get to safety, kid!"

I don't have time to obey before a muscled form covered in brown fur smashes into him. The thing growls, its sharp teeth ripping through the protector's resilient, body-hugging garb like it's tissue paper. He screams. I pant, back away, and the monster on top of him rounds on me, staring at me with bloodshot eyes.

It's a hound, big as a cow, slavering with bloody teeth. It has two heads, one in proportion to its massive body. The second head is smaller and wilder, snapping at the air. I've seen dead mutated animals on the backs of trucks, driven around to scare the populace. *This* is terrifying.

Guns blast, protectors shout, and more beasts growl amongst the trees. Muscled shapes covered in fur blur as they sprint through the orchard.

Oh, geez-us, I swear. *There's a pack.*

The monstrosity before me ignores them, all four of its bloodshot eyes on me. The little head yaps wildly, egging the big head on. The beast bunches on its haunches, preparing to rip me apart the same as it did the protector. I'm dead. It's as simple as that.

"Leave her alone!" Bradie shouts. The idiot clenches an apple. His arm winds and throws the red fruit at the mutated creature. The apple hits the big head square in the brow with impressive force. The apple bursts. The monstrosity yelps, and little head bites big head's ear. The hound shakes it off and turns to face Bradie; he's a toy doll by comparison. He picks up another apple, keeping it where big head can see it. Little head cranes its neck to get a better view.

More gunshots, shouts, and screams rise around us.

The mutated thing steps cautiously toward Bradie, ears back, showing its teeth as a low growl rumbles in its throat.

"Caitlin," Bradie says, "I need you to get the protector's gun."

The hound's tail swishes over the dead protector's booted feet. His gun is strapped in its holster.

"You can do it," Bradie says.

I nod. I *can* do it, but should I? An ordinary citizen brandishing a weapon? That's forbidden. Yet what choice do I have? Bradie's brother is a protector. Does that make this okay?

I swallow my fear, pushing it down my throat to the pit of my stomach as I creep closer to the protector. The little hound head sees me, but before it can bark, Bradie whips an apple and hits the small one between the eyes. Bradie unleashes more apples, grabbing them from the ground and pitching them with surprising accuracy. The big head catches an apple in its jaws, chomping hard. Juice, seeds, and saliva spray everywhere. I bend over the dead protector. The reinforced tensile fabric of his uniform—allegedly as supple as silk yet stronger than steel—was useless against mutated fangs and claws. His rib cage pokes out. I step in a pool of his blood, reach over his torso, unclasp his holster, and pull his firearm free. I lift it and point. My arms shake.

"You need to turn off the safety," Bradie says. "It's on the left side of the barrel."

I spot and thumb a slide switch; it clicks, revealing a red rectangle that presumably means I've followed his instructions correctly.

"Pull back on the barrel to load the chamber."

He sees my confusion.

"The top of the gun! Pull it back!" he shouts, still lobbing apples.

I do, and something snaps into place. The mutant hound loses it and charges Bradie.

"Shoot it!" he shouts.

I point, aiming at the thing, and pull the trigger. A boom fills my ears; the force jerks my arm overhead, and the gun flies from my grip, bouncing across the uneven ground. I slip on the protector blood around my feet, trip over his dead body, and hit the ground. The impact reverberates into my

60

jaw. I gaze at what I expect to be the animal's dead body, killed by my bullet, only to find the beast very much alive. My shot hit it, if barely. One of the little head's ears is blown clean off. It's deathly quiet, staring at me over its shoulder. So is the big one. Bradie hits it with more apples, but both heads ignore him. They emit a low growl and charge me.

The gun is too far away. I grasp the protector's baton and blindly shove it toward the animal. A blue burst of electricity courses from the shaft into the creature's chest. It yelps in agony, the two heads smashing one into the other. It can't pull away, the electricity holding it fast. I push the baton deeper into its body.

I smell burning flesh; smoke rises from the beast's clumpy fur. The baton grows hotter, burning my palms. My jaw clenches, and I squeeze harder. The baton sparks. The electricity grows brighter, then winks out as the battery runs dry. I drop the weapon, and the monstrosity falls dead at my feet.

I pant, drenched in sweat and blood. My senses are wound so tight, the tiny crackle of a branch rings loud as the gunshot. I swivel and face a single-headed hound between two trees; the beast is double the size of its mate. The hound sprints toward me. There's no time to run; I'm too spent to scream. It launches off its haunches. I cover my face, hear a boom, and warm blood splatters my cheeks. I lower my hand. The beast's lolling tongue and blown-open head loom large, pounding me into the ground with all its weight. The stink of wet fur and infected flesh crawling with maggots fills my nostrils. I grit my teeth to keep its hair out of my mouth. I'm sure I'm going to suffocate when Bradie shouts, "Push, Caitlin!"

I do, and with him pulling, I'm able to skitter out from under the thing's mass. Bradie helps me stand and holds me tight. Before I know it, he kisses me, and I kiss him back. The shock wears off, and I feel him grab my butt. I shove him so hard he lands on his ass. I pant, towering over him, fists clenched.

"What was that?" I demand.

"Me saving your life?"

"You kissing me!"

"I don't know," he shrugs. "You seemed into it."

"I wasn't," I say. "Ask next time."

"Next time?" he arches a brow on that dopey face of his.

He holds the protector's gun. A bleeding red wound mars his cheek.

"You're hurt," I say.

"Yeah, well, turns out you're a terrible shot," he replies.

"I did that?" I ask.

"And that," he jerks his head at the electrocuted mutant animal with the two heads.

He gets up and reaches out to me. I step back.

"Relax," he says, waving at himself. "You had your chance at this."

He takes my hands and uncurls my fists. My palms are red and blistering from overloading the baton, matching my Testing Day face.

"You'll be okay," he says. "I've seen worse."

He kisses me again, but this time on my forehead. It's so tender and unexpected and different than the lip kiss, all I want is to curl into him and listen to him tell me everything will be all right.

Those are your daddy issues coming out, a part of me snips.

It doesn't matter. The moment passes, and a group of protectors surrounds us, weapons pointed at our heads.

Bradie raises his arms, and my blistered hands go up in surrender. A protector's dead because of us, *and* we took his weapons. I look for the gun we used. I don't see it. Did Bradie tuck it under one of the mutant hounds? Doesn't matter. We are in a *lot* of trouble.

The lead protector touches the side of his helmet; his visor slides back, revealing his face. He looks at the dead animals.

"You kids did this?"

There's no point in denying it. We nod.

He inclines his head to the side. "Not bad. Maybe you should become protectors."

Never, I swear to myself.

CHAPTER 11

The protector examines my blistered hands and whistles.

"Gross," he says lightly. He takes a tube from the medkit on his belt and squeezes a clear ointment into my palm.

"Rub it in," he says.

I wince as I do.

He wraps gauze around my injured fingers. The cream tingles, dulling the pain to a throb. I've never known a protector to be nice. A wounded hound drags its hind legs behind it, growling as it pathetically comes toward us. The protector pauses in tending to me and shoots it in the head.

I wince at the sound, then look around, hoping to see the members of A.M.M.O.—Anti-Mutant Menace Offensive—swooping in from Jupitar City to save the day.

"Is Captain Light here?" I ask.

The protector chuckles. "Don't fool yourself, kid. The protectors are the first line of defense. We do the heavy lifting." He jerks his head in the direction of Jupitar City. "*They* only come around when the cameras are on."

"Oh," I say with disappointment. I've always wanted to meet Captain Light, and this would've been the perfect chance to ask him about the apple distribution discrepancy. I know there must be some explanation.

The protectors escort us to the train platform. Through the trees, I see more hound corpses. Protectors toss the smaller ones onto the back of a flatbed truck, but some are as big as cars. Abattoir workers in thick, leather aprons stab the oversized mutants with meat hooks attached to mobile hoists, lifting and depositing the corpses next to the smaller members of their pack. One has three tails; another, twin faces mashed together. Its four dead eyes stare at us.

They're not going to feed us that, I assure myself. *Are they?*

There's always talk of what goes into the canned meat we receive as part of our rations. The Bureau of Health assures us deformed cattle are sent to a lab for analysis, like the oddly shaped apples. Surely, it's the same for these monstrosities. Realization smothers worry.

"I *killed* one of those things," I say out loud.

"Yeah," Bradie agrees. "That makes you a badass."

"You killed one of those things too," I reply. "I guess you're also a badass."

He smiles and winks. "*That* was never in question."

Such a brat. It's a step up from idiot.

We scale the concrete stairs to the train platform; cheers and applause rise with us. Many of the students and farmhands saw us from above. They know what we did. Bradie waves at them. I stare like an oaf. The train is waiting, doors open.

"*Please board the train*," a crackling voice comes over the announcement system.

Bradie and I move to obey.

"No, no," the protector who tended my hands says, grabbing us by the shoulders. "*That's* your ride."

He pushes us toward the shiny caboose at the rear of the train.

Workers and trainees stare as Bradie and I board.

Inside, we gaze around at an upgraded version of the car we rode in on. The lighting is perfectly gentle, soothing music plays, and a scent of eucalyptus teases the air. The helpful protector gives us a thumbs up from the other side of a freshly cleaned window. This car must be for officials. When I sit on the vinyl upholstery, which looks new *and* stuffed with foam, I experience a foreign sensation—comfort.

"Well, this is all right," Bradie says.

I watch out the window as protectors herd everyone else onto the train; none of them are let into our car. Once the doors close, the train lurches to life, carrying us back toward our borough.

A grey-clad overseer enters, carrying a pair of dinner trays with foil on top. She sets them down on pull-out tables. Fancy.

"We thought you might be hungry," she says. "And for dessert..."

She hands us each a shiny, perfect apple. I hold it before me, gazing in awe. I want to devour it immediately, but I'm curious what's under the foil. I pull it back and stare at what appears to be real meatloaf (not some mix of oats and animal fat), mashed potatoes, and string beans doused in butter. I've rarely experienced a meal like this; I barely chew between bites as if they might take it from me. Bradie sprints through his meal as well. Neither of us hesitates to lick the trays clean.

I set my metal utensils aside and gaze at the apple, but I don't bite into it. Bradie shows no such restraint, taking a large chunk out of his with his large teeth. His face is pure ecstasy as he chews.

"It's so good," he grunts with delight.

He notices I haven't tried mine.

"If you're thinking of saving it for your family, you can't. They won't let you take it with you," he says.

"What do you mean?" I ask. "Why not?"

He shrugs. "It's another one of their rules."

I get the feeling he caught himself as he was about to say, "One of their *stupid* rules."

"How do you know?" I ask.

"Because my big brother's a protector, remember?" he replies. "He was never allowed to bring food home from the Cube when he came to visit, and that guy is sneaky."

My chest constricts. I'd forgotten his brother was one of *them*. I was wondering where Bradie learned so much about guns, enough to shoot a mutant obscenity square between the eyes. That wasn't luck.

"He's the one who taught you to—"

He jerks forward and grabs my hand, his fingers pressing into my bandages.

"Ow!" I say, but he doesn't let go.

"Has anyone ever told you that you have the most beautiful eyes?"

Bradie's charm almost cons me, but a terrified furrow frames his dark eyes. He's scared.

Before I say a word, the soft music cuts out and dissemination screens around the cabin spring to life. An information clerk in navy blue appears on the monitors, seated behind a desk and reading off a teleprompter.

"A breach today in the farming sector, where brave protectors saved hundreds of lives."

We watch footage of the protectors shooting at rabid and deformed canines hunting amidst the trees. Yelps echo around us, joined by a dramatic musical score.

"Three officers were killed in the incursion, bravely defending the populace from these ravenous beasts."

Smiling headshots of the three fallen protectors appear on the screen along with their names and ages. The youngest was barely older than us. I recognize him. He's the one I knocked over, the one who told me to run. He died defending me. I've grown to hate the protectors so much, I stopped believing how dangerous their jobs can be outside the fence.

That's what they want you to focus on, I hear my mom say.

The information clerk is back on screen.

"And some unexpected bravery from a pair of mentees during that incursion," he says.

Bradie sits up excitedly. "He's talking about us!"

New images appear, taken from the security tower cameras overlooking the fields, including a shot of the dual-headed hound growling at me.

Bradie throws apples at the mutant, and it turns to attack him. Any images of me picking up or wielding the protector's gun are omitted. It cuts to the hound rushing me, right into the baton in my grip. The music swells triumphantly as the beast electrocutes itself.

The images cut out, and up comes Chief Bureaucrat Sannvi Patel, dressed in a beige suit, extolling our bravery, saying how sure she is that we will "grow into our place within the system."

I barely listen, focusing on what the broadcast left out—me firing a weapon, badly; Bradie shooting the second dog, expertly.

Ordinary dregs shouldn't know how to fire a weapon. They shouldn't think of picking one up. I'm sure to be penalized. But Bradie, he's had practice—lots of it. That will earn him the death penalty—or worse. As if reading my mind, Bradie turns pale. The protectors in the orchard seemed so concerned about our well-being, I'd assumed we were in the clear. That was before they reviewed the security footage.

I want to reassure Bradie, but the door to our car slides open. In strides a man in a black uniform with red piping. The insignia on his chest is a red hangman's noose. A woman with that symbol oversaw the protectors taking my dad away. This man in black is an agent of the Cube; he's worse than a protector. He moves like an eel, and with the shaved strips on either side of his grey, slicked-back hair, he looks like one too. A pair of protectors with black piping on their copper uniforms walk behind him. I grip my apple tightly.

"I trust you've enjoyed your meal," the agent says.

"Y-y-yes," Bradie stutters.

"It was delicious," I add quickly.

"I'm sure," he says, wrinkling his nose as if we'd been feeding from a trough. He plucks the perfect apple from my hand, appraises it, then polishes it on his black leather. "I need a word with the young man, in private."

"But—" I hesitate, and a massive protector yanks me from my seat. My toes barely touch the ground as he drags me toward the door. I look at Bradie. He stares at the floor. I think he might be crying.

"Caitlin, my dear," the agent says, "don't let the public broadcast give you any foolish fancies about being a hero. We do like to give the populace the occasional story of hope. We find it minimizes the suicide rate. But we both know you got lucky. By all rights, the beasts should've torn you to shreds. Understood?"

I gape, not saying a word.

"Do you *understand*?" he shouts.

"Yes, I do," I insist quickly. "And Bradie—"

"Goodbye, Caitlin," Eel Man says. He bites into the apple as the protector drags me from the car.

I stare over my shoulder. Bradie's body heaves. I can't hear what the agent says. Apple juice drips down his chin as the door slides shut.

CHAPTER 12

The protector shoves me into an empty cargo car. I screw my nose at the reek of fermenting fruit, and I swat at buzzing flies. The train jostles, dropping me to my hands and knees; pain flares up my wrists. I sit on the bare metal floor for the rest of the ride, staring at the door, waiting for it to open, wishing for the protectors to throw Bradie in with me—but they don't.

We pull into Central Station, where I hear everybody else file off the train. By the time the doors on my car pop open, the platform is clear. I exit, looking for Bradie.

A protector sees me loitering and points for me to be on my way. I obey. What else can I do?

At home, my mom gives me an awkward hug. She saw the information update broadcasting the images of me electrocuting the mutant. I cry, and she thinks it's because I'm scared of what happened. I am, but I'm not thinking of the hounds. I don't know what they've done to Bradie, and I have no way of finding out.

That night, after my mom and brother have gone to bed, I lie in my bunk, staring at nothing. I wonder if I'll ever sleep again. I fish under my mattress and pull out Normand's comic book. I climb down from my bunk, careful not to step on my brother, and go to the window where the light from a streetlamp streams in.

I flip to a page where Tigara is breaking a militia fighter's neck while slitting the throat of a mercenary with the claws on her feet.

I stare at her image and wish she were here to make the agent pay.

The next day at school, classmates run up to me. They all saw me on the information broadcast. My whole life, they ignored, derided, and played tricks on me; now, they act like we're the best of friends.

"Are those claw marks?" Julia asks of the scratches on my cheeks.

"Teeth," I reply dryly. Her eyes grow wide. It's nonsense, of course. They're scrapes from when I fell. If the hound had gotten that close to me with its gaping jaws, I wouldn't have a face.

"Here," Julia says, offering me a plastic cup of gelatinized vanilla pudding with a peel-back lid. I slide it into my pocket.

"Caitlin's sitting next to me in class!" she declares to the crowd. Julia's the new Lilianne and has blossomed into a grade-A bossypants now that her domineering best friend is gone.

Mrs. Cranberry also acts differently toward me.

"Still getting yourself into trouble, I see," she says, but there are no threats of punishment, demerits, or the dreaded "permanent file." Even her baleful glare softens.

It's small consolation. I have no idea what happened to Bradie. I realize I barely know the guy, but I have to help him—and *not* because helplessly watching an agent take him the way agents took my dad hits all kinds of triggers. Bradie risked his life for me. We faced mutant hounds together, plural, and we won—even if that meant breaking the Protectorate's rules.

The thought brings a realization.

I raise my hand.

With an exasperated sigh, Mrs. Cranberry acknowledges me. "Yes, Caitlin?"

"I'd like to skip the rest of my farming apprenticeship," I say.

"Caitlin, I know you had an upsetting day," she snaps, "but that simply isn't done."

I'm undeterred.

"I'm ready for my protector training," I declare.

The class falls silent. She stares at me. Does she feel guilty? Farmhand wasn't one of my options, but she sent me there anyway. *She* put me in danger. Maybe she reasons I'd find a way to get into trouble no matter where I was, but from the way her face constricts, I don't think so.

"I'll look into it," she says.

She breaks us into groups based on our workstreams. Focused discussions guide us through what we've learned, questions we have, and areas we'd like to improve upon. When it comes to my turn, everyone in my group wants to know about the hounds.

"How big were they?" they ask.

"Like a truck," I reply.

"Did they have three heads?"

"Only two."

"Did you see anyone die?"

"Yes." And worse.

It's all a bit silly considering they were there, but I suppose the adult workers kept them from seeing much. We answer multiple-choice questions about the work placement, and we write essays about how this makes us contributing members of society.

Walking home, a cluster of classmates who identify as girls surround me; the boys who like them follow. Julia loops her arm in mine.

"We have got to talk about who your boyfriend is going to be!" she coos. "Or do you prefer girls? What about Cody? I think he likes you."

I glance at Cody, one of the more athletic members of our class, and quickly look away. All I can think about is Bradie.

Red-black wrens swoop through the air, gobbling insects. We pass the library, and I see Normand's unmistakable silhouette. He raises a hand in a wave. I try to do the same; Julia grabs my arm, forcing it down.

"Don't encourage that weirdo!" she hisses.

We keep walking; I glance at Normand alone on the library steps.

Little by little, my classmates disappear into the various tenements near our school. It's down to Julia and me. She hugs me.

"Caitlin Feral, I think you might be the bravest person I've ever met," she says. "I'm so glad you're my best friend."

"Sure," I say, waiting for the punchline.

She giggles, waves, and skips to her family's townhouse. It's been a long time since my family lived in one of those. Before Julia reaches the entrance, her mother opens it as if she'd been waiting for her daughter's return. Behind her is Julia's father, seated on the couch next to a man clad in a black uniform with red piping.

The door slams shut, and Julia is gone.

My heart pumps loudly, and my throat runs dry. It's the same agent who came for Bradie on the train. Eel Man. I hide behind a scraggly bush. A moment later, the agent emerges with Julia. They get into the back of a black car and drive away.

They're taking her too!

I want to knock on her door, but a neighbor pops her head out.

"What are you doing?" she demands.

"Nothing," I say.

"Well, off with you," she orders. "Before I call the protectors."

I blanch at the thought and hurry home.

The next day, I walk briskly to school, frequently looking over my shoulder. I tense whenever a car, van, or hover vehicle drives by, waiting for agents to pour out and nab me off the street.

My nerves are wound tight by the time I get to school, and the screeches of the younger kids chasing balls or jumping rope are cymbals in my ears. I wander among them, searching for Julia; to my shock, I see her.

I smile in relief. Julia's pack surrounds her, not a hint of torture or trauma on her pretty face. She does look different, though. She wears a jaunty beret, which the socialista reports say is all the rage in Jupitar City; her school uniform fits perfectly; hints of makeup highlight her cheeks, lips, and eyes.

I rush over and hug her.

"Julia!" I say. "I'm so relieved to see you!"

She pushes me away. "Hands off!"

I pull back, confused. She straightens her outfit, giving me stink eye.

"Hey, Feral," Cody asks, "kill any more mutie hounds?"

"The *real* heroes are the protectors," Julia interjects. "Don't go taking on airs, Caitlin. Some people say *you* got those three protectors killed."

"What people?" I demand.

"People," she says pointedly.

Her clique goes quiet, appraising and passing judgment. I mutely follow her and her posse into class. Once again, we are divided into our groups. I'm placed with the farm trainees. I put my hand up; before I utter a syllable, Mrs. Cranberry says crisply, "I haven't heard back, Caitlin." My arm retracts.

After attendance, we go for another day of on-the-job training. I am conspicuously alone amidst the packs of teens marching to the train station. I tell myself I'm imagining it, but some of them are giving me dirty looks.

They don't matter, I tell myself.

I scan for Bradie's face and tell-tale banter. I spot several doppelgängers (I never knew our borough had so many people our age with freckles and unruly black hair). None of them are him. I head for my train when someone grabs my arm and shoves me to the ground. A huge teen towers over me.

"Hey!" I shout at the guy, waiting for the protectors to intervene. They all turn their backs.

"I heard how you put everyone in danger in the farmlands, attracting those mutant hounds into the orchards. My *mom* works in the orchards," he shouts, pointing his finger at me.

"I didn't," I insist. "Where did you hear that?"

"Come on," a friend of his says. "She ain't worth it."

He spits on me, and they disappear into the crowd. Nobody helps me. Many avert their eyes. A few glance at me guiltily. It reminds me of our neighbors after the agent arrested my dad. People we'd known our whole lives wanted nothing to do with us. Relocation was almost a relief.

In the orchards, farmhands hose away the blood of the mutant hounds. I pick apples in silence. At day's end, nobody tries to walk me home.

At school the next morning, I stand with the other farm laborers.

"Mrs. Cranberry," I start.

"If this is about the protectors, Caitlin," she says with an edge to her voice.

"No, Mrs. Cranberry," I say. "Sorry, Mrs. Cranberry."

"Good," she snips. "If I have something to say about it, I'll say it."

She shoos us through the door.

I join the next generation of workers coming together into a horde. I search for Bradie and reach the station in disappointment. I hand an overseer my i-dent card. She swipes it in her on-the-go. I wait for it to bleep cheerily. Instead, it honks.

She looks at me closely.

"You're the girl from the info update," she says. "The one who killed the mutant."

"Yes," I say.

"Come with me," she says.

"But... my train," I say.

"This way," she says.

She leads me to a row of booths, all of them shuttered, advertising tickets for sale, from the days when people traveled to far-flung parts of the continent, before bombs and battles turned most of it into an uninhabitable wasteland. She opens a door and indicates for me to step inside.

I enter the small, windowless office. Its original contents have been cleared out, but some of the architectural detail remains—molding, a marble window ledge, and a lamp of rounded stained glass hanging from the ceiling by gilded chains. A single bulb flickers in it, casting shadows over the agent in black seated in a padded chair before a scratched wooden table —the same agent who took Bradie.

"Sit," he says, pointing at a stool.

I lick my lips and do as I'm told.

"Good girl," he says. It occurs to me, I don't know his name. He doesn't introduce himself. In my mind, I continue to call him Eel Man.

"Caitlin, you've had quite a few eventful days, haven't you?" Eel Man asks.

I ignore the question.

"Where's Bradie?" I ask. "Is he okay?"

He shrugs. "Dead."

I struggle to breathe.

"Or alive," Eel Man adds. "I wouldn't know. I'm not handling his case."

My fingers dig into my thighs. He's toying with me.

"It's obvious Bradie knew how to operate his weapon with proficiency," the agent continues. "That's why we took him so swiftly. You, on the other hand, haven't a clue how to use a firearm."

"I really don't," I confess.

"Which is why we let you be a hero—for a little while," he says. "You wouldn't want to get too full of yourself, now would you?"

"I would not," I force myself to say.

"Marvelous. You've had your little moment in the sun. Best you get comfortable with the shadows again. Are we clear?"

"Very much so," I reply.

"Off you go then," he says, brushing the air as if I were a foul smell.

I get up. The sound of the stool scraping on the floor is a razor to my ears. I wince. I walk to the door and open it.

"One more thing," he says.

I stop. Sweat drips down my neck. Here it comes.

"Yes?" I ask, staring at the concourse and it's taunting freedom. I was so close.

"Turn around when I'm speaking to you."

I hate myself for obeying.

"This is for you." He slides something toward me across the table. To take it means walking back into the room. It could be my execution order for all I know. He might expect me to carry it to the protectors myself.

"Come, come," he waves impatiently.

The knob slides from my grasp, and the door whines shut as I step back toward the table. His gloved hand lifts, revealing a trainee armband stenciled with a fist holding the all-seeing eye of a protector. This is my way into the Protectorate. I want to grab the armband and run, but I hear my dad's voice.

Nothing is ever free, Caitlin.

The agent's smirk hardens. "Those who hesitate miss out an all sorts of opportunities," he says. "When you're offered what you've been asking for, you should take it."

I think of Bradie. I need to know what happened to him. My fingers close around the rough fabric, and Eel Man strikes like a viper, grabbing my wrist. He squeezes. I suppress a whimper.

"Caitlin, the rules are in place for a reason," he says. "What are those reasons?"

I force myself to look at him.

"To maintain the peace," I say, reciting the lines I've learned since first year. "To honor the treaty with the Supergenics. To avoid another gene war. To fix what's been broken. To make this a better world."

"Yes," he says. "Maintaining the truce requires sacrifice. There are rewards, though, for those who play by the rules. You requested an early transfer to the Protectorate Novice Program. Well, here it is. What do you say?"

"Thank you," I reply.

A few seconds pass; all I hear is my pounding heart. He releases me and sits back. I hug the armband to my chest.

"You're welcome," he replies.

"May I go?" I ask.

"Of course. Hurry, hurry. The train won't wait forever. Track 2, I believe. Who knows, we may yet put that rebellious nature of yours to good use."

As soon as the door snaps shut, I run toward my train and away from the agent. I crush the armband in my grip for fear Eel Man will change his mind and take it away from me. Panting, I emerge onto my platform.

I clamber aboard the waiting train, where I'm met by rows of seated peers. They stop chattering, staring at me while I walk past.

Ignore them, I tell my burning cheeks, searching for an empty spot. The passengers are in their school uniforms, same as me, all wearing the armband with the all-seeing eye clutched in a fist, all of their bodies bigger than average, regardless of where they fall on the gender spectrum; that includes a couple of goons from my school, known for getting into scraps on the recreational yard—and the brute who shoved me to the ground yesterday. He gives me a dark look and sticks his foot out with zero subtlety.

I stop, look at him, and say, "No."

"Caitlin?" someone shouts, cutting off the brute's response. "Hey, Caitlin, over here! Come sit with us!"

I spot a pair of familiar faces. The guy who's calling and waving is Liam. He's all muscles and square-jawed good looks. He should be in magazines.

"So, what are we doing here?" I ask the brute.

He grudgingly retracts his foot. "Whatever," he snorts.

I walk past and sit opposite Liam and his girlfriend Sandie. She keeps touching her closely cropped, tightly curly black hair. The last time I saw her, she had shoulder-length dreads. I'm the only one on board who doesn't have a severe haircut, reminding me that our days of self-expression are over.

Both Sandie and Liam are star athletes from another school. Everyone was sure one or both of them would Manifest. They were always graceful, strong, and sure. Competing or sitting, they project the elusive ease of those at home within their bodies.

It's a stretch for me to call them friends, but they would always say, "Good job" to me after a discus throw, especially when I beat them—which was not often. If I flubbed a pole vault, they'd assure me, "Next time, tiger."

"Hey, hero," Sandie says, her fingers lounging against Liam's.

I tense. "Please don't call me that."

Neither asks why. They see it in my eyes and hear it in my tone. We are officially dregs unable to fulfill our Gen M promise. We must transition from trying to stand out to learning to fit in.

"Here," Liam says, indicating my armband. "Let me help you with that."

He takes it from my tense fingers and snaps the insignia around the sleeve of my dress jacket.

"Welcome to the club," he says.

His words are paradoxically inviting and alienating. What am I expected to give up to be one of them?

Relax, I insist. *You're not joining, remember? You're playing along.*

Except, I do like these two. At their most competitive, they've managed to be nice.

The train hisses to life. Unlike the conveyance to the farmlands, there's no grinding of gears nor jerking back and forth. It glides along the tracks instead of clawing its way grudgingly toward its destination. I note other differences—plump seats, carpeted floors, clean windows—and remember the agent's words. *There are rewards for those who play by the rules.* And clearly for those who enforce them.

The track takes us parallel to the security fence; lightning flares and thunder rumbles.

"So, your first day," Liam says. "You think gym class was tough? You have no idea."

"Don't scare her," Sandie says, punching his arm. "But seriously, Caitlin, I've never been so sore in my life. If you find yourself needing to cry, sneak into the equipment room and find a spot where someone isn't having a breakdown. It's a thing."

"Okay," I say, wondering if this was such a good idea.

Stay on mission, I order myself. *Find Bradie's brother.*

"Have you met any protectors with the last name Lopez Nettle?" I ask.

Liam and Sandie look to each other and shrug.

"Doesn't sound familiar," Liam says. "But we can ask around."

"That would be great," I say.

I tell myself not to be disappointed. I'll find Bradie's brother soon enough. I believe it until the train rounds the bend; I stare at a gigantic white Cube in the distance. This is it—the Protectorate. I've seen it from afar, towering over our borough, reminding us of the ever-vigilant protectors and agents within.

"Impressive, huh?" Liam asks.

"It is," I agree.

It looms larger, so big, the train pulls into the structure, stopping in the middle of a gigantic atrium. I follow Liam and Sandie off the train and into a concourse of white, polymer tiles. I stare up and up.

Clear glass reveals floor upon floor of training areas. Sweaty male- and female-identified protectors train in hand-to-hand combat, run on treadmills, and shoot targets in firing ranges. Short shorts show more than they hide as muscled individuals bound, crawl, and climb through an intricate, shifting obstacle course. Medics in lab coats oversee what seems to be a meditation room with rows of protectors sitting cross-legged on mats, eyes covered by visors that flash rainbow colors.

A squadron of officers in copper uniforms marches by; black-clad agents slither among the masses.

"Welcome to the Cube," Liam says. "Munitions depot and garage are on the sub-levels. Forget hovercrafts; they've got hover*boards*. Ah-maize-ing!"

I nod, awed and overwhelmed. I try to spot an older version of Bradie, but it's impossible. This is a hive of thousands.

I am so screwed.

CHAPTER 13

"Come on," Liam says. "We need to sign in and get your gear."

They take me to a counter where a puffy matron in an overseer uniform swipes my i-dent card, then hands me two bundles of workout clothes, a towel, and a set of sneakers.

"You wash them yourself," she says. "At the end of your placement, you return them. *Clean*. You lose them, it's 100 credits. Here's your lock. Combo's on the back. Next!"

"One quick thing," I say.

Her glare implies I couldn't possibly have questions after such a thorough rundown.

"What?" she demands.

"Everybody here must come to you at some point, right?"

Her fingers drum the counter.

"And?"

"How would I find a guy with the last name Lopez Nettle?"

"I'm not a dating service," she snaps. "Next!"

She motions for the person behind me to come forward. I look, but no one's there. I turn back, and the waddling overseer disappears through a swinging door.

Sandie laughs, "I can't wait to meet this mystery man. Come on."

We ride up a set of moving stairs Liam calls an escalator. An adjacent escalator carries people down. We follow our peers to a swinging door. Sandie stops me.

"Have you ever been in a mixed changing area?" she asks.

"A what?" I reply.

She drags me inside a room of benches and lockers, all made of the same white plastic that dominates the Cube. Disinfectant and sweat burn my nose. I barely notice, blinded by the mix of genders stripping to their essentials.

"Oh," I say.

"If you got it," Liam shrugs.

His school jacket and tie hang on a hook.

He peels his button-down shirt over his head, revealing the firm mounds of his chest and the delineated lines of his mid-section.

A lot of these teens are visibly fit, Sandie among them. They may be dregs, but they are still genetic winners in the fitness department. The more sports medals they won over the years, the more they were rewarded with healthier food rations, training, and other opportunities that reinforced their athletic success.

I'm not *the runt of the litter*, I assure myself—not that it should matter if I were, but the world is what the world is, especially in this environment.

I'm not here to do well, I remind myself. Mom would kill me if I did.

Several hulks, including the brute who shoved me in the station and tried to trip me on the train, glare at me. I guess I'm going to have help in realizing my underachiever goals.

"His name's Gregor," Liam says, catching the dirty looks. "Total douche."

I turn, wishing Gregor would stop eyeing me while I change. I'm slow to take my clothes off, then quick to get my shirt and track pants on.

I shove my uniform into an empty locker, memorize the combination on my lock, and click it shut. We're all dressed in beige shorts and tank tops as if to make us as indistinct as possible. I follow Liam and Sandie past a row of stainless steel toilets open to one another and a shower area that makes the toilets seem private.

We enter a vast training area with a glass wall exposing us to the atrium —and to anyone in the Protectorate who'd care to observe us. On the other walls hang long banners of the all-seeing eye clenched in a fist, reminding us that the protectors don't just watch the general populace—they also watch each other.

My fellow trainees circle their arms and stretch their legs, warming themselves for the brutality to come. I would do the same, but I see a man with flecks of grey in his hair wearing blue training pants and a matching t-shirt. He's chewing on a whistle while flipping through a datapad. I jog over to him.

"Hi," I say. "I'm Caitlin Feral. Do you know a protector with the last name Lopez Nettle?"

He gazes past me.

"Novice!" he shouts at the youth closest to us; it's Gregor.

He runs over and puffs his gorilla chest.

"Yes, sir!"

"Show your fellow novice how to execute a takedown. Do it until she successfully counters. The rest of you, in a circle!"

I open my mouth to protest the way I would with Mrs. Cranberry—only here do I realize she was patient with me.

"Come on, hero," Gregor says.

He grabs my arm and tosses me to the mat-covered floor. Many in my cohort laugh. Liam and Sandie wince. I get to my feet, trying to remember what I learned in wrestling. I spent most of those sessions escaping drab reality by daydreaming about how wondrous it would be to fly. Gregor makes a twisted version of my fantasy come true, grabbing me by the shirt, lifting me up, and slamming me down.

The impact knocks the breath from me.

"Get up, novice!" the drill instructor yells.

Air floods my lungs. My plan to suck is coming together too well, too quickly. Gregor takes a bunch of steps back, then charges. There are scores of counters for a moving attacker, but I blank on all of them. He closes his arms to engulf me in a bear hug. I instinctively squat, slide through his legs, and pop up behind him. From this vantage point, I've no doubt Sandie could pick from a dozen by-the-book maneuvers to end an aggressor. I can't recall a single one, so I grab Gregor's shorts and pull them below his knees. He turns, face an angry red. He reaches for me; his shorts tangle his legs; he teeters, arms windmilling to catch his balance. I kick the crook of his knee, and he slams to the mat.

The drill instructor blows his whistle. Liam and Sandie cheer, joined by scattered applause. Gregor's friends glare. I don't have time to gloat.

"Clear a hole!" someone shouts in a commanding tone.

My fellow novices open rank for a muscled young man dressed in the yellow and blue tank top and short shorts the protectors wear while training. His body owns the room with every step.

He stops in the center of our semi-circle, contemplates us one by one, then holds out his hand. Our instructor passes him the tablet. The protector swipes it repeatedly, grunting here and there. He stops, lifting his eyes to me.

"Caitlin Feral," the protector says.

"Y-y-yes," I stammer.

Our instructor glares.

"Yes, sir!" I shout.

The protector gives the tablet back to our instructor.

"The girl who took down a two-headed mutt," the protector says, scratching his biceps. I catch the dismissiveness in his voice. "Well, let's see how you do against me."

"She had a baton against the mutt," Liam says.

The drill instructor rounds on Liam and shouts, "One hundred push-ups!"

Liam drops to the ground.

"Your baton," the protector in the tank top says, holding his hand out to the instructor.

I expect the instructor to protest. He smirks as if he's in on the joke. He hands the weapon over, and the protector gives it to me. I hold it awkwardly.

"Well, come on then," the protector says. "Power it up."

I hesitate.

"Now!" shouts the drill instructor.

I flick my wrist, and blue energy sizzles along its length. The protector lunges at me, and I swing the weapon. He evades, grabs my wrist, and twists. Pain runs up my arm. I drop the weapon, and before I know it, I land hard on my stomach, his full weight crushing against me.

He presses his lips to my ear and whispers, "I'm Trenton Lopez Nettle. Stop asking questions about me. Bradie's in enough trouble, and so am I."

"Bradie, is he—" I start.

Trenton presses my cheek deeper into the mat. "Stop talking. My brother's all right. You'll see him soon. Now keep your mouth shut. And, for eff's sake, get a haircut."

He stands, picks up the baton, turns it off, and hands it back to the instructor. Sandie helps me to my feet. I rub my arm.

"There's a big difference between fighting an animal and a person. Remember that," Bradie's brother says.

"Thank you, sir!" the circle of novices intones.

I wait for him to give me a special look, a wink—something to reassure me and cement our newly forged bond. He turns without a word, his muscled back rippling as he leaves. A giddy smile crosses my lips.

Bradie's alive. And I'll see him soon.

CHAPTER 14

By mid-day, bruises cover my body, broken blisters bloody my palms, and a hasty trip to the in-house barber has left my neck itchy and my hair too short to tuck behind my ears.

An overseer ushers us into a cafeteria furnished with sleek white polymer chairs and rounded tulip base tables. I expect a buffet of food, hoarded from the general population, enabling the protectors to gorge themselves while laughing at the less fortunate.

The reality is we lineup at slots in a wall, where I pull out a single foil-covered platter. The servings are larger than school served, and the food is better (in this case, protein-based pasta with meatballs and a protein-enriched brownie for dessert), but it's not a free-for-all. It is enough to fill me, which is a foreign sensation—one that doesn't last. Post-feeding, we endure survival training, obstacle courses, and a torturous form of stretching known as yoga.

We're all so exhausted; the only sounds on the train ride back to Central Station are the whistle of air, the hum of the conveyance speeding along the track, and the *ploff* of rain smacking the windows. Even the perpetual thunder from beyond the fence feels muted. Liam and Sandie lean against each other, eyes closed, her head on his shoulder, his head on her head.

I wish I could do the same, but bruised and beaten as I am from today's training, I'm too wired to rest. Out of everything that's happened today, one moment blares louder than the rest.

Bradie's okay!

After the train reaches the station, I walk with Liam, Sandie, and a few other trainees. It's strange; I think I'm enjoying this togetherness. What's up with that? In ones, twos, and threes, they veer down the streets leading to their homes, until I'm on my own in the rain. A battle rages in my stomach.

Am I fitting in? I wonder—followed by a warning. *Don't get attached. It won't end well.*

I pass a pair of protectors and instinctively salute. They see my armband and salute back. My cheeks flush.

It's okay, I assure myself. *You're playing along.*

A familiar figure reminds me who I am, waving at me from underneath an awning. It's Normand in a plastic poncho with matching rain pants. I walk toward him. I haven't had time to think about Tigara, comic books, or superpowers all day.

He gestures to come and walks away without waiting.

"You are the weirdest," I say, hurrying to catch up.

Normand takes us through side streets and narrow alleys. We turn, and the electrified chainlink fence is in front of us. The radiation and mutant warning signs make my wet skin prickle.

The black storm clouds over the broken city fire lightning bolts like crazy. Thunder throbs in my eardrums. He leans over an e-pad to protect it from the rain. I'd say he got it as part of his tech training, but it can't be standard issue. It's beaten and scratched; decals on the back look like odd i-dent insignias—a black bat, a big X inside of a circle, and a stylized golden eagle. In the middle of them all, and part of the e-pad itself, is a white apple with a bite taken out of it.

"Where did you get that?" I ask.

He lifts his fingers to his lips. Is he shushing me? An instant later, I understand why. I hear the squawk of a pair of protectors talking to each other. I can't see them, but they're approaching the mouth of the alley. If they see us here, it's going to raise questions, but Normand doesn't flinch. He shows me the screen of his e-pad; it's also filled with bizarre icons. They're programs, GRAMS for short, but different from anything we've used at school. One is of a cartoon clown; another is a scowling red bird; a third is a stylized hand showing its middle finger. He taps an icon in the shape of a protector helmet. A map of our borough appears, pimpled by a scattering of red dots with horns and angry faces. He enlarges our location —two red dots get closer and closer.

"Normand!" I hiss. "Are those protectors?"

"Caitlin," he whispers urgently, "I must insist you be quiet or they might hear us."

"*Hear* us?" I demand. "They're going to *see* us!"

He drags an icon of a happy face wearing a blindfold on top of the two red dots approaching the mouth of the alley. The dots change into happy faces with blindfolds. The squawk of their voices projected through their helmet speakers grows louder.

"The protectors can't see through their visors," Normand explains. "Their helmets are equipped with cameras, which project a 360 view of the world on internal screens. Since that visual stream is digital, it can be manipulated. When the protector pulled out your Tigara comic book, I made her see a bureau-approved comic book instead."

I gape. *That's* how I got away with it?

"What if she'd raised her visor?" I demand.

"You would have been in a significant level of trouble," he replies unapologetically.

Understatement! And a GRAM that tracks protectors? It's treason! If I'm caught, they'll do to me what they did to my dad.

"I have to go," I say.

Normand steps in front of me. "That would be a mistake." He shows me his strange-looking e-pad. On the screen is a picture of *Tigara*, issue number two. She's in her full garb, jumping from a rooftop, claws at the ready. My instinct to run is anchored by my desire to stay.

"And then I say to him," a protector's voice squawks through the speakers in his helmet, coming from around the corner. "I say, you call *that* a baton?"

Their electronic laughter rings in my ears.

"What are the chances it won't work?" I demand through clenched teeth. Rain runs down my back.

"I've reduced the failure rate to 22 percent," he says.

"Are you kidding me?" I whisper.

"The audio reconfiguration sequences continuously crash. They shouldn't be able to see us, as long as we keep still, but…"

He points to his ears, stops talking, and makes a slitting motion across his throat. The protectors reach the mouth of the alley and stop. Five measures away, they stare and shine their lights in my face. One of them steps closer. His boot crunches a discarded soda can. He halts. If he were to open the visor's reflective sheath, we'd be eye to eye.

My heart smashes my sternum. I imagine him ordering me to my knees, driving his electrified baton into my gut, and making me taste mud while he cuffs my arms behind my back. The news could kill my mom. And Nate. He's too young to remember what happened to Dad, but it affects the kid. Underneath Nate's outgoing nature, I see the insecurity, the need to belong, and his fragility when he doesn't.

84

I'm so sorry, I think.

"Status?" the second protector asks.

The one shining the light in my face lowers his arm. "Clear."

He steps back, crunching the can underfoot. We watch them walk away, their squawking voices growing distant. I round on Normand.

"What is wrong with you?" I demand, gesturing at his e-pad. "Do you have any idea what they'd do if they caught us with that?"

Normand nods, avoiding my gaze. "I know precisely what they would've done to us. We must step quickly before the next patrol arrives."

He reaches the end of the alley, not bothering to look if the way is clear. He heads for the security fence. I'm about to call out, sure that he doesn't see the electrified barrier beyond the wall of rain despite the brightly colored warning signs on either side of a gate. He ignores the radiation and mutant hazard symbols, confidently positioning a round electronic gadget of shiny metal onto a lock pad. Bands of blue energy rotate over the gizmo's surface.

On his e-pad, he drags a key with a skull and crossbones overtop a symbol of a spider's web. The device on the lock hums to life, spinning one way, then the other. The gate clicks open.

"Effing eff," I swear under my breath.

The fence possesses a mythic quality. It stands between us and the deadly horrors beyond. And Normand—the timid loser at the back of the class— opened it. The mental reconfiguration hurts my head. Who is this guy? Who is he *really*?

Normand tucks his e-pad under his arm and rubs disinfectant into his hands. He looks at his watch, then his e-pad. Red dots move toward us.

"We must go," he says.

He steps through the gate. I wait for alarms to sound and protectors to swarm him. They don't. Still, I don't move.

"Caitlin, how do you think I procured a comic book from before the war?" He gestures toward the Yellow Zone. "A fallen city holds much more than bones."

"I…" It's so obvious now that he's said it. He's a pilferer, scavenging the Yellow Zone for anything of value. That's where he got his electronic pad. If caught, he'd lose a hand.

"The next patrol's running late, but it will be upon us shortly," he says, looking at his watch. "What say thee, Caitlin Feral? Dare ye venture outside the cage?"

No, a terrified part of me cries.

"Ball sack," I swear. Before I can talk myself out of it, I step beyond the chainlink fence.

Normand's lips twitch in amusement, and the gate clicks shut behind us. My heart pounds louder than the surrounding thunder. *I'm in the Yellow Zone.* Protectors shoot on sight for this. I gaze at a charred and half-melted car. This is the single stupidest thing I've done. I look at Normand, waiting for the joke to be over. His twitchy mouth turns into a smile. The weirdest part of all—Normand's not scared. *How can he not be scared?*

"Here," he says, handing me a thin, sticky pad with circuitry embedded in it. "Place this somewhere on your skin."

"What is it?" I ask.

"Motion and heat sensors are positioned amidst the debris to detect mutants and catch runners. This," he gestures at his tech, "will tell the security grid to ignore you."

How many times has he done this?

"Okay," I say. I slip the gadget inside my soaked shirt, pressing it under my collar bone. Microscopic hooks cling to me.

He turns to the swipe pad and drags the icon of a raccoon onto one of a girl with a superhero mask.

"It's syncing," he says.

His pad *bings;* the superhero girl winks and gives us a thumbs up.

"We may proceed," he says.

Walking the orderly streets of the borough, Normand is a snail, but here, in the jumbled ruins of the Yellow Zone, I struggle to keep pace. The rain makes it impossible to see more than a measure in front of me, and the terrain is unstable. More than once, Normand grabs and steadies me.

"Step where I step," he says, squirting his hands with sanitizer.

We climb down a collapsed building and stop in front of more rubble. Normand bends, grabs a twisted metal rod, and yanks.

"Kazamo!" Normand cries, like he's a stage magician declaring abracadabra.

Something mechanical clangs into place. He steps back, and a chunk of debris lifts open on hydraulic hinges. A few pieces of broken concrete skitter off, but the mangled mesh of cement, steel rods, and refuse holds together, revealing a set of stairs leading underground.

"The descent," Normand says, walking down.

I follow. How can I not?

Static electricity pulses through me as I cross the threshold.

"Notice anything different?" Normand asks.

I do. I'm not dry, but I've gone from soaked to damp. It's still raining, but I can't feel it. An invisible shield keeps the storm out.

"Humidity controllers," Normand says, pulling back his hood and stripping off his poncho. "Prevents the water from getting in; otherwise, all this would've flooded long ago."

"What is this place?" I ask.

His avoidant gaze is alight with excitement.

"Come," he says. "Showing you is always my favorite part."

He is *so* weird.

I trip when I get to the last step. Another, more conventional door creaks open, and Normand guides me deeper. Both portals click shut behind us. Darkness engulfs me. I could die here, and no one would know. Maybe something's wrong with Normand; maybe he's funny in the head in a dangerous way; maybe—

Normand claps, and twinkling rainbow lights on dangling strings come aglow all around. I stare in wonder at the impossible. Walls of comic books surround me—hundreds of issues all on display.

And that's not all.

Life-sized statues and glass display cases with busts of unfamiliar caped crusaders and costumed heroines greet us. Dressed in wild costumes, they wield primal elements with dramatic poses. A counter is home to rows of multicolored dice, a toy flying saucer, and fanciful vinyl figurines with huge ears and bellies plastered in floral patterns. Posters of bearded wizards, jacked barbarians, and scantily clad warrior women are pinned to the walls while books and games line shelves.

I want to touch everything, but I'm afraid to touch anything, as if I'm at the museum, and Mrs. Cranberry is ready to yell, "Put that down, Caitlin!"

I close my liar eyes. This can't be real. I blink, expecting the mirage to fade, replaced by my bunk at home, the lumpy mattress waking me from the most wonderful dream. But I'm still here.

I pick up a box touting itself as "a game for terrible people." Nowhere do I see the Bureau of Infotainment's seal of approval. I eye the comic books. I've never heard of a single one of them. Like the statues, I don't recognize one hero, heroine, villain, or villainess on all the covers.

"All of this is from before the war," I realize out loud.

If the Protectorate found this place, they'd burn it to ash.

"Observe," Normand says.

He pulls a drawer. It's the perfect fit for comic books. I gape at the contents—a long row of issues, all lovingly preserved in plastic custom-sized bags with cardboard backings. A hundred or more comics fill the retractable slot, and there are *dozens* of slots.

"What is this place?" I ask with pure awe.

Normand points to a battered sign on the wall, about six measures by two. The name of the store glows, made up of a strange type of tubular lighting.

"I Want Superpowers," I read. "Comic books 'n other kah-rap." A stylized lightning bolt buzzes. The store sign confirms what I already know —this place gets me.

"I dragged it in from outside," he says. "Fixing the neon tubes was shy of impossible."

"Is that how you found this place?" I ask.

"That is a tall tale for another time," he says sadly.

"What even brought you out into the Yellow Zone?" I press.

"Nine-point-eight meters per second squared," he replies.

As if that's an explanation. *Weirdo.*

"Weren't you afraid the telepath at Testing Day would see this in your mind?" I ask.

"There are ways to fool everyone, even mind readers," he replies.

Joshua said as much. I want to ask how, but that's a whole other question.

A display shelf rising to the ceiling holds hundreds of comic book titles, including multiple copies of the *same* issue. My brain short circuits. It seems impossible to choose the first one—though there is no choice to be made. I wander down the length of the shelf, following their alphabetical order to the T section.

There she is—Tigara. I stare at issues 192 up to a giant-sized issue 200. My mind snaps. The series has 200 issues!!!

"You're probably wondering how this all survived," Normand says.

"Yeah," I say distantly, picking up issue 192. Tigara is claw-to-claw with an equally fierce leopard-printed villainess. If only the newest issues are on display, back copies must be in those pullout drawers.

"This portion of the edifice was below grade. It's constructed of reinforced concrete," Normand explains. "In essence, it is a bomb shelter."

"Uh-huh," I say, barely listening.

The comic book opens with Tigara in mid-battle. I flip the page to a flashback. "Two days ago…" a yellow box explains, and I know this will lead to the epic confrontation with "Lady Leopard."

I sit cross-legged on the floor. Above me, a sign declares, "You read it, you bought it! NO loitering." I turn the comic book's pages and forget the pain of my bruises and the dampness of my clothes. Tigara sweeps me into a gritty urban world similar to—and distortedly different from—my own.

At issue's end, Lady Leopard is about to slice Tigara's throat. Normand sits diagonally from me, contentedly reading a tale of a jacked guy with claws coming out of his forearms, fighting another guy in weird metal armor.

I take a moment to soak in the feeling. I'm pretty sure it's happiness, and I think the words, *Thank you.*

I read another issue of *Tigara.* Then another. I'm mesmerized by Tigara's hot/cold love triangle with fellow nocturnal crime fighters Miss Thang, a crime lord trying to mend her ways, and Whamarang, a daytime "billionaire playboy" (whatever that is) by the name of Bryce Dayne, who's atoning for a legacy of "corporate corruption."

They clash with villains like the Ghouligan, Mesquite, and Hairantula. Sometimes the heroes battle each other as the path to justice grows blindingly murky. When criminals run free, and their leaders are untouchable, how can Tigara not play judge, jury, and executioner? Yet if she does, how is she any better than the villains she professes to fight? What is Tigara to do? Can she remain true to her moral code or will the darkness in her soul prevail? And what will that mean for the citizens of Bright Lights Big City?

I'm so caught in such questions, it's not until I reach the middle of the double-length anniversary special that something revolutionary strikes me. My stomach heaves as if from a physical blow, forcing me to lower the issue.

The comic books I usually read are based on real people, like Captain Light. Did Tigara live and breathe? It seems improbable a grown woman would go running around in a tiger-print leotard fighting crime.

It doesn't matter. It's the *idea* of Tigara that burrows into my brain because *she doesn't have any superpowers!* She's an ordinary woman who's trained herself to be *almost* superhuman, but she's *not*—she's a dreg.

Tigara and her world may be fiction, but they spark something very real.

She's like me—DNA regular. Does that mean one day I could be like her? A superhero without superpowers? Can I still be Generation Manifestation?

My other revolutionary realization—super beings, such as the feline imbued Lady Leopard, can be evil, and it's sometimes up to DNA regulars like Tigara to stop them. And Tigara *does* defeat her!

In all the bureau-approved comic books, the heroes are *always* Supergenic, as if with great power comes immediate morality. The villains are always dregs, out to destroy the world out of spite and malice, or mutant animals grown grotesque from the irradiated aftermath of dreg bombs , now ravenous for the flesh of law-abiding folk.

In the approved comic books, the Supergenics, being good and true, always prevail, and the dreg villains pay for their crimes. Yet, according to *this* comic book, Tigara is not only a hero, but a *super*hero, even without enhanced abilities, and Supergenics, like anyone else, can be either good or bad.

I close the 200th issue, my world turned upside down. All this time, I wanted to be Supergenic because I thought it was the only way for me to be special. Enhanced DNA would fix everything wrong with my life. What if I was wrong? What if there's another way? But if *that's* true, is it also true that the Supergenics are sometimes the *real* bad guys? I think of all the food destined for Jupitar City.

My mind swirls with these thoughts when Normand looks at his watch and announces in his abrupt way, "*Terminus.*"

"What?" I blink in a daze.

"Our time here has come to an end," he says.

I want to argue, but he's right. The stiffness from today's training is setting in. It's late. I have to get home. I reluctantly and reverently return Tigara to her appointed place. I can't believe all of this is real.

"Can we come back tomorrow?" I ask.

He nods. "And the day following."

Getting back to the borough is slow going. The perpetual twilight under the clouds is inconsistently lit by flashes of lightning and the crackling, energy-absorbing globes overhead. Finally, we reach the fence. It's still freaky being on this side of it. Normand uses his gadgets and swipe pad to open the gate, and we slip through. I expect a squad of protectors to be waiting for us, guns leveled, but we're alone with a scurrying rat.

"Thank you," I say while walking Normand to the bus stop, "for sharing your place with me."

"You can't tell anyone," he says. His voice and shoulder stare intensify.

"I know," I reply.

"Nobody," he repeats. "Not ever."

"Normand, trust me, I get it."

"Not even Bradie," he insists.

"Of course not!" I say.

"Good," Normand replies. The bus arrives, and he clambers on. "You will find that Bradie is no longer as you remember him."

His words are a brick to my chest.

"What does *that* mean?" I demand.

He swipes his i-dent card in a reader, and the doors close in my face. The bus carries him away.

I cough on fumes and ask no one, "How do you know about Bradie?"

CHAPTER 15

A beam of sunlight fights its way through the dirty window in our tiny flat. My mom, Nate, and I eat protein-enriched cereal puffs with watery powdered milk. Nate knocks one floating ball into another with his spoon, making *puh-RROOM* noises.

"So, how did the protector training go yesterday?" Mom asks.

She's been quiet about it since I told her last night. There was no point in trying to hide it. My short hair was a dead giveaway, and she spotted the fresh bruises amidst the yellowing ones from testing.

Nate catches Mom's tone, grows quiet, and raises his eyes from his bowl. My armband with the all-seeing eye sits on the table, glaring at me accusingly.

"I got beat up a lot," I reply.

"It's so odd that they cut your farmhand training short," she says.

"Mom, I was almost killed," I reply.

"Dozens of farmhands are killed by animal attacks every year," she counters. Leave it to my mom to be so coldly logical. She's right to be worried, though. I haven't told her about Eel Man.

"Can we talk about this later?" I glance at Nate.

She catches my meaning and takes the bowl from him, pouring half its contents into mine, the other into hers.

"If you're not going to eat your food, you might as well go to school early," she tells him.

"Why?" he asks. "So you can talk about stuff behind my back?"

"Yes," she replies.

He looks ready to argue until I shake my head at him.

"Yeah, yeah," he says, grabbing his back sack. No twirls as he leaves, jerking the door behind him.

"What happened?" Mom asks.

"An agent gave me this," I say, fingering the armband.

Her grip on her spoon tightens.

"I'm such an idiot," she says. "Of course, they're going to pick on you. I loved your father, but that man has left us a heap of trouble."

"Mom—" I start to say.

"Okay," she interrupts. "We've been through worse. We dance their little dance until they get bored and decide to pick on someone else." Hands shaking, she takes the armband with the protector emblem on it and snaps the cloth over top of my school uniform.

"Listen to me," she says. "It's critical you fail the protector training."

Tears bubble in her eyes. I hate it when she cries. If this escalates, she'll scream and break things. I never should've told her about the agent.

"It's okay, Mom," I grasp her arm. "Trust me. I'm going to fail."

An hour later, I get the chance to make good on my promise. It's another school day, where we sit in class under Mrs. Cranberry's glare and ruminate on the lessons learned at our work placement.

I'm the only one in my class in the protectorate program, so I'm in a corner alone, answering essay questions along the lines of "How does being a protector make me a contributing member of society?" and "What sacrifices am I prepared to make to keep the peace?"

I think of Tigara and write, "I'm learning to defend the defenseless against the strong" and "I ask lots of questions." They'll hate those responses. I also think about the comic book store in the Yellow Zone, Normand, and what he said to me about Bradie.

I meet with Normand that night in an alley near the security fence.

"How do you know about Bradie?" I demand. My tone is more accusatory than I intend.

Normand holds up his electronic pad and plays security footage of Eel Man escorting Bradie off the train.

"How did you get that?" I whisper as the image freezes. Bradie looks terrified.

"I have many GRAMS," Normand explains.

"Do you know where he is?" I ask.

"Negative."

My shoulders slump, and I wait for him to reassure me. He does not; that's beyond him.

"Let us proceed," he says, leading me to the fence and putting his skeleton key on the gate's security pad.

"Normand, I can't stop thinking about Bradie and the danger he's in," I say. "His brother said he'd be back, but... Normand, what did you mean Bradie would be different?"

The skeleton key spins.

"Agents took him. The experience would alter anyone," Normand says.

"He'll be broken," I realize out loud.

"Broken things can be fixed," Normand says.

His words catch me off guard. I'm sure he has no idea he's said exactly the right thing. The skeleton key stops spinning, and the gate pops open.

I continue obsessing over Bradie while we travel through the Yellow Zone. We reach the debris door. Normand opens it, and we descend the stairs. At the bottom, he slaps his palms together; the lights come aglow, and I marvel at the effort to preserve this place.

"You say you found it like this?" I ask.

"Correct," Normand says as he pulls the door closed behind us. "I postulate the owner of this complex was a billionaire genius. Those of lower intellect might describe him as eccentric."

I walk past a counter with a register. Next to it sit trading cards of unfamiliar heroes and villains. I have similar cards of the different members of A.M.M.O. A pair of metal Baoding balls sit in an ornamental box alongside a scarf with a big red S inside a diamond shape, and a black rectangular device labeled Taser, with two metal rods at its tip. The latter sits on top of a charge pad. I reach for the scarf.

"Stop!" Norman shouts, grabbing my arm. His grip still surprises me.

I hold my hands in peace. He lets go and squirts disinfectant between his fingers. He moves the scarf slightly one way, the metal balls the other, as if somehow that micro-adjustment makes a big difference in the cosmic scheme of things.

"You may touch anything you wish in here, but nothing on this counter. These must stay exactly as they are," he says.

"Yeah, sure," I say. Living with my mom, I've learned to keep the peace.

Two drawers of *Tigara* back issues reward me. I take out the first dozen. I stare at the cover of issue number two. Normand is already leaning against a concrete column reading a comic called *Fighter Foes*.

I join Tigara in her battle against the shirtless, muscled henchmen of the Conglomerate. They surround her. She's outnumbered and outgunned. She takes out two henchmen, dodges machine gun fire, and confronts The Man in Charge.

You think you are helping the oppressed, he says to her. *I help more people in a day than you will in a lifetime.*

At a cost, she says, stalking around him.

Nothing is free, he replies. *There is always a price.*

Yours is too high.

She attacks. He points his gun and fires—end of issue. I reach for the next one, and my hand freezes above the pile. The next issue isn't there. In fact, six issues are missing, resuming with issue nine.

"No," I whisper in horror.

Normand blinks at me. "What is the source of your negative statement?"

"The collection's incomplete," I say.

"Indeed," he says. "I sometimes resort to creating my own."

I shake my head to reboot the frozen data terminal in my mind.

"What do you mean you create your own?"

His brace creaks as he waddles over to the counter. He opens a drawer, pulls out a stack of papers, and shows me scads of drawings. I like to doodle, but my sketches pale next to these. They're amazing, telling the lost tale of the Fighter Foes engaged in battle on an alien planet, determined to save the Martian Princess *and* stop the evil Kahblang from detonating an intergalactic nuke.

"You did these?" I ask.

I flip through the panels. The art is amazing, but the storytelling, not so much. The heroes all sound monotone robotic, barely getting a word in, while the villains' rambling diatribes sometimes take up pages.

"I once dreamed of penning tales," he says. "My father informed me that all comic books come from Jupitar City. I experienced a gravity well in my chest so strong no particle could escape."

"A blackhole," I nod. "Sounds like me when I failed final Testing Day."

I look at his drawings.

"I could do the same for your Tigara comics," he offers.

"We can fill in the blanks," I realize out loud.

My words spark a catalytic sensation; the opposite of helplessness. I can *do* something about this. Is *this* what Manifesting feels like?

In art class, I learned form, color, and storytelling. But we were only allowed to write and draw "inside the lines." We might as well have been solving math formulas. But this, this is…

…*freedom.* The word booms in my mind.

"Okay," I say. "But I want to do the writing."

"Excellent," he agrees. "My narrative talents lie in non-fiction."

CHAPTER 16

My mother eyes me when I get home. She stirs a pot of reheated beans. I enter slowly, gauging her mood.

"Where were you?" she asks.

"The Yellow Zone," I reply.

She snorts. "Can you imagine?"

I smile weakly. "I was reading." So far, I haven't lied.

She nods, assuming I was at the library. I feel a wave of guilt. What Normand and I are doing is dangerous. If we're caught, there will be consequences for more than us. It's not worth the risk. Yet Tigara's all I think about. She even distracts me from worrying about Bradie.

"You must be hungry," Mom says.

"I am," I agree, my stomach gurgling.

She divides the beans into two bowls; I brace myself.

"So, have they cut you from the Protectorate program yet?" she asks.

And there it is.

"Not yet," I say.

Her fingers drum the chipped tabletop.

"Well, I'm sure this will be sorted soon. They haven't given you any pills or injections have they?"

"No," I say, confusion in my voice. "Why would they?"

"Just… don't take them," my mother says. "There's talk."

There's always talk.

She pats my hand. "You're a good girl."

Are you a good girl, Caitlin? part of me asks. *Does a good girl sneak into the Yellow Zone? Does a good girl put her family at risk for the sake of some silly comic books?*

Over the next two weeks, I spend less of my days at school and more at the Protectorate. At night, Normand and I sneak to the comic book shop. We've taken to calling it the Lair.

There, we divide our time between reading comic books of old and creating our own. We argue over plot, dialogue, and character development. For someone uninterested in the nuances of fiction, Normand is surprisingly opinionated on these matters, particularly in the debate of capes versus no capes.

One night at the Lair, he hands me a book from the before days, full of tips on how to write "good story." I learn about the crucible, stereotypes versus archetypes, and I have an *a-ha* moment when the book recommends creating some personal connection between the hero and the villain. Brother fighting brother is more powerful than stranger against stranger. Written in the margins is the question, *What about childhood enemies?*

"You could write about Lilianne," Normand suggests.

I snap the book closed. "Normand! You scared me."

He wheezes laughter.

"Honestly," I shake my head, sounding like my mother and smiling despite myself. I roll his words around my head, not sure I heard him right. "What did you say?"

"We could create a character based on Lilianne," he says, "and then she and Tigara could fight."

Has Normand completely lost it? Lilianne is a Supergenic, and we are not to speak against the Supergenics, not ever. Yet, inside this place of secrecy, maybe such thoughts *are* allowed.

I nod, my smile widening. "Let's do it."

In real life, I'm sure Lilianne's Manifestation has blossomed into something that makes her even more beautiful than I remember. I'm guessing gossamer fairy wings and glittering crystal skin softer than satin. But here, I tell whatever story I want. Here, she does not get off so easy. Here, I can have justice.

After much discussion, Normand does some rough sketches, turning Lilianne into a monstrous creature covered in scales named Venomerella. The only things that remain of the girl she once was are her beautiful eyes and her all-too vicious human tongue. I almost feel a twinge of guilt. Almost.

In our tale, she and Tigara were once classmates, formerly best (if competitive) friends, who become bitter enemies. In an egomaniacal rage, Venomeralla sets off an explosive device that levels five blocks of Bright Lights Big City. She and Tigara fight amidst the rubble.

Who shall be victorious? I write. *Venomerella, with her cruel cunning, chameleon abilities, and poisonous fangs? Or Tigara, who has honed her abilities through hours of training, armed only with a whip and her wits, vowing to protect those weaker than herself?*

I read the words over and over, words *I* wrote, relishing them like the finest of meals, with no Mrs. Cranberry to tell me it's terrible. A slew of possible outcomes dances in my head, each vying with the other. I don't know what's going to happen next.

I can't wait to find out.

The next morning, I'm exhausted. I sit on the train with Liam and Sandie. I'm dying to tell them about Tigara, but that would raise too many questions. Once we arrive at the Cube, thoughts of my comic book heroine stop.

Day by day, the protector training intensifies, both physically and mentally. Some of it's individual; other times, cooperative. I'm supposed to be trying to fail, but during the group challenges—whether it's flag football or an obstacle course—I can't let my teammates down, which is a foreign feeling. I'm a loner, not a joiner... aren't I?

The weirdness compounds. Like, I wind up *enjoying* the challenge. Or, at lunch, someone will call me over to sit with their group. Usually, it's Liam and Sandie, but sometimes it's Denise, Reg, or Bacon (I blush *and* feel grownup when Denise explains how he got the nickname). I expect they're positioning me for social rejection. Instead, they ask me questions—and listen to my answers. I crack jokes. One day, it hits me—I have *friends*. Plural! I half-heartedly remind myself, I only came to the Cube to make sure Bradie's okay.

In the cafeteria, I eat an egg salad sandwich and keep an eye out for his mass of unruly hair. I search through novices and off-duty protectors with no luck, but as I do, I see the law enforcers differently than I used to.

Without all their gear—the guns, the batons, the on-the-go devices they use to report on people—they're not so different from the rest of us. Admittedly, many of them are bigger and more fit than the general population, with straighter backs, clearer skin, and better teeth, but that aside, they laugh and joke with each other. They have their romances. Their failures. I've seen friends become enemies. Enemies become friends. It's like everywhere else.

Stripped of their uniforms, I see the people behind the reflective visors. I'm forced to admit, they do serve our most important function—guarding the fence against the monstrosities beyond and maintaining the rules that uphold our alliance with the Supergenics across the river. Maybe this place isn't so bad after all.

Could I be a part of it?

The irony isn't lost on me. During the day, I'm learning to maintain societal order by shutting down deviant behavior in the adult population. By night, I'm engaging in the very activities I'm training to suppress.

The duality cleaves my psyche down the middle. Like so many of the heroes in the comic books I'm reading, I lead a double life. It raises questions; which is the real me, and which is the mask? And, what happens if one day I have to choose one over the other?

Such dilemmas are on my mind one morning in particular. Three months have passed, and it's the final day of my novice protector training. I'm sleepy-eyed at breakfast. I was up late again, huddled in the Lair with Normand.

We finally finished the battle between Tigara and Venomerella. Venomerella lay dying and bleeding on a shattered sidewalk. Her spine was broken. She grasped Tigara's arm, and with her last breath, she hissed, "They did thissss to me. They made me a monsssssster. Ssssstop them!" Her words shook Tigara to the core because, once again, good versus evil was no longer black and white, but shades of grey.

As for who "they" are, that is a mystery to be solved in another issue. Remembering it makes me smile at the breakfast table as I slurp leftover cereal milk.

When I reach Central Station, I hum and skip until I board the train bound for the Cube. I look at the other novices. The melody dies on my lips. Something's off.

I head for my seat. A few people call, "Hey, Caitlin." I greet them by name and receive friendly nods.

What's different?

I walk toward Liam and Sandie. She won't look at me, staring forcibly out the window. Liam's lips keep twitching. My throat tightens. Practical jokes are part of our bonding, but I can't say I'm a fan.

What are they going to do to me?

My heart beats faster. I try to relax, reassuring myself this is different from when Lilianne would put water on my seat.

This means they like you.

I stop. Someone's sitting in my usual spot. He smiles at me, his parting lips creasing the spray of freckles across his nose.

"Hi Caitlin," he says.

I cover my mouth.

It's Bradie. His face is leaner, and he's put on some muscle, but it's him.

I sit down, not quite believing it. Liam and Sandie smile.

"You're here," I say.

"Yeah," he says, eyes twinkling, "I'm here. Can't get rid of me that easily."

I keep my voice low. "Where have you been?"

He replies at a normal volume, if a little off-key.

"I've been training, like all of you, in a different compound," he says.

His cheeks twitch, and I notice his hand. Angry scars run up his fingers and wrist, disappearing into the cuff of his school blazer. He rushes to explain.

"I hurt it when the mutant attacked," he says. His cheeks twitch more.

"No, you didn't," is my instant response.

He hides the scarred hand behind his back and squeezes my shoulder with his good one.

"I injured it when the mutant attacked. Do you understand?" He says it slowly and meaningfully.

I'm about to argue.

Caitlin, part of me blurts to myself in exasperation. *You need to go with this.*

All of a sudden, I understand why Mrs. Cranberry was so angry with me all the time. She kept trying to give me the rulebook when I had no idea a game was at play. I think of the agent, and what Normand said, *You will find that Bradie is no longer as you remember him,* and it all falls into place. My throat constricts.

"Okay," I lie. "I remember now."

Liam and Sandie nod in agreement, though they weren't even there. *They* know how to play the hands we're dealt.

The train pulls out of the station. I imagined Bradie's and my reunion many times, many ways. Sometimes, I would scold him. Sometimes, we'd exchange teasing jokes. On occasion, I'd let him kiss me. I hadn't considered it would be like this. An awkward space grows between us; we're two people who shared something intense, creating an illusion of closeness, but we're strangers.

All that matters, I assure myself, *is that Bradie's safe.*

"So, how do you all know each other?" I ask, seeking safety in small talk.

"Bradie's brother introduced us at the station this morning," Liam replies. "Said we should all ride together and you'd like the surprise."

I smile in relief. I was worried the agent had a hand in this.

Maybe he did, part of me thinks.

We stick to safe subjects. The lightning strikes beyond the fence. The food at the Protectorate. How sad it is that pre-training is over and how exciting it is that cadet training will soon begin—for those of us who get in.

When the train arrives at the Cube, Liam and Sandie squeeze each other's hands.

"They need to be careful," Bradie says, eyeing the pair walking ahead of us. "They'll use them against each other."

"What does that—" I start to ask.

"Nothing," Bradie cuts me off.

The fear in his voice passes in an instant. Jovial Bradie is back, but not far under that veneer…

I pay attention to the band around Bradie's arm, the one we all wear, of the all-seeing eye clenched in a fist. It makes me wonder if I've been getting too comfortable with that symbol.

"Okay," I say to Bradie, pretending not to worry about him.

Where were you really, and what did they do to you? I wonder. And the scarier question, *How broken are you?*

CHAPTER 17

The rest of the morning is a snooze. We stand in line to hand in our gear, another line to submit blood work and a urine sample, and then the lunch line to get to the food slots in the cafeteria wall.

The one relief from the bureaucratic monotony is Bradie. Despite my worries, his charisma blooms. It took me months to fit in; he does it in half-a-day. I'm relieved—and faintly pissed.

"He's a good one," Sandie says in the cafeteria. We take double trays of steaming pork with rice, with a side of cookies. Oh, the cookies! They're protein-based and sweetened with an inverted sugar that won't spike our insulin, but the bakers manage to get them gooey and chewy all the same. This could be our last meal here, and no puke-inducing workout awaits, so we're going for it.

"Who's a good one?" I ask innocently.

Sandie rolls her eyes toward Bradie. He entertains a gaggle of crushing female-identified cadets and a few moon-eyed guys with an impersonation of one of the instructors from the compound where he trained. He waves a dramatic finger, delivers a flurry of martial arts chops, and unleashes a staccato *hee-yah!*

Sandie nudges my shoulder and winks. "I think you'd make a lovely couple."

"What?" I say. "Bradie? With me? No. We're friends."

She makes an *mm-hmm* sound, not buying what I'm selling.

After lunch, hundreds of us stand at attention in one of the physical education rooms. I note the missing faces from my cohort. The Protectorate is the one pre-work training program one can opt-out of at any point. *Culled* is the word the drill instructors use.

The absentee requested (or begged) for transfers after "tossing their salad," breaking a bone, or worse, withering under the glare of teammates after a failed challenge. Others were summarily cut and sent to more "suitable" workstreams. I expected—and intended—to be one of the latter.

A row of uniformed protectors stands along one wall, helmets buckled to their belts. Bradie's brother Trenton is among them. They salute briskly as a man slithers in, wearing a crisp black uniform with red piping and the insignia of a hangman's noose.

My spine stiffens. Sweat beads Bradie's forehead. He recognizes Eel Man too.

Eel Man assesses our tidy rows. When he speaks, he's a spitting serpent.

"Bravo," he says curtly, "to some. We will invite the best of you to join the cadet program. The top three in this class will do so immediately. They are Liam Nelson, Sandie Marter, and Bradie Lopez Nettle."

My sternum twists. The agents did that to Bradie's hand. I *know* they did. Yet, they're fast-tracking him into cadets? Is that his reward for playing his part? Or is this part of the game, like putting me on the airwaves as a hero, only to turn me into an example?

"Come forward," the agent waves.

Bradie freezes. I nudge him; he steps jerkily, puts on his game face, and follows Liam and Sandie. The agent leads us in applause, his cheeks sagging like heated plastic. Bradie's brother broods as he claps. The agent nods dismissively then walks out of the room. A grey-clad overseer steps forward.

"Congratulations," the overseer says. "The rest of you will now move onto your next vocational stream. As you do, we will be reviewing your results from your time here. Be warned, what you have experienced thus far has been easy. *If* you are offered admission to the cadet program and you have *any* doubts, *do* decline because once you learn how to fire a weapon, there is *no* turning back."

Bradie clenches his scarred hand. His brother stares at nothing, his brown skin turning pale.

"I'd wish you luck," the overseer says, "but luck won't help you."

She salutes, and we salute back. The sound of her boots smacking the floor echoes in the cavernous space; a protector holds the door open for her. The murmuring begins right away. I try to rejoin Liam, Sandie, and Bradie, but a horde of novices surrounds them. I back away, hollow, once more on the outside looking in.

You knew this day was coming, a part of me chides. *This was the plan.*

I hear the words, and I know they're true. Everything worked out. I found Bradie. I made sure he's okay.

Is he? I wonder. His scars run deep. My mom responds in my head. *There's nothing you can do about it, Caitlin. That's that—end of story.*

She's right, and I hate her for it.

People clap Liam, Sandie, and Bradie on the back, and it hits me.

I want to stay.

On the train ride home, Liam and Sandie are way too nice, borderline apologetic for receiving immediate entry into cadets when I did not.

"You're getting in. You'll see!" Sandie says.

"Of course," I reply, not telling her about my abysmal written tests, nor that my mom would kill me if I went on to be a cadet.

I hug them goodbye outside the station, along with a few others. A weird air of competitive camaraderie hangs overhead. Gregor nods and grunts at me, "Good luck."

"Yeah," I say. "You too."

"Walk you home?" Bradie asks.

"Sure," I say.

Liam and Sandie look ready to join us, but Sandie holds Liam back, giving me a thumbs up. Bradie slides his unblemished hand into mine, his palm warm against my own.

"Let's go," he says.

We walk in silence. He looks at me and smiles. I smile back.

"What are you thinking?" he asks.

My gaze drifts down to his scarred hand, hidden in his pocket.

He sighs. "All right, let's get this over with."

"What?" I ask.

He jerks his hand out, holds it up, and pulls his sleeve past his elbow. The scarring ends right below the joint. I reach to touch it; he angles his body so I can't.

I back off. "Does it hurt?"

"Not physically," he says. "The med techs did a good job. Cultured my skin cells for the grafts and injected steroidals for muscular regen. The nerve rehabilitation was the worst."

"It doesn't make sense," I say, trying to logic my way through the story. "They went to a lot of trouble to heal you, so why burn you in the first place?"

His cheek twitches.

"You know why. I broke the law—a biggie. So did my brother. Trenton's got high standing in the Cube, and I've got 'potential,' so they're bending the rules, giving me a shot at becoming someone who *is* allowed to discharge a weapon. But nothing comes free. This…" he holds up his scarred hand. "This is the price for our second chance."

CHAPTER 18

We're quiet after that. When Bradie and I reach my tenement building, our lack of words turns awkward.

"This is me," I say.

With his good hand, he brushes a lock of my short hair, fingers grazing my cheek before retreating.

"I'll see you soon, Caitlin Feral," he says. He disappears around a corner, but his touch remains.

Warmth fills my belly. *Could we make a nice couple?* My humming echoes in the concrete stairwell; my smile swells step by step. I reach my apartment, unlock the door, and go inside.

"Welcome home," a foreign yet sinisterly familiar voice greets me.

It suffocates the warmth in my belly. Within the gloom of our tiny apartment, I make out a silhouette.

Eel Man.

"What are you…" I catch myself and bite my lip.

"No pleasantries?" he asks. "Probably for the best. We haven't much time before your mother and brother get home. I don't imagine you're looking for me to stay for dinner."

"If you'd like." The words are barbed wire in my throat.

He gazes around the flat, appalled. "I'll pass."

He snaps his fingers and points for me to stand in front of the kitchen table. I scurry forward, a trained mutt for its master. He slides a data tablet across the table toward me, and the screen projects a series of holographic files. Bits of my personal data float in the air—my scores from Protectorate training, answers from my questionnaires, a web of lines connecting me to the faces of my friends and rivals in the mentorship program.

"You failed your cadet entry trial by one percent," the agent says.

My jaw clenches. I failed. I'm out. I should be happy. I achieved my goal —to come close, but not close enough to pass. *Yay for me*, I think. But surely he's not here to tell me that.

"I gave you an opportunity," he says. "A gift wrapped up in a bow. And this is what you do with it?" He shakes his head and makes a *tsk-ing* sound.

"I'm sorry," I say.

He contemplates me.

"Can you keep a secret?" he asks.

His gaze bores through me. Does he know about the comic book shop?

"Yes," I reply.

"We allow a margin of error in the trial results. A fudge factor."

My eyes widen.

"Does that mean… I'm in?"

"Dear me, no," he chuckles. "This year's crop of candidates was exceptional, though I'll deny it if any of them ask. Between us, anyone under 70 percent didn't stand a chance."

"Oh," I reply.

"What are we to do with you, Caitlin Feral?" he taps his waxy cheek. "You killed a monstrosity. The angle of the videos can't prove it, and the witness testimony is inconclusive, but we know you discharged a weapon. Your physical scores are well above average. Your psyche profile categorizes you as a solitary, yet during team training your bio readings, heart rate, voice analysis, and brainwaves tell a different story."

He notes my look of confusion.

"Yes, Caitlin, we monitor such factors. It's not enough to excel in combat. The skills the Protectorate teaches, in the hands of someone opposed to the treaty with the Supergenics, and the methods we use to enforce it, well, that could be revolutionary to the current world order. We can't have that, can we? It could destroy us all. These readings help us determine who we can count on."

"And what do your readings say about me?" I ask.

"That putting you in the general workforce could be troublesome," he says. "The Protectorate is good for you. It gives you focus. Clarity. Community."

He slides an envelope toward me with a stamp bearing the all-seeing eye in a fist.

"This is your last chance to be a part of that," he says.

I take the envelope. My heart beats wildly.

"You're conflicted," he says, "because of what we did to your father, no doubt, and your friend's hand. Regrettable actions, but necessary. Your father was about to ignite a second gene war."

I can't hide the surprise in my eyes.

"He nearly killed us all," Eel Man says.

106

"No," I say.

"Yes," he replies. "I have no reason to lie."

I can't hear this.

"And Bradie?" I ask.

"We could've executed Bradie. We showed him mercy—as I'm now doing for you. I trust this will be our last conversation," Eel Man says. He taps his tablet, and it swallows the hologram of my readings.

It's strange watching him walk out the front door. His slithering stride has a dancer's grace, camouflaging the predator within. The door closes, leaving me alone in the darkness.

I think about what Eel Man said about my dad, and I wonder, *Is it true?*

When my mom gets home, she bangs a switch, and a bare bulb flickers to life. I sit and stare at the kitchen table.

"Caitlin?" she asks. "Why on earth are you sitting in the dark?"

She sees the Protectorate envelope in my hand.

"Caitlin." A dangerous edge creeps into her voice.

I tear the envelope open and pull out a thin sheet of paper.

"Attention, Caitlin Feral," I read out loud. "This notice serves as your official notice of early admission into the Protectorate cadet program. If you choose to accept this position—"

My mother grabs the sheet and tears it into confetti.

"You stupid girl!" she shouts. "You were supposed to fail!"

"I *did* fail," I shout back, slamming my fist on the table.

She stops, confused.

"The agent was *here*," I say. "He gave me the letter personally."

My mother leans on the counter for support.

"They're doing this to punish me," she says.

"This isn't about you!" I shout.

"Of course it is," she snaps. "You're a teenage girl. You think an agent's taking the time to oversee your choice of vocation? This is because of your father. As if giving me these blasted migraines weren't bad enough!"

I roll my eyes. She's insane. How many times has she blamed the protectors for something brought on by the fumes at the factory?

"This *isn't* about you," I repeat. "This is about me, and Bradie, and those stupid mutant hounds. I fired a weapon. They're not letting that go." I think of Bradie's hand. With or without evidence, they could've done that to me. "I'm getting off lucky!"

Mom squeezes her eyes and presses her fist to her temple. Could the agents be responsible for her headaches? *Maybe. Or maybe she's conveniently having an episode to get me to do what she wants.* I hate myself for thinking it, and not for the first time; right now, my anger is stronger than my self-recriminations.

"You have to say no," my mom says, "consequences be effed."

"Mom," I reply, "I'm going to say yes."

She grabs a chipped mug from the dish rack and throws it at me as hard as she can. I duck, and it shatters against my closed bunk.

I shake with rage. She *threw* it at me!

"No daughter of mine will ever be one of *them*," she insists.

"They're not all bad," I insist.

Her jaw clenches. "You did not say that. You were there when they took your father. They ruined our lives."

"You're the one ruining my life!" I snap.

Three months ago, I would never have dared say such a thing. Think it, yes; say it, no. That was before I failed my final Testing Day; before I killed a two-headed ravenous hound; before I snuck into the Yellow Zone; before I had friends.

"I want to do this," I say calmly. "I'm happy there. And this is my decision to make."

"This isn't my daughter speaking," she says. "This is them brainwashing you with their chemicals and their pills."

"There are no pills," I say. "Those are stories. They're *all* just stories."

She waves at nothing. "No, you're wrong. It's in the food then—or the water."

"The food is food," I reply. "And the water is water."

"What about the agent? He was *here*," she hisses. "You said so yourself. Coercing a sixteen-year-old girl, turning her against her mother. *That's* what you want to be a part of? That's the kind of person you want to be?"

"Of course not! He's an a*gent*."

"Agent, protector, you think there's a difference?" my mom snorts.

"Yes!" I say. "There *is* a difference. I've seen it."

"No," she insists. "You go back to the Protectorate Caitlin, mark my words, you will do bad things, things you will regret."

108

"No," I insist. "I won't. Me and my friends—"

"Oh!" Mom throws up her hands. "She has friends now. Is that what this is about?"

I think of Liam, Sandie, and Bradie. I think of how I fit at the Protectorate.

"Yes," I say.

"They took your father!" she shouts at the top of her lungs.

"Maybe he had it coming!" I shout back.

My mom looks like I slapped her. I don't care. All these years, she's given me delusional half-truths suited to her version of reality, but what kind of person was my father really?

"Be *very* careful what you say, Caitlin," my mother warns. "There are some things you can't take back. Your father was a good man—"

"Then why did they arrest him?"

"*Because* he was trying to do something good," she says.

"He chose to break the law," I say. "And he left Nate and me without a dad."

"You don't know what you're saying. You have no idea what they were making him do to children like you. Twisting their minds with his devices."

"Enough!" I slam my palms onto the table. "I'm tired of your stories."

"They're not stories," she insists.

"Then why am I only hearing about this now?" I say.

"Their machines, they made me forget… but the memories, they come back with the headaches."

"Convenient," I say.

"Caitlin…"

"You're sick," I continue. "You're not getting better, and I only make you worse."

"Nate, he needs you. He's your little brother," she says. "You can't abandon him."

"Nate's going to leave us. He's going to Manifest. He *is* Gen M. You know it. I know it. All the signs are there. It's simply a matter of time."

She winces at the throbbing in her head, trying to find her cool. "Caitlin, I know you're scared, I'm scared too, but—"

"I'm not scared!" I shout. "I'm *choosing* this, not because of *them*, but because of *me*. I don't want to pick apples, or file requisition forms, or sweep garbage off the streets. I *want* to be a protector. I *want* to be one of *them.*"

I can't believe I said it. I can't believe I mean it. Her arm swings to slap me. The arc is wide, telegraphing her intent. My newly honed reflexes kick in, easily catching her wrist in my grip.

"You do not lay a hand on me," I say. "Not ever."

She tries to jerk free. I grip tighter. For once, I'm in control.

"I don't know you anymore," she says. I relate. In this instant, I'm a stranger to myself. "Get out," she says. "Get out of my house!"

I snort like a true protector. Lines I memorized at school flow more instinctively than my martial arts block. "You don't have a house. You're permitted to occupy this government-owned residence at the grace of the Housing Commission. It *can* be taken away."

"Caitlin," she whines, "you're hurting me."

I assume she means my words—until I realize my fingers are turning into a vice. I release her, back away, and wonder if maybe there *is* something in the Protectorate food.

"I… I'm sorry. I didn't mean… You shouldn't make me angry."

The phrase horrifies me. I sound like someone I recognize all too well. I sound like her.

My mother's quiet at that, so quiet it's scary. When she speaks, it's with a resolute coldness.

"Get out," my mother says. "Get out of this government-owned residence—and don't ever come back."

CHAPTER 19

I stand outside the apartment that was home, staring at the closed door separating me from my mom.

Now what?

I lift my open palm. Do I tap meekly or pound aggressively?

"That was quite the fight."

I whip around and face Bradie's brother. His form-fitting copper uniform accentuates the curves of his muscled form. He holds his helmet under one arm.

"Officer Trenton!" I snap my heels together and salute.

He smirks. "At ease, cadet."

I lower my arm.

"You heard all that?" I ask, standing protectively in front of the door.

"Whole block did, I imagine," he replies.

My mom could be in a lot of trouble.

"She didn't mean what she said," I assure him.

He shrugs. "At least you have a parent left who cares."

"You don't have parents?" I ask.

"Orphans," he says.

I remember now. Bradie lives with his aunt.

"Right. Sorry."

Trenton shrugs. "It is what it is, cadet."

"You keep calling me that," I say.

"Cadet?" he asks.

"Yeah."

"You got your early admittance notification, right?"

I nod.

"So, are you in, or are you out?"

I take a deep breath, and before I change my mind, I say in a quick exhale, "I'm in. Sir."

"Great. Let's get going, cadet."

I hesitate.

"Where?"

"You'll see," he says.

I follow him down the concrete stairs and into the near-empty streets. Evening lamps come to life around us.

We round a corner. Liam, Sandie, and Bradie wait by the security fence. All four of us are in our school ties and jackets. Bradie winks. I try to wink back, but I know it looks like I've developed a tic. Practicing in the mirror hasn't helped. A fourth youth stands with them, wearing the yellow coveralls of a technician with the emblem of a computer monitor and screwdriver on his chest.

"This is—" Trenton begins to introduce the odd man out.

"Normand," I say. My tone is heavy. My heart hammers. *What's he doing here? Is this a trick? A trap? Do the protectors know about the Lair?*

Behind them, black clouds roil, and lightning blasts into the energy siphons.

"You two know each other?" Trenton asks.

"We're in the same class," Normand explains, his avoidant gaze drifting.

"Huh," Trenton grunts. "I should've paid more attention to your files." He looks from one face to another. "Kind of weird you all have a Caitlin connection."

He says what I'm thinking. Trenton shrugs. "One of those things, I guess."

I almost believe he means it.

"Normand's just been assigned to the Protectorate as a techie," Trenton explains. "Sometimes we take one into the field. Tonight is one of those nights."

We look to each other. *Into the field?*

Trenton punches a code into the gate's locking pad and swipes his i-dent card through the reader. It beeps and clicks. He shoves the gate open. We exchange another confused glance. *Is this a test?*

"Last one in, make sure to pull the gate shut behind you," Trenton directs, stepping into the Yellow Zone. Lightning crackles into the energy absorbers set twenty measures back from the fence, lighting him up from behind.

"Is he serious?" Liam asks, staring at a biohazard sign with mutated animal heads on it. "He wants us to go in there, in our class uniforms, at night?"

"The evidence is incontrovertible," Normand replies. He marches past and through the gate.

"Is Leg Brace showing us up?" Bradie asks.

"Yeah," I smile, weirdly proud. "He is."

"Well, balls to that," Bradie snorts, hurrying after him.

"Are we doing this?" Liam asks Sandie.

She takes a deep breath.

"Looks like," she answers.

They snake their hands together, square their shoulders, and I'm suddenly the last one on the safe side of the fence.

"Hurry up!" Bradie yells at us, forging ahead.

"Yeah, okay, we're coming!" Liam shouts in return.

Sandie turns to me. "Come on, Caitlin!"

She holds her hand for me to take. I don't know why I'm hesitating. I've been in the Yellow Zone before. It's not such a big deal. Yet, as I embrace the path of the protector, the one that leads to the Cube and all that it represents, my mom's promise haunts me.

You go back to the Protectorate, Caitlin, mark my words you will do bad things, things you will regret.

"Oh, screw it," I say. *What does she know?* I take Sandie's hand, and she guides me through the gate. I pull it shut, and we set off after the others.

The pulsating globes of the energy siphons crackle and emit an eerie glow. We run, stumble, and crawl over debris and through busted buildings; for all we know, they could collapse at any moment. We chase Bradie, who tries to keep up with Normand, who presumably is following Trenton. We grin wildly.

Normand is surprisingly sure-footed, projecting his knowledge of the terrain. I hope no one else notices. We catch up to Bradie. He offers me his good hand. I take it.

"Can you believe we're *in* the Yellow Zone?" His eyes are full moons, reminding me of Nate. Lightning flares from the perpetual black clouds above.

"Crazy, right?" I say. I've been in the Yellow Zone before, but not with him, not like this.

We catch up to Normand. Trenton's gone. We've lost sight of our borough, and I realize I'm unsure how to get back.

"Guys, are we lost?" I ask.

Before anyone can answer, the sizzling energy absorbers around us go dead, casting us into pitch blackness. Fear eclipses excitement.

"Do you hear that?" Sandie asks.

I do hear it—an animalistic growl. I turn toward it. A pair of glowing red eyes stare at us.

"Arm yourselves," Sandie says.

I reach down. My fingers close around a pipe. I raise it over my shoulder. The beast is almost on top of us. The red eyes wink out, and a pair of blinding headlights flare to life. Trenton's laughter echoes around us.

"Effing eff," he swears, turning on and off a battered animal toy with glowing eyes and a wolfish howl. "You all look hilarious!"

He stands on the hood of a hover vehicle, mocking us.

"Ha, ha," Bradie says, shaking his head. We drop our makeshift weapons. Only Normand didn't arm himself. Figures he'd leave the fighting to us.

"Come on, losers," Trenton says, nimbly swinging over the hovercraft's windshield into the front passenger seat.

A woman sits at the controls. She's got the air of a protector—strong jaw, slicked-back hair, and an arrogant tilt to her head. She's out of uniform, wearing a tight tank top, a silver collar, and, strapped to her forehead, a pair of flight goggles.

"So *this* is the best this term has to offer?" she gazes at us, unimpressed.

"I didn't pick 'em," Trenton shrugs. "Besides, they can't all be as good as our year."

She grunts in agreement.

"Get on," she orders.

We grapple aboard using handles and footholds. We half drag, half push Normand to get him and his bum leg up and over. This vehicle is definitely not accessible. Neither the woman nor Trenton offers to assist. She spits overboard but looks like she'd rather direct it at Normand.

"Techie?" she asks.

"Genius, apparently," Trenton says.

"All right," she says, skeptical. "You're up front, genius."

Normand shuffles forward and sits between her and Trenton. For once, he's not looking at his watch or someone's shoulder. He stares at her breasts.

"Hey! Eyes on the console," she orders. Normand redirects his gaze.

"Everyone, this is Crystal Kapor," Trenton says.

She gives us all the finger, talking only to Normand.

"You know how to use a DRADIS?" she asks.

Normand confidently punches keys on a control pad, and a monitor flicks to life. It shows the surrounding cartography with us as a blue blip. A multitude of red blips move around us. I grip a chair. Liam, Sandie, and Bradie do the same. The red blips are other life-signs. If they're mutants, we're as good as dead.

"Eliminating non-threats," Normand says, typing away. The red dots blink out. "They were mostly rodents," he explains. "Possibly an alley cat."

"Not bad, rookie," Crystal says. "Keep an eye out. We did a sweep today, but you never know when a mutie might slip through. All right, buckle up, grubs."

She doesn't wait, putting the craft into gear. I'm thrown into Bradie's lap. He's belted into a chair and deftly catches me. Sandie does the same for Liam.

"My hero," he says to her.

Bradie puts his arms around my waist. It's not the worst. My gaze drifts to the scarred skin of his left hand. He sees me staring, and he hides the injury under his thigh.

The hovercraft is open to the air. We speed through the broken city, wind beating our faces. The vehicle's headlights illuminate the way as we weave among the lightning-absorbing electrodes.

I crane my neck toward the roiling clouds. We travel deep into what's left of the city; I leave the fight with Mom behind.

"Multiple contacts," Normand says. "Two dozen hovercraft closing in."

High beams shine in the distance. They seem to be coming from the direction of the other boroughs. Some are small craft like ours. I spot a two-seater and several single slings. Others are Juggernauts, capable of carrying up to a hundred people each.

What kind of mission is this? I wonder.

Bradie's grip tightens around my waist.

"Check that out!" he yells above the wind.

Lightning arcs into an energy-absorbing globe set atop a tower that rises from the center of an enormous building in the shape of a curvy bowl.

Crystal accelerates, and we disappear into an opening in the side of the gigantic edifice. We skim along a huge hallway flanked by concrete pillars. At the end is an empty elevator shaft framed by sliding steel doors yanked from their housings, maw wide and ready to swallow us whole.

"I hope you're all buckled in!" Crystal shouts.

We race faster, and Crystal sharply turns the steering bracket. We do a 180, careening past the fallen steel doors and into the portal of darkness. She shoves the gear into neutral; momentum slides us into the hollow shaft. We hover there.

"Ready?" Crystal asks.

I grab a handle, my eyes locked on Bradie's.

"Don't you dare let go," I say.

"Never," he winks, squeezing me tight.

Crystal shoves a gear shift; the hovercraft shudders, and its vibrations stop. We drop straight down the shaft. I scream. So do the others. Trenton whoops wildly. His thrill echoes through us.

The fun turns to real danger. The walls blur; I lift off Bradie's lap; my sweaty grip gives. I'm about to be wrenched into nothingness when Crystal rams the gear shift. The hovercraft vibrates to life, sending up a cloud of dust as upward pressure pushes Bradie's thighs into mine.

We pant, confirm we're alive, and burst into laughter. Normand wheezes happily. He gives me a thumbs up. I mirror it and experience a collective joy as Bradie, Liam, and Sandie do the same.

"Did we lose anybody?" Crystal asks hopefully.

"Negative," Normand replies.

"Well, there goes that bet," she says with disappointment, handing a chocolate bar to Trenton.

Crystal propels the hovercraft through another hall. Multicolored lights flash ahead, and a strange booming grows louder. At first, I think it's the omnipresent thunder, but something's off. It sounds like—

"Music," Bradie says as we burst into the middle of the bowl.

Bradie's right. It is music, but not like the wind and string instruments we learned to play as children. This is deep, then light, pounding, then gentle. It comes in waves, rhythmic and repetitive. It's the thumping of the heart and the sluicing of blood; the inhale/exhale of the lungs; the crackle of synapses firing into an infinitely repeating song. It rises and falls with the ebb and flow of adrenaline, the cascade of hormones, and the dilation of pupils. The music is more than alive; it *is* life.

Normand puts on a pair of tinted glasses with ear covers.

I gaze in wonder as Crystal drives us into the open air space. Trenton is unabashedly stripping out of his protector's gear, down to a pair of short shorts and sneakers, muscled bod bared.

Lightning flashes above, caught by the globe on its concrete pillar in the middle of the gigantic bowl. The electrode's been modified to not only absorb energy but to spit it back out in the form of lasers and light bursts, all in time to the music's throbbing beat. It's beautiful and mesmerizing. I can't believe this is happening.

Seats rise around the periphery. Our various gymnasia have miniature versions of these stands at some of the schools, where the public can fill their short leisure hours by cheering on kids who may yet Manifest, playing team sports, doing gymnastics, or performing at a recital. On special occasions, protectors do demonstration athletics against each other. But this could seat thousands. What kind of games were played here?

Crystal powers down the hovercraft amidst dozens of other short-range vehicles. More of them arrive from various access points. Some of the drivers and passengers wave and holler at us as they pass.

Trenton and Crystal catcall in reply. We help Normand clamber down then walk toward the center of the stadium. The middle is full of people dancing and gyrating. Not regular people—protectors. Like Crystal, out of uniform, they retain a look, with their toned bodies and sure movements. Many wear metal i-dent tags about their necks.

Most are dressed in the short shorts or loose track pants they train in, and little else. Some of the female-identified wear sports bras or tank tops. Others do not. Both the male- and female-identified wear makeup, accentuating their eyes, lips, and cheekbones. A few playfully embrace androgyny or bend binary gender idents, combining bushy paste-on mustaches with long, flowing wigs. Everyone has colorful accessories—bows and ribbons are wrapped about hair, brows, and biceps. I wish I'd put on the yellow bracelet Nate gave me before Mom kicked me out, although I fear it would look childish here—amidst the collars, bracelets, and straps made from shiny metals, shimmering beads, or bands of leather that accentuate thighs, pectorals, and breasts.

I'm mesmerized and horrified at the same time. If regular dregs were to gather like this, they'd be arrested by these same people.

"What is this?" I ask.

"This," Trenton replies, "is something few cadets see or take part in, not until they are protectors themselves. Welcome to Revelry."

Crystal leans her arm on Trenton's shoulder in the way of old comrades, and she adds, "What he's saying is, *this* is where we party."

CHAPTER 20

Crystal holds a cylinder the size of a pinky finger and pops off its cap. She twists, and a red, waxy substance rolls out. She applies it to Trenton's lips, turning them neon, then tosses the cylinder to me.

"Here," Bradie says. "I'll help."

Bradie applies the lipstick to my puckered mouth then turns my chin left and right, nodding in satisfaction. Girls like Lilianne would sometimes wear stuff like this. I never thought I would.

Bradie hands me the tube. "Now you do me."

Crystal has us all add mascara to give our lashes "luster" and then smears a black line with her thumb under each of our eyes. To my delight, the final effect is glam warrior-esque. I'd expected clownish. We leave our jackets in the hovercraft and are about to follow Crystal when she stops us with a commanding hand.

"Not you," she says to Normand. "You're over there."

She points to a group of young techies in coveralls at a multitiered array of consoles.

"That's not fair," I say.

"It's all right, Caitlin," Normand says. "*Someone* has to keep the lights on."

"But—" I argue.

"I would never partake in that drug-addled petri dish of sweat and germs," Normand gestures at the throng of bodies.

Bradie hides a smirk behind his good hand.

"Staphylococcus infections are no joke!" Normand points at Bradie.

"Fair enough, my man," Bradie says, raising his good hand in peace.

Normand straightens his stance and lifts his nose haughtily. His tone turns commanding, making him sound far older than he is. "Whelp! From what alternate timeline do you hail in which I am in any way your man?"

"Easy, tough guy," Bradie replies.

"We shall see who is the 'tough guy,'" Normand bristles. He pulls a marble-shaped data pod from a pocket in his coveralls, holding the device between his thumb and pointing finger. He glares triumphantly, like he's brought a blaster to a knife fight.

118

"Kazamo," he growls.

"Uh, okay," Bradie says.

"Normand—" I start.

"Enjoy the festivities," he snorts, stuffing the gizmo into his pocket. He bows stiffly, throws an imaginary cape over his shoulder, and limps to the double-decked control center.

I've seen Normand spaz before, but never like this. He seems mostly okay with the lightning and thunder in the Yellow Zone, but I bet the stadium's multicolored flashing lights and the pounding music are getting to him.

"He's a bit odd, isn't he?" Crystal asks.

"You should read his personnel file," Trenton says.

Until now, Normand was a part of this evening. Crystal made him up like the rest of us, only to shut him out? It reminds me of how I was treated at school. I feel a tug to go to him, but the selfish side of me wants to stay. Besides, I can't imagine Normand having fun with a bunch of dancing protectors. That would be too weird.

"The techie's right about one thing," Crystal says. "We do need some pharmacological enhancement."

She pulls a pillbox from her pocket and opens it. Inside are six glowing, orange gel capsules.

"What's that?" I ask.

"The chemical composition is dioxymantangulate. We call it Mango Tango."

She sees the concern on my face. "Relax," she says. "It's brain food. It enhances your ability to absorb new information and learn faster under guided conditions. We take it before our Calibration sessions."

"What are those?" Liam asks.

"Guided meditations," Trenton explains. "Only way more kick-ass."

Crystal holds the pillbox to us; one by one, we each take a capsule. I hold the glowing orange gel tab up to the cascading light show. Through the translucent shell, I appraise the throng of dancing protectors.

"This doesn't look like a guided situation," I say.

"That's what makes it so much fun," Trenton says. He knocks his capsule back with a chug from a canteen.

"When you throw a bit of booze into the mix, the effects are hallucinogenic," Crystal winks.

Trenton passes the canister to Bradie; he follows his older brother's lead. Crystal's next, then Sandie and Liam. It's down to me. I take the canteen from Liam, put the pill in my mouth, and suck it back. The liquid burns and sends a rush of peppermint through my nasal cavity.

As the Mango Tango slides down my throat, I remember my mom's words.

This is them brainwashing you with their chemicals and their pills.

Shut up, I tell her. But part of me isn't angry. It's afraid. *What have I taken? What will it do to me?*

But fear is a funny emotion. I forget about the drug's theoretical danger as I face the certainty of something much scarier—the threat of public humiliation.

I was always a disaster in dance class. I had no rhythm, could never keep time with my classmates, and I'd lose track of the choreography. My instructor was relieved when she was finally allowed to flunk me. Humiliation churns in me as we move amidst the sweating, gyrating bodies. I look longingly to the command deck where the techies are overseeing the music and power flow.

Normand got it lucky.

The protectors stare at us. We clearly don't belong. Only Trenton and Crystal abide by their party dress code, not only stripped down to the barest of outfits but unabashedly dancing in the sea of undulating physiques.

"Come on!" Trenton waves at us, disengaging from a boy-girl couple who had him sandwiched and now make out.

He leads us deeper into the crowd. Protectors press him for high fives and fist bumps, which he happily dispenses. Our school uniforms earn increasingly dirty looks.

"Screw this," Bradie says, and he yanks off his shirt, bunching it up into a ball and throwing it into the crowd. Loud cheers rise all around. Trenton beams proudly, grabs his brother, and lifts him onto his shoulder. Bradie still has his tie around his neck, hanging between the surprisingly muscular mounds of his chest.

"This is my baby brother, yo!" Trenton shouts to a chorus of approval.

Liam and Sandie shrug to each other and also toss their shirts away. More cheers ensue. Everyone looks at me. Every bit of insecurity Lilianne and her friends bashed into me over the years floods my reservoirs. I want to run; I'm going to run—until I ask myself, *What would Tigara do?*

I channel the urban huntress, recalling how she was thrown into a coliseum not unlike this to face slavering beasts. My fingers transform into imaginary claws, yanking my shirt open and popping buttons everywhere. I gorge on the screams of approval as I pull my shirt off and twirl it over my head, grateful for my sports bra. A gust of air pulls at the cloth, and I let it go. The updraft whisks the garment away, higher and higher, until a burst of stato-electric energy grabs it and slams the garment into the sizzling electricity sphere above. It makes a *whu-zip* sound and a tiny burst of flame.

Protectors cheer and shove drinks into our hands. I hold a plastic cup filled with a frothy red liquid giving off a thick vapor and the stench of strawberries.

"They're phytochemicals!" Crystal shouts over the music. "They're good for you!"

Trenton calls for a toast, and we all clink our cups, sloshing sticky, foaming liquid over the rims. The fear is gone. The thrill of belonging courses through me. This time, as the bubbly sweet concoction washes down my throat, my mother's voice is wonderfully silent. The music holds sway, and when I catch an illusory glimpse of a man in black watching from the shadows, I don't give him a second look.

CHAPTER 21

A rush of giddy euphoria power washes a lifetime of junk from my mind. I willfully obliterate the choreographed steps from the classes I failed. Tonight, I dance my own dance. My movements are random and wild, arms swinging and hips swaying to the paradoxically predictable yet ever-shifting beat.

Bradie reaches his good hand to me, his scarred one safely behind his back. Our fingers entwine, and I pull him toward me. He grins goofily. I had no idea it was possible to feel so light and free.

What happens when tonight ends? the naysayer in me wonders.

I don't care, is my honest answer.

"Look!" Bradie points a scarred finger.

A floating stage descends, bearing a band, singers, and dancers. The band feverishly plays a slew of electronic instruments, and the dancers are among the best I've seen. The singer's tall and willowy; her voice is melting nougat.

She sings a song we all know, of sacrifice, strength, and solidarity. She adds a verse about the protectors standing tallest and shining brightest against the things that growl and shred in the night. Dozens of smaller hover podiums come down, each with a pole in the center. Athletic physiques costumed in copper undergarments, a protector's helmet, and nothing else are upon each dais, whirling and twirling around the poles in dizzying displays.

Loud cheers rise around. The frenzy of dancers on the main stage thrust and dip hips.

"All the performers are protectors," Crystal shouts into my ear.

Of course, I realize. *This* is Gen M. All of them were once candidates for Manifestation. All of them went through years and years of study to learn these crafts—singing, ballet, gymnastics. None of them have special powers, and yet they are all amazing.

Does that mean I can be amazing too?

I squeeze Bradie's good hand and look for a kiss, but he ignores me. His gaze meets his brother's. Bradie points to himself, then at the main stage, hovering right before us, ten measures off the ground. Trenton laughs and shakes his head. Bradie's eyes widen into full moons; he nods vigorously. Trenton sighs, shrugs, and hands his drink to Crystal. She rolls her eyes.

"Clear a hole!" she shouts above the music. Nearby protectors step back, their smirks full of curiosity.

Bradie pulls his hand from mine. "Wish me luck!"

"For what?" I ask.

"For this!"

He sprints toward his brother. Trenton crouches, hands cupped together. Bradie jumps his right foot into Trenton's grip. Trenton's hips thrust, propelling his arms upward and launching Bradie into the air. His perfectly aligned body's a missile, and, as if it's the most natural thing in the world, he flips and lands on the stage. He holds his arms out to the side; the crowd goes wild. My lungs swell with pride; unbidden, I think, *He's my boyfriend!*

Is he?

My heart trembles.

I don't know.

Into the euphoria creep black pits of neediness.

But you want him to be, don't you?

I escape answering by gulping my strawberry elixir; it rescues me with a gentle numbness.

Bradie flips, turns, and somersaults. The crowd screams in approval. He dives into splits and bounds out of them. It's part dance, part acrobatics, and pure wondrousness. The band plays off of him, and he plays off of them.

He builds to a climax—a dozen flips in a row from the far left of the stage to the far right. In a dizzying twirl, he rips his pants off to everyone's amazement. Down to his sleek, moisture-wicking underpants, he slides toward the crowd on his knees. He throws his arms wide, panting and covered in sweat.

We fall silent; the music stops. The crowd's awe gathers itself, about to erupt in thunderous applause fit to deafen the roiling storm clouds above.

I'm poised to lead the charge, but before any of our palms can clap together, screeching feedback bursts from the sound system. The acoustic assault makes us gasp, wince, and cover our ears. We hunch in pain and collectively gape. Lightning strikes the globe atop the electric rod in the center of the arena, but the device no longer sprays a technicolor light show.

The orb absorbs and cages the energy; it demands release. The sphere whines, an overfilled cell ready to burst. People back away.

"Please turn off all cell phones and any other mobile communications devices," an antiquated computerized voice counsels us from the loudspeakers, "so that everyone can enjoy the show."

The groaning in the power-absorbing sphere peaks, and it shoots an arcing bolt of lightning to the rear of the stadium. A lone figure stands on a floating dais in the lightning bolt's path. I recognize his dropped shoulders, the girth of his waist, the out-turned leg in a brace, and the tinted glasses with ear covers.

"Normand," I whisper, followed by a shriek, "Normand!"

I want to look away; the lightning is too fast, and I'm too slow. It's going to electrocute him. The memory of his burnt husk will wake me with nightmares for years to come.

Except, the lightning *doesn't* kill him. He holds up a palm with a metallic disc strapped to it. The lightning breaks into smaller bolts, cresting around the disc like a wave smashing against a rock. The streams of electricity dance about him. More of the weird metal discs cover his torso, arms, and legs. The data pod he showed us menacingly is fastened to a circlet about his brow.

The energy forms a crackling sphere above his open palm. From the center of the arena, the energy-sucking globe fires another bolt at him. He harnesses it same as the first, creating a second sparking globe above his other extended hand.

His floating podium moves toward us, and his voice projects into a microphone strapped about his head. He sings an opera in the gibberish he's prone to.

Is he speaking one of the old tongues?

The assembled protectors are glassy-eyed with wonder. We can't understand a word, but it's beautiful. His voice! Who knew he had such a voice? It vibrates, sending shudders up and down my spine. It's raw beauty, ugliness, triumph, and failure.

He moves his arms in sinewy arcs, and his lightning globes crack like eggs. Sizzling, whiskered snouts capped by wide eyes force their way out. The orbs are hatching a pair of energy dragons! Their confining shells disintegrate. The creatures snake and twirl around Normand's arms, then about each other in the air before him. He looks down at me, and I up at him. I give him a double thumbs up. He draws his arms back, and the dragons land like trained hawks, crouching on each of his forearms. The crackling dragons hungrily bite the air, eyes on their meal—me.

"Normand! What are you doing?" I demand. He doesn't flinch.

From the stage, Bradie sees the danger. Normand's lost it.

"Caitlin!" Bradie screams. He somersaults off the podium and runs toward me.

"Stay back!" I shout at him, "Everybody, get away from me!"

The protectors closest to me edge away in panic. Normand winds his right arm—and throws a lightning dragon directly at me. It travels at the speed of light; for me, everything slows down. Trenton grabs his near-naked brother, jerks him off his feet, and holds him tight, one arm around his neck, the other about his lean waist. Bradie struggles futilely, calling my name. Sandie buries her head into Liam's chest; he turns away, unable to watch. Crystal's eyes widen, head shaking in disbelief, her scream of "No!" echoing in my ears.

"Kazamo!" Normand shouts.

The lightning hits me.

CHAPTER 22

I expect the agony to be unendurable—an instant of ultimate suffering as my central nervous system overloads and my blood boils in my veins. Bradie elbows his brother in the face, slips free, and runs toward me. Except, I'm not in pain.

I look at the follicles on my arms rise gently. The screaming stops. People stare in wonder. Bradie's goofy grin gets a fifth wind.

"Your hair," he says. "It's sticking up."

Normand's outstretched arm continues channeling energy into me, but it's not lightning—it's amazing. His song continues, subdued but building.

Bradie reaches my side.

"Are you okay?" he asks.

"I am," I reply. A halo surrounds me. I feel like a superhero.

Bradie's so mesmerized, he reaches for me with his scarred hand. I mirror him, my fingers a digit from his—until he catches sight of the mottled tissue winding up his forearm to below the elbow. Trauma infiltrates euphoria.

I see the alert sounding in his eyes, blaring, *Retreat, retreat!*

"Stay," I say.

His shoulders soften.

"Okay," he says.

I hold my glowing fingers a breath from his scarred hand. He presses the pitted flesh of his fingertips against mine, and Normand's song hits a crescendo. The luminescence around me spreads to Bradie, dancing up his arm. Steam rises off him, our heat evaporating the sweat covering his muscled form. He laughs, entwining his fingers in mine.

The touch of his other hand on my cheek sparks a gentle exchange between his skin and mine. Electricity flows betwixt our approaching mouths. Our lips meet; the tingly current travels down my spine, and the pulsing warmth curls into a ball in the center of my hips. Our bodies press together.

Time is gossamer; the world fades. I want to swallow him and be swallowed by him. When the sensations overwhelm, I tuck my head into his shoulder, clinging to him with pure need—and he clings to me. It's what I crave, and he gives it to me. It's what he needs, and I give it to him.

We deep dive; he strokes my hair, and we grudgingly come up for air.

He whispers into my ear, "Should we share this with the rest of them?"

The selfish part of me wants to say no, but I nod. Keeping hold of his scarred hand, I withdraw my torso from his; a million microscopic connections come undone. Bradie reaches his palm to his brother. Trenton takes it, curiosity on his face. The glow spreads into him, and Trenton's smile widens. Crystal entwines her hand in his and joins our effervescent ranks. I hold my free hand to Sandie. She takes it, still holding Liam. They glow.

Normand's current spreads. More people join our circuit, some taking hands, others pressing palms to a neighbor's shoulder, back, chest, or hip. Normand's song rises and descends; soon, we are all linked, shining from within. Mist rises from us, and we look up to him as if he were the mightiest Supergenic.

He lifts the second energy dragon.

"*Volant!*" he cries. It wiggles its bottom and launches upward.

The dragon takes on the shape of an electrified bird with a forked tail, soaring in a circle of blazing light. The crowd gasps, and murmurs ripple through our ranks. "It's a hawk!" some say. "No, it's a phoenix!"

I shake my head. It's a fork-tailed shadowren, winged rodent of the Yellow Zone. It's an odd choice.

Normand squeezes his fingers tight, extinguishing the light that fills us. We gasp collectively. The stadium goes pitch black. For the first time in my life, the clouds above are lightning-free; the towering electrode in our midst looks like it's blown a fuse. Our silence matches the darkness. If not for Bradie's hand in my own, I would think this was the afterworld—not that there is such a thing.

I count a full ten seconds. Then, as if someone's flicked a switch, the lightning rears to life in the clouds once more, firing into the glass orb; it flares and emits a rainbow light show, and speakers blare synthesized music.

Everyone cheers and dances more frenetically than before, jumping and pounding their fists in the air. Normand and his floating podium are gone.

"Did you like it?" a familiar voice asks.

We turn. Normand's there, covered in the discs that enabled him to manipulate the energy, the circlet with the data pod about his brow.

"Wow," Bradie says. "That was *awesome!*"

Normand stares over my right shoulder; a twitching smile broadcasts his pleasure.

"What are your thoughts on the matter, Caitlin?" he asks.

"Magnificent," I reply. "I wish I could live in that moment forever."

"That would be dangerous," he replies.

Trenton claps him on the back.

"How epic was that?!" Trenton declares.

Crystal pushes him aside, takes Normand's cheeks in her hands, and kisses him on the lips. I expect him to freak and deliver a diatribe about how the mouth is the most bacteria-filled part of the body. He puts a hand on Crystal's thigh and leans into her kiss.

They disengage, and Crystal slings an arm around his shoulder.

"Kazamo," Normand murmurs.

"You got that right," Crystal says. "You are definitely coming back next year." A shadow crosses Normand's face.

"That is 365 days away," Normand answers. "I should rejoin the other technicians."

"No way," Trenton interjects. "You're going to party."

He shoves a frothy strawberry drink into Normand's hand. He sips it tentatively and eyes Crystal's figure. She thrusts her breasts.

Bradie laughs. "Caitlin, I think you're jealous."

"What? No," I insist. "Crystal who?"

Bradie laughs more. "It's okay. It's pretty obvious the guy's at least a little in love with you. And I gotta give him props. He definitely showed me who's who. I can't compete with that."

It takes me a moment to process. Normand's not in love with me, is he? And what does Bradie mean he can't compete? Is there a competition? Am I the prize? I should be horrified. I'm not some object. Yet, I smile.

"Oh geez, there goes the girl's ego," Bradie rolls his eyes.

"Hush," I say, in a way that means, "go on." "Normand's not like that. He's different."

"Caitlin, he's a guy. Trust me. He's like that."

Normand shuffles awkwardly; Crystal dances suggestively.

"I should rescue him," I say.

Bradie holds me back. "Dude does not need to be rescued."

"But—" I try to argue.

"Let him have this night," Bradie says. "And we can have ours."

He kisses me, and when he does, I feel the electricity all over again.

CHAPTER 23

Morning comes too soon. Roiling clouds hide the sun, but protector timepieces start beeping all around, alerting us to the arrival of a new day. The celebrants look at their alarms, the music and lasers cut out, and the electrode above returns to feeding energy into the power grid instead of spitting out a technicolor display. Many moan in disappointment but all dutifully head to their hovercrafts.

Normand gives Crystal a big hug. She kisses him on the lips. I wave and watch him leave with the other techies.

"He's a character, that one," Bradie says.

"He is," I agree, glad that Bradie didn't call him a weirdo or a donk. Only I'm allowed to do that.

We find our ride amidst all the others. Crystal drives us toward our borough. Liam and Sandie doze in each other's arms. Liam's tie dangles from around his forehead. Bradie and I cuddle. Dressed only in underwear, his near-naked body radiates heat. Trenton is up front, monitoring the DRADIS and chattering with Crystal. Across the river, the sun rises beyond the towers of Jupiter City, where there is no perpetual storm full of thunder and lightning.

So this is happiness, I muse. I know it can't last; I wonder to what lengths I'll go to get it back.

The closer we get to the security fence, the more relevant that question becomes. I remember the fight with my mom. I have no idea how I'm going to fix things with her.

"Sorry, future Caitlin," I yawn, "that's your problem."

The euphoria of the evening is wearing off, and all I want is to sleep.

We skim parallel to the fence, toward the giant white Cube gleaming in early morning light. Cleaners dangle from ropes attached to the roof and squeegee the polymer building.

The protectors at the guard tower nod, gates slide open, and our hovercraft passes through. Crystal guides us into an underground parking garage. Fuel fumes catch in my throat; a flickering overhead light assaults my bloodshot eyes; a rusted jeep waiting to be junked reminds me of life's depressing impermanence.

I don't care. *I'm home.*

"Come on, grubs," Crystal says. "We need to get you washed and into uniform."

We stumble out of the vehicle and along the concrete floor, bump into each other, and giggle childishly. The Mango Tango pulses in my temples; my body tingles pleasantly. Crystal directs the four of us to stand side-by-side in front of a concrete wall.

"Face me," Crystal says. "Yup, that'll work." She aims a fire hose and blasts us with freezing water.

I screech. I'm not the only one. Bradie, Liam, and Sandie curse as Trenton unleashes a second stream of brutally frigid water. They increase the flow, knocking us off our feet. My hip slams into the concrete floor. I crawl away; the torrent of water follows. Crystal turns her hose on Sandie, granting me brief relief—until the stream returns, blinding and searing me. Who knew water could hurt so much?

More hovercraft zoom in.

"Grubs! Grubs! Grubs!" out-of-uniform protectors chant. Their hoots and hollers echo.

Trenton and Crystal cut the flow of water. We cough and sputter.

"On your feet, grubs!" Trenton yells.

We shiver yet force ourselves to obey. Our skin is red and painfully numb.

"Clean yourselves up, grubs," Crystal yells, pelting me with something hard as stone. I pick up a bar of soap. It slips through my cold, numb fingers. They make us strip naked, and we pass around the brick of cleanser. I dip my hands into the puddles of murky water at our feet to rinse away the lipstick, eyeshadow, and mascara.

"Good enough," Trenton shouts, hitting us with another spray that shears a layer of skin along with the soapy film.

Trenton shuts the tap. We drip, teeth chattering. Crystal gathers our school jackets and dumps them in a pile. She pours fuel on them, then drops a burning match. They go up in flames.

"Say goodbye to your old lives, grubs, and hello to the new," she smiles.

Trenton tosses us towels. I barely grab mine before it falls into a puddle. Draping it over myself, the sandpapery cloth scratches my already battered flesh.

The protector onlookers from the party disappear into several elevators.

"Get dressed," Trenton says, and he drops four foil clothing packs in front of us. They splatter on the wet concrete. "Come find us. You've got ten minutes."

Trenton and Crystal enter the last elevator.

"Find you where?" Bradie asks.

The doors close on Trenton and Crystal giving us the finger. Signs light above each elevator, declaring them, "Out of Service."

"Effing eff," Bradie swears.

Sandie yanks and pulls on her foil pack.

"How the deuce do you get these things open?"

She tries with her teeth, but no go. Bradie races over to the junked jeep and slices the edge off his packet using a jagged fender.

I expect the package to contain disposable track uniforms similar to what we use on Testing Day. Bradie pulls forth a fun fur animal hat in tiger print, with matching trunks.

"Seriously?" Liam asks, freeing a similar leopard-inspired outfit. Sandy's is zebra striped and comes with a matching bra. Mine is snake skin.

"Sssssexy," Bradie winks.

The get-ups are worn and patchy. One is missing an ear. They smell funkier than the exhaust fumes seeped into the garage's concrete floors. We dress, and I try not to think about where the ensembles came from or how many cadets have been forced to wear them.

"Hustle!" Liam orders, and we hurry to the stairs, slipping on the slick floor in our bare feet.

We open the stairwell door and gaze up and up.

"We don't know where we're going," Sandie points out.

I look at how we're dressed. "Yes, we do."

Gasping and drenched in sweat, we reach the desk where we got our novice gear months ago. The overseer lowers her glasses reprovingly and slams four cadet uniforms onto the counter.

"Have you seen a pair of protectors by the name of—" I ask.

"No," she snaps and resumes reading a book.

"Guys, there they are!" Sandie points.

Trenton and Crystal wave at us from dozens of floors below.

"Really?" Bradie demands.

We grab the uniforms and run.

We stumble into the glass hallway where Crystal and Trenton sit on a white polymer bench, sipping tea and laughing at a video on an e-pad. From the audio, it's them hosing us down.

"You're out of uniform," Trenton snaps at us.

We strip and change into baby blue unitards made of a form-fitting webbed material. Our furry costumes make a sad carcass on the floor.

"Line up," Crystal orders.

We comply, backs to the wall, wondering what fresh torture awaits.

"So," Trenton asks. "Who's first?"

We look at each other. Liam steps forward.

"I'll go," he says.

"Enjoy," Trenton nods. A door disengages from the wall, hissing open on hydraulic hinges to reveal a medic in purple with the emblem of a syringe.

"I'm Sewzanne," she says. "Welcome, welcome. Your first Calibration. How exciting!"

Behind her is a lie-back chair surrounded by data monitors. Needles attached to IVs dangle from suspended canisters alongside a circuitry-enmeshed helmet on a retractable arm.

"Ah yes," she says, noting our inquisitive looks. "The Chair."

Bradie's eyes grow wide; his scarred hand clenches.

"Is everything all right?" the medic asks him.

"Everything's fine," Trenton replies. "Isn't that right, grub?"

Trenton nods at his brother, eyes full of meaning. Bradie steadies himself.

"Yes," he forces himself to say.

"Yes, *sir*!" Trenton corrects.

"YES, SIR!" Bradie echoes forcefully. Sweat beads on his forehead.

"All righty," the medic smiles comfortingly. "Officers, it's time for you to join your squadron for group Calibration. Please take the props with you."

Crystal dutifully gathers the furry outfits.

"You go ahead," Trenton says to Crystal. "I'll be there in a hot flash."

She raises an eyebrow but says nothing.

I expect Trenton to reassure his brother.

"Cadet Feral, walk with me."

Bradie's eyes beg me to stay.

"I'll be right back," I say.

"Okay," Bradie says meekly.

132

I follow Trenton around the corner. He checks to make sure no one is listening.

"I need you to keep an eye on Bradie," he says.

"What's up with him?" I ask.

"Nothing," Trenton says defensively.

Things had been going so well, I'd forgotten—Bradie's broken.

A pair of protectors walk by. Trenton nods at them. They smirk, assuming he's concocting an extra-special initiation for the grub.

"Help him keep calm," Trenton instructs. "Can you handle that?"

"It would help if you told me what was going on," I say.

"He's fine," Trenton says. "Jitters is all. But I've been looking out for that kid for a long time; old habits and all that."

I'm neither convinced nor comforted. Trenton grows more brusque.

"Well, grub, what are you standing around for? Back in line!"

He's worried. I can tell by the lack of rigor in his dismissal. I'm not feeling it myself.

"Yes, sir," I salute half-heartedly. He doesn't call me on it. He waves me away, and I dutifully join the others around the corner.

"What was that about?" Sandie asks as I sit next to Bradie.

Bradie's foot taps rapidly, making his leg shake. I press my hand on his knee to make him stop.

"Trenton being a dick," I reply. "Bradie, you okay?"

He looks at me, forcing a smile. "Yeah, fine. You?"

His tawny brown skin is several shades paler than usual.

"Is anyone else hot?" he asks.

Sandie shakes her head.

"What a party last night," I say to change the topic. "Bradie, I can't believe what an amazing acrobat you are. You were *epic*."

Nate's king of the ego stroke, but I have my moments.

"Did anybody else notice how none of the older protectors were there last night?" Bradie asks. "Don't you think that's weird?" His other leg catches the shakes.

He scratches the scars on his hand, leaving long, red marks. His breathing quickens.

"I guess they're too old for it now," Sandie suggests, watching him closely. "Or maybe they have their own party. You know, with fancy stemware. The women wear slinky dresses, and the men talk in funny, deep voices, like in the screenings."

Bradie wrings his hands.

"Could be," he says doubtfully.

"Maybe we should go for a walk," I suggest.

Bradie shakes his head, stands, and paces.

"It doesn't make sense. Why let us have a party at all?"

"To let off steam?" I suggest.

He waves his finger at me. "This is the Protectorate, and we go out into the middle of the Yellow Zone where techies turn an energy siphon into a light show for protector acrobats on poles as if we were still kids who might one day be special enough to Manifest? Am I the only one who thinks that's off?"

He keeps looking at the door hiding the medic and Liam.

"I guess they want us to get it out of our systems," I suggest.

"Does that get it out of our systems? Or does it make us want it more?" he presses. "What's their end game?"

My brain's exhausted, but I know he's right. Last night, the brightest, best moment of my life, so alien to anything I've experienced, what was it really about?

The door to the chamber hisses compressed air and slides open. Bradie flinches, and his cheek twitches uncontrollably. Liam emerges relaxed and refreshed. His lethargic state should reassure Bradie nothing horrible's going on in there—but he's not paying attention to Liam. Bradie stares at the Chair with its helmet, sensor pads, and needles dangling from tubes.

"I can't go in there," Bradie whispers. His chest heaves. His freakout is different than my mom's, but I know what I'm seeing.

"Who's next?" the medic asks.

"I'll go," Sandie replies, rushing forward and using her body to block the medic's view of Bradie.

"Bravo," the medic says.

"Is this going to hurt?" Sandie asks.

"Quite the opposite," Sewzanne assures her.

Sandie nods, giving us a worried look over her shoulder as the door slides closed behind her. Liam cocks his head, smiles a goofy smile, and contemplates Bradie.

"What's up with him?" Liam asks.

"I'm not sure," I say.

"Hey, it's okay, buddy," Liam says, rubbing Bradie's back. "Relax. It's chill in there."

"That Chair," Bradie says, "It's—"

Like Testing Day, I think.

"It's just a chair," I assure him.

Bradie's throat constricts.

"I can't breathe," he gasps. His scarred hand digs into his thigh.

Liam remains calm. Is he high? "Maybe we should get the medic out here. She was cool."

He heads for the door leading to the lab.

"No!" Bradie rasps. "You can't. They can't know about this, or they'll kick me out."

"Okay, man," Liam says, holding his hands up in surrender.

Bradie's face turns red; his knuckles are white.

"I don't know if I can do this," Bradie says.

I pretend I'm Nate after one of mom's tirades—I sing to Bradie.

"…blue moon…" It's an oldie. I forget some of the words, but I do my best. Bradie looks like he's drowning. I keep singing.

"…blue moon…"

I take his arms and wrap them around me. His slack limbs tighten, clinging to me like I'm a lifeline.

"Sing with me," I say.

I repeat the refrain; he struggles to join in. After a few lines, he hits the notes. His grip on me slackens. I hold his cheek.

"You got this," I say.

Bradie nods, wiping tears from his eyes.

"I'm good; I'm good; I'm good," he says to himself. He's still saying it when the door hisses open.

The medic guides Sandie out. She has the same dreamy look on her face as Liam.

"Everything all right?" the medic asks.

"Fine," I nudge Bradie.

"Yeah," he stands, staring at the Chair beyond the open door.

"Nothing to be afraid of," the medic says.

"Sure," he says, stepping into the chamber.

He quietly sings, "…blue moon…" and the door steals him from view.

CHAPTER 24

I wait with Liam and Sandie, my stomach clenching in a way I've only ever felt for Nate when he's late coming home from extracurriculars or before he steps on stage.

The door slides open, and Bradie staggers out. His shoulders and eyelids sag. His cheek spasms. He looks nothing like Liam and Sandie when they emerged. They beam. Bradie's jaundiced.

"What's up, buddy?" I ask.

"Tired," he answers.

The medic pats him on the shoulder. "It gets easier. Let go and the Chair will do the heavy lifting." The way she appraises him reminds me of a butcher deciding if they can salvage a crummy cut of meat. "Okay," Sewzanne motions at me, "last one."

I follow her in, glancing over my shoulder. I expect Bradie to give me a thumbs up. He stares at the plain white wall. The door slides shut.

"Is he okay?" I ask the medic.

"Perfectly normal," Sewzanne replies. "About 20 percent of subjects have that kind of reaction. It's temporary. Come, come. Your turn."

She directs me to the Chair. I slide onto its smooth surface. Above my head dangles the circuitry-covered helmet.

"Is this a physical?" I ask.

"More like a 'mental,'" she winks, attaching sensor pads to my body. She rolls up one of my sleeves. "Make a fist."

She taps my forearm, finds a vein, and uses a needle to insert a clear tube running out of a canister. She tapes the tubing in place then flicks a switch. The container vibrates, pumping a glowing orange liquid into my arm.

"Dioxymantangulate," she explains.

"Mango Tango," I murmur.

She touches her tablet, and it projects a holographic image of my insides alongside readings labeled heart rate, cerebral output, and pulmonary function.

"Electrolytes are low. I'd say someone had a good night," she winks.

"I haven't slept," I admit, watching the bright orange liquid feed into me. "Maybe we should do this after I rest."

"On the contrary, cadet. You are both physiologically and neurologically primed."

"For what?" I ask.

"For Calibration. Watch your noggin," she says, guiding the helmet over my head and strapping it under my chin. An opaque visor lowers in front of my eyes.

Inside the helmet, I barely hear Sewzanne's lacquered nails pecking at her pad, igniting 3-D geometric images across the inside of the visor. Shifting spirals bulge in and out. I try to speak, but pulsating music cotton-balls my mouth through my ears.

Lightness buoys me… and then the images and sounds are gone. The helmet vibrates and lifts off my head.

"Well done, cadet," the medic says.

"But, I didn't do anything," I say.

"Exactly!"

"Nothing happened," I insist. First, I fail Testing Day; now this? I think of how Lilianne gets to be the best of Gen M while I remain Generation Loser. "Put me back in, and for longer. That was barely two minutes."

"Would you believe it was an hour?" the medic asks.

I gape. "For real?"

"It's one of the longest first sessions I've done. Even longer than Trenton's! But don't tell him," she winks. "You're lucky. Not everyone takes to Calibration this quickly or deeply."

I struggle to process.

"I'm good at this?" I say more to myself than her.

"You're a natural," she smiles. "You must have a good imagination."

The part of me that drove Mrs. Cranberry crazy with questions immediately blurts out, "A natural at what?"

The medic drains the excess Mango Tango from the rubber tube into a disposal vat.

"We're optimizing your brain for learning," she says. "The better you do in here, the better you're going to do out there. And you did *very* well in here."

"But… I don't remember any of it," I say.

"Not consciously," she agrees. "But it's there. Trust me. Physical and mental skills are going to come *very* naturally to you, much more so than your fellow cadets. As the sessions progress, so will you. The trick is to stay

137

receptive. We can only insert what you're open to receiving. Keep going like this, and you'll be on the fast track for group Calibration."

I open my mouth, an endless stream of questions ready to pour out. She presses a finger to my lips.

"You feel good, don't you?" she asks.

I nod.

"Go with that, and let's see what happens."

"Okay," I mumble from behind her finger.

"Good luck, cadet," she says, nodding at a mural of the all-seeing eye in a fist. "I'll be watching you."

Over the next week, we do more Calibration sessions, and the medic was right—I do notice a marked acceleration in my protector training.

In the padded combat center, I run through physical drills, including hand-to-hand. My body moves as if it were engineered to spar. I easily turn Bradie's weight against him, tossing him to the floor then wrenching his arm behind his back.

"Auntie! Auntie!" he cries.

The next day, in the weapons range, Trenton shows us how to load a sidearm. I slide the clip into place like I've been doing this my whole life. I aim at a paper outline of a man hanging 20 measures away. I vividly recall my inability to shoot a giant mutated hound at a distance of only five paces. Liam, Sandie, and Bradie watch. I should be nervous, yet as soon as I lift the gun, it's a part of me. I squeeze the trigger; the bullet hits the target through the heart.

"Beginner's luck," Trenton snorts.

I fire again. The bullet pierces the target's forehead.

"Huh," he grunts at my success.

Confidence surges through me. I blow Trenton a kiss, aim, pull the trigger three times, and a trio of slugs rips through the outline's baby maker. Trenton's brow rises; his jaw drops.

"Wowzer," Liam says, clapping me on the back.

Trenton gives me stink-eye. "Moving on."

The changes go beyond my physical skill sets. The ceaseless questions that buzzed around my mind like a hive of agitated bees grow quiet and still. I'm at peace. Why was I always throwing up resistance when it's so much easier to go with the flow?

At the end of the week, Bradie, Liam, and Sandie all go home for Recuperation Day. I consider visiting Nate and trying to smooth things over with my mom. The thought skitters along the surface of my mind and sinks.

Next week, I assure myself.

Instead, Normand and I sneak into the Yellow Zone to hang out in the Lair. It's our first opportunity to do so since I moved into the Cube. As we descend the concrete steps and clap on the twinkling strands of lights that illuminate the displays of comic books, I wait for the usual rush of excitement.

Huh, I think to myself. *That's odd.*

Coming here used to be magic; now, it's as if there's a haze over the whole store. Numbness presides. The disconnect extends to my friendship with Normand.

Little things grate on me—his creaky brace, the smell of hand sanitizer, the OCD checking of his watch followed by strange proclamations like "*Nunc futuri.*"

His nonsensical "codes of conduct" are the most annoying. Most stuff in the Lair I can touch; some, I can't. I intentionally move the scarf with the red S in a diamond to watch him freak and fussily put it back.

Over the next several weeks, I cut our visits to the Lair shorter, space them out longer, and frequently cancel at the last minute. I passive-aggressively wait for Normand to realize I'm phasing him out. He doesn't get it.

The day comes when we finish creating our last issue of *Tigara*. I stare at the concluding panel. In it, our heroine hangs up her costume. Her days of fighting the forces of evil in Bright Lights Big City are over.

"Normand," I say. "We can't come back here anymore."

"*Affirmativa*," he says, a sad resignation in his voice, "I am aware."

I guess he did see this coming.

"You'll have to destroy your e-pad and erase the GRAMS you've created," I say. "Otherwise, I have to turn us both in."

I brace myself, expecting him to argue, beg, and rationalize. He does not.

"We shall require my duplicitous devices one last time," he says. "To get back to the fence undetected."

"Agreed," I say.

His brace creaks as he shifts his weight and slings a satchel over his shoulder.

I take one last look, scanning the shelves of comic books, the costumes on the wall, the posters, games, screening discs, and busts of imaginary superheroes with impossible ideals and shoulder-to-waist ratios. A faint wave of nostalgia tinged with sadness passes through me, and then it's done.

I guess I'm growing up.

By unspoken agreement, Normand and I ignore each other after that, and as more weeks pass, our time together in the Lair grows faint. Meanwhile, my Calibration sessions grow longer.

"Any vivid dreams at night?" Sewzanne asks as I sit in the Chair.

"Yes," I admit.

"Good," she says. "Your subconscious is working things out. It has a lot to process. You're setting records with the length of your Calibrations."

"Longer than Trenton's?" I ask.

"I'm not saying yes," she winks, "but I'm not saying no."

The rubber tube running into my arm swells my veins with Mango Tango and my heart with pride. Everything's coming together—almost. While my sessions accelerate me into hyperdrive, Bradie limps at subsonic. Later that day, I'm eating with him, Liam, and Sandie in the cafeteria. Bradie gripes about a migraine after his Calibration today.

"You have to relax," I tell him. "It's easy."

He pushes around a protein-based chocolate pudding with his spoon. Liam and Sandie tense at my words.

"You don't know what it's like," he says. "It's as if they're trying to hammer a square peg into a circular hole *in my head.*"

He looks ready to curl in on himself like a dying bug. Was he always this whiny?

"You must be doing something wrong," I say. He gives me cut-eye. So touchy.

"Hey," I say, "the new grubs."

More than a hundred teens file in, all in baby blue uniforms. They've completed their final placements and are the last group in our age level to make the cut for cadets. I recognize a bunch of them from novice training, but most come from other cohorts. I wonder which ones will make it to protector and which will wash out.

140

"We should say hi," I say.

Bradie eyes me in a way he's been doing of late—part suspicion, part glare.

"How sociable of you," he says.

"It is, isn't it?" I agree.

"That machine is changing you."

"Yes," I agree. "For the better."

"Says you," he counters.

"Says my test scores. You're jealous because you can't keep up."

Liam's and Sandie's pudding-filled spoons freeze in the air. My temples throb, and my cheeks burn. I've gone too far, and I know it.

"I'm sorry," I say. "I didn't mean—"

"Yeah," he says. "You did."

I wait for him to remind me he saved my life once, but he doesn't.

"Excuse me," he says. "Probably best I hang with someone my speed."

Liam and Sandie are *very* focused on their pudding. Bradie stalks out. I half-heartedly wonder if I should go after him. The new cadets eye Bradie; I expect him to crack jokes and cozy up to them. But that Bradie has checked out. He exits through a set of sliding glass doors, not looking back.

The Chair is changing him, too—definitely for the worse.

"He's struggling," Sandie says. With his difficulties in Calibration, he's barely keeping up with training. He's getting by on his natural athleticism—for now.

Pull it together, Bradie, I think. Guilt flickers within my impatience—first Normand, now him. *You can't let them hold you back,* a part of me insists. It's an uncomfortable thought, so I focus on the recruits.

"I'm going to introduce myself," I say. I pick up my tray and walk over to the newbies. As I sit down and shake hands, I notice Bradie on the other side of the glass wall enclosing the cafeteria. He's talking with Normand.

Bradie says something, and they both laugh—Bradie in his gregarious way, like the Bradie I first met on the train, while Normand's shoulders bob up and down, wheezing the way he does when he finds something amusing.

When did they become so tight? I wonder.

I force myself to focus on the cadets bombarding me with questions.

"What's training like?"

"Who's the toughest instructor?"

"Are we allowed to date other cadets?"

I answer their questions in order.

"Training is awesome. It will challenge you like you won't believe. Trenton is the worst. And can you date another cadet? I am, but no PDAs." They lean closer, eyes shining like spotlights.

So *this* is what it's like to be a Lilianne. Who's to say which of us is the *real* Gen M?

Within the next few weeks, a third of the recruits is culled. A lot of our training is all together, but sometimes they take Sandie, Liam, Bradie, and me apart from the rest. The training masters position us as examples. That gets some of the other newbie grubs sucking up. Others show their jealousy with petty remarks or going out of their way to get in our space. I make a point of sparring with each of them to prove I'm superior—and I am.

None of this is easy. Each day is more grueling than the one before. They are also the most rewarding of my life. I climb through, over, and under obstacle courses with electrified wires, icy waters, thick mud, and brick walls. I engage in hand-to-hand combat. I learn survival skills, electronics repair, and how to read body language. Considering my mother's shifting moods, I could teach the latter.

I grow stronger, faster, and deadlier. I no longer think about Tigara. I don't need childish fantasies. I've got me. During Calibration, my brainwaves are going deeper and deeper with impressive real-world results. I fast track like crazy.

The next hurdle to pass is my cadet field trial.

When the time comes, protectors grab me without warning from a sound sleep in my bunk. They tie a bag around my head, my wrists behind my back, and drag me in my skivvies down flight after flight of stairs, smacking my ankles with each downward step. My heart is a train flying off its track.

You're ready for this, Cadet Feral, I assure myself.

I better be. This is the hardest challenge before a cadet can graduate. My abductors toss me into a cold metal container, put noise-dampening headphones over my ears, and fill my world with the grating sound of rusty nails scraping on stone. The floor vibrates and pushes into me—I'm in the back of a hovercraft.

We bob along—for an hour? Two? Time loses meaning. When we stop, they shove me out of the still-moving vehicle. I hit the ground, knocking the breath from me. I recover, feel around, and cut my bond with a sharp stone. I yank off the headphones and the bag covering my head, then cough on exhaust as the hovercraft speeds away. Lightning bursts overhead, followed by the rumble of thunder. Rubble surrounds me. I'm alone in the middle of the Yellow Zone with no food, water, or compass. A basic survival kit lies on the broken sidewalk next to me, along with a cadet uniform and a note in Trenton's handwriting.

Get the flag. Bring it back. Good luck beating my record. 73:41:15.

Seventy-three hours, forty-one minutes, fifteen seconds.

He's goading me, hoping to make me reckless in an attempt to beat him.

Forget about him, I tell myself, and I do. Ish. I enter Trenton's score into the timepiece around my wrist. The clock counts down.

I search and see the red flag fluttering at the top of a towering building. My stomach contracts. The edifice is ready to topple. I have to scale it, capture the flapping crimson fabric, then find my way back to the Cube.

"Ready, set, go," I say.

I dress, grab the survival kit, and sprint to the hollowed-out skyscraper.

Four hours later, I'm back on the ground, scraped, bruised, and bloody, flag in hand.

For the next three days, I navigate the streets like a stealthy urban cat. I buried Tigara deep in my mind, but here, alone, she digs free. I feed off birds I capture and seeds blown in from the farmlands. I test for radiological dangers and take shelter from deadly windstorms. By day three, the borough is in sight. My cracked lips burn, dirt fills every exposed pore, and the inside of my mouth is more desiccated than a prune.

I ignore the discomfort. I stride streets dotted with white weeds and mushrooms poking through crumbling asphalt. Reaching the Cube is the only thing on my mind when something catches my eye. I stop, not sure why, but I've learned to pay attention. If something seems out of place, it probably is. It's not my sight and hearing alone that have become sharper; my whole body is a vibrating sensor pad. I stare at a familiar mound. My belly warms. I smile childishly. It's the Lair.

Only now do I realize how successfully I'd forgotten it. Between severing my friendship with Normand and focusing on my training, there was no reason to think about this former place of escape.

What exactly is the Mango Tango doing to my brain? I wonder.

The point is to rewire it, to make it better, but what does that mean? The thought is a pebble skittering into a deep dark lake, lost with barely a ripple.

I continue staring at the mound of concrete hiding the Lair. It's been months since I've been inside.

Well, now's certainly not the time, a part of me snorts, egging me to pick up the pace. I check the counter on my wrist—more than enough time to beat Trenton's record. My eyes move back to the Lair.

You could go in, another part of me says. She sounds like the old me, lonely and needy, yet whimsical and full of dreams. We haven't spoken in a long time.

No! the cadet in me snaps. I ignore her. Being out here, alone, has rubbed me raw inside and out. Tigara helped me get through. My brain detached her from the Lair, but without it, we'd never have met. I clutch the red flag in my fingers.

The sensible thing would be to go, beat Trenton's record, and truly forget about this place, forever. Yet, unfinished business tugs me. The cadet considers this. *All right*, she says. *Take a look.*

Thought and action are one; I yank a rusted steel bar. The door to the Lair releases a hiss of air and swings open. I pull it shut behind me. I'm down the stairs and inside the store within seconds. I clap, and strands of lights twinkle like stars. The smell of paper and dust fills my nose, and larger than life heroes and heroines gaze at me from the posters on the wall. I wait for the sense of wonder that flooded me my first time here. Instead, it's as if an ice cream scoop's hollowed out my chest, and someone's poured concrete into the pit.

I take in the ceiling-high displays of comic books, the costumes on the wall, the stack of antiquated screening discs.

Burn it, the cadet in me whispers.

I hold a packet of matches. *When did I take it out of my survival kit?*

Do it, the cadet urges. *Burn the past. Burn it all.*

I strike one of three remaining matches and let the flaming stick fall onto the stained carpet. The moisture controllers keep the place so dry, the fibers immediately catch alight. Yellow licks of flame dance at my booted feet.

It's beautiful.

I sigh, relishing the thought of that rising flame burning away the ridiculousness of my former life.

Freedom, the cadet thinks. I used to think that word meant an escape from rules. My definition has changed.

The counter on my wrist beeps unexpectedly, snapping me out of my reverie. I look at the ticking clock—I have just enough time to make it back to the Protectorate to beat Trenton's record.

I smell smoke and see the tiny fire at my feet.

"Geez-us!" I curse.

I stamp out the flames with my boots; the acrid odor of burnt fabric makes me sneeze. *Normand is going to kill me!*

For a second, I'm the old Caitlin, the one who would lose herself in this place of fantasy. The schism in me jousts. I swore I'd never be back, so why do I care if it burns? Why do I care what Normand thinks?

Because you believe as long as the Lair's here, you can change your mind about being a protector; that comforts you, a part of me says. It's followed by Sewzanne's pre-programmed voice, explaining in her hypnotic tone, *To truly move forward, you must burn the attachments of the past. You must burn it all.*

I gaze at the comic books, horrified at the thought of it all going up in flames. I turn and run. I stagger up the stairs, stumble outside, and seal the door shut.

I sprint toward the Cube without looking back.

With moments to spare, I drop a tattered red flag in front of Trenton's face. He grunts his way through a set of shirtless push-ups in one of the training areas in the Cube. We're alone. The alarm on my counter chirps, echoing in the cavernous space.

I smirk. I win.

"Congratulations," he says. "If you'd been just a little sooner, you'd have beaten my record."

My eyes widen, but I keep my mouth shut. He lied on the note he left me, leading me to think I had more time than I did to best him. If I hadn't stopped at the Lair…

He moves into side-plank, showing me his sweaty back and reaching his free hand to the ceiling. I wait for him to revel in his victory. The silence stretches on.

"You're dismissed, cadet," he says.

"That's it?" I ask suspiciously.

"That's it," he replies. "You know the drill. Mission complete. Report for Calibration."

I shrug and obey.

"A word of advice," he says. I pause. I knew it wouldn't be that easy. He hops to his feet, picks up a jump rope, and takes himself through a series of skipping patterns. I force myself to smile.

And here it is.

"Be careful how good you get," he says.

"I'll keep that in mind," I reply, clenching my jaw to keep my honest response in check. As much as it galls me, I recognize he's an officer while I'm a mere cadet for a while longer. Graduation can't come soon enough.

He chuckles, but there's no humor in his eyes. "You've got a lot to learn, little bird, about this place, about what it takes to survive here."

"I'm doing fine," I reply.

"No," he corrects. "Fine would be perfect. But you're not doing fine. You're excelling. Fast. Winning. Lots."

He drops the rope and switches to air squats.

"Scared I might be better than you?" I ask.

"One day, we may get to answer that question *if* I can keep you alive long enough."

"What's that supposed to mean?"

He advances to one-legged pistons.

"Caitlin, you need to pay attention to the *real* rules of this game. After you shot the mutant, they put you all over the information updates. Made you sound like a regular hero. Then what happened?"

I think of the agent visiting me, warning me to watch myself, but I don't share this with Trenton. From the way he nods, I don't need to.

"Yeah," he says, "that's what I thought. First, they propped you up. Then they knocked you down. Want to know why?"

He moves through a pattern of stretches.

"Yes, sir," I say sarcastically.

"Do you know what happens to an object when you heat it, then freeze it, over and over?"

I don't answer.

"It expands and contracts, again and again. It develops fault lines. And that's how they want us—brittle. It makes us easier to smash. Then they sweep us aside and repeat with the next generation. We're not Gen M. We're Gen Disposable."

Is Trenton right? For those of us who don't develop superpowers, is that what it means to be Generation Manifestation? He sees the doubt in my eyes.

"They want us to be good enough to keep the population in check," he continues, "but not so strong that we would overthrow the bureaus—or worse."

I don't ask him what could be worse than a coup. There are some things one doesn't talk about—like challenging the Supergenics.

"Sounds like you're afraid," I say.

"I am," he agrees. "Killing you isn't the worst thing they can do. I learned that the hard way."

"Is that why you're clinging to your records?" I challenge.

He snorts. "Trust me. I'm holding back. You need to as well. Be good, Caitlin, not great, and maybe you'll survive."

"Thank you for the teachable moment," I say.

He air punches a breath from my face, again and again, his knuckles getting closer and closer to my nose. I refuse to flinch.

"One last thing," he says between sharp exhales. "I'm looking out for you because you saved my brother's life, and he seems to have a thing for girls with flat chests and no hips and whatever it is that's going on with your face. I'd do anything for that kid. But if he ever gets hurt because of you, if they ever punish him for something you did, we'll find out how good you are."

His next punch is about to connect. I move aside just in time; as he overextends his reach, my instinct is to grab his arm and toss him to the ground. He waits, biceps grazing my cheek, daring me to do it. I barely restrain myself.

"Noted," I say.

I brush his arm aside, turn my back on him, and walk away.

He's full of crap, I scoff. At least, that's what I tell myself.

CHAPTER 25

I shower, change, and head for Calibration. Sewzanne hugs me like the mother I never knew I could have. I hug back. There's a comfort to sliding into the Chair and the drill that follows. I'm so used to it, I help Sewzanne attach the pads to my body and correct her when she misplaces one. We gab about who's dating who in the Protectorate, along with various other bits of dish. It's a mindless relief.

After Calibration, Sewzanne's eyes mist over.

"What?" I ask.

"I'm so proud of you," she says.

It's the first time anyone's said that to me.

"I'm glad someone is," I deflect.

"Trenton?" she asks.

"Trenton," I agree.

Her eyes twinkle mischievously.

"Caitlin, dear, how would you like to become the youngest cadet to go on a field mission?"

My eyes widen with hope and disbelief.

"When?" I ask.

"Before Trenton can do anything to interfere," she replies.

She gazes at me meaningfully.

"Wait," I say. "Do you mean right now? But I'm barely back from my field test."

"If you don't think you can handle it…"

I hop up out of the Chair.

"I'm in," I insist.

I can't believe I'm getting this opportunity.

Wait 'til Trenton finds out.

I'm jonesing during the elevator ride to the subfloor where the hover vehicles are parked. The suddenness of this assignment is hard to believe.

The doors glide open; Crystal's squad does last-minute vehicle and weapons checks. Six protectors are dressed in their copper uniforms with the all-seeing eye in a fist. I'm in cadet blue. Crystal hands me a baton and a sidearm. I fail to conceal my look of surprise. I check the barrel of the gun. It's loaded.

"Don't get too excited," she says. "They're stunners. Rubber laced with a paralytic. Still pack a wallop, though, so be careful where you point that thing."

"Understood," I say, holstering it to my thigh. I eye the multi-variant rifle poking up from Crystal's back.

"Don't even think about it, grub," she says. "But, you do get one of these."

She hands me a protector helmet. I slide it over my head; darkness blinds me until six holographic images hum to life, providing a 360-degree visual of what's around and above me. We've been practicing with these. It can be dizzying and takes getting used to. Liam threw up the first time he put one on.

I clamber aboard the hovercraft. Crystal moves icons around on her tablet to sync all our communicators. I hear the protectors checking their mics. It gets to my turn, and I dutifully say, "Cadet Feral, check." Half-a-dozen voices reply, "Check," "Check," "Check."

Crystal has me sit next to her. The engines whir, and the hovercraft rises. We zoom up a ramp and into the open air.

"Guard tower delta, patrol niner on approach, anything to report?" Crystal asks. We whisk toward the gate separating the boroughs from the Yellow Zone. I can't believe this is happening. The chainlink barrier draws aside, and we skim out into the broken city. Lightning flares and crashes into spherical energy siphons on rearing pylons.

The wireless crackles in response. "We've got some anomalous readings in sector 18-dash-G."

"Acknowledged guard tower delta. Sector 18-dash-G. Will check it out. Over," Crystal says. She switches her COMM to address me alone, "Probably a sensor glitch, but we'll make sure the area's clear. If it's something simple, we'll fix it ourselves; otherwise, central will send out a tech crew to deal with it."

"Understood," I reply.

We whoosh along the streets of the broken city in a grid pattern.

"Nothing on DRADIS," the navigating officer reports.

"Approaching sector 18-dash-G," the helmsperson replies.

"Eyes sharp," the navigator says. "I think I've got something."

On one of my internal screens is a smaller version of the DRADIS readout. I see a trio of blue dots huddled together until a sharp buzz of feedback rages through our helmets. We all grunt in surprise and momentary pain. The DRADIS crackles in and out. The navigator gives it a couple of smacks; it pops back on. Its circling cone of light now shows zero contacts. The protectors pull out their weapons. My heart hammers. Something's out there, and it knows how to hide.

"Patrol niner to guard tower delta, we have a potential mutagenic animal presence in sector 18-dash-G," Crystal says into the wireless. "Suspected chameleon creature."

"Confirmed patrol niner," the guard tower replies. "Mobilizing back up. Over."

The helmsperson stops in an open square next to a row of blown-over merchant carts painted with pretzels, sausages, and patties. The hovercraft lowers to the ground. The *whoop-ah whoop-ah* sound the vehicle makes slows; it shudders as the engine cuts out. We stand, visors scanning the vicinity, ready to dismount.

"You stay here," Crystal says to me.

"But—"

"Don't make me repeat it," she interrupts, sweeping away any thought that I'm a full-fledged protector. "Eyes and sensors peeled, cadet. You see anything, you think you see anything, you let us know. The rest of you, beta formation and fan out. This is recon only until back up gets here."

Working in pairs, they disappear into the surrounding rubble. I scan the landscape through my visor. The screens before me show crumbling walls, a car with its roof caved in, and a wire pushcart. I switch to infraspectro vision, casting the dead city in dull tones of green. The small infrared outlines of rodents and felines light the view screens, along with a flock of shadowrens that suddenly takes flight. I ignore them, turning my body to scan in a circle—which only serves to make me dizzy. I've already got a 360-degree view.

You have to learn to trust the screens, Trenton told us. *Remember which one is front, which one is back, which one is left, which one is right, and which ones are in between.*

A jut of concrete fizzles then snaps back into focus, much like the DRADIS earlier. Suspicious.

"Lead Officer," I say into my mic. "This is Cadet Feral. I may have found something. Repeat, I think I found something. Over."

"Understood," Crystal replies.

I switch back to high def view and take out my sidearm. I take two steps toward the pile of concrete.

"Stay put," Crystal says, her voice coming clearly through the ear-jacks.

I stop, raise my gun, and a man bursts out from within the concrete as if he'd somehow been a part of it. He's dressed in worn grey clothes, helping him to blend with the urban blight.

"Freeze!" I shout. He ignores me, sprinting past.

My finger tightens on the trigger, but before I can fire, an invisible force knocks me up and over. I fly three measures and land on my side. I shake my head. My gun is on the ground, a measure away from me. I grab it and fire three shots. Two go wide, but one hits the man square in the back. He staggers, trips, catches himself, then runs a few more steps, slowing as the paralytic takes effect. I'm about to shoot again when something smacks the gun from my hand.

I twist around, making the screens swirl. My gut wrenches, but only for a moment. I'm ready to fight hand-to-hand—if only there were something to fight. No one's there. This time, I remember to look at the screens instead of turning my head this way and that. Behind me, the man who ran is flat on a busted sidewalk. I eye my gun a few measures away. I crouch and reach for the weapon; a sharp electrostatic shock runs through me. I jerk back.

Something blocks me from touching the gun.

Force field? I wonder.

My eyes widen. The field contracts, crushing the gun into a twisted ball.

"Lead Officer," I say into my mic, "this is *not* a mutated animal. I've tagged one runner. Adult male. There's also a Supergenic. I have not made visual. Suspected abilities include invisibility and force field manipulation. Repeat, we are dealing with a Supergenic. Over."

I wait for Crystal's reply, but nothing comes through. "Lead Officer, do you copy?" I ask. "Does anybody copy?"

No response. Something's interfering with the signal.

"Crap," I swear to myself. I run toward the hovercraft—it has more powerful transmitters—and I smack into an invisible wall. I stagger back and hit another unseen barrier. The screens in my visor show nothing there. I reach up and down—the smooth, unseen blockade encases me. To my

151

horror, it pushes my outstretched arms inward. It's closing in on me. I stare at what's left of my gun—a crumpled metal ball. I'm next. I bang on the shrinking cage, shouting into my mic, "Crystal!"

A pair of protectors emerge from the rubble, pointing their rifles at the man I shot. One of the protectors grabs the man by the hair and pulls him onto his knees. He's conscious. He stares at me. I pound harder on the invisible enclosure, but no one can hear me.

Is he the Supergenic? I wonder. *No.* He'd be using his powers on his captors instead of me if that were the case.

I look at the concrete mound the guy seemed to burst out of. I think about the visor sensor glitch when it passed over that one area. That's where the Supergenic is hiding. It's probably his kid. The dad ran to draw us away. The kid must be terrified. I look at the protectors. They must think the dad is alone, a desperate fool who believes the stories of habitable lands and a better life beyond the fence. The punishment for his crime is immediate and summary execution. The protector holding the guy's hair puts a gun to the back of his head.

I slam the bottom of my fist into the shrinking shield. It's forcing me to crouch and curl into myself. The kid must be too far away to use his/her/zirs power on the protectors. I kick futilely at the field closing around me. I shout. The protector pulls the trigger. I barely hear it; a muffled pop, and a red bullet hole blooms in the guy's head. He falls dead onto the cracked concrete. The shield around me evaporates, and I fall sideways in surprise.

"Papa!" a wail rises from behind me.

A kid a few years younger than Nate runs out from the slabs of concrete where his power kept him hidden. A woman dressed in grey chases after him, her limping stride unable to catch up. His mother, I presume, concealed by the kid's power until he freaked out.

"Mattaius!" she screams.

More protectors emerge in a wide circle around us.

"He's Supergenic!" I yell into my mic. "I repeat, the boy is Supergenic!"

He passes the hovercraft, and an expanding force rips it apart from the inside. It explodes; shrapnel flies everywhere. Screams of pain from two protectors echo in my helmet. An invisible force slams into the protector who stood by while the kid's father was executed, sending the man flying off his feet.

Crystal arrives on-scene. She opens her visor.

"It's okay!" she shouts at the kid. "We're not here to hurt you!"

An unseen power rams into her gut, throwing her back. She lands a few measures from me, unconscious.

"Mattaius, please!" the mother cries.

The kid corners the protector who acted as executioner. The mother reaches the boy's side and hugs him tight. The protector slowly puts down his gun. The protectors who are still on their feet do the same, holding their hands up in peace. The kid lifts his hand, and an unseen force lifts the protector who killed his dad. The protector clutches his throat as if grasping a noose. His visor cracks, and he screams from the pressure on his skull as something beyond dreg sight compresses his head.

"Please stop, Mattaius," his mom begs. "Please!"

Mattaius jerks his arm to the right, and the invisible force slams the protector's body against a pile of asphalt. The kid punches the air to his left; throwing the protector into the side of a collapsed building.

"Stop this at once!" a commanding voice booms.

I open my visor and stare at the floating radiance of a muscled man who is impossible not to recognize, dressed in form-fitting silver, with a lightning bolt on his chest. It's Captain Light. He floats ten measures off the ground in a glowing globe. Of course. Protocol when any child Manifests is to contact Jupitar City. Still, I can't fully wrap my head around it. He's *actually* here!

Mattaius glares. "He killed my dad."

"No," Captain Light shakes his head. "The man you call 'Dad' provided the seed that helped give you life, but he is *not* your father. He selfishly tried to keep you from your *real* Supergenic family. He tried to run. The punishment for that is death. The protector was doing his duty."

As the Captain speaks, an undulating grey mist drifts along the ground like a low-lying fog. A light breeze fails to disperse it. It swirls around the boy's ankles, ignoring the mother at his side.

"That's a load of crap!" the kid shouts.

"Please," the mom begs. "Please don't take him away."

"We're not taking him away," the Captain replies. "That's what you were trying to do. We thank you for providing the egg and the womb that led to this boy's birth. But he is not your son. He has loving parents waiting for him in Jupitar City. You would've been richly rewarded for your service. But kidnapping cannot be permitted. Runners *will* be punished."

Captain Light holds his palm toward her and fires a beam of energy. I expect it to slice her in half or disintegrate her or burn her to dust. It's surprisingly gentle, forming a wall between her and her son—one that pushes her away. She beats at it with her fists; it relentlessly forces her back. Gravel skitters under her heels as she digs them into the ground. From the wail that rises from her lungs, I think she'd rather die than let the boy go.

"Mom!" the kid cries, trying to go after her.

Captain Light fires a second beam from his other palm. The energy wraps around the kid like a tether, holding him back. The mist swirls around his feet.

"Your *real* parents can't wait to meet you, Mattaius," Captain Light says. The mist seems to nod in agreement.

"No!" the boy shouts. "I'm not going anywhere!"

He lifts his palm toward Captain Light. I can only guess that a shield forms around the muscled figure, cutting off the beams of light. The kid's mother trips to her knees as the photonic wall disappears. She scrambles to her feet and is about to run to her son when a smokey hand rises out of the earth-bound grey cloud, hovering in front of her in the well-recognized symbol for STOP.

She does, blinking in surprise. Tentatively, she passes her hand through the incorporeal one, and the movement makes the phantom shape disperse.

"Mattaius," she breathes, stepping forward.

She's too late. The mist swirls up the boy's body, into his mouth and nostrils. He inhales the twirling air; his arms drop listlessly to his sides, and his head falls back. The whites of his eyes show; he stumbles, sleepwalking.

"Thank you, Cloud," Captain Light says, clearly freed from the kid's power. He floats closer to the ground.

"Mattaius?" the kid's mom calls. "Mattaius!"

She rushes toward him, her legs flailing through the low-lying fog, and Captain Light fires a beam of light that smacks her off her feet. He's not so gentle now. She hits the side of a crumbling building. She grunts and tries to get up, but a pair of protectors grab and hold her. She struggles against them, sobbing in a way that reminds me of my mother.

"Noooooo!" she cries.

Captain Light slings the boy over one shoulder as if he were a sack of potatoes.

"As per our treaty, we will leave you to govern your people while we take our leave with ours," Captain Light says to us. Cloud swirls into the air, undulating around him. They rise higher into the sky and float across the river to Jupiter City, leaving a phosphorescent trail in their wake.

The woman sobs. I want to reassure her it's going to be all right, but she broke a fundamental law. She failed in her duty. I turn away. I don't want to see what happens next.

"Mango is the new tango," a voice speaks through my earbud. It's Sewzanne. The words are a switch in my brain. Without thinking, I press the button on my helmet, and my visor lowers. The screens pop to life. The mom is on the display that shows what's behind me. To do what I must do, I have to face her. I turn in her direction, and the screens change. What was front is now back, and what was back is now front. I'm getting used to this.

I stare at the mother held by the protectors.

I step forward, a puppet in a dream, and pick up Crystal's rifle. The runner woman is begging, but I can't hear her. As if this were nothing more than target practice, I aim and fire. Her head whips back, and the protectors drop her dead at their feet. I lower the rifle.

You killed a woman, a part of me says in horror. *A mother trying to hold onto her son.*

The rest of me should be equally horrified, but it's not. I know that's not how a normal person reacts after taking a life. *This isn't real*, I assure myself. I tap the side of my helmet; my visor slides open. I stare at the face of the executed woman. I drop the rifle from listless fingers.

What have they turned me into? I wonder.

I tried to warn you, I hear my mother reply. *Now, it's too late.*

CHAPTER 26

Back at the Cube, protectors escort me to a debrief room. It takes all of ten minutes for a pair of overseers to take my statement and dismiss me. I step into the hall, and Sewzanne bustles over. She beams and hugs me tight. I don't hug back.

"I knew you were ready," she says. "Caitlin, I'm so proud."

This morning, those words made me shy with pride. Now, I struggle to feel anything.

"The boy, is he all right?" I ask.

"The Supergenic child?" Sewzanne replies, releasing her hold and arching a plucked brow. "He's with his own kind, where he belongs."

She sounds relieved we are rid of him. She touches my arm in her conspiratorial way, her signal that she has some juicy tidbit to share. "The boy was unusually young to Manifest," she whispers as if that were some great secret. "Some people are saying we should be testing younger than we do."

I nod, trying to feign interest; all I can think is, *I killed his mom.*

"I should go eat," I say.

"Yes, yes, you must be starving," Sewzanne shoos me away amiably. I nod, turning toward the elevator. In truth, I have no appetite.

I go to my locker, strip, shower, and change into a fresh cadet's uniform. I close my locker door and punch it as hard as I can. Something crunches— either my fingers or the door. There's so little feeling in me, I can't tell which.

"Tough day?" Bradie asks.

I wheel about. He sits on a bench in a corner. I lower my fists.

"I killed a woman," I say matter-of-factly.

"I heard," he replies. "Figured you'd need to talk. How do you feel?"

"How do you think?" I reply as if it were the most redundant question in the world.

He shrugs. "Honestly, with the way you've been changing, I have no idea."

His words are a needle pricking my heart.

How can he say that? a part of me asks.

156

Because it's true, another part answers.

"Numb," is what I reply. "Like I have to keep reminding myself it happened. Like it would be easy to do again."

He comes over and takes me in his arms. My instinct is to shove him away. I try to remember how good this used to feel.

"Caitlin," he says, brushing my cheek with his scarred hand, "are you still in there?"

I shake my head.

"I don't know," I say. My voice trembles, but I can't say why. It's as if someone else is speaking.

I take his wrist and gently remove his hand from my face.

"Don't pull away, Caitlin," he says. "Please."

"I can't go back to being the girl I was," I say. "But I don't want to be who I've become."

"Who says those are your only choices?" he asks.

I struggle to find an answer.

You don't deserve him, a part of me realizes.

"I'm going to get some air," I say. I need to be away from this place. Maybe if I give myself room, the part of me that's gone dormant can come crawling out.

And then what?

The truth is, I don't know. Everything's such a mess; people are dead, and the words "they broke the law; they put us all in danger; they could've ruined the peace" are not enough.

He nods. "I'll come with you."

"No," I say. I push him away, gently but firmly. "I don't think I can be around people right now."

"Which is exactly when you should be around people," he answers.

He's right, but it's me, so I don't listen.

"I'm not going to do anything stupid," I assure him. "I need space to clear my head."

He takes my hand and stands on tip-toe, kissing me on the forehead. It's tender and familiar, reminding me of the Bradie I first met, and of the Caitlin he first met. I wipe at my eyes reflexively, expecting tears.

Nope.

Outside, moments later, I take a bus to the center of the borough. It passes a huge billboard of a beaming muscled teen boy in short shorts and nothing else, sticking to a sheer wall with his bare hands and feet. He looks over his shoulder, staring right at me. Bold words declare, DON'T BE DNA REGULAR! BE GEN M!

The bus rumbles to a halt, and something about the sign bids me to get off. The door whines open; cool, crisp air slaps me. A balding man with hunched shoulders disembarks. His jacket is worn, and he coughs frequently. He eyes my cadet's uniform. He wears orange coveralls.

"Don't expect them to take care of you once you're no longer of use to them," he says.

He doesn't wait for a response, limping down the street. I assume he was once a protector, injured in the line of duty. Now he bears the symbol of a toxic-waste worker.

I wander, seemingly aimlessly, until I'm standing in front of the security fence separating the borough from the Yellow Zone. I stare at a mutant hazard sign on a gate.

My eyes burn. I touch my cheek, wetting my fingers.

Weakness water, Trenton calls it.

I laugh and swell with relief. If I can cry, I can feel; if I can feel, maybe I can find me amidst whatever Sewzanne's shoved into my head.

"Hi, Caitlin."

I whip around at the familiar voice. It's Normand.

"What are you doing here?" I ask.

He puts his skeleton key on the gate's punch pad. With a swipe of a new tablet, the lock clicks with a merry chirp. I watched him destroy the old contraband e-pad, but clearly, he kept copies of his GRAMS. He hands me a motion detector suppressor—like old times. Normand jerks the gate open and steps through.

"Will you join me?" he asks.

I hesitate. It's my job to report activity like this. We're creating all sorts of risks. And for what? So I can read children's comics books? This is a self-indulgence. *Duty before all.*

What about the woman you killed? a part of me asks.

That settles it. I follow Normand.

The first time he brought me into the Yellow Zone was less than a year ago; a lifetime seems to have passed. Then, I was halting and tripping as I followed him. Now, I lead, sure of foot, moving with an agility he'll never match. I scout ahead, watchful. Excitement flickers in my breath as we get closer to the Lair—only a flicker, but it's there.

Pay attention, the cadet in me orders, extinguishing the delicate glimmer with a cold iciness.

This time, she's right. I'm in the Yellow Zone. This isn't a playground. My eyes rove everywhere for threats—traps leftover from the Genetic Wars, sinkholes, and for mutants that got past the outer wall. Thankfully, all I see are shadowrens.

We reach the Lair and enter. I brace myself, not sure what to expect. Part of me worries that I came back in a fugue state and burnt it down after all. Normand claps, and the strings of light twinkle. It's still here—the comic books, the costumes on the wall, the posters, the busts, and the board games.

Normand shuffles to the counter and adjusts the position of the scarf with a red S on it. The comforting familiarity of it makes me want to hug him, if only for a second.

I wait for Normand to freak out over the scorch mark on the carpet. He doesn't, and not because he hasn't noticed. This is Normand, after all.

He forgives me, I realize. I'm not sure if I can forgive myself.

I wander around the store, too amped to read, and I find myself drawn to the costumes covering the store's rear wall. There's a giant rubber hammer, a green lantern, more masks than I care to count, along with capes, wigs, fangs, and crazy contact lenses I definitely would've worn on Testing Day given the chance.

One costume calls to me. I lift it off its hook and hold it before me. The cadet in me sees it for the ridiculousness it is—a clingy blue top with a strange insignia emblazoned in gold on the chest and a red mini skirt with matching knee-high boots. The thawing dreamer in me loves it.

I remove my uniform. I don't want to be a cadet right now. Nor can I handle being Caitlin. I want to be this superpowered heroine with abilities and a backstory beyond imagining, who always does the right thing and never fails to save the day.

I slide the satiny top over my skin and slip into the skirt, enjoying how the fabric clings to me. I don the belt and boots; lastly, I drape a cape over my shoulders. I gaze at myself in a cracked stand-up mirror. I'm surprised at how well it fits, showing off the muscles I've developed over the last year. I pull on a blond wig with curls that tickle my shoulders and neck.

Normand stares.

"How do I look?" I ask.

"Like a hooker," he says.

My jaw juts. His mouth widens into a smile.

"So, you do sex jokes now?" I ask.

"Situational specific spiritedness," he corrects.

"Is that what we're calling it?"

"Bradie's been teaching me," Normand replies. "Did you know you can pre-plan such drollery but make it seem impromptu?"

"I did not," I confess.

"Bradie also says anytime someone asks how they look, they want a compliment, so first you give them a little insult, smile so they know it's in jest, and *then* communicate something complimentary. I fail to understand why, but recent social interactions indicate it's an effective interpersonal lubricant."

Normand's rationale makes me feel lighter, more innocent, like we're back in the world we inhabited before we entered the Cube.

"I'm waiting," I say.

"For what?" he asks.

"You said first you insult me, then you say something nice."

"Indeed. That is the formula. Well, you do have the appearance of a woman who barters for sex…"

I roll my eyes, but keep quiet. I get the sense that saying the words "hooker" and "sex" is making Normand feel like a bad boy. We'll be having a talk about respect for women; for now, I indulge him. I owe him that much.

"…but only because that's the way so many superheroes dress." He waves his hand at the shelves full of comics with muscled men and large-breasted women on the covers, villains and heroes both, all in skin-tight clothes that reveal more than they conceal. "Which means you look like a superhero, which means you look awesome."

His words bring unexpected tears to my eyes.

"Bradie says when people cry, it's sometimes because they're happy, sometimes because they're sad. What is your current emotional status?" Normand asks.

"Both," I smile, wiping the tears away.

I've missed him, I realize. *A lot.*

"You should put on a costume too," I say.

He shakes his head, wrings his hands, and squirts sanitizer into them.

"That option is closed to me," he says.

"Nonsense," I say, using Normand-speak.

"None of the costumes can accommodate my proportions," he explains.

"That sounds like something a quitter would say. And we," I wave at us, "are not quitters."

I go through the packaged costumes in the cubbies beneath the display wall.

"Caitlin. I'm simply stating the facts," he insists. "I'm too big."

I wave my index finger at him, having none of it.

"Small, small, medium, large," I mutter, reading off the labels.

"Caitlin! This is a waste of time," he fumes, and I'm starting to think he's right. I find an extra-large of some furry blue creature who is into cookies, but even that won't accommodate Normand's girth. I look around the shop in defeat.

"You must concur," Normand says. "My assertion is correct."

"No," I say. I'm on a mission to do something nice for my friend, my *best* friend, and I *have* to complete my mission.

I stare at the cash register. Something about it catches my eye, and I've learned to pay attention to my instincts. I walk toward it.

"Remember the rules, Caitlin," he says. "That is a no-touch zone."

A warning edge sharpens his voice.

"Yeah, yeah," I say, sounding like Nate.

I stare past the forbidden objects. Normand watches me circle around the counter. Under the register is a bin on wheels labeled, RETURNS, housing a pile of toys, games, and books. I dig through—and find a miracle within. I pull out a triple-extra-large set of beige coveralls with lots of pockets on it. As if it were an official job in the borough, it has a round emblem on it—a red circle and slash over a white cartoon ghost.

"Hey, weirdo," I say to him. "Check this out."

He sees the voluminous costume hanging in my hands; his brace creaks as he shuffles to my side.

"*Impossibilis*," he murmurs. His eyes are a mix of hope and fear. "Do you think it will fit?"

"Only one way to find out."

We struggle to get the coveralls over his leg brace, but, after much tugging and swearing, he finally zips it up.

"*Miraculum*," he murmurs in disbelief.

"This is part of it," I say, helping him don a square padded backpack with a cord attached to a fake rifle. He looks both ridiculous and awesome. I cheerfully punch my fist into the air and shout, "Ghost Fighters!"

He pretends to fire the plastic rifle with *pew-pew* sounds, annihilating a slew of unseen foes. When did he get so playful? That's when I realize what's most different about him.

"Normand, are you making eye contact?" I ask.

He blushes but doesn't look away, staring at me so intensely it's uncomfortable.

"Bradie taught me how," he replies. "He says avoiding eye contact makes people think they can't trust me. It's body language for 'I'm hiding or lying about something.' People give away a lot with their body language."

"They do," I agree.

"Want to know a secret?" Normand asks.

"Sure," I say.

"I'm not looking you in the eyes."

"Is that so?" I ask. I move my eyes one way and then the other. His gaze doesn't follow. "Then what are you looking at?"

"Your forehead," he says proudly. "It was Bradie's idea. He has learned much from me as well."

"I have no doubt." Part of me is jealous they've become such pals. It makes me the outsider again.

What did you expect? I chastise myself. *You neglected them both. They found each other.*

"Normand, I'm sorry for being such a bad friend."

"We've both had hectic itineraries," he replies as if it were simply a question of scheduling.

I think that's his way of saying he forgives me. It prompts another confession.

"Normand, I don't think I can be a protector," I say.

He nods. It looks mechanical and rehearsed, like he's initiated a program in response to preset circumstances. "Do you want to talk about it?"

I laugh a bit. Who is this person?

"Did Bradie teach you to say that?" I ask.

"Yes," Normand replies, factual and straight-faced.

"There's the Normand I know," I say.

"Where else would I be?" he replies. He blinks like his eyelids are flipping through the pages of a book. He stops. "Is this where we discuss what happened while you were on patrol?"

His words open a vacuum inside me. "Normand, how do I live with myself? I turned a kid into an orphan. I don't deserve any of this."

"Clarify," he says. "What is it you do not deserve?"

"This!" I yell, gesturing around the comic book store. "The escape from what I've done. You," I point to him. "You being nice to me. You should be telling me I'm garbage."

Only then do I realize how right Lilianne was about me all along.

Most people would say I had no choice, that I did what I had to do. Normand is not most people.

"I have a proposition for you," he says. "I move that we commence working on a new comic book project."

It's a preposterous suggestion. A comic book can't fix this. Yet guilt fights with intrigue.

"Yeah? Like what?" I ask.

He makes a few quick pencil strokes on a pad of yellowed paper.

"This," he says, holding it up.

It's rough, but the images are clearly of him and me. He's drawn me in the lycra outfit I'm wearing and himself as a muscled doppelganger of himself in a form-fitting version of his anti-ghost jumpsuit. My heart hammers. Our own comic book. Of us. Not as we are or were or how the Cube wants us to be. But as we choose to imagine ourselves. Mind blown.

"Yes," I say.

He checks his watch, and we commence. We spend the next hour lying on the floor, him drawing, me filling in the thought and word bubbles of the premiere issue of our very own series. I've missed our collaborations. I hold up a full-page panel. My superheroine alter ego has an evil henchman in a headlock while kicking another across the face. Normand's ghost brawler is holding off a battalion of henchpeople with his blaster gun. I stop. The way he's drawn the henchpeople, they look very much like protectors.

"Normand," I say. "Have I become a villain?"

He stares at my forehead and says, "Yes."

With anyone else, I'd fly into a defensive rage; with Normand, I've trained myself to hear his truth because there is no filter and, as far as I can tell, no agenda. It's like getting mad at a data pod. Satisfying for a moment, but ultimately futile.

Sourcing a word he would use, I say, "Elaborate."

Normand puts a finger to his temple. "Accessing files," he says, then he makes *beep, boop, bop* sounds.

"I may punch Bradie for teaching you that one," I say.

Normand holds up the middle finger of his other hand. My jaw juts. His smile is definitely that of a guy who is feeling like a badass.

"Data retrieved," he says. "Based on my readings of thousands of comic books from hundreds of titles, I have determined the different classifications for heroes. There are those who have powers, and those who have honed their normal human abilities to near-superhuman levels. Many are guided by high-minded moral principles. Others are best described as 'anti-heroes,' meting out violent justice to those who escape the punitive arm of the judicial system. Some are born to greatness; others have it thrust upon them by a quirk of fate. But they all have something in common. They stick up for the weak. The broken. The powerless."

"And those who don't..." I begin.

"...those who don't," he continues. "Even if they have good intentions, those are the villains."

I'm quiet. He goes back to drawing me evading a henchperson's laser fire then draws himself blasting our foes with goo.

"Stop," I say.

He keeps sketching until I put my hand atop of his.

"Stop," I say again.

"But, I'm almost done," he replies.

"I need you to do a different drawing for me."

He doesn't ask why. He doesn't ask what. He shakes with repressed excitement and says, "Finally."

164

CHAPTER 27

I ransack the wall of costumes, my hands a blur as I grab anything made of black or red lycra. I'm more ruthless in the weapons section, taking knives, a mini-crossbow, short swords, fighting sticks, and a projectile grappling hook —all light-weight plastic props ready to crack if I squeeze too hard.

I pull off the blond wig, strip out of the star-spangled spandex, and don my selected gear. It's red, intermixed with swathes of black. I attach weaponry all over my body.

"Here," Normand says, handing me a dark red wig.

I put it on. He adjusts it, moving locks here and there.

"How do I look?" I ask.

I wait for him to compare me to a sex worker, but he doesn't. I think he grasps we're not playing anymore.

"Inspiring to the good. Terrifying to the bad," he answers.

He gets it.

I strike a pose with the fighting sticks. Normand draws with quick, sure strokes.

"What are you going to call yourself?" he asks. "The red hair and costume, it's like a—"

"Shadowren," I finish for him.

He nods approvingly. "Many consider the species rodents with wings because shadowren not only survive on the ashes of the broken city, they thrive where little else can. They are fierce and loyal. I saw a flock massacre half-a-dozen rats to defend a single nest."

He *really* gets it.

He shows me the drawing; I scarcely breathe. I knew Normand was a talented artist, but this is something else. Normand's captured my essence in a way a mirror or photograph never could; they are mere reflections of the physical, and this goes so much deeper.

This is the version of me I need to see, a larger-than-life character, perfectly formed and battle-ready, Generation Manifestation in fact and name—not a conflicted, brainwashed teenage girl. The lettering is bold, ink-blot graffiti. *Shadowren*, Issue 1. A heap of defeated agents and protectors lies at her feet.

At my *feet.*

I pin the drawing to the wall. I'm not sure how long I stare at it. I never want to look away.

"*Tempest est ire,*" Normand says in his matter of fact tone. "We must depart."

I reluctantly undress and don my cadet's uniform, burning the idealized image of Shadowren into my brain, memorizing the feeling of being her, willing her to override anything Sewzanne and her Calibration procedure uploaded into my mind.

"The obvious course of action would be for you to tender your resignation," Normand says. "You're not a protector until you're a protector."

I think of the man from the bus, in his toxic-waste coveralls.

"I know how to shoot," I say. "If I quit, I'll be assigned a job with a 100 percent mortality rate."

"Would you prefer to be put in a position where you are required to destroy another family?" Normand asks.

Walking away is tempting. I'd have a few years of misery and then die— the punishment I deserve, followed by the ultimate freedom.

I look at the Shadowren drawing. "And then what?" I ask. "Pretend I don't know what they do to cadets during Calibration? Do I let those brainwashed cadets become protectors? My father knew what was happening. I think he was involved. My mom tried to tell me, but I wouldn't listen. He died trying to stop it. Maybe now it's my turn."

Normand nods. "Spoken like a true hero."

"Yeah," I snort. "I execute a woman trying to keep her son. I join the organization that killed my father. I turn on my mom, on Bradie, and you. And then I come here to play dress up. I'm a real hero."

"With that being the case, what is your anticipated course of corrective action?"

"I don't know," I reply. "How do I unbrainwash the brainwashed? And then what? Fight the Supergenics the next time they come to take a kid away? It all seems so impossible."

"That sounds like a quitter talking," he says, using my own words against me.

"I know, it's just…" my thought trails off, eyes landing on an issue of *Tigara* in which she's fighting the mesmerizing hypnotic powers of

GazeFatale. The villainess wears a skin-tight outfit of swirling circles. It gets me thinking dangerous thoughts.

"Normand, hypothetically, from a techie perspective, would it be possible for us to insert our own program into the Calibration data bank?" I ask.

"Affirmative," he says, following my stare. "I have something I believe you will find useful."

He takes me behind the counter. I give a wide berth to the forbidden objects. He pulls out a book and hands it to me. On the cover is a dove transforming into an eagle. I read the title. *The Power of Suggestion: A Guide to Hypnosis, the Subconscious, and Trance-Formation*, by some guy named Eugene Towers. In his creepy bio pic, an ill-fitting suit sags around him, a drooping mustache stains the space above his lips, and shaggy hair harasses his shoulders.

"Am I to understand the fate of the world rests in this guy's hands?" I say.

"Negative," Normand says. "It rests in ours."

We change back into our dreg clothes then silently climb the concrete stairs leading out of the comic book shop, weighed down by the magnitude of what we are about to attempt.

"Normand, do you think this is our last time at the Lair?" I ask, opening the outer doors.

Rumbling thunder drowns his response.

We duck to avoid a patrol then sneak our way back to the fence. I glance at *The Power of Suggestion* book, outlined inside a pocket of Normand's coveralls. He swipes a few GRAMS on his tablet to put the security camera on a loop, and we slip through the gate.

"Finally," a familiar voice says.

I stare at Bradie leaning against the wall, eating a nutrition bar.

"Bradie!" I stammer, searching for a workable lie. "We were on a special patrol."

He snorts. "A cadet sneaking out from behind the fence with a techie, and *that's* your cover story?"

"It's not like that," I insist.

"Yeah, it is," he says, squirting sanitizer in his palm. He rubs it in, jerks his head in a brotherly way toward Normand, and holds a hand up.

"Hey, buddy."

"Salutations," Normand replies.

They high five. I look around nervously. Another patrol could come at any moment.

"Bradie, you shouldn't be here," I say.

"Neither should you," he replies.

His eyes twinkle, not as brightly as when we first met, but like me, he's still in there. It's not too late. For him. For me. For us.

"Bradie, you're not going to tell on us, are you?"

"Depends," Bradie replies.

"On what?" I ask.

He shrugs. "On whether you're ready."

I look to Normand. "I am as bemused as you." His voice warbles. Is he lying?

"Ready for what?" I ask Bradie.

He gazes at the Cube in the distance.

"A revolution."

CHAPTER 28

At training the next morning, Bradie-classic is back. While I fill my water bottle at a dispensing station, I eavesdrop on him regaling the other cadets while we wait for the drillmaster.

I join them and catch the tail end of his anecdote.

"...and then she says, well, maybe if you could levitate. Womp womp."

They laugh. I force myself to smile. It's a good story, one he nuances with every telling. The edge in his voice adds to the drama, but he rushes the punch line, laughs too loud, and grins too wide. He's nervous. Me too. If anyone notices...

Steady, Caitlin, I tell myself. *Steady*.

He winks at me. Despite the skills I've gained in Calibration, my return wink still feels like I've developed a tic. Hopefully, Normand's doing better.

The drillmaster's whistle pierces the air, and I sweat through swings, push-ups, tumbles, jumps, and flips, losing myself in physicality. I'm no mere pawn of the Protectorate. I'm Shadowren. I channel her, pushing harder when exhaustion weighs me down, growing supple when I require finesse, and strategically retreating when necessary to regain an advantage.

I'm not sure what Bradie is channeling. We spar, and he kicks my feet from under me. His Calibration sessions have gone terribly, but he's a natural, which is why the trainers haven't culled him from cadets. I land on my back, and he pins me. I don't fully mind, but Shadowren does. I get him in a headlock. He flips me. I roll. He counters. And on we dance.

In the showers, I notice his muscles. In my mind, I dress him in a mask and tights with a crow sigil in the middle of his chest—a fitting match for his Shadowren girlfriend. He catches me looking and blows me a kiss. I give him the finger. He responds with a moon-eyed "awe shucks" look and presses his hands over his heart.

I see the mottled flesh running up his fingers, knuckles, and forearm. The skin looks raw and always will. He catches me staring. He curls his scarred hand into a fist and punches it into his other palm.

I nod. It's payback time.

In the afternoon, I report for my first group Calibration session. Hundreds of protectors sit cross-legged on the white rubber floor of a large glassed-in chamber overlooking the atrium. The male-identified wear short shorts and little else, while the female-identified also have their sports tops on. Above each hangs a helmet with a visor.

A slew of technicians and medics bustle around, attaching sensory pads to the protectors' bodies. Sewzanne waves me over.

"Caitlin," she says, hugging me. "Big day! How are you?"

"Ready to do my duty," I reply.

"That a girl. Let's get you hooked up. As long as group Calibration goes well, you'll be a full-fledged protector in no time! CeeCee?" she asks, looking around. "Honestly, where is that... CeeCee!" Sewzanne shouts, gesturing impatiently at a rotund woman with her hair pinned in a top bun. She chats animatedly with a muscled shirtless protector in the lotus position. Her hand lingers on his biceps.

"CeeCee!" Sewzanne shouts again.

CeeCee holds up a "just a minute" finger to Sewzanne, says something that makes the handsome protector laugh, then shimmies over.

"CeeCee, this is Caitlin, the girl I was telling you about. CeeCee's one of my best," Sewzanne prattles. "She'll take excellent care of you."

"Come on, Cay," CeeCee says.

She loops her arm into mine, winks at her handsome protector, and whispers in my ear, "Massive," showing me a space between her palms one measure long as she leads me to a dangling helmet. I'm flustered and blushing. *Is making me uncomfortable part of the process?* I wonder. *Does it make the Calibration more effective?*

It's hard to say what's an act and what's genuine anymore.

Game on, CeeCee, I think. *Game on.*

I strip down to my short shorts and tank top.

"You had quite the day yesterday," CeeCee says, sticking monitoring pads to various points on my body. "Runners, nasty business that."

She falls silent, letting the uncomfortable lull in conversation drag. Interrogation instructors taught us this technique. Most people will automatically rush to fill the quiet and will often let slip something they didn't intend. CeeCee is good with her disarming off-kilter and flirty manner. One of the best, as Sewzanne promised.

I take a moment to calm my heart, to let any tension drain away, and then I answer, "It is what it is."

CeeCee looks at her datapad. No bleeps betray what I'm thinking. She nods. The system can be fooled.

"All set," she says, handing me a gel cap with a bright orange liquid in it. Mango Tango. I swallow it with a swig from my water canteen.

"Good luck," she winks.

I sit cross-legged like everyone else. The helmets lower, and we ease them over our heads. They quiver to life, and I already know something is different from individual Calibration. I sense the others around me. It's subtle, as if we're all humming the same mantra with our minds. Occasionally, someone warbles off tune. Sometimes that person is me, sometimes a neighbor, but each of us is guided back by the vibrations of the others. Within a few minutes, we're all in harmony.

Images flash inside the visors, and gentle instructions guide our bodies and minds deeper into relaxation. I read Eugene's book, so I understand what's happening. The images and vocal induction are quieting down my conscious mind, prepping my subconscious for new input. In theory, they can't input anything I don't believe, and they can't make me do anything against my will. But, according to Eugene, each person's psyche is composed of different parts, some of which might be diametrically opposed.

The Calibration process focuses on the parts of me that want to be a protector, the parts in support of upholding the treaty with the Supergenics at all cost, and it makes those aspects of myself louder, brighter, and stronger, programming them to kick in on autopilot. Bit by bit, the process quiets my other parts, the ones that question, hold autonomy as a virtue, and are inclined to rebel, ultimately turning them off. The Mango Tango intensifies the trance-formation. But even drugged, we have agency.

Who you are, and who you will be, Eugene wrote, *is ultimately up to you.*

In this moment, I'm done wondering who that is or what Gen M means to me.

I am Shadowren, I intone in my mind. *Shadowren is me. Shadowren defends the weak. Shadowren is a hero.* I think it over and over. My heart flutters, and I fall out of sync from the intricately choreographed calibration that relies on all the players doing the same moves at the same time. I mentally step my own steps, bumping into the psyches around me. I throw them off, and they jostle surrounding dancers. I'm a pebble thrown into clear waters; the ripples spread outward.

I picture myself in the Shadowren costume, blood-red with slashes of black, standing between Captain Light and the boy he took away. The vision sends vibrations into the calibration system. Brainwaves spike, exposing kindred spirits. They mimic my steps, creating a new harmony that challenges the one imposed on us. Others join in; our invisible circle expands. We agitate the larger group; they yield to the old steps one moment, then trip and incorporate a few of ours. Discord ripples through our ranks.

It's working, I think—until the hum dies out. The images on the inside of my visor go dark, and the inductive tones in my earbuds fall silent. My helmet tugs at my ears, pulled off my head. I blink in the sudden light.

Is that it? I wonder.

The protectors are equally confused.

"My apologies," Sewzanne says from the front of the room. "Technical issues. We'll reschedule for later in the week."

We file out, and I overhear CeeCee say to Sewzanne in a hushed tone, "I don't know where the anomaly came from." Her eyes flick at me. "I'll take a techie to the data towers and run a diagnostic. Probably just a faulty node or processor pod."

It's both a victory and a defeat. My thoughts were able to affect the protectors around me. Some of them, anyway. Can we level up to reach the entire Protectorate? And how do we stop Sewzanne from realizing the protectors' brainwaves are changing?

Over the next several weeks, Normand, Bradie, and I plan and scheme. One day, we meet inside a custodial closet. Brooms and mops are hooked to the wall; scrub pads and vats of industrial cleaner line metal shelves. Normand holds his hand before us; we stare at a round processor pod sitting in his palm.

Bradie takes it and holds it up, turning it this way and that. A dense network of circuits glint in the LED light. "This isn't a regular processor pod," he realizes in awe. "It's got *way* more connections. How'd you get your hands on this?"

"I forged it," Normand replies.

For a moment, Bradie gapes, then he laughs. "You almost had me there. I don't know how you stole this without anyone noticing, but... respect."

"Didn't you have that at Revelry?" I ask.

"Affirmative," Normand confirms.

"You used it to create the link between everyone on the dance floor."

"Overly simplistic," Normand chides. "The union I engineered at Revelry also required a power source—"

"The lightning," I realize.

"Routed through a converter to modulate the energy into the amplitude and frequency of human brainwaves—"

"Your energy discs," I say.

"And a connection interface to transmit the unifying current—"

"Us touching each other," I conclude.

"And... kazamo!" Normand raises his fist to the air. "You were joined as one."

"It was so cool," Bradie sighs.

"So why don't we just—"

Normand holds up his hand before I can finish my thought. "Do not embarrass yourself by suggesting we reprogram the entire Protectorate using that methodology."

"I mean, obviously not," I snort. "But, maybe explain why to Bradie."

"Nah, I get it," Bradie says. "The reconditioning messaging we're going to use to un-brainwash the protectors is too complex for the simple emotional connection badass Bamford created at Revelry."

"It would be like trying to use a child's word toy as a supercomputer," Normand wheezes. Bradie laughs with him. I force myself to join in, louder than either of them.

"Okay," I say. "Now that we are all equally in on the joke, our next step is to..."

"Populate the pod," Normand says, holding his hand toward me, "which we will then insert into an actual supercomputer."

"Right!" I say, remembering our actual plan. I dig in my pocket and pull out a pilfered data cylinder the size and shape of a pill. The simple storage device is way easier to come by than a processor pod, so it's unlikely anyone will realize it's missing. If they do, it should be too late by then. Should be. I hand it to Normand. He slides it into a round port on the device he used at Revelry. A red light blinks three times.

"The upload is complete," Normand declares.

"You sure this will work?" Bradie asks.

"Affirmative," Normand says so emphatically, I can't help but believe him.

"I guess we're going to find out," Bradie adds.

"Tomorrow, when you hear the perimeter breach alarm, that's the signal," Normand says.

"You're going to activate the perimeter siren?" I ask. "I thought we didn't want to attract attention."

"I can assure you, no one will be paying attention to us," Normand says. "A powerful mutant is headed for the Yellow Zone. It will be *very* distracting."

We don't ask. In Normand we trust, him and his hacking GRAMS. He must've jacked into the longer-range sensors. Bradie flexes and stretches his scarred fingers.

"All right," he says, "Let's do this." He hovers his hand at waist height, palm down, in the center of our triangle.

I put my hand on top of his. His scars radiate heat. Normand makes a delighted squeal.

"This is precisely like issue 52 of the *Aerobots*!" he explains, squirting the top of my hand with disinfectant then adding his palm to our pile.

"We're doing this," Bradie says. A glassy look overtakes his eyes; shallow breaths dominate the rise and fall of his chest.

I don't need to be a telepath or an empath or a siphon to know what he's feeling. I'm feeling it too. Scared... and powerful.

"Kazamo," Normand says confidently.

"Kazamo," Bradie and I echo.

The next day, though I know it's coming, I'm caught off guard when the wail of the perimeter sirens pierces my ears. We're in the outdoor training yard running laps. A light drizzle mists us. Bradie and I make eye contact. It's time.

"Mutant alert! Repeat, mutant alert!" the loudspeakers boom. "Seismic sensors indicate a subterranean approach!"

A squad of protectors runs toward us, visors down, rifles in hand.

"Cadets, into the hall! Now!" our instructor shouts.

We run toward the Cube, our two rows of cadets parting to either side of the squad of protectors sprinting the other way. The ground shakes, knocking cadets and protectors off our feet and tossing us together like grizzled meat churned into a stew. I slam into a protector in full uniform and fall on top of him.

My arm flails and hits the side of his helmet, causing his visor to slide open. It's Trenton. He glares as if he blames me for this and far more. I'd forgotten about the little heart to heart we had. He has not. He presses the button that slides his visor shut and shoves me off.

"Move cadets!" he shouts at us through the speakers in his helmet. "Protectors, with me!"

We are trained dogs, scrambling to get out of the way, but even the most beaten canine would stop and look back at the destructive force bearing mercilessly in our direction. The unseen underground creature's burrowing throws chunks of broken concrete and beat-up vehicles in the Yellow Zone into the air, leaving a trail of upraised streets and sidewalks in its wake as it races closer to the surface—and us.

The rising ridge snakes toward the fence—and stops 10 measures from the barrier. Everything is silent except for the wail of the proximity siren—until the ground shakes worse than before; chunks as big as a tank explode outward. A rusted car flies over the security fence and crashes a few measures from us.

A sinkhole forms in the Yellow Zone, collapsing downward and releasing a thick cloud of dirt. From within, an enormous paw ending in jagged claws reaches up and out, stabbing into the ground like it's soft butter. A second paw follows; its deadly talons grip the base of a concrete pylon with an energy sphere on top. The creature flexes and pulls itself up. Bright spotlights along the fence spin toward it, casting huge shadows as the beast emerges.

It's gigantic, about 20 measures tall, lumbering on legs thicker than tree stumps. Its grey skin is rough and thick. Beady eyes poke out of its bestial face; a wide snout rises into a gigantic horn. It reminds me of pictures of an extinct species called a rhino. I've seen mutated animals, but nothing like this. It releases a terrifying howl.

Lightning arcs from the billowing black clouds above, striking the beast. Protectors cheer as the animal writhes, defeated by a stroke of luck before it could do any real damage. But the celebratory notes die as we realize something's wrong. The same strike of lightning is still hitting it.

That's not right.

Giant pustules rise all over the mutant's body. They pulse with an inner glow. The thing huffs and snorts, like a hound slavering over the most delicious of T-bones. It's feeding off the energy from the clouds. When the lighting flares out, the mutant animal's entire form is aglow.

"All units, mutant threat can absorb energy," Trenton says, his voice piped through external speakers. "Repeat, the mutant threat can absorb energy. Ballistic weapons only. No plasma rifles or photonics. I repeat, ballistic weapons only!"

The thing roars, and the energy it absorbed surges out of its mouth. It fires a blast of pink electricity at the closest guard tower. The pink power cascades through the structure. Spotlights burst, and the protectors on the platform writhe in agony.

The sirens grow louder. Beyond the Cube, those who work in the borough scramble for the mutant raid shelters. The schools and factories have underground bunkers. I think of Nate and Mom hunkering down with classmates and coworkers. Someone grabs me. I assume it's Bradie; I stare into the drillmaster's angry face.

"Move!" he shouts, pushing me in the direction of the protective walls of the Cube.

I run, searching for Bradie. He finds me, the mottled flesh of his injured hand snaking into mine.

Normand was right. No one is paying attention to us. In fact, I momentarily forgot about our plan. Ahead of us, the rest of the cadets flee into the Cube. A burst of pink lightning flies over our heads and slams into the compound's sleek surface. The energy sprays outward, shattering several white panels and spraying glass onto a cadet below.

He screams, protecting his face with his bare arms. He bleeds; exposed wires spark and smoke.

The beast roars and fires a bolt of green electricity. It hits the Cube a dozen floors up. The lightning cascades outward along the building's surface. It seems to fizzle out—until the uncovered circuits a few measures away spark with emerald energy.

It traveled!

I shove Bradie inside the Cube and jump in beside him as power the color of radioactive limes shoots out of the exposed cables—into our fellow cadet. His body shakes uncontrollably, fried by the current. The surge stops; his scorched corpse topples to the ground.

The rhino monstrosity glows all colors of the rainbow. It lumbers toward the fence; a hover attack vehicle zooms between, firing a missile. It strikes the rhinonstrosity and explodes. The creature staggers back, banging into one of the concrete pylons supporting a power absorber.

Lightning flares from the clouds into the orb. The beast reaches its thick fingers toward the crackling globe; energy bursts out of the sphere, arcing into the creature's outstretched hand. The mutant grasps the bolt of power and swings it like a whip, cutting the hover vehicle in half. The front skids along the ground, the back tailspins, smashing and exploding against a half-collapsed building.

The protectors at the fence crouch behind plastic shields and fire their ballistic weapons. The bullets sound like pellets as they bounce off the creature's thick hide.

The mutant roars—and the door shuts behind us.

Flashing red lights cast a demonic filter over the cadets bunched together down the hall.

"To your bunks!" the drillmaster shouts.

"Hurry," Bradie says, pushing me in the opposite direction.

We skitter down a stairwell, turning sharply at each landing until we get three floors below.

Something's burning—we reach a smoldering medic lying facedown on the floor, one palm fused to the handle of the door we need to get through. Her other hand is melded with her smoking i-dent card, which is partially melted into the security swiper.

"That's problematic," Bradie says.

The door opens from the other side, breaking the medic's charcoal arm at the wrist. Normand stands there. He checks his watch.

"You need to accelerate your pace," he says. "We're off schedule."

"That means crank it," I translate.

"I speak Normand," Bradie says.

I grab his hand, and we jump over the dead medic. Normand's all business, limping as fast as he can, brace creaking like crazy. He navigates us through the underground maze, taking lefts and rights through white corridors that all look the same to me, except for the occasional number with a letter to identify where we are. He doesn't use his e-pad—"too much interference from the EM waves."

I convince myself we're the only ones down here. Everyone else is fighting the rhinonstrosity or confined to their bunks. We round a corner and face a pair of protectors with their helmets strapped to their belts.

"*Deodamnatus*," Normand huffs. "They were supposed to be in the next corridor. That's the problem with—"

"What are you doing here?" the bigger one demands.

"We—" Bradie starts.

I take two running steps and propel myself off the ground. My legs wrap around the protector's neck before Bradie can say another word, and my swinging weight topples the guard to the floor. I grab his baton, roll to a lunge, and shove the weapon into his stomach. He writhes in a spastic dance. I pull the rod away, and the cold barrel of his partner's gun presses into the back of my head.

"There's two of them," Bradie points out.

"I assumed you'd deal with the second one," I reply.

"I was going for smooth-talking our way out of this," he says.

"Noted," I say.

I spin with greased precision as all the skills Sewzanne rammed into me during Calibration snap into auto. I smack the gun from the protector's hand. It fires. Bradie kicks the protector's legs out from under him. We've got the jump on him, and it's two against one, but the guy's bigger and has more training than us. He drops, rolls, and is back on his feet, kicking me in the gut so hard I slam into a wall. Bradie unleashes a flurry of blows into the guy's kidneys, and he punches Bradie across the jaw. His head snaps back.

"Not cool," Bradie says.

"I'm going to enjoy kicking your—" The protector's words cut off, his body quivering like a bowl of shaking jelly. He drops to the ground. Normand stands behind him, baton in hand. He shudders, shaking off the heebie-jeebies. His body settles.

"I'd rather not do that again," he says. He looks at his watch. "Let's press on."

"What do we do when they wake up?" Bradie asks.

"They won't be sharing tales," Normand replies. "Come."

Bradie and I look at each other. The protectors aren't dead, so what's Normand talking about? I know I won't get an answer now. He stops in front of a door that blends seamlessly with the wall. We flank him, standing guard. He presses his card to the door's surface, and a square keypad lights up. The door hisses open. We go in and stare at banks of processor drives stacked one atop the other. The whir of fans hums in our ears.

Normand looks at his watch. "Here it comes," he whispers.

A loud beeping fills the room.

"Get down," Normand says.

We duck, and pink electricity surges through the towers. I imagine what's going on up at the surface. The rhinonstrosity must be putting up quite the fight. The towers spark, the power surge dissipates, and the processors return to humming. I look to Normand.

"All clear," he says.

He leads us unerringly through the maze of smoking towers and stops in front of one computer drive in particular. Cooling fans run louder than before. Many of them are misshapen from the pulse of energy, yet they still try to do their duty. Normand unholsters a mechanized drill from his belt. It whirs as he undoes six screws. He pulls off a panel. Inside are rows of round processor pods. Several of them are smoking from the power surge. He gently touches one blackened pod.

"Worry not," he says to the burnt-out node. "You have served nobly. Your duty is now at an end."

He grips the damaged spherical device, which fits nicely between his thumb and index finger. He twists and pulls it free. He places his processor pod in its stead, snapping it into place with a decisive turn. It whirs to life, spinning one way, then the other.

"So that's the thing that's going to spark a revolution," Bradie says.

"The revolution *is* sparked," Normand replies, staring at my shoulder. "This is the fuel to the flame."

CHAPTER 29

Two minutes later, Normand finishes screwing the panel back into place.

"It seems so easy," Bradie says. "*Too* easy."

He winks at me like a clichéd hero in a comic book.

"We should go," Normand replies. His voice is weary, and he won't look at either of us in our foreheads. If it were anyone else, I'd assume he was up to something. Since it's Normand, my best guess is he's stressed.

We leave the room of processor towers. I think the worst is over and dare to believe we got away with it. I envision a world where those who enforce the law are not brainwashed puppets; a future where strangers from Jupitar Island can't take Nate away if he Manifests; a generation *not* defined by a pass or fail on Testing Day.

And it all starts here.

So I think as we enter the hall of white panels outside the processor room—until I find myself in not only a metaphorical cage but a literal one.

Left and right, white polymer security barriers block both ends of the hall.

"Guys, are we trapped?" Bradie asks.

Normand nods, weirdly calm.

"When the power surge ripped through the data banks, the area automatically sealed off," he explains. He suspected this would happen and apparently assumed we would as well—must mean he knows how to get us out. It would've been nice if he'd mentioned it during our planning sessions.

The two protectors we knocked out are locked in with us. They stir.

I grasp one of their batons, ready to zap them.

"No!" Normand shouts at me. "Throw it away!"

"I need to knock them out again," I say. It's a short-term solution to a long-term problem—they can identify us. Normand grabs my weapon and yanks it from my hand.

"It might as well be a lightning rod!" He tosses it to the far side of the hall.

I look at him, confused. He similarly gets rid of his tool belt and takes off his watch, setting it on the floor and stepping back. His gaze locks onto the timepiece. It's counting down. 10... 9... 8...

"Against the security gate," he says. "Tight as you can."

"Normand," I argue, but he's not paying any attention.

... 7... 6...

He drags me toward the synthetic security door.

"Five," he says pressing his back against the barrier. To appease him, Bradie and I do the same. The guards shakily get up.

"Normand," I say.

"Four..." he replies, following his chronometer.

Bradie takes my hand.

"... three..."

The bigger of the protectors pulls out his blaster.

"... two..."

The other protector picks his gun off the floor, finger tensing, ready to fire.

"What are you counting down to?" he demands.

"... one," Normand says. A panel between us and the protectors explodes off the wall. Black lightning shoots out of it, snaking into their metal guns and ripping into their arms. They spasm, the seams of their uniforms burst with tiny pops, and smoke rises from the breaches. The smell of cooking flesh fills the room. The black lightning blinks out, and the protectors collapse to the floor.

Black scorch marks mar the floor, walls, and ceiling where the lightning hit. Normand's watch, tool belt, and e-pad are fried. We were standing in the one safe place in the pen. Bradie and I pant. If I'd kept the baton, I'd be dead. I look at Bradie. He's thinking the same thing.

"You're okay," he assures me. "Normand, can you get the security gates open?"

"No," he replies.

"What do you mean 'no?'" I demand.

"We will require assistance," he says, "From someone on the other side. Bradie, there's a communication console in the wall."

"Normand, who do you think he's going to call?" I ask.

"My brother," Bradie replies. "He's going to kill me."

And me, I realize.

Bradie goes to the console and dutifully punches in Trenton's COMM code. The connection comes to life. The sounds of firing and animalistic growls emanate from Trenton's end.

"Trenton, it's Bradie," he says.

"Bradie? What the eff! Get off my COMM line!" Trenton shouts.

"Trenton," Bradie says, forcing the words out. "I'm in trouble."

Trenton is silent. More shots, explosions, and a monstrous howl echo. Protectors scream in pain.

"Where are you?" Trenton asks.

"Sending you my location," Bradie replies, pressing the tap pad. "We're sealed in by drop doors."

Trenton doesn't curse. He doesn't yell. His anger seeps through the preternatural steadiness of his voice. "What are you doing on sub-level 3?"

Bradie doesn't answer.

Trenton releases a defeated sigh. "I can't. You're on your own."

"Please," Bradie says. As if he's been saving this for the most desperate of situations, he adds, "You owe me."

He's so broken and beseeching, I try to go to him, to hold his hand, to squeeze it in mine. Normand grabs and drags me away. I look at Normand in confusion, jerk my arm free, and turn toward Bradie. Pink sparks flicker around the console.

"Bradie," I shout, "get ba—"

Pink lightning bursts from the COMM, slamming into Bradie and pinning his flopping body against the floor.

His head snaps back, jaw locked in a silent howl. His uniform smokes; I smell his smoldering hair. The pink lightning crackles out; he collapses.

"No," I breathe. "No, no, no, no, no!"

I drop to my knees next to him. An animalistic howl shreds its way out of my lungs. I cradle Bradie's head. I sob. Blisters rise all over his skin, red, raw, and angry. He gasps like a fish yanked from water.

"Bradie? Bradie!" I shout. "Hang on." I turn to Normand. "We have to get him to sickbay."

Normand's shaking. If I didn't know better, I'd say there were tears in his eyes. It must be from the smoke. He stares and says, "My deepest regrets, Bradie."

"Bradie? Bradie!" It's Trenton's voice. The COMM is somehow still working. "Bradie, are you all right? Caitlin, what's happened?"

"He's been hit!" I blubber. "An energy surge. He's covered in burns."

Broken blips of swearing rip through the COMM; it fitfully flutters on and off—then goes dead. Is Trenton coming for us? I don't know.

182

"Caitlin?" Bradie sobs. "It hurts."

"It's going to be okay, baby," I lie.

I doubt he hears.

After what seems like forever, compressed air hisses, and the security barrier slides up. Trenton stands there. His visor is open. He takes the scene in at a glance. If Bradie weren't alive, Normand and I would be dead.

"You blasted morons!" Trenton swears, kneeling beside his brother.

He checks Bradie's pulse and scans his brother's injuries.

"We have to get him to sickbay," I say.

Trenton glares at me. He's thinking what I'm thinking, what neither of us will say out loud. Bradie is going to die.

Trenton scoops his brother in his strong arms, and we run for the elevator.

Come on, I think as we wait for the doors to open. They finally do. Several floors up, we arrive at the health unit and step into chaos. Burned protectors are everywhere, crying and screaming. Doctors and medics rush amongst them. Trenton places his brother on a gurney.

Trenton grabs a passing doctor. His light purple uniform is splattered with blood.

"Where are you hurt?" the clinician asks Trenton, looking him up and down.

"I rescued these cadets," Trenton replies.

"Well, get back to the battlefield before that thing gets through," the doctor shouts.

Trenton is ready to punch him in the face. I put a restraining hand on his arm. He rounds on me with the fury of a brother's pure love, ready to kill me. I want him to. This is my fault.

"Go," I say. "You can deal with me later."

"Don't think I won't," he promises.

The doctor fills a syringe with a blue liquid. "We need a drip!"

A medic inserts an IV into Bradie and places sensor pads atop his heart and other organs.

The doctor injects Bradie "for the pain," and then half-a-dozen protectors stagger in. Most are covered in electric burns; one's been mauled; his arm dangles by threads of flesh; his screams fill my ears. The doctor rushes to him.

A medic cuts Bradie's clothes and peels them off. They come away dark with blood and skin. He's so burnt and swollen, I don't recognize him.

"He'll need grafts," the medic says, wrapping him in gauze soaked with a steroidal cocktail. "Lots of them."

She covers him head to toe in the bandages, then abandons him to help a screaming protector squirting blood from his neck. Two stocky orderlies pin him; the medic tries to stem the flow of blood. I gaze at Bradie.

"I want to hold his hand," I say to Normand, "but I can't because that will hurt him more."

"Would you like me to hold yours?" Normand asks. "Is that the appropriate course of action under the circumstances?"

"Yes," I say, nodding fervently. "Yes, it is."

He squirts a clear disinfectant onto my palm, rubs it in with his fingertips, and only then takes my hand in his. I laugh and cry at the same time.

"You're a good friend," I say, squeezing his hand.

He doesn't squeeze back; such nuances are beyond him.

"Thank you," he says. "I appreciate the positive reinforcement."

That does me in. I think I'm going to laugh; my throat catches and breaks into sobs. My eyes pour tears, and I fold into Normand's soft body. He puts his arms around me, like he's been taught. They rest on me like heavy dough.

"There, there," he says as if reading from a script Bradie gave him for when someone cries. "There, there."

CHAPTER 30

All night, I refuse to leave Bradie's side. I sit in a padded chair and stare at his mummified form, wracked with guilt. Whatever numbness the Chair granted me, it's gone. I have no idea what Trenton will do to me when he gets back, but I'll be here for whatever punishment he dishes out.

At some point, exhaustion overtakes me, and I doze. When I wake, sunlight streams in from a translucent window. The first thing I see is Bradie in his medically induced coma. The second is Trenton with two protectors, their copper uniforms laced with black piping.

I knock over my chair as I get to my feet. A medic shushes me then sees the protectors with black piping; she squeaks and scurries away. These are not ordinary protectors. They work directly with the agents.

"Trenton," I say. "What have you done?"

"It's *Officer* Trenton, *cadet*," he replies. "And *I* did my duty."

"Come with us, cadet," one of the protectors says.

I walk past Trenton and glare; he grabs me by the arm.

"I warned you," he says. "I would do *anything* for my brother."

"You're going to get him killed," I whisper.

"Good," he replies. "Because my brother's better off dead."

Trenton shoves me into the protectors. They push me toward the elevators. *What did Trenton tell them? What does Trenton know?* His words echo in my ears. *My brother's better off dead.* A part of me wonders if he's right.

The protectors take me several floors up. When the elevator opens, the Cube's ubiquitous white walls, floor, and ceiling are gone, replaced by shiny black. Hidden speakers fill the hallway with instrumental music. The protectors propel me forward. I trip, roll, and right myself.

I brace to counter-attack when a hidden door hisses open to my right.

A greasy smile greets me. It's the agent who took Bradie away on the train and coerced me into joining the Protectorate cadet program—Eel Man.

"Caitlin, he says, "do come in."

He sits at a black desk and turns to a holo projection of an infocast; it's been running nonstop since the mutant attacked. A soft glow from the emitter reflects off the red logo of a noose on his leather uniform. Fixated on the infocast, he snaps his fingers in my direction and points at a curvy black chair.

I enter and sit. Still staring at the image of the rhinonstrosity slaughtering protectors, Eel Man waves dismissively at the guards. They salute stiffly, and the door clicks shut behind them.

In the corner of the holo update is Informant Aarav Chandar, providing details of what took place. He's handsome, with a square jaw and slicked-back hair, dressed in a muted yellow jacket buttoned up to its short collar. The emblem on his chest is a microphone.

"As you can see here, a valiant, though futile, effort on the part of protectors to defend the boroughs against this beast, ironically birthed in the aftermath of the very war we dregs initiated so long ago."

I gaze at the images of the mutant slaughtering dozens of protectors, smashing through hover tanks, blasting energy into heli-fighters, and ripping a protector to pieces in its jaws.

"It's almost too much to watch," the agent says without blinking.

"Yes," I agree, "it's—"

Eel Man snaps his fingers at me. "No talking. Ah, here it comes."

In the holo image, a ball of light launches from Jupitar City's gleaming towers, flying like a comet across the river.

"Ever the humanitarians, the good denizens of Jupitar City don't leave their weaker neighbors across the river to fend for themselves," Informant Chandar beams on the infocast. "You can see here, Captain Light is reporting for duty."

As the comet gets closer, I see the outline of a muscular man with a form-fitting cowl hiding his face. My memory flashes to him taking the boy from his family when they tried to escape. Captain Light gets within 50 measures of the gigantic mutant and releases a ball of light the size of a fist. It drops, falling fast. Twenty measures from the ground, it jerks to life and fires like a missile toward the rhinonstrosity. Protectors fall back.

The howling creature siphons energy from the surrounding power collectors; a battalion of corpses lies at its feet. The mutant squints then roars at the energy ball racing through the air. The glowing sphere shoots into the beast's mouth and down its throat. The look on the creature's face is almost comical, reminding me of Nate when he swallowed a bug.

The creature burps, staggers, and scowls. The ball bounces around the creature's innards, making the animal's gut bulge cartoonishly with every strike. In a corner of the screen appears a box with a bald man wearing a bright blue suit and thick spectacles—an expert from Jupitar City.

"Some of you dregs might be wondering why this mutant creature doesn't absorb the energy of Captain Light's projectile. Clearly, it's the creature's *epidermis* that has the necessary cellular configuration for that ability. Its internal digestive system is limited to absorption of a more conventional kind." The image of the expert fades away.

Captain Light floats in a luminescent bubble above the suffering mutant. The photon ball burst out of the rhinonstrosity's chest, and the creature falls dead to the ground. The deadly globe sizzles, burning off the creature's blood, then arcs upward, coalescing with the larger aura surrounding Captain Light's densely muscled physique.

The protectors cheer. Captain Light salutes them and, without a word, flies back across the river.

"Classic Captain Light," the informant says. "Not a word. He says it all with a simple salute. What a hero!"

I stare at the dead protectors surrounding the mutant's corpse. Eel Man hits rewind, pausing the footage as the rhinonstrosity belches up a stream of pink lightning.

"The beast killed more than a hundred protectors. Unfortunately for you, Officer Trenton was not one of them," Eel Man says.

I stiffen.

What did Trenton tell him?

"Did you know a second mutant slipped through the breach last night?" the agent asks.

"No," I say with surprise.

"It failed to make the info broadcasts, but let's see," he says, tapping at the smooth surface of his desk. The holo image of the rhinonstrosity fizzles and is replaced by another. Dozens of protectors fire plasma weapons at a gorilla-sized mutant with white fur and tusks. It evades them with dizzying movements, disappearing amidst the debris of the Yellow Zone.

"Not what we pay them for," Eel Man says. "They will face disciplinary action. We've also been tracking a third mutant that broke through the outer perimeter using the fissure the first monstrosity created, but it's dropped off the grid. Our best intel places it somewhere in the Yellow Zone. It'll turn up. But listen to me go on. Why would I tell you such a thing?"

"Because I'll be a protector one day?" I offer.

He laughs gaily. "My dear! Here you are sitting in the office of an agent after rather questionable behavior, and you believe you're going to be promoted? Caitlin, I'm telling you this because you've obviously figured out it's no coincidence that three mutated animals breached the perimeter soon after runners tried to make off with a Supergenic child. We're being punished."

"I... What? By who?" I ask.

Eel Man eyes me as if I can't be serious. "How utterly clueless," he says with shock. "The Supergenics, of course. We almost let one of theirs get away. They're not going to let that stand."

"But, it's not our fault!" I insist.

"Isn't it? If our security measures were tighter, our propaganda more effective, our citizens more cooperative, there would be no runners."

I stare at the bodies of dead protectors on the hologram. I know those people. They're dead to teach us a lesson?

"I had no idea," I admit.

Eel Man swivels in his chair one way then the other. He stops and wags his finger at me.

"Well, you and your friends were certainly prepared for the distraction the mutant provided, allowing you to do this."

He taps away on his computer and up pops a security feed of me, Bradie, and Normand.

"I had to do quite a lot of digging to recover this footage. Someone is very good at covering their tracks."

Not good enough. I watch the images of us taking down the two protectors who caught us outside the processor room. I zap one with an electrified baton, and he falls to the floor. The footage cuts out for a moment, then resumes with us emerging from the processor room.

"The cameras inside the processor chamber short-circuited from the electrical overload," the agent says, "but according to the timecode, the three of you were in there for roughly ten minutes."

"I can explain," I begin.

"Can you?" Eel Man replies.

I reach for a lie—I've got nothing.

188

"While you're at it…" he presses more buttons on his desk. The projector sucks away the image of us, replacing it with another. I stare in shock.

No. Please no.

Shadowren stares at me from the cover of her premiere issue.

"My son is a sucker for comic books, but I'm not familiar with this title."

The agent flips to the first page—a black and white drawing of a beaming girl dressed in a skirt, cleavage-revealing top, and a cape.

"A young girl dreams of Manifesting superpowers," the agent reads the text box. "But alas," he gasps melodramatically, still reading, "she fails her final Testing Day. She must face reality. She is nothing more than a mere dreg! This is the future she has to look forward to."

The panel shows a twisted version of the first. The girl stares at her shoes, shoulders hunched in defeat. She wears baggie coveralls and sweeps contaminated waste.

"Aww," the agent says. "You mean she's going to have to *work*? How awful."

He flips the page to the next series of panels.

"Such would have been her fate, but walking home one day, she sees protectors beating her neighbor, Mr. Fantome. The protectors are taking away his grandson because the boy has Manifested."

The girl lifts her broom and smashes it over the protector's head. The protectors chase and corner her against a wall.

"You're going to wish you hadn't done that," the protector says. His looming shadow towers over her quaking frame until…

"I'm through playing with you," Mr. Fantome says. He holds the two pieces of broken broom handle. He attacks, twirling them like cyclones. In a series of *BAMs! WHACKs!* and *POWs!*, the old man lays the four protectors low.

"What happens when the protectors wake up?" the girl in the comic book asks.

"Grandson," Mr. Fantome says. "Can you make them forget?"

"I can try," the little Supergenic boy replies. He holds up his hands and uses his powers to strip the protectors of their memories.

From there, old man Fantome offers to train the girl in the ways of the warrior. She accepts. A montage shows the withered man teaching her how to fight hand-to-hand, scale walls, do flips, and use an array of blades.

"When they look at me, they want to see a broken old man, so that is what I show them," Mr. Fantome says in a dialogue bubble. "You will wear a mask of a different kind."

I mouth the words along with Eel Man, so engrossed, I forget I'm sitting in his office in mortal danger. The story takes a turn. In a bid to infiltrate the protectors, the comic book girl joins their ranks—except little by little, she's brainwashed. She betrays her own ideals—and old man Fantome. She turns him in, and to prove her loyalty to the protectors she once vowed to defeat, she beats him to death.

"Only then," Eel Man reads aloud, "as he dies in her arms, she realizes what a monster she's become. Protectors should protect the weak—not make them live in fear."

The issue ends with the girl vowing to make right her wrongs. She dons her Shadowren costume, a graffiti-style sigil of her namesake on the brick wall behind her. Her thoughts appear in bold letters.

We can be more than they will allow. You *can be more. The Supergenics use us as indentured servants. They turn us against each other. They take our children, our brothers, our sisters, then expect us to thank them for it. They try to break us, but we are stronger than they know.* You *are stronger than you know. We ARE Generation Manifestation. It's time to show them what that means.*

The image of Shadowren hangs there. I will face the death penalty for this. So will Bradie and Normand. Yet, I can't help myself. I'm dying for issue number two.

CHAPTER 31

We stare at Shadowren, floating there with her graffiti bird sigil in the background. Several heartbeats pass. I cough. Eel Man taps his chin.

"So, I don't get it," he says. "If the little boy can make the protectors forget, why doesn't he do so in the first place? And old man Fantome, if he's so rough and tumble, why did he need this girl's help?"

I say nothing.

"Well?" he demands. "You went to a lot of trouble to sneak this into the Calibration system. Defend your plot holes."

I lick my dry lips. I was ready for the agent to put a gun to my head, not belittle me with a critique. Normand and I worked super hard on this.

"Come on," Eel Man says. "I'm a fan. Do tell."

"Well," I say hesitantly, "the little boy doesn't fully control his mental powers. And, the protectors *will* start to remember what happened, causing some to hunt Shadowren, others to turn to her cause."

Eel Man arches his brow. "It's plausible, I suppose. And the old man?"

I shrug. "He's an old man. They caught him off guard. It happens."

"It does," he agrees soberly. "So, what am I to do with this?"

Shouldn't I be in an audit room? I wonder. *Why am I in his office?*

He's trying to trick me, I realize. But to what end?

"I've had the cadets and protectors run through their Calibrations with your little embedded story. I was… curious," he says.

"And?" I lean forward, emoting my excitement.

"And… nothing," he replies. "All the readings are normal."

My smirk might as well be an evil laugh. His eyes narrow.

"Your gimpy friend added a subroutine to alter the output results," he realizes out loud. "Clever. And that light show of his at the Revelry, this breach is a sophisticated version of that."

Eel Man was at Revelry. *I knew it!* And he seems to be putting all the pieces together.

He walks to a side table by the window. Steam drifts from a teapot flanked by dainty cups and a three-tiered plate with scones and jelly-filled pastries. He pours himself a cup, drops in a sugar cube, and adds cream. He sips loudly, not offering me any.

"The caffeine is hell on my nerves, but decaf is swill," he says, confessing the guilty pleasure as if we're the best of confidantes. He flips the holo pages of the comic book back to the cover. He stares at it. "The question is, do I let this run its course, or do I shut it down?"

My heart hammers in my ears. Did I hear right?

"The latter would be easier," he continues. "Safer. I'd have to execute you and your friends, of course. I've certainly made greater moral compromises."

I grip the arms of my chair.

"Do your worst, monster," I say.

He waves his finger. "Careful. You have no idea what my worst looks like. Hint—it's ugly." The insignia on his chest reminds me it's not a casual threat.

I chew the insides of my cheeks to keep from saying any more.

"My quandary is this," he muses. "I recruited you, and a few others like you, over the years; children with specific brain wave patterns that could upset the group Calibration process."

I cock a brow and snort. "Specific brain wave patterns? You make it sound like I'm Supergenic."

He considers this. "Tell me, what is the difference between a mediocre Supergenic and an exceptional dreg?"

I have no answer to a question I'd never thought to ask.

"That's the thing about genetic variation," he says. "It's varied. Even in dregs. Not that it matters. Although your uniqueness allowed you to create a bit of a stir during your first group Calibration, it had no lasting effect. But this! You've inserted suggestions into the Calibration process to create dissent. If I expose you, the new security protocols will be impossible to hack. We'll never get another chance like this."

The truth hits me. Eel Man's a rebel!

"So, you're *not* going to execute me?"

He sips his tea and admits with disappointment, "No. I'm not. Your pulp fiction is crude but effective."

I struggle to process.

"You're going to let this play out," I say. It's not a question. He sets down his teacup and stares at the huge hole the mutant created in the Yellow Zone. Bulldozers slowly fill it in.

"Yes," he agrees. "I suppose I am."

CHAPTER 32

I feel like I'm on sedatives when I exit Eel Man's office. The agent's guards stand in the hall. They tower over me, visors closed. It must be a let down to see me alive. I want to sprint to the elevator, but they're predators. If I run, they'll hunt; it's their nature. I see a sticky strip on the floor with a cockroach stuck to it. I relate.

What have I gotten myself into? I wonder.

Eel Man is a subversive. He wanted me in the Protectorate to stir up trouble. Now that I've exceeded expectation, what does that mean? We're not partners. Are we allies? Am I his lackey? The latter seems most likely. I reach the elevator. I imagine the protectors' stares boring into my back.

"Come on, come on," I mutter, willing the lift to get here already.

The door opens. I board, turn, push the button for the medical floor, then wave to the protectors down the hall. I can't help myself. Makes sense Mrs. Cranberry couldn't stand me.

The sliding doors steal them from view. I lean against the slick wall, cup my face in my hands, and allow myself this momentary weakness for the count of three floors. Tears build for my wealth of mistakes—and the compounding consequences.

If I fall apart now, more people will pay the price.

I sniffle, wipe my eyes dry, and force my head up.

"Medical bay," a computerized voice announces.

I face my mess. Moans rise from those injured in yesterday's battle. They lie in cots separated by flimsy white curtains.

I go to Bradie. Trenton is there, eyes bloodshot, holding his kid brother's hand. A machine bleats next to him, monitoring the faint pulse of Bradie's heart.

"Caitlin," Trenton says.

He's not surprised to see me. The agent's already been in touch with him. Trenton looks ready to kill me himself.

"I guess you heard," I reply. "All the EM waves corrupted the security stream; it's unwatchable. The agent thinks you're mad with grief, desperate to blame someone for Bradie's injuries."

I choke on Bradie's name, but I have to see this through.

I hope Trenton buys my lie, for his sake. He's a complication. He could try to expose Normand and me. Eel Man's solution was to kill Trenton.

"I got the message," Trenton says. "I guess your little techie friend had something to do with that. The agent may buy your story, but I don't. You weren't lost during the attack. One way or another, you're going to pay for what you did to my brother."

"Yes," I agree. "I know."

I look at Bradie. Whatever Trenton plans to dish out, I deserve it. I hope he doesn't get himself killed in the process. I want to take Bradie's other hand, the one the agents burned to punish him what seems a lifetime ago, but I can't. That hand is gone. The doctor amputated his arm above the elbow. If he survives, he won't be a protector anymore.

Once you learn to fire a gun, there's no turning back. I'm surprised they haven't cut their losses and put him out of his misery. I suspect Trenton has something to do with that.

We were such stupid idiots.

I loop the memory in my mind—Bradie at the panel, calling his brother for help, me reaching for him, Normand yanking me back.

I gorge myself on the images to figure out what we could've done differently—and to torture myself. I've been compulsively doing this since the incident, but this time I pause. Maybe it's Trenton mentioning Normand. Maybe it's Eel Man talking about the light show at Revelry, the one that calibrated everyone to each other, the one that was created by one person alone.

"Normand," I whisper.

When Bradie was electrocuted, the same thing could've happened to me. It didn't because Normand pulled me away from the COMMs panel. If not for him, I'd be lying here, my skin covered in ointment soaked bandages, my central nervous system fried, and my extremities turning necrotic. It's what I deserve. If that were me lying there, Trenton wouldn't hesitate to pull the breathing tube from my throat and press a pillow over my face.

Instead, I'm healthy and haunted by a horrible thought.

Normand was so sure of himself when he jerked me away from the panel—as if he knew the power would surge. I rewind further, to when the two protectors were drawing their guns on us. Normand *insisted* I throw away my baton *and* that I press myself against the wall. Seconds later, energy pummeled the protectors.

Effing eff.

I can't be thinking what I'm thinking, and what I'm thinking can't be right. Yet, Normand knew the mutant was coming—before the rest of the Protectorate. He knew it was going to cause electrical havoc within the Cube, and he knew which node would burn out.

Eel Man pointed out the final piece of evidence. He reminded me of Normand's light show at Revelry. I relive that moment and see Normand on a floating platform above a crowd of protectors in the arena in the Yellow Zone. Lightning pulsed around him as if he were a god, and he transformed it into a different kind of energy. I thought he did it with tech, but what if he didn't? What if he didn't need gadgets and gizmos to manipulate electricity?

What if Normand's Supergenic?

Trenton glares at me. I barely notice.

Normand can control energy.

I reel at the possibility. Trenton stands. Do I share my suspicions with him?

"You need to leave," Trenton says. His fingers turn to fists.

That would be a "no."

"Sure," I say. My mind's working fast, searching for flaws in my "Normand has powers" theory. Normand failed his final testing, but false negatives happen. Yet, if he knows he has powers, why keep them a secret? Why not move to Jupitar City?

Because he's Normand, I think. *He is such a weirdo.* And a rebel. He's here because he wants to be here, where he can take down the Protectorate. My theory's riddled with holes—like, how could he do this to Bradie?

Trenton steps threateningly toward me.

I hold my hands up in peace. "I'm going."

I retreat to the elevator, the impossible racing through my mind. More pieces fall into place. When we were trapped outside the data node chamber by the drop-down walls, the lightning hit Bradie only *after* Trenton refused to help us. Normand knew there was no way Trenton would leave his brother suffering if he was critically injured. To get the king you must sacrifice the pawn.

Trenton was right about one thing. Someone *is* going to pay for what happened to Bradie. That someone is Normand.

CHAPTER 33

I search for Normand all over the compound. So many systems are either fried or rebooting, I can't track him down using internal sensors. I ask around, but the Cube is huge, and the techies are working triple shifts to get it all fixed. Most are keyed on amphetamines and have no patience for a cadet.

"If you have a work request, put it through the proper channels," says a sallow-faced tech girl, defiantly flipping a knitted, lime-colored scarf around her neck. "We'll get to it when we get to it."

By midday, my hunger flares. I can't remember the last time I ate. In the cafeteria, Liam slides in next to me.

"I ran into your tech friend," he says.

"Normand?" I ask, dropping my spoon into my split-pea soup. "Where? When?"

"Twenty minutes ago," he says. "He had a weird message. Says if you want your questions answered, meet him in your special place."

My hand tightens on a knife. Liam notices.

"Caitlin, if something's up, if you need back up—"

"I don't. You want to stay out of this."

He nods. "Aight."

He'll have questions later. I'll answer with lies. I'm good at that. I hurry into the hall, past all the tech squads with their soldering equipment and lengths of cable. I get outside in time to see Normand's distinct figure hobbling onto a bus. He says something to the driver, and they wait for me.

Panting, I pull on the handrail to board. Normand gazes at my forehead.

"Come," he says curtly, limping past half-a-dozen people to the rear of the bus.

I stare at his back, barely restraining myself. He sits. I force myself to take the seat next to him.

"I know what you did," I say between clenched teeth.

"Not here," he replies. "Too many eyes. Too many ears."

It galls me, but he's right. The ride lasts ten excruciating minutes. Normand pulls the notice cord, a bell dings, and the "Next Stop" sign alights. The bus jerks to a halt; we exit in front of the billboard of a muscled spider guy encouraging teens to "BE GEN M."

The sun sets, and the street lamps light. We walk side by side to the security fence where Normand uses his swipe pad and skeleton key to open the gate. I follow him into the Yellow Zone and see him differently forevermore. I should've known better than to trust him. Heroes and villains are both outsiders in their own way; the difference is, we look up to heroes. Villains are outcasts—like Normand.

We move undetected amidst the motion sensors. The trick is avoiding the sightlines of the crews repairing the fence damaged by the monstrosity and the heightened patrols searching for the mutated animal that may still be in the Yellow Zone.

"Crouch down," Normand says, gesturing for me to duck. I do, the pair of us cramming into a moist alcove.

I hear the *whumf* of displaced air and a hovercraft zooms by. I'm tempted to shove Normand in front of it. The protector patrol passes. He didn't even look at his swipe pad or the illicit GRAM that allows him to track protector movements. Maybe he doesn't need to. Maybe he never did. If he can control electricity, perhaps he can sense it too, tuning into the cells that power the hovercraft or the helmets and body packs the protectors wear on patrol. The hovercraft passes beyond hearing, leaving only the echo of my labored breathing in the confined space.

"Let us continue," he says.

We're both in our uniforms—he in his coveralls; me in cadet's blue. My baton bounces at my side. We reach the Lair, pull back the door, and walk down the stairs. We're unusually quiet as we enter the old comic book shop. The suspicious part of me wonders if this is a trap.

Normand turns to face me; I whip my baton free and assume a fighting stance. He doesn't move, doesn't lift his hands to fire lightning into me, doesn't break character. Framed by rows of comic books and a wall of plastic shields, blasters, and capes, he sighs sadly.

"*Nunc futuri*," he murmurs in what I once thought was gibberish. Now, everything he does or says is suspect.

"What does that mean?" I demand.

"Future now," he says. "Today's the day—again."

He sounds tired beyond the three shifts he worked in a row, as if his soul had grown weary—not that there's any such thing as a soul.

He looks around the store. He picks up an issue with a muscled man in a loincloth swinging on a vine on the cover. He puts it down.

"You blame me for what happened to Bradie," Normand says, staring at my forehead.

I had a whole ranting speech planned.

"Is it your fault?" I ask.

"Yes."

I wait for him to elaborate. He doesn't. He is *so* frustrating!

"Explain," I demand.

He looks at his new timepiece, an antique-style pocket watch, then back at me. "Caitlin, as you have guessed, I am Supergenic."

My grip tightens on my baton. *I knew it!*

"I'm going to kill you for what you did to Bradie," I say.

Normand cocks his head, surprised by my words. "That's not what you say. You're supposed to ask me why. Why would I hurt Bradie? You're supposed to remind me he's your boyfriend." That *is* what I was thinking. It's like he can read my mind. Can he read my mind?

I raise my baton and lunge at him. He cowers and raises his arms over his head.

"I did it because of you!" he shouts in a panic.

I freeze, baton in the air. I'm shaking. "Don't you put this on me!"

Yet, despite my rage, I know the truth. It *is* on me. Everybody said Normand had a crush on me, but I convinced myself it was harmless. He and Bradie became friends; Normand had a bigger crush on Crystal, and whatever he felt for me, it was never weird with us—meaning it was always weird with us because Normand's weird.

"I know you think I hurt Bradie out of jealousy," Normand says.

If he can read my mind then—

"Caitlin," he interrupts my thoughts. "I know the future. That's how I ascertained when and where the lightning would strike, how to evade the patrols, and which node would burn out. It's how I knew when the mutant would attack. It's how I know some of what you're thinking, because in the future, you tell me."

I shake my head. "There's no such thing as precognition. The Supergenics say so."

"It's rare," he says. "And most precogs go insane from what they see, or from trying to change what's to come."

"But not you?" I say skeptically.

198

"My brain works differently. I'm a weirdo, remember? But yes, it will mean my demise in the end."

"You failed your Testing Day," I object.

"The tests are flawed," he replies. "And telepaths can't seem to access the temporal anomaly in my mind."

I punch a cardboard cut-out of a robot.

"No!" I shout. "I came here to punish you, not to listen to this crap."

"My punishment is coming," he assures me. "There's so much I wish to tell you. About how I Manifested. The things I've seen. The lives I've led. And to confess the horrible things I've done in those futures that will never be."

I shake my head. "The lives you've led? What does that mean?"

"That's how my power works. I only see *my* future. Perhaps 'see' is the wrong word. I experience it. I *live* it. That future is then fed back to me in the past, at which point I can let it play out, re-live it the same as before, or change it, then new me can travel back into my past self again. Out of all those lives, this is the first time Bradie and I form a platonic bond. I'd rather hurt myself than hurt him."

At the mention of Bradie, I decide to believe everything Normand's telling me. Normand can change the present by going into his past; he can fix everything.

"Save him," I say. "You tell your younger self to save Bradie. You do it, and you do it now. This future, it never happens. Do you understand me?" I expect to disappear as Normand erases this present like the mistake that it is. But nothing changes. I remember everything. The robot remains indented by my fist.

"Why are we still here?" I demand.

I grab Normand, shove him against the wall, and pin him between a rubber mask of a grey-haired guy with a big chin and a white-faced grinning villain. "You can save Bradie, so you do it."

"No," Normand shakes his head.

He gazes at his pocket watch. It's not some OCD tick. He's counting down. He knows what will take place. He knows *when* it will take place. His watch isn't a watch. It's a timer.

"What is it?" I demand. "What's about to happen?"

He shakes his head. "If I tell you, you won't pull it off. I must use care when and how I interfere. Changing things versus *not* changing things is a delicate tightrope."

I don't have time for Normand's nonsense. "Save Bradie."

"*Deus ex machina*," Normand murmurs sadly.

My heart throbs. My face burns. My fists prepare to lash out. "What?!"

"You're asking me to be the god in the machine," he explains. "It's a contrived story device in which a great power suddenly appears and solves an otherwise hopeless situation. If only I could claim such a title, I *would* save my friend, but I assure you, my presence is anything but sudden, and my abilities are full of limits. I've attempted to keep Bradie safe, again and again. In every timeline where we rebel against the Protectorate, Bradie ends up mortally wounded. Time is… tricky."

"Time is *tricky?*" I demand. "What does that mean?"

"It means—" he tries to explain.

"Shut up!" I yell, thinking fast. He said something important.

In every timeline where we rebel against the Protectorate, Bradie ends up mortally wounded.

"What happens to Bradie if we don't rebel?" I ask. Normand's silent.

"Tell me!" I demand, but he doesn't have to. I see it in his avoidant gaze, unable to look me in the forehead. Has Normand saved Bradie, in an alternate future, an alternate past? I'm not sure what to call them.

"Then stop us," I say. "Stop us from defying the Protectorate."

"No," he replies.

"Why not?" I slam my palm onto the wall next to his face.

"Because you won't let me," he replies.

I step back. He's terrible at reading facial expressions, but even he sees my confusion.

"In earlier timelines," he explains, "you and Bradie have a daughter. She Manifests. The Supergenics take her, and they change her."

This is absurd, yet the comic book girl in me needs to know.

"What do you mean they *change* her?"

"Her power is intermittent. The gene therapy required to make it 'take' beastializes her and drives her insane, so the Supergenics dump her in the Yellow Zone to attack the boroughs."

Now I know he's full of it. "They wouldn't. Not to one of their own."

"Yes, they do. Where do you think so many of the monstrosities come from? Some Supergenics are more animal than human. Not fit for civilized society. But they still have their uses. To attack us. To remind us, we need heroes to come to our rescue. To keep us so afraid of what the fence is keeping out, we accept that it's keeping us in."

"You're lying," I say without conviction. And then I beg. "Please, tell me it's a lie. Please, tell me you'll save him."

"You're not on-duty when your daughter attacks," Normand ignores me, "but you and Trenton are competing for number of kills, so when you hear the mutant alert siren, you bribe someone to switch shifts. In the Yellow Zone, your daughter's tracks are hard to follow, but you're the best. You corner her and fire a kill shot. Ready to claim her head for your wall of trophies, you recognize her—eyes? A scar? Something—too late. Mad with a mother's grief, you turn on the Protectorate. You're terrifying but hopelessly outnumbered. I manage to reach you in your cell. I convince you of my powers, and you beg me to prevent that future from happening, no matter what—not just for your offspring, but the other children like her. I believe that moment primes you on a subatomic level to rebel in every timeline that follows."

"This isn't happening," I insist.

Normand looks at his watch. "You should go."

"I'm not going anywhere until you change all of this!" I shout.

"That's why we're here, again, to fix things, for *all* of Gen M."

I shake my head. "I can't have known what this would mean for Bradie. How could I? You can't hold yourself to a promise I've yet to ask of you."

"That's what I'm efforting to explain," Normand says. "I have attempted to talk you out of your plan to challenge the Protectorate—*ad nauseam*."

"*My* plan?" I demand.

"Indeed," he agrees, failing to read my tone. "I've warned you of the consequences. Bradie will never regain proper function of the right side of his body; he'll lose bladder control; the headaches will drive him to chemical dependency; he'll come to blame you for his broken body, mind, and life before taking his own. You thought I was making up horrible things because I was jealous. You shut me out, went ahead with your rebellion, and you were both caught and executed."

"Enough!" I can't hear this; I can't—because I don't know what's worse; if Normand's telling the truth or if he's lying.

"I hate you," I say.

"I know," Normand says sadly. "But I love you. And this is one of the hard things I have to do because of it."

"You know nothing about love, and you never will," I rage.

I wait for him to crumble, this man with his soft and weak body, his out-turned leg, his eyes that need glasses as thick as a deck of cards. Instead, he stares me in the eyes—not at my forehead, but in the eyes—and speaks unflinchingly.

"A lot of people think love is that wild sensation they get in their belly when they see, think about, or touch their other person. That isn't love. That's infatuation. *This* is love. When things get hard and ugly, and the one you love stumbles under the weight, and you take it on yourself so that other person can keep going. My love for you has deepened over many lifetimes. You have no idea of the adventures we have shared; the battles we have fought; the dark times you have seen me through. My love for you is not the romantic kind. It runs so much deeper than that. You saved me from myself. Now I will help you do the same for yourself."

His refusal makes me snap. I want to hurt him the way Lilianne would. With my words.

"You will always be alone," I say.

He nods. "There is but one future where I experience romantic love." He looks around at the comic book store, at the images of muscled men and busty women in their tights. "In a way, you introduced us. She loved me, and I loved her. But some lives can be lived but once. I can't return, not without losing myself and causing suffering beyond your ken. Nothing is free. This is the price I must pay."

I look at "the no-touch zone," the countertop where everything has to stay in its exact place. I sweep my arms across it, shoving everything off. The metal balls clang against the floor; I stomp on the red S on the scarf, and I kick the Taser. My actions are stupidly childish and, for a heartbeat, utterly satisfying.

I turn on Normand and hold my finger a breath from his face. He's not looking me in the eyes anymore. He stares at the floor.

"This isn't done," I say.

I turn my back on him. A poster of Tigara hisses at me. I rip her down, step over the burn mark in the carpet, and yank open the door to the stairs.

As it whines shut behind me, I catch Normand looking at his watch. He never did tell me what he was counting down to.

He mutters to himself, "She better not be late."

CHAPTER 34

I emerge into the open air knowing this is my last time in the Lair. I can't come back. It's more tainted and ruined than the rest of the Yellow Zone.

I told you to burn it, a part of me chastises.

I duck to avoid the sightlines of the crews repairing the security fence. I crouch and plot my route, so distracted I almost don't notice a piece of rubble skittering off a wall behind me. In this city that's ready to collapse, falling debris is commonplace—yet I experience an odd sense of familiarity, as if this moment's played out before. I'm no Supergenic, but I trust my Protectorate-honed dreg senses.

There's not a shadowren to be heard or seen.

Except for me.

I take the baton from my hip, turn, and scan the wreckage of the Yellow Zone. My gaze assesses and dismisses non-relevant items, glancing over a fire hydrant leaning at a weird angle, a utility pole that's remained upright all these years, and a busted sign for "oca-Cola." There's no one here.

Yes, my instincts insist, *there is.*

I won't be fooled by an invisible foe a second time. I flashback to the runners—the executed dad, his son freaking and throwing force fields left and right; Mom chasing after him; me picking up a rifle and...

I shake off the memory. I won't hurt anybody, not this time. *Could Normand have prevented that? Could he still?* I set the baton down and step back. Someone must've taken advantage of the damage to the fence to get out.

"It's okay," I say. "I'm going to help you."

In the space between booming thunder rises a low animalistic growl. That's not a runner. It sounds big, whatever it is. Too big to be one of the feral tomcats that live in the Yellow Zone.

"Easy there," I say as if it were a trained dog. I eye my baton a measure in front of me.

Only now do I remember what Eel Man said. *We've been tracking a mutant that broke through the outer perimeter.*

At first, it's hard to see the thing. It's got grey scales with flecks of brown that help it blend with the surrounding concrete and rusty metal rods sticking up from the collapsed buildings all around. Like many of the mutated animals that make it through the outer fence, it's disturbingly human in its proportions, with long, lean arms and legs, rounded buttocks, and well-proportioned breasts.

It's a she, I realize. Not that it matters.

The mutated animal sniffs the air through a pair of nostrils on a bump in the middle of her face. I'm downwind, but I don't think it's me she's smelling. In the distance, I see a series of hovercrafts whisking toward us.

She hisses. I'm expecting a forked tongue, but it's round and pink, and her eyes aren't yellow with vertical pupils. They're hazel and circular at the center, with flecks of gold. They're beautiful.

Doesn't matter.

My fear turns to something else—I need to kill something. I want it to be Normand, but this monstrosity will have to do.

She crouches low, skin shifting with every move. She's got chameleon abilities sophisticated enough to fool the motion sensors. I lunge and grab my baton. It's firm in my grip. I strike—too slow. She's gone, and I hit the concrete where she stood a moment ago, sending reverberations through the stick and up my arm.

Where is she?

I spin, and she lands a solid blow, slashing me across the back. If not for the reinforced lining of my training uniform, I'd be shredded from my shoulder blade down to my opposite hip. As is, I stumble and roll.

I catch a glimpse of rippling air, and I sweep my foot across the ground, knocking her legs out from under her—for all the good it does me. She lands on all fours and launches herself at me.

She's on top of me, her smooth reptilian palms wrapped around my throat. As she chokes me, I realize I have to stop thinking of it as a her. She's a thing. Yet, her hazel eyes are hauntingly familiar and all too human—not reptilian at all. And the way she fights, something's not right about it. She's got claws and razor-sharp teeth, so why is she choking me? It's like she doesn't know what to do with her arsenal.

She lifts me by the throat, one hand drawing back, claws growing longer. She looks at them. She's figuring it out. I grab hold of the thumb around my jugular and crush it on itself. She hisses in pain, and I break her hold. I land a solid kick to her abdomen, sending her slamming into a jagged piece of concrete; she leaves behind a telltale smear of blood. Caught in freeze-frame, the scene looks strikingly like a panel from one of Normand's and my comic books.

Cheers rise behind me. Protector hovercrafts stop, bobbing in a semi-circle 15 measures away. Outside the fence, a crowd of local workers and retirees grows larger. The mutant hisses at them. The protectors point their rifles at the creature, but they don't fire. All of this is against protocol. They should be killing her, *it*, and arresting me for being in the Yellow Zone without permission. But they're not. Many of the protectors have their visors up. There's something in their eyes, like they need me to do this, hand-to-hand, to prove that we too have power, to make my story about a dreg hero true.

Maybe the Calibration program we inserted is working. The mutant comes at me. *And maybe I need to focus on staying alive.*

I smash the baton against her face. My audience demands more, and I intend to show them how powerful I've become. I brace to deliver a skull-crushing blow.

Stop!

The thought is a combination of my mom, Nate, Bradie, Normand, and me. I hesitate. The lizard shakes her head as if the blow cleared something inside of her. She stops hissing and looks at the crowd differently. She appears... confused. Déjà vu haunts me. She gazes at me. In a voice that is disturbingly familiar, she whispers, "Puddle Pants?"

I stare into gold-flecked eyes I realized long ago camouflaged a monster. Now, the monster is revealed for everyone to see.

"Lilianne?" I murmur.

It can't be. Lilianne's not a mutated animal. She's a Supergenic, and I've been beating the crap out of her! That's an offense punishable by death. Then again, so are most of my offenses. But this time, I'm *really* caught, with dozens of witnesses. She sees the fear in my eyes. She looks back at the crowd. Is she searching for her parents? Her friends?

What is she doing here? Why does she look like this? The things Normand said about my unborn daughter dumped in the Yellow Zone, could they be true? Are the Supergenics doing this to their own? Out of all the fantasies I've had of kicking Lilianne's ass, I never imagined this.

Yes, you did, a part of me says.

I realize why all of this is so familiar.

"Venomerella," I whisper. Normand drew this—a version of it anyway—but I wrote the story.

Lilianne looks at me. I wait for her treacherous *I got you now* smile.

"Hit me," she says quietly.

"What?"

"Hit me, as hard as you can. Then you rescue me. Do you understand? Do *not* let them hurt me. Not again."

People are watching. The protectors see something's changed. The hovercrafts close in.

"Make it look good," she says. She lunges at me, hissing, "Come on Puddle Pants."

I swing my baton, smashing her one way, then again with a backhand. Twin cracks echo, joined by the ever-present rumbling of thunder.

Venomerella falls unconscious to the ground and loud cheers fill the air.

CHAPTER 35

The protectors chant my name. I always wanted the world to witness and acknowledge all the specialness within me. I didn't figure on it being like this. I drop the bloody baton. It clatters against asphalt. The anger and adrenaline dissolve, leaving me hollow.

None of this will help Bradie. None of this will fix my broken friendship with Normand. Mending things with my mom seems easy by comparison. And none of this explains what the eff Lilianne is doing here. I can't bring myself to believe Normand's story. I look at her unconscious, scale-covered form. With her eyes closed, she looks pure animal.

What did they do to you? I wonder. *All that jealousy over the years, and for what? To see her end up like this?*

A black-clad female agent leads a swarm of protectors through the gate. The shouts of my name die.

"Get that filth back!" she yells to her detail, pointing at the people gathered by the gate. Protectors with plastic shields grudgingly force the onlookers away. The red noose on her chest glares.

A protector assigned to the agent shoves me away from Lilianne. I expect them to shoot her like the mutant animal they believe her to be. Instead, they manacle her arms and legs, then toss her into a holding van.

Do not let them hurt me, Lilianne said. *Not again.*

I step toward the vehicle; the agent grabs my arm.

"You've got questions to answer."

Half-a-dozen of the agent's cadre surround me. I stare at the distorted reflection of my face in their visors. No one's cheering now, but the other protectors clench their weapons.

Are they thinking of helping me?

Six of them step forward. I shake my head, and they stop. The agent's protectors shove me into the back of a black SUV. The agent slides in next to me.

"I can explain," I say.

"You tell me *nothing*," she insists.

"I don't understand," I reply. "I thought—"

"That I was going to interrogate you?" she snorts. "Do I look like I have a death wish? You've pissed off some *very* important people. The Supergenics are sending a telepath to mind audit you and anyone who's been in contact with you, so whatever's in your head, keep it to yourself. I'm not going down with you."

I stare out the window at the river separating us from Jupitar City. A hovercraft with the lightning bolt insignia skims across the water toward the Cube.

This is about Lilianne, I realize. She's a secret—an important secret. When I hit her head, she changed. She was no longer a wild animal. *I'm supposed to think she's a mutant.* She was sent to keep us scared of what's outside the fence—at the cost of her life.

The Cube looms ahead of us. We disappear down a ramp and into the parking garage below. The protectors shackle my hands and throw a hood over my head. I stumble blindly until they shove me into a seat and yank off the covering. The restraints they leave on. The door hisses closed behind them. I'm alone, in a room of all black, lit by a purple glow that comes from the seams in the ceiling. The air is intentionally warm and damp. This is an interrogation chamber.

"You might as well make yourself comfortable," the female agent says over an intercom. "The telepath will be here shortly."

Normand claims it's possible to trick telepaths. Joshua said the same. Neither explained how.

I'm guessing an hour goes by before the door opens. The moment the man with the grey flecks in his hair steps in, I know I'm as good as dead. He wears a crisp uniform of blue with bands of yellow and carries a black case. It's the man from my Testing Day, the one who filled Joshua with pain and fear—and nearly killed me. It's Mole Man. His insignia is not a tester's, though. It's a lightning bolt atop a brain. He's a mind auditor.

"You," I say in surprise.

He arches a brow and sets the case on the floor. "We have never met," he says. "Though I understand your confusion. According to my records, my twin brother was in charge of the team that tested you. Fair warning, he's the weak one. All he can do with his abilities is cause pain. I'm capable of that and so much more."

"I'm not afraid of telepaths," I lie.

"You will be."

He's trying to scare me. He needn't bother. I'm terrified. I've heard the stories of mind auditors. Part weasel. Part snake. I'm the hen in the house. A one-way mirror along one wall gives me a view of how screwed I am.

"That was quite the display you put on out there," he says. "Hand-to-hand combat with a rabid mutant."

She's not a… I catch myself and start singing in my head.

Blue moon…

He grabs my throat with the swiftness of a viper and lifts my whole body out of the chair. He's impossibly strong. Despite all my training, I flail helplessly as he slams me to the floor. I try to kick him, but my mind is mush. Even shackled, I'm deadly, but all the moves ingrained in me are gone. He rips at my clothes, pawing at my breasts. His hand moves lower.

"Stop it!" I yelp like a pathetic mutt.

I'm back in the chair. Despite the experience of a second ago, I never left it. I pant, drenched in sweat. My uniform is exactly as it was when I walked into the room. Dirty, bloody, and ragged where Lilianne shredded it with her claws, but Mole Man's scarier brother hasn't added to the rips.

He is touching me, if barely, the tips of two fingers against my left temple.

"I can make you see and believe anything," he says. "I can fill your mind with all sorts of horrors—agents torturing your brother, your mother in an asylum, or worse. I can make you believe Bradie is healed. You'll be overjoyed by the miracle. And then I'll take it away, and you'll hear him scream from the pain of his burns, the endless skin grafts, the humiliation of soiling himself. Do you understand?"

I nod.

"Say it," he insists.

"I understand."

"Good. Then no more melodies or attempts to hide your thoughts. Say it again."

I force the words from my mouth. "I understand."

"You fought the mutant instead of calling for backup. Why?"

I don't dare hesitate or lie.

"I was angry."

"Yes, I see that. You had a fight with your socially awkward friend, Normand. You're in a store, surrounded by contraband. My, my, and you've been going there for some time now."

My fingers tighten into fists behind my back. A coil of blinding agony sears down my spine. A moment later, it's gone.

"Say you'll play nice," the mind auditor commands.

"I'll play nice," I say, panting and wincing at an echo of pain.

"Good girl. Now let's see. For some unfathomable reason, this Normand has developed an attachment to you, not that he's a prize himself. And you've infiltrated the Calibration system, implanting it with subversive programming. You've been a *very* naughty girl," the auditor says nonchalantly. "But that's not what I'm looking for. I've watched the security footage of you fighting the mutant. At the end, it looks like you're speaking with the creature."

"I—"

"Shhtt," he hushes me, raising a finger for silence. He moves his head to one side as if listening to a sound only he can hear. "There it is."

Against my will, I replay Lilianne staring at me with her gold-flecked brown eyes. *Do not let them hurt me*, she says. *Not again.*

His face darkens. "So you know," he says quietly. "Not everything, but far too much. What is it with the girls from this borough? Such troublemakers."

"Why?" I ask. "Why send Lilianne back to die? She's a Supergenic."

"We all have to follow the rules," he replies. "Lilianne was given everything—a new life, a new family, a new home, but she's proven... difficult."

I know I'm not leaving this room alive, but I won't go down without a fight. I try to launch myself from my chair, but nothing happens.

"I've cut off your access to the motor control centers of your mind," he explains. "It's time for you to serve your sentence. Mere execution is too simple."

He opens his black case and removes a needle filled with a glowing green liquid. "Most of the creatures who attack your borough *are* mutated animals grown in size and ferocity by the radiation unleashed by the Genetic Wars. Some form packs. A few are crafty or have powers. Occasionally they evolve into a new species. But it's not enough to convince you dregs you need us. Sometimes we give a helping hand. Peace is pricey."

He flicks the needle to get the air bubbles to rise to the top and squeezes the syringe until a drop of liquid dribbles out. "This won't give you powers, but it will turn you into a monstrosity. We'll set you loose on the outer fence, and the protectors will gun you down. It gives them a sense of purpose."

"You're evil," I seethe, futilely trying to fight the paralysis.

He snorts, sliding the needle into my vein.

"I forgot that you fancy yourself a hero. You are a terrorist."

He squeezes the syringe, sending green liquid toward my bloodstream.

The door hisses open; he looks in surprise. So do I. My head can still move. Normand stands there, dressed in his coveralls with the emblem of a computer and a screwdriver.

"The accomplice," the mind auditor says.

"Accomplice?" Normand snorts, drawing himself to his full height and speaking in an imperious tone, "I'm the mastermind."

I head butt the telepath. He staggers back, jerking the needle from my arm. Blood squirts; Normand hurries over and grabs a cotton ball from the black bag on the table and puts pressure on the pinprick in my skin.

"Forget that," I say. "Get him." I'm still furious with Normand, but, priorities.

"I will," Normand replies calmly. He tapes the cotton ball in place, then places his electronic skeleton key on my shackles. He pulls out his swipe pad, drags an icon of a key onto a lock, and my restraints pop open.

The telepath winces and touches his nose; his fingers come away bloody.

"I am going to eviscerate your minds," he says.

"You may begin with mine," Normand challenges.

He speaks with a cold finality I've never heard in him.

"Normand, you don't want him in your head," I warn.

"I'm fairly certain I do," Normand assures me.

He stands between the mind auditor and me, but not the way a protector would.

Fighter's stance, I want to bark at Normand, willing him to smash his e-pad across the auditor's arrogant face like a set of brass knuckles.

Normand looks down at himself, distractedly patting his coveralls as if he's lost something.

"Where did I put that…"

If this is a tactic, it works. The mind auditor hesitates, unsure what to make of this odd behavior, so different than the fear he's used to inspiring.

"What are you up to?" the mind auditor asks.

He's confused. Normand's mind is not so easy to read.

"You can't keep me out of your brain forever," the auditor says.

"I very much look forward to letting you in," Normand replies.

He pulls out a familiar metallic disc from a pocket.

"Catch," he says, tossing it at me. My fingers close around its smooth surface. It's from the outfit Normand wore at Revelry, the one that filled me with energy that temporarily linked me with all the protectors who were there. I could use that connection with my fellow protectors now, maybe use it to emotionally amp the Shadowren program we inserted during Calibration.

It's a futile hope. Normand's tech relied on physical touch with the protectors to create a conduit for the unifying energy to spread from me to them. So why would Normand give me the gadget?

Because he's already been through this, I realize, which means there *is* a way for me to reach the protectors with what's in this room and, I hope, trigger the Shadowren program we snuck into Calibration. I look at the mind auditor differently. He reads my thoughts.

"You think *you're* going to use *me* as a conduit to connect with the protectors in this base to activate some silly story you've embedded in them?" he snorts. "You're going to be a catatonic drooling imbecile by the time I'm done with—"

I don't let him finish. I grab his wrist.

"Bring it," I say.

CHAPTER 36

I wait for light to emerge from the disc in my hand, filling me so I can use the mind auditor's telepathic abilities to reach the protectors. Nothing happens. At Revelry, Normand had his custom processor pod. Do I need that to make this work? The auditor smiles wickedly. He twists his hand and clamps his fingers around my forearm.

Pain sears through me. My fingers spasm; the metal disc clatters on the black floor, and I drop to my knees. I scream. Normand fiddles with his e-pad.

"And... activate," he says.

Through a haze of tears, I catch the nimbus glow growing around the disc. I grasp it, and the energy flows into me, pushing the pain away. Luminescence dances along my skin, penetrating my veins, my cells, my synapses. I pull forward the image of Shadowren from the data pod that is my mind. In the mirror on the wall, I see the radiance around me change, growing wings, beak, and a forked tail.

I imagine that image clawing its way into the auditor, and through his telepathic power, reaching the protectors in the Cube. I expect it to be like diving into a pool; I slam into a brick wall.

"Stupid girl," the auditor mocks. "You thought a mere dreg could turn my power against me? Allow me to show you how it's done."

He grins and scorches me with deeper pain. I howl in agony—and defiance. I lock more firmly onto my Shadowren self and push back. The pain gives me strength. I grit my teeth, dig in my heels, and with a will I didn't know I possessed, I force the light into the auditor.

The wall keeping me out crumbles, and the mind auditor's form glows. Through him, I sense the protectors in the Cube. At least, I think I can. It's subtler than group Calibration. Is it enough to trigger them? I imagine Shadowren in all her fierceness. I'm about to send her out into their minds; the metal disc glows brighter, and... its light dies out. The sense of unity with the protectors fizzles, and the shadowren silhouette evaporates.

The mind auditor barks a laugh. "You failed." He grabs me by the throat, nails digging into the side of my jaw. I squirm.

"Oh, the fun I'm going to have with—"

A deafening boom drowns his words. The room rocks. Dust filters from the ceiling. He staggers, loses his grip on me, and falls to one knee. I hear gunfire and shouting.

"Kazamo," Normand says.

The auditor stares at the ceiling as if he sees through it.

"It can't be," he says in shock. "The protectors are rebelling."

"Some of them," Normand agrees.

"No," the mind auditor insists. "I stopped her psychic transmission."

"Indeed," Normand replies. "And you were wise to disengage the cameras and mics from this room. But I turned them back on. While Caitlin distracted you, I broadcasted your interrogation to the entire compound. They know what you've been doing to children like Lilianne—the ones you were supposed to be taking to a better life, the ones you changed and sent back for the protectors to kill. Many protectors are *pissed*." He says this with bad-boy emphasis. "Most of them take pride in protecting us from the dangers outside the fence. Turns out, that's you."

A third explosion goes off above us. The mind auditor's disbelief transforms to rage.

"You have no idea what you've done!" he shouts, grabbing Normand's face in both his hands. "I will destroy you for this!"

Yet it's the mind auditor's eyes that twitch. "What... what are you?"

"I've lived the future," Normand explains calmly. "Many of them."

"That... that's not possible," the auditor says.

He tries to pull his hands away, but Normand grabs the auditor's forearms and holds him fast.

"Normand, what are you doing?" I ask.

"I'm showing him everything," he replies.

"But you can't," I say. "You said telepaths have a blind spot for your..." What did he call it? A temporal anomaly?

His wheezing laugh turns into a racking cough. Blood trickles from his nose—and the mind auditor's.

"The divides in my mind, the segregation of memories from past, present, and future, from all the timelines that once were but will never be, it's all collapsing together. The cell membranes are breaking down. My synapses are misfiring. Things are leaking all over the places as the quantum singularity in my brain implodes."

"Normand, you have to stop," I say. "Please!"

Whatever anger he sparked in me before is gone; I can be furious with him *after* he lives. He shakes his head.

"I told you my powers would kill me one day. *Really* kill me. Today is that day. No more do-overs."

The mind auditor and Normand cough blood in unison, spraying each other with red droplets. They both lower to their knees.

"Please," the auditor begs, his eyes blinking uncontrollably. "Please stop."

"My brain's pulling you in," Normand responds. "Like a black hole. Hurts, doesn't it?"

Normand chokes. Blood bubbles out of his and the auditor's mouths.

"Tastes like iron," Normand says.

"Don't go," I say, grabbing his shoulder. "I take back everything I said. You know how to love more than anyone, and you'll never be alone because you'll always have me."

He pauses. "Sounds like you love me too."

I nod vigorously. "I do. I love you. Now stop. Stop downloading from the future, be here with me now."

"I'm not downloading from the future because I have no more futures. I'm uploading from the pasts that were my futures. All those memories, of timelines redone, of moments never to be, they're all coming back."

"It's too much," the auditor sobs.

"He's right," Normand agrees. "The human mind, even a Supergenic one, even an oddity like me, can only handle so much."

"You can't die here," I insist. "You told me all about things yet to come. That means you live through this."

He and the auditor cough more blood in unison. When Normand talks, the auditor says the same on the slightest of delays. It gives Normand an otherworldly echo.

"I lived longer some times," Normand says, his voice more mechanical than ever. He stares at the auditor's forehead. "Different decisions, different outcomes, different life expectancies."

"But then how do you know this is the right decision if you don't see how it turns out?!"

They shrug. "I don't. I'm neither omniscient nor omnipotent. I can't be everywhere, everywhen. I've done what I can to be of service, but this is your story. You must see it to its finale."

"How can you say that when you've been pulling my strings this whole time?" I demand. "You don't get to abandon me after turning my whole life into a predetermined sham!"

I pant, buffeted by rage, fear of abandonment, and a sense of betrayal.

"Non-time travelers," Normand sighs, "you're so linear." Next to him, the auditor stops speaking in tandem, lost in some psychic hole. Normand ignores him. "Yes, Caitlin, when I deemed it safe, I prodded you so we could skip over filler and get to the good parts, such as you coming up with the idea of Venomerella."

My swirling emotions freeze. "And then Lilianne showed up covered in scales."

"My resets can cause déjà vu. That likely offered you inspiration. But freewill was always yours. When I changed circumstances to steer you in a new direction, you found ways to circumvent me. You're very frustrating."

"*I'm* frustrating?"

"Indeed," he agrees. "Your every move, left or right, fight or flee, live or die, was yours to make."

"Live or die," I murmur. I remember Testing Day and imagine the spinning hula hoop tearing me apart. "If you hadn't warned me, Mole Man would've... I died, didn't I?"

Normand nods gravely.

"You gave me a second chance."

"I gave you *many* chances," Normand says in an accusatory tone. "Finding a way to convince you to willingly accept your genetic limitations took numerous rewinds, forcing me to relive my testing dozens of times."

I think of how battered he was, and yet he went back, repeatedly, for me.

"Wait," I say, mapping the events of Testing Day. As if we were hashing out an issue of *Shadowren*, nerd Caitlin takes over. I point out the flaws in his narrative. "You were tested;" I raise my thumb, "you returned to class beaten up;" I lift my pointing finger, followed by my middle, ring finger, and pinky as I count the beats, "I helped you to your desk; you begged me to live; I left with the testers. When you found out I'd died..."

It's so weird saying that.

"... why rewind all the way to your testing?" I curl in my thumb. "Why not stop and hit play *post*-testing to avoid it altogether?"

Normand *harumphs*. "Are you asking me to explain the finer points of temporal mechanics with my dying breath?"

"Kind of," I admit.

"I already told you. Time is—"

"Tricky," I finish for him, pretending to grasp 'the finer points.'

"Correct," he coughs, "and rife with danger. By repeatedly circling to the same moment, I caught myself in a loop. I barely broke free."

I remember Normand at his desk, spasming over and over.

"That's what you meant when you said you couldn't go back for another round of testing." I shiver at the thought of him trapped in that nightmare, circling through testing over and over.

"I gave up on you," Normand admits. "When you returned, I couldn't believe my glasses."

"I didn't want to believe it either." I relive how crushed I was to be on the DNA-regular side of the Gen M divide. So much has happened since then—more than once, apparently. As if in my own time loop, key moments flash through my dreg brain as I try, and fail, to make sense of this Supergenic mind storm.

"I don't get it," I say.

Normand tilts his head quizzically. Apparently, I can still surprise him.

"Why would you go to so much trouble to save me? Unless…"

I appraise him. His leg brace, stilted speech, and OCD make it easy to forget he's lived who knows how many times. The auditor spasms and spits blood in the wake of Normand's assault, reminding me he's not some vulnerable innocent. He's a time-traveling, computer-hacking, mind auditor-killing genius; he knows things, and knowledge is power.

But what might he have learned about me that would make me special enough to risk a time loop? My cheeks harden, and my fingers curl into fists.

"You bragged to the auditor that you're the mastermind."

"I couldn't resist one last dramatic entrance," he agrees proudly.

Another explosion rocks the compound.

"You know the Supergenics will come here to end this revolt," I insist. "That's what you want. This is an elaborate trap—for Captain Light, I bet. After so many lives, you must have all kinds of grudges. But you couldn't have done it without my brainwaves disrupting Calibration. *That's* why you needed me to survive Testing Day."

I wait for Normand to stammer in denial or laugh maniacally in admission.

"You read too many comic books. If I wanted to quash Captain Light," he sounds older as he tilts his nose with imperial arrogance, "I wouldn't require you, and it would be cataclysmic beyond your imagination."

Before I can respond, Normand shudders; his tone and expression soften.

"Apologies," he says. "I *do* need you, but not for a revenge stratagem or world-altering machinations."

My hands clench. "Liar."

"Caitlin, I'm dying. What kind of trap is that?"

"You're *not* dying!" I shout in denial. He waits for me to accept the truth. He avoids my eyes, but I see it in his. I go numb. All I can feel are my fists. "But… if you're not using me for some plot, why risk everything for me?"

"Is it not obvious?" he asks. He's not being rhetorical.

"No, Normand, it's not!"

He shrugs. "I wanted to be friends."

Of all the answers I might have predicted, it was not that. "That's so—"

"Pathetic?" he offers.

"Human." I consider my own social isolation before joining cadets. I rub at my eyes with my knuckles. "Being the only one to remember all those timelines, it must be—"

"Magnificent," he says grandly. His voice softens. "But also lonely."

Can his motivation really be that teenager?

"No," I say. I was a loser; no one would want to be my friend that badly—would they? "There *has* to be more to it. Infiltrating the Calibration system—"

"Was always your idea," Normand says. "I participated so we could spend time together on a new project."

"You used *Tigara* to turn me into Shadowren," I insist.

"You aren't Shadowren because of *Tigara,*" he corrects. "I gave *Tigara* to you *because* you are Shadowren."

I struggle to wrap my head around this. "So when you took me to the Lair—"

"I wished to share it with a fellow connoisseur of the graphic arts."

"What about the time when—"

"Caitlin Feral," Normand interrupts, sounding disturbingly like Mrs. Cranberry. "It's time travel. Don't overthink it."

"But—"

"I know you don't remember those other lifetimes," Normand sighs. He sounds impossibly tired. "And you question the decisions of this one, especially the ones that hurt Bradie, but try to accept, you *are* worth saving."

His words are a sucker punch to my gut. *Do I really think so little of myself?* I remember how willing I was to give up everything to Manifest. I dug deep to achieve that goal—and died. That's the value I put on me without superpowers. Thanks to Normand, I got one last chance to dig deeper. I didn't strike gold, but I did hit something solid.

"I… I needed a friend, too," I admit, speaking my 'pathetic' truth.

"*Te gratissimum*," Normand replies.

Plasma blasts echo. I need to get out there, but I can't leave him.

"This last life was one of the good ones," Normand assures me. "*Exempli gratia*, Bradie and I became friends. I did not see that coming. And I achieved my goal—I was a hero, not a villain."

I don't want to ask, but I do, "Does it hurt?"

"The temporal anomaly in my brain is collapsing," he and the auditor reply, once more talking together with a slight delay. That can't be good. "It pinches. But there is an odd beauty to it. My lives are flashing before me, and I confess, I find myself thinking how nice it would be to fall in love one more time. Oh, and Revelry. The music was too loud and the lights too flashy, but making out with Crystal was *awesome*."

The Bradie-speak makes me smile. Blood dribbles from Normand's and the auditor's ears.

"And here I thought I was the only girl you liked."

"I like lots of girls," they say. "I'm a dude, remember?" More Bradie-speak. Such a pair of tools. I think that is Normand's dying breath, yet in death, as in life, he finds a way to be verbose. I wish he'd go on talking forever.

"I've been thinking about how to help Bradie," Normand and the auditor say together. "I've made arrangements. I hope they work out."

"What do you mean arrangements?" I ask.

"No time to elaborate," they say. "Take my skeleton key and electronic pad. The GRAMS are very intuitive, and you've used them in other timelines. Even if you don't consciously remember, on a sub-atomic level, some déjà vu may help. Also, I've left a surprise for you. Don't ask."

I clench my jaw to keep it shut.

"And, remember," they say, "*Nunc futuri*."

"Future now," I echo.

He and the auditor burp, blood bubbles from their mouths, and they collapse dead to the floor.

CHAPTER 37

"Normand? Normand!" I kneel next to him; I shake him; I press repeatedly on his chest and breathe into his mouth like the medics taught.

"Come on!" I yell, pounding harder on his sternum.

The door behind me hisses open. I don't look. I don't turn. I keep trying to save Normand. I know it's too late—for us both. I wait for the pop of a gun and the sharp smack of a bullet blasting open the back of my skull.

A hand squeezes my shoulder. My instincts kick in. I grab and throw the person over me, grasp the needle with the glowing green liquid, and press it to Eel Man's throat. He holds his hands up in peace.

"I'm ever so glad we're on the same side," he says.

I whip the needle into the corner and get off him. He jumps to his feet. My hand shakes.

"What's happening out there?" I ask.

"Half the base is fighting the other half."

My brain's working fast.

"The other bases are sending attack squads against us, aren't they?"

He nods.

"We'll be slaughtered." My voice is matter of fact. I sound like Normand. I look at his lifeless face covered in blood. I don't want to leave him here. I also don't want his sacrifice, his *many* sacrifices, over countless lifetimes, to be in vain.

"The base is the most secure stronghold we've got. If we manage to take it, how long do you think we can hold out?" I ask.

"Against other protectors? A few days. Against Supergenics? An hour, if we're lucky."

I nod. They'll burn us in fire, light, and acid; they'll choke us with toxic gases; they'll shred us with claws and pulverize us with brute strength. Our bullets will bounce off flesh made of organic steel. Our cries for mercy will be lost in sonic screams turning our brains to pulp. Our carcasses will be strung up and used as an example to any dregs who would defy those more powerful than themselves.

We could run, but never fast enough to outrace their speedsters, flyers, and teleporters. We could hide, but they'd find us with sniffers, readers, and trackers. And, it won't only be those of us who picked up arms who will suffer; it will be our families as well—the entire borough.

I say the unthinkable.

"We have to surrender."

The agent looks at me in shock.

"We won't get another chance like this," he says.

"The only chance we have of winning," I reply, "is to give up."

"You're not making any sense," he says.

He's probably right, but I look at Normand to find my courage. He gave me this one last reset. I have to try something new. Surrender is the last thing I would ever do—so here's me doing it, I'm assuming for the first time.

"I've got a plan," I insist.

I talk fast. The agent nods, mumbling "very well" and "indeed" in a way that lets me know he's getting it.

"It's rather daring," he says when my torrent of words finally ebbs.

"It might work," I say more defensively than I intend.

"Perhaps," he agrees.

I close Normand's eyes. *I'll come back for you*, I promise him, *if I survive*.

"Your friend did an utterly brave thing," Eel Man says.

"Brave doesn't cover it," I reply, wiping the weakness water from my eyes. I force myself to turn my back on Normand. "All right. Where are the holding cells?"

"You're quite certain about this?" he asks.

"We need her," I reply.

"She's one of *them*, you know."

"No," I disagree. "She's Generation Manifestation. She's one of us."

Tectonic plates seem to shift in the agent's head.

"Very well," he concedes. "Go save the lizard girl. If you'll excuse me, I've got a rebellion to destroy."

CHAPTER 38

The agent and I sprint down a hallway in opposite directions. I use Normand's swipe pad. A blinking dot leads me through the maze of underground corridors. Unlike him, I don't have the place memorized. I think of him dead on the ground. His blood is on my lips from the mouth-to-mouth. I sprint harder to run from the memory. The world mimics my volatile emotions, and a wall explodes in front of me, throwing me off my feet. I hit the floor, ears ringing.

A group of rebel protectors back out of the opening. They fire rifles and are fired upon. A pair of them kneels and provides cover for the rest. Once clear, they break and run toward me. The one in the lead sees me and points a blaster at my face. He's not wearing a helmet. He's young, barely older than me, hair shaved to stubble. Handsome. I hold my hands up.

"You're the girl from the broadcast," he says, lowering his weapon.

"Assemble!" someone shouts. He turns and kneels along with the rest of his cadre. They fire at a squad brandishing plasma rifles, the *wuppa-wuppa* of their automatic weapons thudding in my ears. I duck against the wall. A plasma beam bursts through the air, barely missing my face. I smell scorched hair, skin, and muscle. The rebel protector who recognized me is on his back, staring at the ceiling, a charred hole the size of a fist burnt through his chest.

"Retreat!" someone orders, and the surviving rebels fall back. I lie next to the dead, pretending to be one of them.

Loyalists give chase, their boots beating the ground. Black soles run past my nose, heading toward more gunfire, shouts, screams, the twanging sound of plasma bursts, and someone yelling, "To me!"

I struggle to my feet and step over the bodies, expecting pools of blood. A few splatters is all. The plasma beams cauterized the wounds even as they tore through the protectors' vital organs. I stagger, sweating, panting, looking over my shoulder for fear of what might be coming behind. The corridor bends to the left. I turn, and a pair of women stumble into me. One is a protector. She grasps her bleeding shoulder and can barely hold her injured arm to point her gun at me. Her visor is cracked, and a cut crosses one leg. She's been in a knife fight.

222

Sewzanne holds her up.

"You," the medic sneers. "You've destroyed us."

I'm not her favorite anymore. The injured protector's finger tenses on the trigger. I become a thing of violence. My leg whips, kicking the gun from the protector's hand. She growls, coming at me. My punch to her injured shoulder distracts her. I smack the side of her helmet, and her bulletproof visor recedes. I stare into her surprised eyes, swelling with bruises. Her nose is broken. I think she'd be pretty on a better day. I grab her other gun from its holster and shoot her in the forehead.

I point the weapon at Sewzanne.

"Mango is the new tango," she says.

The switch flicks in my brain.

She smiles. "Kill yourself."

I'm far away as I point the gun at my head.

"Ironic, isn't it?" Sewzanne fishes in the pocket of her lab coat and pulls out Normand's spherical data pod, the one we used to hijack the calibration system, the one she clearly found—too late. She holds Normand's tech like it's rotting meat. "There are protectors who have cast off years of programming after your little worm got inside my calibrator, but not you. You're my prize pupil. You soaked up my Calibration like a sponge. You tried to overwrite it with your silly story, and you failed."

The barrel of the weapon I hold is cold against my temple.

"You can't make me do anything I don't want to do," I say. "You said so yourself."

"I fibbed a bit." She holds the thumb and index finger of her free hand a space apart. "With the pharmachemicals and a bit of psychoanalysis to identify your trigger points, we can make you want to do pretty much anything—once I know what buttons to push. Info flash—I know all your buttons. For instance, you want to kill yourself because of all the horrible things you've done."

I think of Normand. I think of Bradie. I think of abandoning my mom and Nate. Sewzanne sees it in my eyes.

"That's it," she says. "Punish yourself."

Sewzanne is right. I deserve to die. I squeeze the trigger, more relieved than afraid. Finally, I'm going to pay for my failures. Finally, this can all stop. My finger tenses, I hear the pop of the gun firing, and Sewzanne falls dead at my feet. Standing behind her is her subordinate CeeCee, a smoking sidearm in her hand. The data pod rolls and stops next to my foot. I continue pressing the gun to my temple.

"Lower your weapon, soldier," CeeCee says.

"I can't," I say. My arm's frozen in place.

"You're stronger than the Chair's programming."

I press the gun more firmly against my head.

CeeCee takes a deep breath. "I've seen the story you've written for yourself. You're not Caitlin Feral, you're Shadowren. And this is not how or when Shadowren dies."

The medic's words flick another switch in my brain. Normand's drawing of that red- and black-clad renegade comes to life in my mind—strong, focused, and relentless. The gun trembles against my temple. It would be so easy to end it all.

You're not done fighting, Shadowren says to me.

That may be true, and yet my finger pulls on the trigger.

I call to mind that moment in the audit room, when I grew wings of light and a sharp Shadowren beak. I imagine her essence welling inside of me, and she says, *You are worth saving*.

My trigger finger relaxes. The barrel of the weapon pulls away from my skull, and my arm drops limply; the gun shakes against my thigh.

Under different circumstances, I suspect CeeCee would take the weapon from me for my own safety. Not today.

"Go," she says. "Finish what you've started."

I run. I use Normand's e-pad and GRAMS to follow the Cube's layout. Blinking dots tell me where most of the protectors are located, helping me avoid the fighting. It's not perfect. Not everyone's in uniform; the ones in their sweats when the battle broke out don't show on my screen, but I steer clear of the worst of the conflict. I see clusters of dots wink out as other clusters of dots annihilate them.

The Supergenics won't have to kill us, I realize. *We're killing each other.*

I reach the holding cells. Doors are open all along the hallway. My heart spasms. I'm too late. I walk slowly, looking in each room, gun at the ready. Each chamber holds a thin sleeping mat on the cold floor, a refuse bucket reeking of human waste, and a dead political prisoner dressed in a coarse, sack-like garment. Most of the victims are skeletal, making the most food-deprived members of our borough seem meaty.

The first few look like they were made to kneel before being shot in the back of the head. The further I go, the more rushed the executions became. Two tried crawling to the door before bleeding out.

I search for one body in particular, covered in scales. My heart hammers harder. I don't see her. Lilianne is not among the dead, or so I pray. I used to mock my mom for clinging to superstitions, but not now. If there is a God, please let Lilianne be alive—or many more of us will end up like this.

The hall seems to end, but I spot a nearly undetectable door, given away by the slight seam where it connects with the wall. I place Normand's skeleton key atop a hidden push pad. The door opens. Inside, lights flicker from a power surge, illuminating a full surgical suite, including an operating table and vicious-looking tools for poking, prodding, and cutting. A knocked-over tray of scalpels and needles litters the floor.

Beyond is a holding room made of clear, impregnable glass. The pen is stark, with barely enough room to walk six paces between a bench and a rubberized bucket for relieving oneself. Otherwise, the cell is empty.

"Mother effer."

A patch of fuzziness appears on the grey plastic wall of the prison. A blurry outline steps forward and solidifies into Lilianne's green-scaled form. She presses her webbed hand to the glass. Her claws don't make a scratch. She's saying something, but I can't hear her. I use the skeleton key, and the barrier slides back.

"It's about bloody time," she snorts. Even as a lizard, she has a way of making me feel inadequate. Despite her words and tone, she wraps her sinewy arms around me and hugs me tight against her surprisingly smooth scales.

"Let's get out of here," I say as we disengage.

She picks a scalpel off the floor. I step back, gun raised. She pays no mind, feeling around on the side of her skull.

"There it is," she says.

She cuts into herself.

"They were controlling me..." she pauses, concentrating. "...with this." She pulls out a small metal chip. I must have disrupted it when I hit her with my baton. She crushes it and drops the remains of the bloody circuit into a metal bowl.

"There," she says. "That's better."

"Good," I say. "Now, we have to get you out of here."

CHAPTER 39

"What's the plan?" Lilianne asks.

"Stand by," I reply.

I look at Normand's swipe pad and flick to the home screen. A slew of icons are on it—all of them his personalized GRAMS. One is of a ninja wearing a headset. Underneath, it says COMMS.

"I hope this works," I say.

Lilianne blinks at me with eyes that still incite jealousy. What can I say? They're more gorgeous than ever against the green of her skin, which ripples with flecks of gold.

"What do you mean, you *hope* it works?" she asks.

"It'll work," I reply, trying to sound more confident than I am. I press on the ninja's face and up come audio feeds from all over the base.

"… we're pinned down! I repeat, we are pinned down…"

"… we need back up!"

"… the rebels are targeting the munitions depot…"

And screams, lots of them.

I double-tap to silence the voices; they continue echoing in my head.

"What's happening?" Lilianne asks.

"Chaos," I reply.

"So, we use that to get out."

"It's not that simple," I reply.

"It is for me," she says, walking toward the door.

"You won't make it," I warn, searching Normand's e-pad. I double-tap an icon of a guy with antique binoculars for eyes. Underneath, it says CAMS. Hundreds of security feeds pop up in quick succession, showing me every camera view in the building.

"Effing eff, Normand," I curse. "I don't need to see this much."

"Now that I've got that chip out of my head, they won't find me or hurt me ever again," Lilianne insists.

Normand's right about his GRAMs being intuitive and there is a weird familiarity. I don't know about subatomic déjà vu, but the programs operate not that differently to the protector communications software I use every day. Still, I'm nowhere near as adept as Normand with his tech. I close one security feed at a time, far too slow in my search for something I can use. I miss Normand looking at his watch, counting down.

"I wouldn't be so sure of an easy get away," I say to Lilianne.

I show her the pad, and we gaze at an armored short-range jet landing on the roof. A lightning bolt stenciled on the side of the craft glitters next to the letters A.M.M.O. The jet's starboard door opens, unfurling a set of stairs. Five Supergenics emerge, clearly identifiable by their silver suits with a lightning bolt emblazoned on their chests. Captain Light is among them.

"No," Lilianne says. "No, no, no. I won't let them get me. I won't!"

She trembles, tears welling in her eyes.

"They won't," I say, hoping to eff I can keep my promise. *Please let this work.*

I swipe faster through the camera feeds.

"Come on, come on," I say. I find what I'm looking for—a group of agents and protector loyalists firing at a small cadre of rebel protectors and cadets defending the communications bay. I minimize the rest of the windows and look for another GRAM. I see one with a stylized version of my Shadowren mask. It's labeled, CAITLIN, USE THIS ONE.

"We have to get out of here," Lilianne says.

"No," I reply. "We have to wear a mask."

She looks at me like I've hit my head.

Normand would've gotten my comic book speak, I think defensively.

Lilianne and I may be allies, but I doubt we'll ever be friends.

I drag the Shadowren icon atop the window with the rebels and loyalists fighting each other. Another window pops up. A computerized voice says aloud, "Establishing COMM link. COMM link established."

"Flank the rebels!" their leader orders. I've patched into the loyalist's communications bandwidth.

"Normand, you brilliant, beautiful bastard," I whisper.

"Pin them down!" a loyalist shouts.

"Belay that order," I say in a commanding tone.

"Who the hell is this?" the loyalist yells at me.

"Check my i-dent specialist," I snap. I cringe in the intervening silence. Lilianne has an "I didn't know you had it in you" look on her face. I'm betting (and hoping) that Normand's program has created a false authentication signature for my audiograph.

In a corner of the screen, I watch the feed of Captain Light pointing at something on the roof.

We're running out of time, I imagine Normand saying.

"What are your orders?" the agent asks.

"Reroute to the roof. We've got rebels up there about to take the whole Cube down," I reply. "They're armed with blasters and explosives. You need to go in hot. I repeat. You need to go in hot. You open fire immediately. Understood?"

"Understood," he says. We watch the loyalists pull back and disappear into a stairwell.

"You think they're going to shoot at Supergenics?" Lilianne asks.

"They will if they don't realize they're Supergenic," I reply.

I look at an icon of a ghost inside a red circle with a line through it. I think of Normand in his Ghost Fighters costume. The GRAM is labeled VISUAL RECONFIGURATOR.

What seems a lifetime ago, before I was put in an accelerated learning chair, when I was mousy Caitlin Feral walking home from the library with a contraband issue of *Tigara*, Normand used this GRAM to fool a protector into seeing a bureau-approved comic book. Now it's my turn.

"Here goes everything," I say.

I drag the icon over the image of the loyalist squadron headed to the roof. A dozen windows activate, and I see what they see inside their visors—a 360-degree digital view of their surroundings. Since it's code, I can manipulate it, like the Protectorate manipulated me into executing the woman trying to flee with her Supergenic son.

"You screw with me," I say. "Now, I screw with you."

A few taps of my fingers, and it's done. The loyalists reach the roof and blow open the door. Normand's swipe pad feeds a false image to their visors. Instead of Supergenics, they see a group of rebel protectors.

"Open fire!" I shout.

They do. Bullets and plasma beams fly.

One of the silver-clad members of A.M.M.O. is hit and falls. The other Supergenics cringe, ducking in fear and surprise. Captain Light's photonic force field pops up around them. The spray of bullets and the undulating power streams bounce off, right back at the loyalist protectors. They're wearing protective suits, but the backlash packs a punch. Copper-clad protectors stagger, grunt in pain, and clutch themselves where they've been hit. The smarter of the loyalists realize something's wrong. I've disabled their microphones, so they can barely hear each other through their helmets, but several of them slide their visors back. They stare in horror at the Supergenics.

"Hold fire! Hold fire!" someone shouts. More visors open, revealing growing looks of terror. Guns are placed on the roof and hands go up in surrender. Captain Light's energy shield drops, and a man with red blistered skin steps forward. He holds his palms toward the loyalists and blasts them with fire. They scream, and their smoldering body suits fall around skeletons of brittle ash.

CAM windows go dark one by one as their helmets burst from the heat. I take a shuddering breath.

"What am I doing?" I ask.

Lilianne puts a webbed hand on top of mine. "What you have to." We're both shaking. I'm not sure if she's trying to convince herself or me. I think of Normand. I think of Bradie. I think of Nate.

"We can't change the world in a day," I rationalize. "But I *will* make sure this rebellion has a tomorrow."

I find a second band of loyalist troops on the swipe pad, then a third, and a fourth. I take another ragged breath. *This isn't their fault*, I reason. I ignore the guilty side of me and send hundreds of people to the roof to die.

CHAPTER 40

Their screams rise through the COMM link. They will haunt me, like so much else I've done. Maybe I can blame this on Sewzanne and her Calibration. Maybe. I turn to Lilianne.

"Now, we go."

We escape through a combination of service tunnels and air shafts, using cunning, cruelty, and luck. Normand's e-pad shows me which way to go, but, without Lilianne, I wouldn't get far. She blends with the walls and strikes at bands of loyalists without mercy. With her chameleon abilities, she's practically invisible. A dozen protectors block a hatch we need to access. She slithers from a vent and knocks them off their feet. Her tail chokes one while her claws slice another across the throat.

She ducks and dodges bullet fire, turning one guy into a human shield. His body shudders under a spray of slugs. She careens off the walls then clings and drops from the ceiling. She reaches her arm over her head and grabs a chin as she lands, jerking it and filling the air with the sound of a snapping neck. The dead protector falls. His baton flies from her hand, hitting one woman while Lilianne drop kicks another. It takes less than a minute.

And she wasn't lying about not being trackable. She can hide her thermogenic signature. She's silent as death. For all I know, even telepaths can't detect her. No wonder they put a chip in her and sent her to die—they don't want people they can't control.

We reach the Cube's outer wall. I push open an emergency exit; thunder cracks the air, and lightning flares on the other side of the security fence.

"I never thought I'd miss that sound," Lilianne says.

The chaos inside the compound is matched outside. Loyalists and rebels shoot wildly at each other. Lilianne pulls me inside the door and points upward. Captain Light blazes off the roof and into the sky. Small balls of luminescence drop from his body, falling several measures before coming alive and blasting into the mouths of fighters on both sides. Their bodies glow and spasm as the photonic pellets beat them to death from the inside. He can't tell friend from foe, so he kills them all.

I huddle down. On the swipe pad, I open a file labeled INTEL, revealing a slew of personnel folders, including ones for me, Bradie, and Normand. Another is labeled AGENTS. I open that. A whack of headshots pop up of people dressed in black. I find the agent who got me into this in the first place—Eel Man. AGENT SAMSON, it says. It's the first time I've seen his name. I want to read everything about him—later. I patch through to him.

"Agent Samson," I say.

"Caitlin," he replies. "You're alive." I'm not sure if he's surprised, irritated, or relieved.

"You need to surrender to the Supergenics," I say. "Convince them of your loyalty before they slaughter everyone."

I can't understand his garbled reply. I have no idea if my message went through, or if he remains in command of the communication center. I want to go back to protect Bradie, but I have my mission. If it fails, we're all of us done.

"Come on," I say to Lilianne, and we scurry for the fence.

We escape into the Yellow Zone through a section in the chainlink damaged by the fighting. Once we're in the broken city, Lilianne all but disappears, her green scales shifting color to blend with the busted concrete. I'm far more conspicuous. Fortunately, no one is paying attention to what's beyond the fence.

The sounds of gunfire, explosions, and screams grow distant, but don't disappear. I jump over a crumbling wall and freeze. We're not alone out here.

I point my gun. A family stares at me—two Moms and twin boys with stuffed travel bags, eyes filled with fear. I lower my gun.

"What are you doing here?" I demand.

Mom One's mouth works soundlessly, trying to force a plausible lie. The answer is obvious. They're runners, taking advantage of the chaos to escape from the boroughs. They're headed for certain death, or so we've been told.

I remember the woman I executed as she tried to flee with her Supergenic son. Free of Sewzanne, I make my own choice, and I leave these moms to theirs.

"Good luck," I say. I hope they make it out there, beyond the Protectorate's squeezing grip and the Supergenics' choking leash.

They scramble away, unable to believe I'm letting them go. I don't look back.

We reach the Lair. I will always call it that, and it belongs to Normand and me, never mine alone.

Lilianne grabs my arm. "Your scent, it's all over the place. I think this is what drew me here when I attacked you."

"There are no coincidences," I reply.

"But I'm smelling a male as well," she says. "Stronger than the rest."

"Yes," I say sadly. *Normand should be here.* "I know."

I open the door. Lilianne goes ahead, slithering down the stairs. I follow, closing the entrance behind me. Down in the store, I clap, but the lights don't turn on. Have they been damaged? If so, I have no idea how to fix them—or anything. How long will this place survive without Normand to keep it running? A worry for another time, if I should live so long. I bump into Lilianne. Her tense body's a wall of muscle. I feel weak next to her.

You hold your own, I assure myself.

"Someone's here," she says. I turn on my flashlight. Her large nostrils on her tiny nose flutter rapidly.

A faint *whuzzphm whuzzphm* sound breaks the silence.

Dart gun!

Lilianne grunts and bumps into me drunkenly. I grab her, but my grip slides off her smooth scales; she thumps to the floor.

The tiny lights on strings come to life. Trenton emerges from behind the counter with the register. Lilianne said she smelled a male. She wasn't talking about Normand.

"It wasn't easy finding your hiding place," Trenton says. "But I kept wondering, how did Caitlin get to that lizard mutant so fast? And what was Caitlin doing on the wrong side of the fence? I checked the sensor logs, and there's no record of you passing through a gate, and the motion detectors didn't pick you up until all of a sudden, you were just there. Led me to the front door. And now here you are *with* the mutant."

I knew one day we'd outsmart ourselves with Normand's technology tricks, foolishly believing we were beating the system, but it never occurred to me Trenton would be the one who figured it out.

He fires the dart gun at me.

Whuzzphm whuzzphm whuzzphm.

I drop and roll. Three darts hit the wall. He tosses the gun with its empty cartridge aside.

"Trenton, don't do this," I say. "Bradie—"

"You don't get to say his name," Trenton growls. "He's why I'm here. I would do anything for that kid. *Anything*. Because of you, he'll never walk again; he'll have a bag for a gut; he'll be lucky if he ever forms a complete sentence. You took my brother from me."

"I love him, too," I say.

Weakness water wells in Trenton's eyes.

"You love him? Really? You think as much as me? Did Bradie tell you how he got the scars on his arm?" he asks.

I swallow hard, thinking of how vulnerable Bradie felt letting me hold his injured hand, and how pained he was by the wound long after it physically healed. There were the scars I could see, and then there were the other ones.

"He told me that was his punishment," I say. "For firing a weapon."

"Do you want to hear the whole story?" Trenton asks. His jaw juts.

My heart hammers. *Yes*, I want to reply.

"No," I say to my surprise. "That's for Bradie to tell or not tell."

"That's where you're wrong," Trenton replies. "*I* did that to him. Literally and figuratively. He had to be punished for firing a weapon, but I'm the one who taught him how to shoot. To teach *me* a lesson, the agents gave me a choice. I could watch them sledgehammer Bradie's knees and ankles before they dumped him in the Red Zone to be picked apart by mutated scavengers, or I could shove his hand into boiling water for 30 seconds."

I struggle to respond.

"Trenton, I—"

"Shut up!" he shouts. He wipes tears and chokes on his words. "They strapped him in a chair in a Calibration chamber. I had a thick rubber glove on so *I* wouldn't get burned. They made sure of that. The pain they wanted me to suffer was not my own. I held his hand over a boiling vat. Bradie gave me the go-ahead—a quiet nod and a look—but he didn't know what he was in for. How could he? He screamed. Oh, man, did he scream. He begged me to stop. *Please*, he said. But I kept going. I had to. I could smell it *cooking* him. It killed, me Caitlin, but to save my brother, I'd do it again. So what do you think I'm willing to do to you?"

Trenton's story enrages me, and I've plenty of blame to throw back at him.

"I'm not the idiot who taught him how to shoot," I say.

His lip tightens. I try a different tact.

"Help me," I say. "Help me stop the people who hurt him—and you. The people who hurt her," I point at Lilianne.

"I'll deal with that thing later." Trenton cracks his knuckles. "It's going to feel so good when I snap your neck."

He was always fast; now, he's like a bolt of lightning. I try to run toward the stairs, hoping to draw him away from Lilianne. In two bounds, he closes the distance. He kicks my legs out from under me; pain fires through my ankle.

I drop, roll, and kick. He catches my foot in his hands. He smiles. He's enjoying this. He lifts my whole body off the ground, wrenches my leg and hip with a harsh twist, and twirls me like a toy. I crash into a shelf, and a slew of plastic figurines topples on me.

"Don't do this," I say. "Don't be their puppet. We have a chance to be free."

He flicks open a knife. "Tell that to my brother."

I search for a weapon of my own. Everything in here is useless props.

He charges. My hand closes on the scarf with a red S on it—the one Normand insisted I never move. After I fitfully threw everything on the counter to the ground, he made sure to put it all back—for me in this moment. That's why everything near the register had to stay in its place. *This* is his final gift.

Thank you, thank you, thank you.

I yank the scarf off the countertop. The fabric's so old, I'm sure it will rip down the middle, but it holds. I dodge left and press the scarf against Trenton's wrist, deflecting his assault. I slide behind him and wrap the cloth around his neck. He turns and smashes me in the face with his open palm.

I roll with the punch, but he's too fast, and so strong his glancing blow sends me off my feet. I try to sweep his legs out from under him. It's like kicking a concrete wall. I yelp in surprise and pain.

He once told me his strategy for avoiding the wrong kind of attention was to hide the full extent of his skills. Now, he's showing me everything.

He grabs my throat, lifts, and squeezes—cutting the flow from the carotid artery to my brain. I attempt to crush his thumb as I did with Lilianne. He smirks. I have seconds before I pass out. He lifts the knife and aims it at my eye. I reach blindly, my fingers wrap around a plastic object, and I shove it into his temple.

Blue electricity flares from the Taser in my hand. The refurbished battery doesn't pack much punch and quickly fizzles out.

Still, he staggers back, breathless and bent over. I fall, gasping, to the ground.

"You are dead!" he spits.

"I don't think so," I reply, and I smash him across the face with the metal balls Normand left for me on the counter.

Trenton reels dizzily. I hit him again. The balls come away bloody. His body wavers, arms flailing comically, grabbing at nothing in an attempt to keep his balance. It's a lost cause. He uses what control he has left to drop to his knees.

"You can't win," he says. "The system, it's too big. Those on top, they're too powerful. They can read minds. Turn invisible. Smell our lies. We can't keep secrets from them. We can't run. We can't hide. We can't fight."

"I know." I look at lizard Lilianne on the floor. "That's why I need as many of them as possible to join us."

Trenton's eyes flutter. *Did he hear me?* No idea. I wrap my arms around his neck in a sleeper hold. When his form goes limp, I gently lower him to the ground and bind his arms with the scarf.

I go to Lilianne, pull the darts from her torso, and toss them aside. She comes to quicker than I expect. It must be something in her Supergenic DNA. She blinks groggily, smiling like a little girl. She knows how to work an audience. No wonder she got away with so much growing up. She processes where she is and suddenly sits up.

"Where is he?" she demands, sniffing the air.

"Taken care of," I reply.

She sees Trenton unconscious on the ground.

"Can I eat him?" she asks.

"Maybe," I reply.

Neither of us seems sure if the other is joking.

"Lilianne, I don't know how much time we have."

She nods. "I think you're crazy. I've always thought you were crazy. But I'm ready. Let's do this."

I insert a data key into Normand's tablet and then set it up to do a video record.

"Ready?" I ask Lilianne.

"Caitlin," she smiles her lizard smile. "I was born ready."

When Lilianne finishes, I press stop, pull the data key from the tablet, and hand the recording to her.

"Do you think this will work?" she asks.

"I guess we'll find out," I reply. She stares at the key. Will it open a door —or lock it shut?

I reverently lift the pile of yellowed papers that comprise *Shadowren*, Issue 1, drawn in black and white by Normand, written by me. Pencil marks show through the ink. I spot the occasional spelling mistake. Some transitions are questionable at best. Compared to the glossy and slick computer-rendered comic books all around us, our work is rough and raw. To me, these pages are the most exquisite of all the things.

"Here," I say. My hands shake as I hand it over. I can't believe I'm going to part with it. Have I ever, in those other timelines? This feels new, and right, but I have no way of knowing. Will anyone on Jupitar Island appreciate it? From what Lilianne's said about the way things work there, they'll take the original more seriously than a digitized copy—I hope.

"This is how we spread a revolution?" Lilianne asks skeptically, flipping through the pages.

"This is your story," I point to the data key containing the video recording we made of her. "The rights the Supergenic leaders violated; the laws they broke; what they were willing to do to one of their own."

"That I get," she replies. "But the comic book?"

"The video will give the people of Jupitar Island a reason to rebel," I explain. "The comic book—I hope—will show them how."

CHAPTER 41

Lilianne helps me get Trenton's unconscious and ridiculously heavy body back inside the perimeter fence. The sounds of explosions are gone, replaced by a loudspeaker flaring to life.

"Citizens, the terrorist attack against the Protectorate has been terminated. For your safety, return to your homes for further instructions. Anyone remaining in the streets will be deemed an agitator and will be met with maximum force. I repeat…"

It's Agent Samson. An edge creeps into his voice. He's scared. So am I. We haven't gotten away with this yet. The metaphorical Supergenic missile casually pointed at us from across the river flew over and remains aggressively aimed at our gates.

"This can work, right?" Lilianne asks.

I shrug. Her guess is as good as mine.

"Do your part," I say. "I'll do mine. Let's see where that gets us."

"Yeah," she agrees emphatically, twisting my words into something more rah-rah than they are. "We'll show them."

"Gen M," I say.

She hugs me. Before I know it, I'm hugging her back. It's hard to remember this is Lilianne, my childhood nemesis. Nor is she the Venomerella I imagined. I think of the things she told me happened to her on Jupitar Island—the things that landed her back here with a chip in her head. She's more badass than I ever would've imagined. I hope she's got more where that came from.

We disengage. As darkness descends, I try to watch her slither and coil her way toward the river, and I quickly lose sight of her camouflaged form.

The next morning, I stand next to Trenton inside the Protectorate. He's strapped into the Chair in a Calibration chamber. A tube feeds a bright amber liquid into his bloodstream. The helmet over his head covers half his face, but not his lips. His jaw twitches and his body tenses.

CeeCee watches his vitals.

"We can't erase memories," she says. "At best, we can overwrite them. We've experimented with dissidents, but the results are inconsistent."

I think of my mom, of how I didn't believe her.

"I understand," I say.

Trenton wakes in sickbay. He blinks at me, confused. I wear a full-fledged protector's uniform. My mom's worst nightmare has come true.

"What happened?" he asks.

"There was an uprising," I reply. "You were hurt in the battle."

I appraise his tone and expression; sensors track his vitals. If he fakes believing me, we should know.

"Did we crush them?" he asks.

"Of course," I reply. "But you suffered a head injury. We found you in the Yellow Zone. What do you remember?"

"There was… a mutant. A lizard. I… I think I killed it," he says.

I nod. "That's what happened."

"What about Bradie? Was he hurt in the attack?" he asks.

"Yes," I say, "badly."

Trenton blubbers. "I have to see him."

"For sure," I say, snapping my fingers at a medic. "She'll take you to him."

"What about you?" he says, surprised.

My earpiece beeps.

"They're here," Agent Samson tells me.

"I'm on my way," I reply. To Trenton, I add, "I have to go."

I walk through a hallway of melted polymer. The scorched and distorted resin looks like a tunnel of petrified magma. Dozens of half-melted protector helmets and pieces of body armor are melded into the twisted walls. The elemental Supergenic scorched his way through here, boiling the blood in the protectors' veins and burning their bodies to the bone. What's left has to be hacked out.

I get to the elevator and avert my eyes from the glare of blowtorches. Repair crews work behind yellow hazard tape, welding broken mechanisms. I take the stairs and pass the imprint of a giant fist smashed into a concrete wall. A steel railing bulges outward from the passing of a huge form. Debris is everywhere. Fingerprints five times the average human size indent the solid metal of a door ripped off its hinges. I emerge into the sub-basement. The audit rooms are here.

I choke on the fumes from chemical disinfectants. I could put on my helmet, use the built-in respirator, but I refuse. People died here—my people. Even the ones we were fighting; they were ours; they just didn't know it. Maintenance crews have removed the bodies and power washed the hall. I run my hand along the slash marks in the plastic walls from claws and tusks. The Supergenics sent a pack of animalistics down here, with their heightened senses and primal urges, surely to hunt down Lilianne.

There'd be no escaping them, except she doesn't leave a scent, I think with relief. *You do,* another part of me warns. *They could follow your trail to Normand's secret place.* I snort. *That's the least of my worries.*

I'm about to be brain raped, and there's nothing I can do about it.

I enter an audit room and wait. I stare at myself in the one-way mirror. For all I know, the mind auditor is on the other side, already doing his/her/zirs dirty work. Then again, maybe not. I know more about telepaths than I used to; they're rarer than the propaganda would have us believe; the weaker ones need physical contact to pick up a single thought, and the most powerful telepaths, the ones who can rip a mind to pieces, rarely survive long after Manifesting, suffering from aneurysms, strokes, and neurological disorders, their brains exploding from being inundated by other people's thoughts.

I think of Normand, and his ability to fool telepaths, a talent I don't possess. What a manipulative liar he was.

Man, I miss him.

"Focus," I tell myself—not that it will make any difference.

Hopefully, Lilianne's doing better than me. There's no sign that she made it to the other side of the river. Such worries evaporate the moment the door opens. I could play a tune in my mind, but I don't. Not today.

My interrogator comes in, and recognition jolts me. It's the same young man who was there on my Testing Day—Joshua. Unless he, too, has a twin. He wears a mind auditor's uniform, showing off every curve of his muscled form. Judging by the stiffness in his walk and the way he keeps pulling at the collar, he's not used to it. His hair is longer and slicked back. It still shines gold.

"Caitlin Feral," he says. "We meet again."

It *is* him.

"Hello, auditor," I say. "Congratulations on the promotion."

His golden cheek twitches as if the title pinches tighter than his outfit.

"Yes," he says. "There was a sudden vacancy."

I nod. "I heard."

Joshua's forehead creases in confusion.

He doesn't know about the video, I realize.

"What video?" he asks, catching the thought. This is going to be brutal.

"Have a seat," I say, gesturing to the chair on the other side of the table as if I'm the one about to interrogate him. "I have a lot to show you."

He sits, pursed lips projecting equal parts curiosity and concern.

"You know, I'm here to find traitors who will be put to death," he says. "Under article 20.2 of the Peace Treaty—"

"Let's not waste any time," I cut him off.

I reach across the table and grasp his hands. He tries to pull back, and I tighten my grip.

"No need to be squeamish," I say. "You once told me skin-to-skin contact intensifies the psychic connection, even for you."

He blushes rose gold.

"That's correct," he says.

"Good," I say. "Let's begin."

I scroll back through my memories, and the telepath pulls at one of me and Bradie in the hospital.

"We'll get to that," I say. "But it will all make more sense if we start at the beginning."

I focus on my trip to the library, on that long-ago day when Normand slipped me a forbidden comic book. Joshua arches his brow, confused and surprised.

"That's the day you and I met," I say, though spoken words are unnecessary. "I'd just failed my final Testing Day."

I allow my story to unfold. I let Joshua feel what I feel. The more excruciating the emotion, the more hopeless or hopeful, the longer I linger on it. By the time we get back to Bradie lying in his hospital bed, I'm crying openly. Joshua's eyes grow moist. He doesn't try to break contact. He doesn't interrupt. He listens, he watches, and he feels. I get to the interrogator who was his predecessor assaulting my mind. The telepath flinches and tries to pull away. My grip tightens.

Is that what you want to become? I ask.

No, is his gentle reply.

He hears his predecessor's confession to the crimes against teens like Lilianne, and I see the rage on his face.

He didn't know, I realize. *How is that possible? He can read minds.*

"We have rules about where and how we use our powers," he explains. "And on whom."

"And they didn't prepare you for what you might find here?" I ask.

"They did not," he says. "My guess is, they're testing me."

Sounds a lot like dealing with the agents. But it does give me a spark of hope. Joshua continues sifting through my brain, transfixed by my memories of Normand rescuing me from that other interrogator, dragging him down into a psychic vortex.

It ends with me beating Trenton and sending Lilianne back to Jupitar City with the seeds to foment rebellion. Then, and only then do I let go of Joshua's hands. We've been at this for hours. He wipes away his tears and then gazes into my eyes.

They're going to execute you for this, he projects into my mind.

Only if you tell them the truth, is my reply.

"What would you have me do?" he asks out loud.

"Lie," I say.

Joshua's mind audit of the Cube lasts a week. He reads a cross-section of minds to determine who is a "loyalist" and who is a "traitor." He's not the only interrogator, but he is the only telepath.

Hundreds of protectors are found guilty of terrorist acts. I am not among them. Neither is Agent Samson. Joshua singled out the loyalists instead. They are the ones to be executed, not the rebels like me.

He's taking our side, I realize, and he may be more powerful than the Supergenics know. I suspect he's changing the memories of his subjects as he goes and is mentally manipulating his fellow auditors to skew their results. There may be rules about using his telepathy on fellow Supergenics, but he seems to be ignoring them. By audit's end, no one remembers me as "the girl from the video." She becomes some amorphous person of lore no one can quite describe. The video itself has been wiped from the drives. What people do recall is a masked red-headed woman leading the rebellion. Her name—Shadowren.

On Joshua's last day at the Cube, I am among the entourage of protectors escorting him to his hovercraft. So is Liam.

Sandie is in sickbay, recovering from a burn to her arm. As our boots thud on the tarmac, I hear Joshua's voice in my head.

The protectors who were found guilty are going to be put to death for doing their duty, he tells me. *That's on you.*

Yes, I reply. *I know.*

You really have changed from that girl on Testing Day, he says.

You wanted a legend, I reply.

Remind me to be more careful what I ask for, he says. *And you be careful not to change too much. You don't want to become what you're fighting.*

Our escort stops twenty measures from the hovercraft.

Are you aware that I will be subjected to a mind audit of my own when I get back? he asks me.

Why? I ask.

Now that I know the truth, they will need to be certain of where my loyalty lies.

Can you fool them? I ask.

I can try, he answers.

And if you fail? I demand.

Then I imagine we'll all be dead within a matter of days.

He crosses the final distance alone. I watch his shapely back, expecting him to turn around, to wink or wave. He doesn't. It was a childish thought. I'm surprised when I hear him in my mind one last time. His voice is fainter, and I make a note of what his limit must be.

This rebellion of yours could destroy us all, he says.

So why are you helping me? I ask back.

I don't get a response. Maybe he's gone out of range; maybe he's not sure of the answer.

He climbs a set of drop-down stairs onto the deck of the hovercraft and disappears into its hull. We watch it float a measure above the tarmac then skim across the river. Night is falling, the air is chill, and we are about to turn back toward the compound, but something across the river catches my eye. I squint at the bright lights of Jupitar City.

"What's the matter?" Liam asks.

"That," I say, pointing at the skyline.

"I'm not sure…" and then he sees it too.

The lights in the tallest tower are winking out, floor by floor—then the next building goes, and the next.

"What the deuce?" Liam says. "Is one of ours doing this?"

My heart beats faster. Soon the whole island city is dark. "Yes," I say. "She is."

A projection fills the night sky, and the accompanying booming audio easily carries across the river. A hologram of a lizard girl with hazel eyes flecked with gold stands tall as a tower. As usual, Lilianne is shining large while Caitlin Feral fades to the background. Still, as different as we are, as much as our paths have diverged—then converged—we are both Generation Manifestation.

"Hello citizens of Jupitar City," Lilianne's video projection says. "My name is Lilianne Whisper… And this is my story."

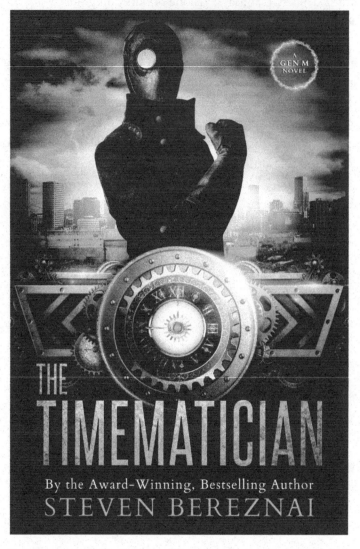

Want to know more about a certain
Gen M character's backstory? Order
The Timematician and add it to your
Goodreads want-to-read list today! For
updates on this and other future releases
(and free gifts!) join Gen M at
www.GenerationManifestation.com

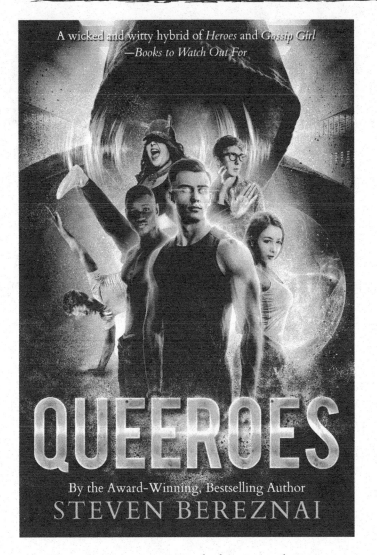

For more young adult superhero
adventures, order a copy of *Queeroes*, where
a group of gay teens must face their darkest
fears to become their truest selves.
Think *American Horror Story* meets
Smallville and *Queer as Folk*.

If you enjoyed this book, please take a moment to write a review on your favorite retailer site and **Goodreads.com**. This helps the author a lot! Also consider buying a copy as a gift.

The author is hard at work on more books in the *Gen M* series. The more positive feedback he gets, the more he'll know people are interested, and the quicker he'll get them done.

Posts on social media are also very encouraging. Feel free to tag and/or follow @StevenBereznai and @GenerationManifestation.

Also by Steven Bereznai:

The Timematician (A Gen M Novel: Book 2)

Queeroes

Queeroes 2

How A Loser Like Me Survived the Zombie Apocalypse

The Adventures of Philippe and the Outside World

The Adventures of Philippe and the Swirling Vortex

The Adventures of Philippe and the Hailstorm

The Adventures of Philippe and the Big City

The Adventures of Philippe and the Magic Spell

Gay and Single…Forever?—10 Things Every Gay Guy Looking for Love (and Not Finding It) Needs to Know

Author's Bio:

In grade two, I wrote a not-so-breathtaking poem for my school's literary anthology. I've been a writer ever since. My experience includes writing/ producing for CBC TV, a short film and reality stint at OUTtv, and penning some award-winning, bestselling novels.

I came out in my late teens and feeling like an outsider has deeply impacted my sensibility. I love writing that combines sass, heart, speculative fiction, and (where appropriate) abs. Basically, shows like *Buffy*, *Teen Wolf* and *She-Ra and the Princesses of Power*.

I'm Toronto-based and can be reached through my website www.stevenbereznai.com.